ONE HUNDRED PERCENTER

Bryan Soroka

PublishAmerica
Baltimore

At the specific preference of the author, PublishAmerica allowed this work to remain exactly as the author intended, verbatim, without editorial input.

ISBN: 1-4241-3715-2
PUBLISHED BY PUBLISHAMERICA, LLLP
www.publishamerica.com
Baltimore

Printed in the United States of America

This is dedicated to my mother, Cyvia, whose life was cut too short, and my wife and children, whom I live for.

-1-

Time.

It's a silver streak during periods of pleasure. It's a cat on a hot tin roof when you've got purpose on your side. Emmit Rhoe was clinging to that by his fingernails. For almost four years he'd been flailing away, trying to latch onto intention. Trying his best to remember what it was like to play a useful role. Like most people, he'd always been a much more contented soul when he was working toward some goal, any goal, no matter its scope or origin. This held especially true at the moment because his current station in life was about as necessary as areolas on a razorback.

Aside from marching on, time also has the inevitable quality of favoring the determined. Just as much, it holds youth in an impossibly high regard. Emmit belonged to neither group for longer than he cared to remember, or perhaps even could. And while time had turned its back on him, he had an ironic surplus of it. In fact, when he made the mistake of sitting back and mulling it over, that's all he really had.

Time to think. Time to wonder. Time to consider how uncompromisingly meaningless his existence had become. If it wasn't so sad, he might have been able to crack a smile. He just might have found the strength to curl his thin, cracked lips upwards, marveling at how ridiculous it was—how he had reverted to…

No.

He was doing it again. Thinking in time frames. Frames of time. Emmit had been through so much. Too much. More than enough to validate his efforts to fight off the rapid synapses that still fired through his brain, and wrestle them into submission like he'd done to those countless threats to his country's way of life.

5

"Excuse me. Mr. Rhoe?"

The familiar voice brought him crashing back down to the physical world. Emmit turned up to look at his newly arrived company with a faint expression of resolve. "How many times do we have to go over this, Frank?" Emmit said to Francis Albertson, Timberlake Villa's chief orderly. "I feel old enough without you chipping in. So please…call me Emmit."

"My apologies. I forgot," the portly overseer said. "Sorry to interrupt—EMMIT, but we're closing the gardens for the evening."

Emmit rubbed the back of his wrinkled neck. He sighed just under his breath and looked on at Frank for a moment, trying to look deep into his eyes—through his eyes more—to see what was really going on inside.

He used to be quite good at that.

All he could read was what Frank had for dinner that evening (some sauce from the vegetable lasagna served for the latter day meal was still clinging to his lower lip).

Slowly (and quite a bit less surely), Emmit raised himself up from the bench overlooking the lush gardens that seemed to go on without end. "What time is it?" he asked, though not really caring.

Frank pulled his silver pocket watch out and popped its top. "Closing in on ten o'clock."

Emmit felt his left knee, the one he'd blown out during the campaign he led in Nueva Loja, buckle. It tended to soften up in warmer, damper weather, and that evening was A-typically as such. "It does fly, doesn't it?" he stopped all forward motion, taking the moment to steady himself on Frank's shoulder. Settled in, he let Frank take the lead as they made their way back into the main building.

"It's got a nasty habit of doing that," Frank said.

Later that evening Emmit found himself in a most familiar territory—sequestered in his room roaming through the dial. He didn't know why he bothered anymore. No matter how many channels he flipped through, the results were always the same. "Crap," he muttered. "Nothing but crap."

Undaunted (and unable to contemplate any other pastime) he kept pounding his ample thumb on the channel change button, racing through the endless seas of unimaginative, me-too pseudo-entertainment. The only reaction it got out of him was coming up with a different tantamount for shit. He settled on The Tonight Show, or Jaw-nny Jowlson as he called it. He refused to refer to it by its rightful nomenclature. That particular title belonged to Mr. Carson and Mr. Carson alone.

After Mr. Jowlson got through with his less-than-inspiring interview with Bryant Gumble, he kindly asked viewers *not to flip that dial.* As the commercials rolled on by, Emmit just sat there so disinterested he'd lost the will to blink. Reaching down to the side of the armchair he was sprawled out in, he pulled the faux-wooden lever to activate the built-in leg rest. Spreading his legs out with his feet hanging over the edge, he rubbed his hands along the fabric of the chair. As the commercials droned on, he crept back into his databanks and thought about how long it had taken him to sit his butt down in such a piece of furniture. He'd always wanted a chair like that. Ever since Percy told him such a fixture might be hard on the eyes, but goddamn was it comfortable! However, Celia, Emmit's wife of over 35 years, would never even let him in the store to take a look. With her, aesthetics always overrode succor.

"You're not bringing a monstrosity like that into my home," she would say with righteous anger.

Every now and again, Emmit would forget who he was talking to and claim it was his home as well, and that he had every right to appoint it with furnishings to his liking. But the fight was over before it began. Emmit may have been one of the most powerful creatures on the earth, but he was nothing compared to Celia when her décor was jeopardized.

The thought of her was enough to make his day. Remembering the tone she'd hit when he attempted to walk through the front doors of the Lay-Z-Boy dealer in the Grambling Gates Mall. Or how her face turned fire engine red when they'd come home and he'd race for the bathroom because of his fear of public restrooms and then in his haste, dry his hands on one of the guest towels.

He thought about her often. More than that, he wondered what she would have thought about his current situation. He surmised she wouldn't be nearly as distressed about it as he, since she'd never been a big fan of his extraordinary vocation. She never voiced it, never in a direct manner, but he could see that she worried about him whenever he was sent out. And from the moment he returned to the time he left again, she was on him to put an end to that part of his life. Yes, he was serving a noble purpose. But as selfish as it may have been, Celia reckoned Emmit her husband and her children's father first and guardian of the free world a distant second.

While they fought and scuffled and teased and taunted, the two developed an uncommonly strong union, and the mere thought of losing him was too much for her to bear.

The paradox wasn't lost on Emmit that she was the first to go.

* * *

The show's credits started to roll. Emmit, still motionless, stared blankly at the screen, until he gathered the strength to tap the on/off button of the remote. He eased the Lay-Z-Boy back into its natural position and headed for the bathroom to get ready for bed.

Following a hearty exhibition of brushing and flossing, Emmit stowed his toothbrush in the medicine cabinet and took a swig of Listerine. He took another, washed his mouth out with a cupful of water and dried his face with a fresh towel. He did his best not to look at the man staring back at him in the mirror. But as far as he'd fallen, he was still drawn to that pale version of himself. There was still an unmistakable resemblance there—a surefire representation of the man he always aspired to be.

"What are you looking at?" he said.

That reflection didn't have an answer. Not one that would satisfy Emmit's curiosity, so he quickly turned away and called it a night.

Sleep had become a precious commodity. Not so long ago Emmit had been able to put head to pillow and that would be that. But ever since he'd stopped paying tribute to his true self, getting a decent night's rest was more of an altercation than a natural occurrence. Whether or not this had anything to do with arriving at Timberlake he wasn't sure. But from the moment he strolled through those imposing rod iron gates, sleep and him had become fast enemies.

Unfortunately, it was moments like this; when the world was still and quiet enough to be mistaken for dead that his mind started racing. All those thoughts of what was and regrettably what could have been tore through his consciousness, all vying for control.

It wasn't until the clock struck three that Emmit's eyelids starting to droop. He laid there in the bed he'd shared with Celia—back to the mattress, eyes to the ceiling and thoughts to the past. His eyes began to flutter like an incensed hummingbird's wings and at three-oh-seven, he was finally out and ready to be treated to another familiar vision. That's what they'd become after all these years—a series of washed out vignettes that still had a faint semblance of truth to them, but had taken on a decidedly more surreal identity.

February 1965

It was an early, bitterly cold morning in Pleiku, a pint-sized village located in central Vietnam. Frost settled on top of the land, covering it in an icy and unforgiving coating that claimed the life of anything still hearty enough to raise a pulse. This would soon prove to be more than simply a forecast for the weather. It was an estimate of the grisly events to come.

It was on that fateful morning that the Viet Cong decided to up their ante by launching a ferocious assault against the American military barracks in Pleiku. While small in stature, the diminutive settlement boasted a highway junction of roads going east to Quy Nhon, west toward Cambodia, north to Da Nang and south leading all the way to Ho Chi Minh City. It was this ideal series of roadways that spurred the U.S.'s decision to construct a major base there, and it was the attendance of U.S. military advisors frequenting the camp that incited the attack.

Following the brief but brutal encounter, eight officers were fit for body bags. Needless to say this did not go over very well with the U.S. delegates, especially with then President, Lyndon Baines Johnson. Upon his order, the Americans retaliated by bombing North Vietnam. This proved to be the spark that lit the fire for the Vietnam War.

Emmit was all of 22 years old at the time. He'd just graduated from the University of Maryland and was preparing to embark on a career in journalism. He was on his way to an interview with Jim Pallock, the assistant editor for the Boston Herald, when the news of the attack played out on the car stereo.

Emmit eased the car onto the side of the road and listened intently to the broadcast. At least he tried to. The car's radio had been giving him nothing but static lately and it took some finesse to manipulate the dials in order to hear what the announcer was saying. A strident series of pops and hisses filled the cabin of his father's Ford Fairlane. In between the inaudible cracklings, Emmit could just make out the announcer's voice. For some reason, the news jarred something loose from deep within. Emmit wasn't opposed to a war in Vietnam nor any other encounter the U.S. had been involved with over the past 20 years. If anything, he supported his country (blindly for the most part). But up until that moment, his backing had always been philosophical as apposed to corporeal.

Emmit's family was steeped in military tradition. His grandfather served in WWI, and his father spilled blood in the Second Global Onslaught. He was proud of this familial heritage. Whether or not he ever told anyone. He'd never considered slinging a rifle over his shoulder, even though his father had been relentless in his efforts to get his only son to join up with the Rhoe Armed Forces.

It wasn't so much that Emmit was more of a lover than a fighter (though he always felt he was), but he just didn't have that killer instinct. He couldn't imagine taking the life of another human being, and he couldn't fathom any scenario that would make him wish otherwise. But after hearing about the attack on Pleiku, his innate sense of patriotism forged to the front lines. It was always there, he supposed, but lay dormant until a powerful enough force came along to jolt it awake. He was right about that. And wrong. There was something sleeping inside of him. Something that was always there and something that would soon attain consciousness. But it wasn't a sense of nationalism or partisanship.

It was something much, much more.

May 1966

It was day 66 of Emmit's 365-day tour. Just another thigh-chafing, lip-blistering morning in balmy South Vietnam. From the moment he hopped out of the Bell UH-1 chopper, Emmit had been trying his best to put on a brave face. He tried fighting through the pain and suffering. He frantically attempted to mask the fear and uncertainty (an enemy much more fearsome than the flesh and bone equivalents) that hungrily awaited him at every turn. But for the most part, his pigment sank into an unmistakably gray pallor that was offset with expressions of inimitable fear and uncertainty.

He had yet to engage the enemy and his imagination (which was vivid) created images of golden, soulless ghouls and goblins that ate the flesh straight off the American bone. The stories he'd heard, which never seemed to end, told tall tales of the dreaded Viet Cong. He'd never heard the moniker up until he enlisted. When he'd first heard the name, he thought he was getting ready to butt heads with some Ray Harryhausen creation. As it turned out, though, both his imagination and knowledge of arcane Hollywood trivia proved to be well off the mark.

Emmit kept trying to slap a full-nelson around his anxieties. He starting taking deep, controlled breaths—in through the nose, out through the mouth. He was starting to feel a little bit better, and that good sensation kept on rolling when he thought about how he and the third platoon of 'A' troop commanding the 35th tank infantry were out in the bush. Dealing with the implacable humidity and pest population was a pain to be sure. But it was a hell of a lot better than having his olfactory senses assaulted with the stink of diesel-soaked soldier shit back at HQ.

Emmit popped his head out of the main hatch of the tank and took another deep breath, still trying to shake off the Boogeyman. He took his helmet off and wiped the fresh layer of sweat that had gathered on his forehead and looked all around, noting how dissimilar the surroundings were. Not just to Boston, but to anywhere he'd been or read about. Vietnam might have very well been on Mars for all he knew, or for that matter, cared.

The tracks of the tank gripped the soft ground. They kicked up chunks of dirt and shot clouds of dust high into the air. It sucked out the rest of what oxygen remained after the humidity had its way. But Emmit still couldn't complain. Riding on the bell cap of the 17-ton Sheridan was considerably more appealing than barreling through hostile territory on foot along with the rest of the scout squad.

The troop was in a line formation save for the command and mortar tracks, which trailed some 150 meters behind. They'd been humping for the better part of the morning. Starting off was never so bad. They usually left just before sunrise, so the air was still a bit cool and forgiving. But as time marched on right along with them, the sun began scorching the earth and all those on it, until breathing became a chore all on its own.

The needle made its way past 104° when the troop arrived at an isolated area just northwest of Cu Chi. It was there that the division base camp was situated.

Emmit swabbed away another coat of perspiration when Lieutenant David Hearnes, a 36-year old warhorse enjoying his second tour of duty, slipped his helmet on and stood beside Emmit.

"Lovely morning for a stroll, isn't it?" David said.

"I've seen better."

David playfully shoved Emmit aside. "You ain't seen shit. Not in just two months you haven't."

Emmit puffed up his chest and proudly proclaimed. "It's 66 days, and yes I have."

David never had much patience for wet nursing fresh recruits. But he'd taken an immediate liking to Emmit and not just because they both agreed Wilt Chamberlain wasn't fit to wash Bill Russell's jock strap. There was something about the young private that David naturally gravitated toward. The L.T. was a tremendous judge of character. It was obvious that Emmit had yet to embrace the killer inside, however, David was certain it was only a matter of time before Emmit and that ultimate soldier shook hands.

He would never know how right he was.

"Know what they call this place?" David said in that broken-glass Tennessee drawl that earned him the moniker, Scrapegoat.

Emmit scratched his head and with a distinctly sardonic tone said, "I dunno? Hell?"

"Some circles, yeah. Others call it the Mushrooms."

Emmit waved the thick clouds of russet-tinted dust out of his eyes and looked down at the ground.

"You're not going to find any, dummy," David said, his tone ogling Emmit's mordant stance. "They just call it that."

"Why?"

"Who the hell knows? But it fits in with the rest this place's logic system, don't you think?"

The roadsides were shrouded with trees and hedgerows, some shooting seven feet high. The ground was more of less flat, making it ideal tank country. That was a good thing because the enemy used the area to stage its operations, and the 35th had to sweep through the locale on a regular basis just to keep its opponents in check.

The troops continued on for the next 20 minutes. Members were spread out over nearly a quarter mile of real estate. Emmit was still head-above-tank when he heard a call come over the horn. The scrambled voice reminded him of the radio in his father's car. Bending his ear further, Emmit heard the tinny voice declare that the left flank platoon had come across what appeared to be a freshly baked bunker. After a brief conversation with the higher-ups, a sergeant from first platoon decided it was a good idea to investigate the trench further. The rest of the troop was ordered to stand pat.

Serving in Vietnam was definitely not a nine-to-five gig, which meant grunts and officers took every opportunity to grab some shuteye, take a shave or fill their bellies whenever they could. As soon as the call came through, the troops snapped up their rations and toiletry kits and went to work. David, who had ducked below to relay the message to the driver, rejoined Emmit and poked him in the ribs. "Hey...psst," he whispered. "Check it out."

Snapping his head left and right, David pulled his free hand away from his vest and unveiled a host of class eight and six rations—two cans of Coke, some Oreos and a bottle of Jack Daniels with a couple of good swigs still left in it.

"C'mon. Let's party," David said.

Again looking all about to make sure nobody knew the wiser, David secured the rations under his vest and braced himself on the lip of the open hatch. With one fell allez oop, he pushed himself out and landed on the dusty trail. Emmit, on the other hand, carefully lifted himself out and bunny hopped beside his L.T.

Slowly walking down the main path, they watched their fellow soldiers go about their chores and duties.

"Looks good over there," David said pointing out a dense assembly of trees lining the path the platoon had been crawling along.

David and Emmit headed in that direction, while most of the other men hunkered down in front of the tanks. Emmit assumed David didn't join them because he didn't want to share his cookies or hooch. But the real reason why the lieutenant sought an alternate perch was because he never felt comfortable sitting out in the open. That, and of course, he didn't want to share his cookies or hooch.

Settling down right beside a thick cluster of trees, David leaned against one of their gnarled members and scratched his back, rubbing to and fro while he purred like a saber tooth. Emmit kneeled down beside his commanding officer and reached out for a cookie. Before he could grab hold of one, David slapped his hand away.

"Hey!" Emmit yelped.

"Now, now. No dessert until we find out if we have company," David said and radioed for infantry support to inspect the tree line that was causing his well-honed sense of self-preservation to hum. It was a perfect place to enjoy rations, David supposed, and an ideal piece of territory for the enemy to lay in wait.

Emmit took advantage of David's divided attention and reached out for another cookie, though David's peripherals easily picked up an incoming assault and he slapped Emmit's hand away yet again. While Emmit rubbed the feeling back into his mitt, a reply finally came back over the radio. The soldier said there were no grunts available to conduct the menial task of rooting through the tree line.

"We got a whole mess of bunkers to check out," the Unknown Soldier said. "You want to see what's up, you're gonna have to find someone else."

David dropped the radio to his side. "Figures," he said gruffly. Holstering the radio, he scouted about for other possible suitors. "Yo…Al! Georgie! Do me a solid and go check out what's what in that tree line, 'kay?"

Allan Winnick, a driver, and George Franscicus, one of the loaders, looked over at their superior officer. They'd just taken a load off in front of one of the tanks and were getting ready to crack open a couple of cans of mystery meat.

"Aww…c'mon, L.T. We were just gonna grab some rats," George mewled.

"Stow it," David said. "You can chow down after you've checked things out."

George set in to launch another objection but Allan pulled him back knowing full well the Scrapegoat wouldn't be denied. Allan snapped the tin can out of his mate's hand and along with his own, placed them on the dusty ground. Like a pair of huffy pre-teens, they grabbed their rifles and headed for the trees.

David carefully watched them go, letting them know he was doing as such. George and Allan were balls-to-the-wall in a firefight and could always be counted on. But that didn't change the fact that they were two of the laziest sons of bitches David had ever crossed. They were much like any other grunt that had served the bulk of their tour, feeling that they were somehow above such meager assignments. In David's opinion, though, there was no such thing as meager. Not in Vietnam.

Still keeping a fierce bead on the two soldiers, David fought off the urge to blink until he was certain they were on the case. With George and Allan out of sight, David returned his attention to Emmit. "Now…where were we?"

As it turned out, absence did make the heart grow fonder. Especially when it came to Oreos. Emmit had never been big on sweets. He'd always had a penchant for the salty treats. But after nearly two months of creamed corn, creamed hash and a cornucopia of other foods never intended to be served creamed, Mr. Christie certainly made some good fucking cookies.

Emmit twisted the top off another Oreo and started running his tongue over the creamy white filling when all of a sudden he heard George shout out, "WE GOT SOMETHING!"

14

David dropped his precious rations save for the bottle of Jack, which he gently lowered to the ground. He ran over to the tank and motioned for Emmit to hop-to. Leaping up onto the 35,000 pound iron monster, he disappeared inside its belly. Emmit stepped up to the tank and kicked away at the meandering clouds of dust until David reappeared, holding onto his .45 sidearm and a rifle. "Here…" David tossed Emmit the M16.

Weapons in-hand, they jogged to the tree line. David brushed away the leaves and branches as they made their way to the others, while Emmit did the same to the chocolate residue coating his lower lip. A dozen or so determined strides later, and they spotted George and Allan standing 25 meters ahead.

"Over here!" George yelled.

David and Emmit stopped just shy of where the driver and loader stood.

"For the love of God, will you keep your goddamn voice down?" David growled.

Emmit set in to comment on the fact David again managed to praise and blaspheme the Almighty in the same sentence. But he pulled back because it appeared there was serious work to be done.

"Sorry, L.T. But I think we got a situation here," George said and pointed down to a large hole in the ground.

David stared down at the familiar looking breach. A heap of customary scenarios raced through his mind as he bent down to one knee. He ran his hand along its fringe and looked up to the others. "Mmhmm. Looks as though you were right, Georgie," he said straightening out to his full six feet. "For once anyway."

"So what do we do?" Emmit asked while he desperately tried to fight off his pale expression from returning.

"Well…that all depends," David said. "Do me a favor and hold this." He handed Emmit his .45 and bent down again, this time on both knees. He looked down into the hole, making sure there was nobody hiding in the immediate darkness. He then dipped his head into the hole and filled his lungs with air. Sucking in another deep breath, he jumped back to his feet. "Smell that?"

Emmit looked at George, George at Allan and Allan back to David.

"Smell what?" Allan asked.

David grabbed Allan by the back of his jacket and forced him down to the ground. "Breathe," he ordered.

"What the fuck're you…?"

"Just do it!"

Allan looked at David curiously then did as ordered. Once David was convinced he'd taken in enough, he let him go.

"Jeez, L.T. You could'a just asked."

David took his gun back from Emmit. "Did you smell it?" he asked.

"Did I smell what?"

The lieutenant cocked his .45. "You can put away your rats, boys. Looks like we're having Vietnamese for lunch."

Emmit stepped back allowing David to walk past. In stride, the lieutenant grabbed his walkie and called in for some grunt support to check and secure the area. Like before, his request was shot down as all *swinging dicks* were indisposed.

"You believe this nonsense?" David said.

"Well, yeah but…"

David put up his hand and stopped Emmit in mid-sentence. "Rhetorical, boy. I thought you were supposed to be some kind'a wordsmith?"

David stepped back and thought about the situation for a moment. He looked around the area, then down into the hole again. "Do me a solid, kid…keep Tweedle-Dee and Tweedle-Dumber here company while I go fetch us some hands? I find it hard to believe every soldier in this platoon's got such important matters that need tending to."

"No problem," Emmit said. "I'll keep them in line."

David jogged back out to the main path. Before he disappeared behind the trees, he looked back to Emmit and smiled. Somehow the simple gesture always made Emmit feel much better.

"You can take it out now," George said.

"Come again?" Emmit asked.

"I said…" George squeezed in tight up beside him. "YOU CAN TAKE IT OUT NOW."

Emmit rolled his eyes, hoping George would take the inference and forget about whatever quip he was ready to drop. As usual, he didn't.

"Okay. I'll bite. Take what out?" Emmit asked reluctantly.

"Your tongue from Scrape's ass."

He smiled that shit eating grin of his, while Emmit stepped away feeling once his pheromones were out of nose-shot, George would lose interest.

David had only been gone for a few minutes, but with the company Emmit was keeping it felt more like perpetuity. Emmit looked down at his watch, the waterproof Timex his mother gave him before he was shipped off to boot camp in Virginia, hoping somehow the timepiece would take mercy on him and speed things up a bit.

"I called in a Cav," David said suddenly appearing from the underbrush. "Should be here in a few shakes of my tail," he hustled to join the others and stopped just shy of the hole in the ground.

Ten shakes later actually, an ACAV, or Armored Cavalry Assault Vehicle, bullied its way through the underbrush. The troops dismounted the vehicle and David directed them to form a large circle around him, which they did with their weapons primed and ready.

"Keep on your toes, gentlemen," David ordered.

The lieutenant cleared his gravel-loaded throat to get everyone's attention as he revealed the smoke grenade he'd taken from the ACAV. He waved it for all to see while he explained how he was counting on the explosive's acrid yellow smoke to seep out from the hole of the bunker and reveal the accompanying exit. Once he'd brought the class up to speed, he pulled the pin and tossed the explosive into the hole.

Then he waited. And waited some more. Thirty seconds came and went. Nothing happened.

"What now?" Emmit asked.

David held up his hand. "Give it a minute."

A few more ticks went by when someone hollered…

"Over there! GOOK!"

The troops spun around and spotted a man wearing a pair of tattered brown shorts and a straw-hat tear down the path behind the ACAV. David looked back and spotted the tree the man lifted. It had been planted in a pot fitted over the entrance of the tunnel, which sat a few dozen yards away from the accompanying hole Allan and George discovered.

David turned to one of the troops, a fresh young thing not much older than Emmit. "Don't just stand there with your tongue wagging, boy. Fetch!"

The nubile soldier shouldered his rifle and set off after the man. Within ten strides he caught up with him. "Freeze!"

The man kept running. The soldier shouted out again with much the same results.

"This isn't *Hawaiian Eye*, motherfucker," George said starting in on a sprint.

Like the young soldier, George quickly caught up with the fleeing man. He grabbed him by the shoulder and threw him to the ground. "He said danh t," George hollered. He turned to the young troop and explained. "That's Slope for freeze."

George brought the man back in tow and tossed him to the ground in front of David, who shot George a wicked glare. The lieutenant didn't care for the enemy, but he was even less enamored of the cruel reputation too many American soldiers had rightfully earned.

The situation was growing a bit too tense for David's liking. In his experience, which was vast, tension created uncertainty and the last thing you wanted to be out in the jungle was unsure. He pulled back to give his troops a chance to collect themselves. While they did, the man who surfaced wiped off the smoke residue from his eyes and mouth. David reached into his rucksack. "Here...take this."

He tossed the man a fresh towel and allowed him to finish the job.

"Cam o'n lam," the man said in between gasps.

"Don't mention it," David said. He evened out to a non-threatening tone and continued, "Anh kia, tên anh là gì?"

Emmit leaned over to Allan and whispered, "What did he say?"

"Asked what his name is. 'Least that's what I think he said."

Two times right in the very same day. It was a new record for Allan.

David asked the man what his name was again. The man just stared him down with tight lips and fierce, narrow eyes. David continued to talk to him in his best Vietnamese, which wasn't all that good. A few broken sentences later the man replied, "I speak English."

David heaved a sigh of relief. "Well why didn't you say so?" he said, feeling even more comforted that the man's English wasn't much better than David's Vietnamese.

"You look like you're parched there, partner," David unfastened the canteen from his vest and popped the top. He took a healthy gulp. Wiping his mouth dry, he offered the man a swig. "Go on. Take it."

The man looked around at all the troops and their contemptuous stares.

"Go on now. It's hot as Hades out here."

Hesitantly and with a trembling hand, the man reached out for the flagon. Before he set his lips to it, he wiped the neck off with the towel David had given him. The lieutenant turned to look at Emmit. "You believe this nonsense? Got more maladies running through these trails than a brothel in Calcutta mornin' after payday...and this dude's worried about me carrying something."

Emmit laughed nervously while the man tossed the towel aside and began to greedily chug the canteen's contents.

"Take it easy," David said.

The man kept sucking it back with a vengeance like he hadn't been treated to a spot of H2O in days.

"C'mon now…" David said a bit annoyed.

He reached down and wrenched the canteen out of the man's surprisingly strong grip. "Slow it down, partner. Don't want you cramping up on us."

David stowed the canteen and sat down beside the man and asked everyone to step away. Once they were out of range, he returned his attention to the man. "All right. Now we can get down to it," he turned to look down the hole as he spoke. "How many more of your pals are down there?"

The man raised his eyes up to the sky, then back to David and held up four fingers.

"Good. Good. You think you can do me a solid and ask them to come out here and join the rest of us?"

This time the man's response was instantaneous. He quickly shook his head from side to side.

"Why not?" David asked.

The man's nerves kicked into overdrive. The rest of his body joined his hand and began to shudder.

"Well, I'm sorry to say you really don't have much in the way of a choice," David said.

He stood up and motioned for the man to join him. He shook his head again. David bent down and pulled him up, easily hoisting his 115-pound frame up off the ground. They walked toward the hole Allan and George discovered. The closer they got, the harder the man fought. He pulled back, digging the heels of his sandals into the ground.

"C'mon now. Putting up a fuss'll only make things worse," David explained.

The other troops watched their esteemed lieutenant drag their enemy nearer to the hole in the ground. While David would never cop to the fact, he was starting to get a bit edgy himself because he knew where this was headed.

"Okay. I get it," David conceded.

He let the man go and thought about his next move. "Emmit. Front and center."

Emmit trotted up to the lieutenant. "What's up?"

"Be a dear and keep this guy on ice for me, would you?"

Emmit put his hand on the man's shoulder. David grabbed up another grenade and turned to face his troops. He looked over their numbers and said, "You…and you…"

The two troops he'd pointed out thumbed their chests.

"Yeah. Gimme your vests."

They both looked at him curiously.

"C'mon now. Time's got better things to do than wait on the likes of you two."

The soldiers did as ordered and handed their military-issue gear to David. "Good. Now you…what's your name?"

The taller of the pair, the one with the red hair and nanny goat chin hair said, "Jim. Jim Bre…"

"Whatever," David said. "You go cover that hole," David said pointing out the breach the man had suddenly appeared from. "And you…"

The other soldier said his name was Devin and kept it to that. David tossed him the two vests and told him to cover up the exit hole once he gave word.

Jim jogged to the hole. He placed the pot back over it and replanted the tree into the pot. Devin, with vests firmly in hand, approached David and waited for him to toss the grenade.

"Make sure you do it nice and tight now," David instructed and tossed the explosive down the hole.

Devin dropped the vests over the opening. He looked up to David for further instruction. Not seconds later, haggard coughs and wheezes filled the air. Devin didn't wait for any word as he quickly scuttled backwards, sifting through the underbrush for his rifle.

The rest of the troops primed their weapons and aimed for the holes. David followed suit, albeit in a considerably calmer fashion. His .45 leading the charge, David shouted in Vietnamese, "Get out of the hole! Now!"

The only response he received was another series of gasps and choking sounds. David's modest reserve of patience was bled dry. He stowed his weapon and jogged back to the ACAV to get a trip flare. A quick about face and a dozen paces later, he ignited the device and tossed it down the hole.

"That'll roust 'em out of there," David said confidently. "Those sons of bitches burn a lot hotter and brighter than grenades."

He was right about that. But what the lieutenant didn't know (and wouldn't find out for a few minutes yet), was the tunnel was quite small. A lot smaller than most of the passageways he'd navigated during his first tour as a platoon tunnel rat, or pineapple as they were also known as. Like the Mushroom reference, David wasn't quite sure why they were referred to as such, though he'd heard it was because tunnel rats gained their notoriety digging around an area southwest of Saigon nicknamed the Pineapple Region.

Another few strokes of the minute hand came and went and there was nothing new to report. David picked up his walkie and called for a rat to secure the area. His third request was also dismissed. He wanted to avoid doing the deed himself, appreciating that most of the troops were still drying the backs of their ears. If he was right about what was going down, and he knew he was, he wanted to be there to point them and their weapons in the right direction. Unfortunately, fate still outranked him and he was forced to investigate the matter himself.

"Well, like my daddy used to say," David gripped his .45 and fumbled for the flashlight he kept tucked away in his rucksack, "you want it done right...do it yourself."

The lieutenant plopped down on the ground and flipped the flashlight on. He aimed it down the center of the hole and scoured the vicinity. Casting the flashlight back and forth, he came across a pair of legs. He kept the light homed in on them to make sure whoever they belonged to wasn't in any shape to get back up on them. "Okay. I'll be back in a sec," he said and quickly dipped out of sight.

More time, not a lot, sloughed by. Emmit peered down at his watch. "You think someone should go down there and see if he's all right?" he asked.

"Naw. Scrape's gone more klicks underground than most of us have above," George said assuredly. "He'll be..."

Before the loader could finish his sentence a dull bang rang out. The ground shook. Emmit steadied himself and looked around trying to figure out what happened. Then he thought of David. The troops scrambled to secure the area. George ordered Emmit to go back to call for help but Emmit had plans of his own. He checked his weapon's magazine, secured his helmet and made a mad dash for the hole.

"Where the fuck're you going?" George hissed.

Emmit cocked his rifle and got ready to jump. "L.T.'s still down there. He needs help!"

"I gave you an order, you little shit. Now..."

Before George could reaffirm his position, Emmit placed either arm by his side and vanished beneath the surface. Just before he did, he cordially extended his middle finger and thrust it at George.

Down below, Emmit pushed his way past the body David spotted at the mouth of the tunnel. He'd been so intent on finding out whether or not the lieutenant was all right, he hadn't even checked to see if he'd stowed his flashlight. Frantically, he ran his hand along his beltline.

Nothing.

He slid his other hand inside his pack. He felt better when he brushed up against the shield of his flashlight, which he'd wrapped inside a hand towel. He brought it out and turned it on, casting the light down the narrow channel. He was fighting the urge to shout out to David, but even he knew better than to call attention to himself before he knew what was what.

Further down the tunnel, no more than a half dozen strides, Emmit came across another two bodies. He wasn't sure since it was so dank, but it looked like they were wearing green uniforms. He took a deep breath and redirected the flashlight dead ahead. The tunnel was narrowing. Every step he took the closer the walls came to his shoulders. Another 10 paces and he had to turn semi-sideways to keep en route. Small chunks of dirt and debris rained down on him. Emmit continued to shuffle down the tunnel path, when all of a sudden a bright light flashed in his eyes.

"Tha…that you, kid?"

Emmit tilted his flashlight downward and saw David lying in a heap. He raced over and knelt down beside his lieutenant. At once, he was elated to have found him but when he shone the light on the L.T.'s midsection and saw a sucking chest wound the size of a VW hubcap, his joy reverted to panic.

"You gotta go, kid. They…they're coming…"

Emmit looked up. He heard footsteps and muffled voices speaking in their enemy's tongue.

"I'm not leaving you," Emmit said doggedly.

"Yeah, you…are," David took a firm grip of Emmit's hand. "Been hit…enough times to know…when to give it up…"

He never imagined disobeying an order from the L.T. before, but as his brain processed his limited options, Emmit quickly came to the conclusion that there was no time like the present.

"Sorry, L.T.," Emmit said as he secured the flashlight under his arm, "you can court martial me when we get out of this mess."

Emmit gathered his strength and resolve and grabbed David's vest. Just when he prepared to hoist him up the chamber filled with an impossibly brilliant light and…

Everything went black. Pitch black.

Emmit opened his eyes and looked about trying to get his bearings but he couldn't see a thing. He wondered how long he'd been laying there in the dark, pinned under what felt like every last ounce of earth the planet could muster.

He remembered those voices. Those droning, chattering voices that were getting closer and closer.

He remembered dropping David and snatching his rifle from his side, and how he barely had enough room to set the butt into his shoulder and take aim at the three Viet Cong guerrillas that had their sites set on him.

He remembered squeezing off a series of shots, praying the training he'd received paid serious dividends.

He remembered how his weapon lit up the fabricated night and how the lead man fell to the ground, then the second, then…

That's when the world came caving in on him or at least the portion that included the tunnel.

Emmit reached down for his flashlight but it wasn't there. He tried to turn his head to look for David but he was pinned tight. So he reached out, sliding his hands through the earth until his palms landed on something that felt like a garbage bag filled with minced steak. It was David. Emmit called out his name but there was no reply.

The air was getting thin. He hadn't noticed before but now that his lungs were starting to burn and his throat was constricting, he realized that if he were ever to see the blue sky again he'd have to get out of there in a hurry.

"C'mon, L.T. I told you…I'm not leaving without you…"

Emmit cleared the dirt until he could move a bit more freely. He kept burrowing away until he had enough room to pull David to his side. He clawed his way upward, inch by agonizing inch. He kept going no matter how much he hurt. No matter how much his body protested.

He wasn't sure how long it was before he saw those spires of light cut through the shadows. Maybe minutes. Maybe hours or even days. But it didn't matter because he'd managed to pull himself and his commanding officer—his friend—to safety.

Emmit broke through the surface like some extra in a George Romero movie. Sucking in an impossibly delicious lungful of fresh air, he gathered the modest reserve of strength left at his command and pulled his legs free. He collapsed on the ground then. But just for a moment. Another deep breath and he dipped back inside the hole to drag David out. The lieutenant hadn't moved a stitch since Emmit first shined his flashlight upon him.

The whine of tank engines and the scattered commands of American troops could be clearly heard. George, who was digging a foxhole for the firefight intelligence forecast a few hours earlier, caught Emmit out of the corner of his eye. "Holy shit!"

George dropped his shovel and ran over to Emmit. "Hey…kid, you okay?"

"I'm fine. But L.T. needs a medic…"

Half an hour later, Emmit was laid out on a stretcher waiting for a chopper to come and transport him back to the medical barracks back at HQ. He was slipping in and out of consciousness but he could see George and Allan sliding David's body into one of those thick, black plastic bags. The platoon's loader and driver then walked over to Emmit.

"You ready, kid?" George asked.

Emmit tried to nod but he didn't have it in him. George and Allan bent down to take hold of the handles of the stretcher. The chopper Allan called in arrived and began to descend; its eight-inch thick propellers blowing the branches of the many trees into a manic dance. The pilot eased the steel bird downward until it made contact with the dirt path and he waited for the human cargo to be loaded.

"On three," George said and they heaved Emmit up off the ground.

Braving the chopper's hurricane, they rushed Emmit over to the open bay and carefully slid him in. George and Allan backed up and waved the pilot off. The chopper's turbines revved to full burn as it started gaining altitude. Shielding themselves from the flying debris, the two members of the 35th were joined by the medic who tended to Emmit's wounds.

"That was some pretty amazing shit," the medic yelled.

The helicopter's engine drowned out his voice.

"What's that?" George shouted.

"I said," the medic leaned in closer to George, "that was some pretty amazing shit!"

The chopper was far enough now that they could speak in a relatively normal pitch.

"No doubt," George remarked. "That kid can't weigh more'n 160 pounds and he dragged the Scrape at least 10 feet straight up."

"That's not all he brought back with him," the medic said.

George and Allan turned to face the medical officer.

"He was hit three times," the medic continued, his tone now decidedly dramatic. "Three shots straight to the head."

-2-

Emmit woke up. Right when the chopper touched down at HQ and the medics carted him into the infirmary.

Leaning back against the headboard, it took him a few seconds to remember when—and where—he was. Unfortunately, he was back in his room at Timberlake. For a second, he shuddered considering his current backdrop was more worrisome than being back in Vietnam.

Rubbing the sleep out of his eyes, he looked out the window. It was shaping up top be a beautiful day. Sad to say, looks often had a bad habit of being less than forthright.

He got out of bed and stretched the stiffness out of his muscles. Grabbing his bathrobe off the post of the headboard, he slipped it on and went into the bathroom. The room was warm but the tile floor was set to chill. Emmit raised himself up on the balls of his feet. He turned the water on, waiting for it to warm up along with the thick skin lining the soles of his feet.

As usual, he tried not to look in the mirror, but his old self always seemed to crave his attention. He opened the medicine cabinet and took out his toothbrush. Running his thumb along the bristles, he noted they were starting to fray.

"Looking the worse for wear my old friend," he said just loud enough to make out. "Pick a new one up at the pharmacy after breakfast."

As he began to clean up for the day, his mind crept back to that night's vision and the events that would lead him to the man he was always supposed to be.

Following the tunnel incident, Emmit spent the next three weeks recovering in the medical barracks in Da Nang. And while he didn't appreciate the fact that he was still alive and kicking until the morphine drip subsided, he grasped how incredible it was that he'd heard the medic talking to George and Allan.

Every word. Every syllable.

Emmit even caught the inflection in the medic's voice and how he dragged his 'S's. He'd heard it all, even though the chopper was shrieking loud enough to wake David.

His mind played the rest of the scenario out as he got dressed and left his room for the dining hall.

It was just after eight in the morning. He was running behind schedule. He often wondered why he even bothered keeping one. It wasn't like five or ten minutes made any lick of difference (or a few months for that matter). But he kept one at any rate, as adhering to a set agenda gave him something to do even though it wasn't rooted in anything even the slightest bit meaningful.

The one thing he couldn't complain about was the food. Forty-five hundred dollars a month was quite the nut, but at least the payment brought forth a bevy of tasty treats that gave Emmit something, if anything, to look forward to.

After swallowing down the last of his eggplant omelet, Emmit filled his travel mug with that delightful Vanilla French Roast they served on Tuesdays. He pulled on the cap to make sure it was properly fastened (he'd been extra-wary of being singed by hot beverages ever since that lady sued McDonald's for her blazing encounter). Satisfied he was safe, he turned around and made his way out to the gardens for his morning walk.

Much like the meals, the Timberlake grounds were undeniably sumptuous. With painstakingly groomed greenery and textured concrete walkways, it was a cover image straight out of *Better Homes and Gardens.*

The lush environ comforted Emmit. When he found himself casually strolling through the myriad formations of greenery and stone architecture, he was at peace with himself and his thoughts. It was a most welcome experience and a bit unnerving at the same time because the area was so reminiscent of the jungles of Vietnam.

Folding one arm behind his back and taking diligent sips of his coffee, Emmit wandered past the perfectly lined trees running along the periphery of the textured cobblestone path. The wind was stiff but warm. The sun was still hiding behind a formation of thick, puffy clouds, but according to the forecast (which confirmed Emmit's initial calculations) it was going to be a bright, beautiful day. He continued down the path, not thinking about anything in particular, when suddenly it dawned on him that he'd been looking at things the wrong way. All at once he considered, *if I look at it from a different angle, then maybe, just maybe, I can find some scrap of happiness.*

It was like making the best of a bad situation. Or getting a lump of coal for an anniversary and having the patience and strength to squeeze a diamond out of it. Besides, it wasn't like his residence at Timberlake was predicated by his inability to take care of himself. Nor was it prompted by an ungrateful child's wish to avoid wet nursing chores. If anything, Hanna and his younger daughter, Rachel, pleaded for him not to move into Timberlake. Well, Hanna did anyway. Rachel and Emmit hadn't been on very good terms before Celia passed and following that, they'd cut all ties. Hanna, on the other hand, made a concerted effort to keep up relations with her father no matter how emotionally distant he chose to be. In accordance with that, she'd invited Emmit to move in. He appreciated the offer but at the same time, he didn't want to be a burden. Even if he chose to look past that, he didn't feel comfortable soliciting her aid considering his duties had pulled him away from most of her formative affairs. As much as he was ever capable of, the one thing he could never do was be in two places at the same time. He was rarely there when Hanna or Rachel needed him, and he didn't feel right suddenly barging in on their lives when it seemed like he was the one in need. So, in his opinion, moving in to Timberlake was as much for Hanna and Rachel as it was for him.

Well, that wasn't necessarily true either.

Emmit had to get out of the public eye. He'd made too many enemies, most of which were still in their destructive prime. And even though his legislative benefactors guaranteed his safety, he wasn't quite naïve enough to buy into their hollow promises. So, appreciating his limited days would be cut that much shorter if he stayed out in the great wide open, he packed his bags, cashed in his savings bonds and stocks, and took his place amongst the Timberlake populace.

It was closing in on one o'clock. Emmit had been walking for hours and his hamstrings felt like freshly lit fuses. He hadn't noticed the pain until then. He'd gotten lost in his thoughts yet again. Maintaining his brand new glass-is-half-full demeanor, he took comfort in that the main building was only half-a-klick away. That, and not so long ago he could beat out Secretariat by a good furlong without the slightest grievance from ligament or tendon.

July 1966

Emmit had been a civilian for the better part of two months. Before he'd left for home and while he was recouping in Da Nang, he'd considered finishing his tour. But after David was killed, he just couldn't gather the resolve. His body and mind proved to be stronger than his seemingly indestructible sense of partisanship after all. The more he thought about it, the more he wanted to pack up and get back home to the life he started to build before he went to answer the call of his country.

The tunnel incident changed him and not just in a psychological sense. Emmit could feel something growing inside of him, something he'd always been cognizant of, but hadn't paid much attention to.

Not until then.

He wanted to get to know his new self—his true self—and he couldn't do it in the jungles of Vietnam where every sight and smell made him want to wretch.

Emmit came to a screeching halt at the intersection at Charles and Beacon Street. The stench of burnt rubber filled his nostrils. He looked down at the pair of Chuck Taylor's he'd purchased not a week prior and was discouraged to note the soles were already worn down to the nub.

It was his third pair that month.

Tapping one nostril shut with his finger, he blew the stench out and found cover behind one of the tall buildings. Peeking around the corner, he spotted the van he'd been following turn the corner onto Beacon Street.

Here goes nothing, he thought, and prepared to find out what he was really made of.

He'd first crossed paths with Michael Ditko three days earlier. It was just after 12 o'clock, and Emmit decided to enjoy the beautiful spring day by heading out for lunch. He didn't like spending his midday meal breaks in the office. After he'd secured his position at the paper, it wasn't long before his colleagues expressed their dislike for him. It wasn't that Emmit was an extreme introvert, which often made it appear as though he was an equally acute narcissist that set them off. Rather, it was his merciless work ethic. He'd come in at seven and stay 'til eight or nine most nights. He never believed in a nine-to-five mentality. Rather, he subscribed to establishing a loose schedule, which was dictated by the workload at hand. This proved to piss off the other worker bees to no end, as nothing could get under their skin more than such a hard-working and conscientious collaborator.

Making his way out onto Commonswealth Avenue, Emmit took the right onto Berkeley Street and headed for the Bean Village Café three blocks away. It had quickly become his favorite midday meal destination, and not just because he didn't enjoy his co-workers company.

Emmit pushed his way through the twin glass doors and started to look for his absolute favorite item on the Village's menu—that pretty girl with the short brown hair. A few quick takes and Emmit saw her standing by the coffee machine behind the lunch counter while she waited for a fresh pot to fill up. Emmit stopped just shy of the countertop, looking at her trying to seem like he wasn't. She turned around and did the same. As her eyes locked onto his, he casually looked the other way while he cracked a half-smile.

Before he turned away, he noticed she was wearing that bejeweled butterfly hairclip, another one of his favorites.

While there was no denying her bodily qualifications, Emmit's attraction to her was based on something much more than the mere physical. There was something indiscernibly special about her, something that came from deep inside and spoke to him in a language only he could speak. Much like David (but to a much greater extent), Emmit had a talent for reading people, knowing much more about their character without ever having to take the time to find out. But lately, this ability had grown exponentially. It was almost as if he could read people's minds, like he could shut out the rest of the stimuli the world was broadcasting and zero in on a singular person's thoughts, feelings and motivations.

Once the hefty man wearing the tattered workman's overalls dropped his tip onto the countertop (an 11% gratuity according to the check Emmit could clearly make out thirty feet away), Emmit made a beeline for the lone available seat.

That's when his recently upgraded clairvoyance kicked into overdrive.

Currents of supercharged electricity shot through his nervous system. It felt like his organs were being deep-fried. Emmit sat down and tried to corral the impulses. He focused, directing his thoughts and desires inwards and down into his deepest recesses until the feeling started to ebb. He straightened in his seat when another wave hit, this time even harder. He closed his eyes and honed in on his heartbeat. He'd discovered doing so helped him reel in the feeling—his power—and gave him control of it rather than the other way around. A few minutes of that and he was feeling a bit better.

The girl with the short brown hair arrived. She was carrying the pot of coffee, along with a smile so beautiful it made Emmit want to cry. "You again?" she said playfully.

Emmit choked back his tears and put on his best blasé face. "You say that like it's a bad thing."

"Far from it," she said and upturned the mug sitting in front of him. She filled it to the brim. "It's just that for a place with such lousy food, you sure do come by a lot."

"I guess that means there's another reason why I'm always here," he said knowingly.

As much as he flirted with her, it occurred to him that he didn't even know the girl's name. He'd never gathered the courage to ask. But that was the old Emmit. The run-of-the-mill version that got scared at the drop of a claymore. But a lot had changed for him in the past few months. Any resident doubt he was forced to suffer had been replaced with a smoldering sense of self-assurance.

He was about to finally ask what her name was, but another customer waved her down and she left to see what he wanted. As she hurried off, Emmit took the opportunity to steal back inside of himself so he could figure out what triggered the previous episodes.

Enter Michael Ditko.

When Emmit first walked into the café he'd felt Ditko, or his intentions, which according to the burning sensation in the pit of Emmit's stomach were all but good. Emmit took a sip off his mug and settled deeper into his chair. He aimed his energies toward the small circular table near the rear of the café, where Ditko and his running mate, Sandy Trimpe, were holed up.

Emmit tuned out all extraneous noises. People's voices were drowned out. Clattering dishes and jangling cutlery were stifled. All he could hear was the readily identifiable and frantic pounding of Trimpe's pulse and the steady throbbing of Ditko's arteries.

On one hand, Trimpe's exasperated blood flow made perfect sense. It was a natural, if not typical, side effect brought on by periods of heightened tension. And that described what was going on inside Trimpe to a 'T'. Again, that added up because he and Ditko were discussing the final details as pertained to their heisting the diamond exchange down on Beacon Street.

But Ditko?

He was the personification of calm, cool and collected. His breathing was easy. His heartbeat every bit as offhand. *Planning a big job like that doesn't mean all that much to such a salty dog*, Emmit supposed. *That or the man doesn't have a heart at all.*

Emmit kept digging until the girl with the short brown hair returned. "Do I even have to ask?" she asked/said.

"Only if you've got something in mind besides a grilled cheese sandwich," Emmit purred.

She cast off another tear-inducing smile. "Coming right up."

Emmit picked up his mug and waved it to her. "And a fresh cup when you have the chance."

She nodded and went off to call in the order, while Emmit cursed just under his breath because he'd again forgotten to ask her name. He resigned himself to finding out when she came back and returned his prodigious attention to Ditko and Trimpe.

May 2004

Emmit's eyes snapped open just when he slipped out from behind the building and readied himself to take down Ditko and Trimpe. A bit disappointed he woke up when things really started cooking, he got out of bed, washed up and headed down to the dining room.

For some reason or another, he'd been very hungry lately. Ravenous, actually. Like his ability to get to sleep, he'd lost most of his appetite since he'd joined the Timberlake population. But for the past few days, Emmit was his usual voracious self, which made the eggs benedict, 11-grain toast and raspberry torte all the more enjoyable.

It was Wednesday, so he filled his cup with the Columbia Narino Supremo blend. As per his hopelessly-ingrained routine, he checked the lid of his travel mug while he made a sharp about face from the coffee bar. With a casual, even stride, he journeyed to greet the most beautiful day that awaited him. Unfortunately his path to the oversized leaded doors leading to the gardens wasn't clear.

"Shit," he mouthed and bit his lip in anticipation of another insipid encounter with Angela Yablans.

"Well, well, well. Look who it is?" Angela said like she'd discovered some sort of rare species.

Emmit stopped in front of the longtime Timberlake resident and hoped his smile looked a lot more sincere than the feeling behind it. "Hello, Angela. How are you?" he regretted the question halfway through its enunciation.

"Pretty well. Though my back's been acting up. And I can't seem to remember where I put my reading glasses. Though I suppose that's not too bad considering…"

"Why don't you give me your prescription," Emmit interrupted. "I have a friend…his son's an optometrist. He gives me pretty good deals on whatever I need and…"

"Really? All right. I've got my prescription form in my room. I'll go and get it right now."

Emmit starched his grin. "No hurry. I'm just going for a walk. Why don't you give it to me at lunch?"

She thought about it for a moment like she was deliberating over some peace accord. Emmit waited, his tautening lips set to crack.

"Okay," Angela conceded.

"Terrific. I'll see you then."

Emmit waved goodbye as he walked off, this time with long, sweeping strides. He was glad to be rid of Angela but a bit worried about how he was going to get that prescription filled. He didn't have any friends he kept in regular contact with, let alone one that had a son who was an optometrist.

Stepping off the patio and onto the shortly-cropped lawn, Emmit turned his face up toward the sky and felt the sun warm his face. He kept looking upward while he walked down to the cobblestone path when he heard Frank wheezing from behind. "Excuse me…Mr. Rhoe…"

Emmit turned around and shot him a disapproving look.

"Sorry…Emmit. I don't mean to bother you, but I've got a letter here for you," Frank waved a small lavender envelope.

"Letter? From who?"

Frank jogged up beside him. Just out of breath, he said, "I'm not sure. I found it lying on the counter at front reception this morning."

He handed over the envelope, which had Emmit's name scrupulously printed on it.

"Here you go," he gave it over to Emmit. "And here I go. Enjoy your walk," Frank tipped his imaginary hat and waddled off.

Meanwhile Emmit just stood there, trying to stop his lower jaw from landing on top of the new pair of Birkenstocks he'd ordered from that mail order catalogue.

It wasn't unusual to get a letter. Not if your name wasn't Emmit Rhoe. He'd never had a visitor or correspondence of any kind. Not since he arrived at Timberlake. That was because nobody was supposed to know he was there, save for Rachel and Hanna. Based on the immaculate script, it definitely wasn't penned my either one of his daughters.

Staring down at that pretty purple envelope, he was amazed at how heavy it was; heavier than David's corpse; heavier than the rear end of Ditko's van.

The muscles in his forearms and fingers knotted and trembled. He just managed to open it and unfurl the neatly folded piece of stationary inside, which read in a most elegant handwriting:

The world still needs you.

That's all that was written, save for the telephone number at the bottom of the page.

-3-

Unlike the previous few nights, Emmit didn't get much, if any, sleep. That note—what it meant—kept him up until the sun crested above the pale, indigo cloud line hovering above his windowsill.

As if getting out of bed weren't already difficult enough, not sleeping the entire night made it all the more of a challenge. Emmit focused, braced himself and on his third try, the phone rang. Sitting up and leaning against the headboard, he stretched his arms out wide and let out a deep, cleansing yawn. The phone chirped again.

"All right. All right. Keep your pants on," he said and reached for the receiver. "Hello?"

"You didn't call."

Emmit shot up straight as a nail. He hadn't moved that quickly in years. "Who is this?"

"I'm afraid this is going to be a lecture, Mr. Rhoe. So please…for both our sakes, listen carefully to what I have to say, yes?"

For the first time in over a year Emmit set foot off the Timberlake grounds. Much like his decision to live there, remaining on property was a choice he'd made for himself. He could have left whenever the mood struck him, either on his own or on one of the excursions to the local malls, racetracks or casinos. But he felt old enough without taking part in any of those geriatric field trips. So for all that time he stayed firmly put. However, staving off feeling like Methuselah wasn't his primary motivation for not wandering past property lines. After all, the last thing he needed was to run into a KGB foil at the CambridgeSide Galleria, or an impromptu face-to-face with a rebel merc at the Sterling Suffolk Race Course.

The voice instructed Emmit to meet him at the Boston Public Garden on Boylston between Arlington and Charles Streets. "The northeast corner," he said. "Please be waiting by the cement bench overlooking the statue of George Washington at two o'clock tomorrow afternoon."

While Emmit didn't appreciate the cloak and dagger routine, he was somewhat gratified that the stranger did say please.

Emmit looked down at his watch—the gold and diamond-encrusted Barthelay Senator Elias gave him following the successful hostage retrieval in Ad Diwaniyah. He didn't really care for the timepiece. It was much too ostentatious for his liking. But it represented one of the few occasions anyone other than a civilian showed him any modicum of appreciation, so he wore it every now and again even though it made him feel like a Liberace impersonator.

It was going on two o'clock. Emmit pulled his sleeve back down and redirected his attention towards the statue of his country's Founding Father. He wondered if Mr. Washington had any inkling what history had in store for him. Continuing to gaze upon the regal looking figure, he felt that old sensation creep up from within. It was just a tangential impression at first, like when an arm or leg starts to fall asleep. But it wasn't long before the feeling intensified to that fiery pins and needles stage, and it began clawing its way out of Emmit just like he did from that tunnel.

He'd been feeling a lot like that lately—like his old self was growing sick and tired of lying about—ignored and unappreciated. Like that image in the mirror, it was trying to reassert itself. However, this time is was dissimilar in that Emmit recognized what was happening. Back when he first encountered his true self, there was a getting-to-know-me stage. A period of trial and error sprinkled with uncertainty and denial. But Emmit had 40 years of being *himself* securely fastened under his belt, and he was all too wary of what was transpiring from within.

Insofar as what was triggering the reemergence, he wasn't sure. He figured it could have been the letter. But when he considered he'd started to feel as such days prior, he was again left guessing at square one.

Two-oh-two. Emmit was still spying about trying to spot the face belonging to the voice when...

"You really have lost it, haven't you?"

Emmit spun around like a runaway top. "Who...?!"

"Settle down, Mr. Rhoe. I mean you no harm."

The man staring back at him was eerily recognizable. Emmit clenched his fists ready to fight. "Dr. Jayne?"

The familiar stranger shook his head and spit out a schoolgirl's giggle. "Indeed. I'm Dr. Jayne, Mr. Rhoe. But not the one you've come to loathe. My name is Henry. Henry Jayne," the gaunt-looking man stuck out a surprisingly firm palm. "Pleased to finally make your acquaintance."

Emmit was too shocked to return the sentiment.

"I can't say as I blame you for your lack of propriety, Mr. Rhoe. I've been told my resemblance to my father is...unnerving, yes?" Henry took a seat on the bench. "I've always thought I looked more like my mother, but that's neither here nor there." He tapped the empty space beside him. "Please. Sit."

Emmit took a load off without taking his eyes off Henry. He nearly missed the seating surface of the bench as he descended. Settled in now, there was an awkward silence until Henry looked at Emmit thoughtfully and said, "He certainly does cut a mean figure of a man, doesn't he?"

Emmit kept his watch over Henry.

"Remind you of anyone you used to know?"

Still locked in on the doctor, Emmit's expression hardened like the statue Henry was admiring.

"You're his son?" Emmit said.

Henry nodded.

"Of Doctor Samuel Jayne?

Henry nodded again.

"He never said he had a son."

Now Henry smiled, the kind brought on by understanding rather than appreciation.

"You should know better than most my father kept matters close to the vest," Henry said. "His family situation withstanding, yes?"

"What do you want?"

"Didn't you read my letter?"

"What's that got to do...?"

"With who I am?" Henry interjected as he pulled a slender silver case out of his pocket.

Reflexively, Emmit pulled away.

"Please, Mr. Rhoe. I was being truthful when I told you I mean no harm," Henry slowly opened the case to reveal a neat row of hand-rolled cigarettes. "Not to you at any rate."

Henry plucked one of the cigarettes between his full lips and reached into the breast pocket of his mohair blazer for his matches.

"So you say," Emmit said feeling a bit more at ease. "But given your alleged family's history, how did you expect me to react?"

Henry mulled the query over. He dragged a match on the surface of the concrete bench and offered, "I'm not quite sure. Surprised. Curious. Concerned?"

"More disinterested," Emmit braced himself and stood up trying to make it seem like it was no mean feat. "I'm done with living in the past, my good doctor. If you're so interested in ancient history, the Boston Public Library's a few blocks west of here on Boylston."

Henry watched intently while Emmit strode off. "It appears as though I was correct in my assumption, yes?"

Emmit slowed but didn't stop. "Assumption?"

"Yes, Mr. Rhoe. The assumption. The one I've made concerning what's happened to you."

He hated to acquiesce but Emmit's sense of curiosity was soundly piqued now. "What the hell are you talking about?" he turned around. "And how did you find me?"

Henry took a long, steady drag off his cigarette and blew a near perfect series of rings into the calm afternoon air. "I really don't think that's relevant right now."

Piqued reverted to pissed.

"Look…I may not have the old stuff," Emmit said tightly clasping his hands together, "but judging by that scrawny neck of yours, I'd say I can still wring it easily enough."

"Undoubtedly. But I think we'd both be better served if we concentrated on something a bit more positive," Henry said almost lyrically. "Especially considering the precarious position our future is in."

While Emmit's English degree gave him an appreciation for the depths of Henry's vocabulary, he didn't feel nearly as respectful of the doctor's unremitting Mulberry Bush routine. But as hard as he tried to focus the energies that roiled inside of him, he wasn't able to establish what to make of Henry or his motives. All he was certain of was the urge to wrap his mitts around Henry's reedy neck so he could squeeze the truth out of him.

"We must deal with the here and now, Mr. Rhoe. With what's happened with you. Or rather…what hasn't happened," Henry said with a tinge of sorrow.

"Come again?"

"With you, Mr. Rhoe. What isn't happening with you. How else can you explain my being able to sidle right up behind you without you knowing any better?"

He was right of course. But even though, Emmit wasn't ready to tip his entire hand. Not yet.

"Maybe," Emmit said, hoping he sounded a lot more sure than he actually was. "But even if that's so—and I do mean if—why do I have any reason to be what I once was?"

"Rest assured, I again must say that I pose no threat to you, Mr. Rhoe," Henry dropped his cigarette to the ground. He raised his leg and crushed the butt underneath the heel of a pristine Florsheim. "In fact, my intentions are quite the opposite."

"Is that a fact?"

"Indeed. Allow me to explain," Henry pulled back to thumb through his impressive lexicon. "Let me begin by apologizing for that letter I sent you yesterday. This world is cryptic enough without having to suffer through such drivel. And believe you me…I would never have entered into such an Agatha Christie-inspired melodrama if it weren't absolutely necessary."

"Looks like you share more than just a face with your old man. He took a millennium to get to the bloody point, too."

Henry held up a lissome hand. "Again, please accept my most humble apologizes, Mr. Rhoe. But you must believe me when I say there are some valid reasons as to why I have contacted you, yes?"

Emmit waved him on.

"But of course. Now…where was I? Oh yes. The letter."

Emmit's suspicions concerning Dr. Jayne Jr. were in no way assuaged. But he started to think Henry was right in his declaration, which had taken him the better part of an hour to get to.

"You haven't lost your gifts," Henry explained. "You've simply forgotten how to open them."

Emmit told Henry he admired the craftsmanship of his similes, but their timing certainly left much to be desired.

"Please…allow me to explain, Mr. Rhoe," Henry cleared his throat and got ready for the big number, "You see, what you are…at the core of your being is something that I have only recently come to understand."

Emmit looked at him doubtfully. "You're telling me you figured out what your father and all of those white coats at Berkeley couldn't?"

"Yes. I've read the white papers. Every last one of them. And they were on the right path. But like my father, they never arrived at any indisputable conclusion."

"And you have?"

Henry's chest jutted out ever-so-slightly and his chin peaked. "Indeed, Mr. Rhoe. I most certainly have."

Emmit was justifiably interested. But it was only when Henry revealed why his father developed such a hatred for Emmit that his ears pricked up to full attention.

"You must appreciate this, Mr. Rhoe. You were everything he was not—strong, confident, self-reliant. But more than anything, you were an...anomaly. Yes. That's how he used to put it. You were an anomaly. Something not yet defined by medical science."

Emmit wasn't sure he agreed. "I always thought I left a bad taste in his mouth because I never sided with him and his political agenda."

"That did play a part in it, yes. But at the risk of condescending, Mr. Rhoe, the reason behind his feelings toward you is really quite simple. My father was mad. There's no denying that. And cruel. But above all, he was a physician. As such, he was rooted in a world of formulae and procedure. Every question has an eventual answer. Every query a final solution. You were the first thing—the first person—he ever failed to rejoin."

Emmit nodded meekly. "I guess."

"No, Mr. Rhoe. I'm sure of it. He told me so. In no uncertain terms, I might add. And I don't mind telling you it drove him insane."

"I don't think he needed any help with that."

"Indeed. Insanity is an unfortunate derivative of genius. My father had stockpiles of both. But I didn't contact you to discuss my father's psychological standing. Nor did I come here with the intention of playing the hackneyed role of the deluded offspring in search of vengeance for his maker's ultimate disgrace."

"Thank you. I think."

"You're quite welcome," Henry stretched out his legs and stood up from the bench. "The long and the short of it, Mr. Rhoe, is that I have gone to such considerable effort to contact you because your special gifts are desperately needed. And they are needed now."

May 1966

Following Emmit's release from the hospital in Chu Lai, he was granted a full discharge. Aside from the field medic's astonished reaction (and how Emmit was able to take note of it), he hadn't thought much, if at all, about how amazing his escape at the tunnel was. All he knew or cared about was that he was free to start a life of his own choosing. What he didn't know was the U.S. military set its sights on him, and would soon be knocking down his door to solicit his one-of-a-kind talents. For the time being, though, they were content to patch him up and send him on his merry way while they prepared to take the next step.

Dr. Samuel Jayne was the presiding surgeon who removed the bullets from Emmit's skull. Subsequently, he was chosen to lead the coming study that would attempt to validate why Emmit found himself above ground as opposed to six feet under.

Like Emmit's family, Samuel's was steeped in military service, albeit in a much different fashion. Emmit's ancestors were all warriors, while Samuel's intimates were healers. Samuel had taken up his kin's tradition by leaving the Miami NeuroScience Center at the Baptist Hospital in South Florida, and joining the 1st Medical Battalion as it attempted to deliver on its motto of helping *to conserve the fighting strength.*

Samuel began his tour in September 1965 only a few months after the U.S. Marines established the Chu Lai Combat Base some 56 miles south of Da Nang. With these marines came 'B' Company, 3rd Medical Battalion. Their primary mission was to form the hub of the medical facility, which was assigned to support the activities in southern I Corp. Initially, this beach unit operated out of sparsely-appointed tents, but soon moved up and out to the rocky bluffs that overlooked the South China Sea. A few months later, the 1st Medical Battalion joined Chu Lai, incorporating the 'B' Med originals into a much larger and capable medical unit.

Rapid expansions continued with a tripled bed capacity, new wards and casualty sorting and treatment areas. New operating rooms were also constructed, along with permanent living quarters. Samuel was one of the first to take residence in these private areas. It was there where he would meet the man that would change his life in ways he (and the rest of the world) could not possibly imagine.

* * *

After only two weeks and some days, Emmit was ready to leave the Chu Lai Base. His wounds had miraculously healed, and the only reason he was still there was because Samuel stalled his release. But there was no reason for Emmit to remain and to keep him there would just raise further suspicion.

While Emmit finished packing the few belongings into his army-issue duffel, Samuel appeared through the canvas flap that hung over the entrance to the ward.

"All ready to go, I see," Samuel said doing his darnedest to veil his disappointment.

Emmit slipped the plastic bag filled with his toiletries into the duffel and turned to face the doctor. "Yessir. Just grabbing my stuff and I'm a memory."

It was all Samuel could do not to throw Emmit onto the bed, strap him down and prod, jab and stick him with any medical device within reach so he could find out what was winding Private Rhoe's clock. Samuel wanted to know everything about the young man, inside and out. What kind of family did he come from? What was his background? What were his interests? Samuel wanted to know it all so he could start building his character profile and find out how the young man standing before him was still able to stand. But he'd been given strict orders from the higher ups not to ask or reveal syllable one. Not until the military could figure out what to do with their most extraordinary private.

"How are you feeling?" Samuel asked softly.

Emmit slung the duffel over his shoulder. "Fine, all things considered."

Samuel walked up to Emmit and reached out, inspecting the unnecessary dressing wrapped about Emmit's forehead. "No headaches or dizziness?"

Emmit shook his head.

"Nausea? Blurry vision?"

"Nope."

Samuel stepped back and jotted down a few notes on the clipboard he always kept at his side. "Well, I guess you are a memory then," he extended his hand.

Emmit shook it and thanked Samuel for tending to his most grievous wounds.

"Just doing my job," Samuel said, and released Emmit from Chu Lai but never from his thoughts.

June 1966

Samuel had been called to attend a meeting with General Lionel Umbridge, a well-respected if not notorious military figure. The five-star general was revered and reviled at an equal pace, though his monstrous ego never allowed him to recognize the latter sentiment. While he was indeed a tyrant, misogynist, racist and bigot, his military background was unmatched and his ability to get the job done was every bit as supreme. That explained why his superiors put him in charge of this particular movement, and why they had every reason to believe that it would succeed even beyond their most lofty expectations.

Samuel thought it strange such a high-ranking military envoy requested his presence, though he didn't doubt for a moment what the general had on his mind. Umbridge requested that Samuel meet him in Hanoi City, which was a far cry from Chu lai both in vicinity and character. Samuel had never been there, though he'd heard some interesting if not racy tales concerning the city. He was eager to see what all the fuss was about with his own eyes.

Stepping out of his tent he couldn't wipe the smile off his face no matter how foolish he felt wearing it. He was very much looking forward to the trip. He couldn't wait to stride down a walkway paved in cement rather than dirt. He was excited by the prospect of breaking bread in a hall that didn't serve its meals out of oversized metal bins.

He stood there in silence, enjoying the solitude and wondering how accurate those stories he'd heard were, when an MP officer pulled up in a Jeep.

"Dr. Jayne?"

"Present."

"Sorry I'm late, doctor. There was a backup at the motorcade. You all ready to hit that dusty trail?"

Samuel picked up his travel bag and waved it at the driver. "Willing and able."

The Jeep turned onto the crudely fashioned dirt road. Slowly creeping past the med tents, the MP officer turned onto the main road that headed due north and would take them past Phu Bai, Quang Tri, Dong Ha, then veer past the DMZ and Vinh. A nonstop journey would have taken over three hours, but Samuel's delicate inner workings soon proved to make a perpetual trip impossible.

An hour later, the MP officer was forced to pull off to the side of the road. "You okay, Dr. Jayne?" he asked again as he tried to stop his eyeballs from rolling free of their respective sockets.

Samuel wiped his mouth with a fresh handkerchief and slinked back into the passenger seat. "Yes. I think so," he said. "Sorry about this, but I've suffered from motion sickness since I was a child."

"Don't sweat it," the MP officer said now biting his tongue. "A lot of people don't like riding in these pogo sticks. 'Specially for such long stretches."

He put the Jeep back into gear and slowly made his way back onto the road, wondering how joyous (and moist) Samuel's chopper ride into Vietnam must have been.

Not quite four hours later, the Jeep passed the Gulf of Tomken and was approaching the outskirts of Ninh Binh. Samuel just managed to keep hold of the remainder of his breakfast as the driver pointed out Hanoi, which was five klicks ahead.

A few minutes later, the MP officer gingerly pulled up to the curb and shifted the gear stalk of the Jeep into neutral. Samuel snapped up his travel bag and carefully stepped out of the vehicle. He was still woozy, but was feeling much better having finally settled onto solid ground.

"You sure you don't want me to wait around?" the MP officer asked.

Samuel shook his head. "No. That's all right. I think I'll take the time and walk around a bit to clear my head." He thanked the officer for the ride and tipped his fedora while the Jeep merged into traffic.

The streets were teeming with motorcycles, mopeds and dilapidated European-made autos. The sidewalks were just as animated, so much so Samuel could barely see the pavement underneath his feet.

Umbridge told Samuel to meet him and Captain Sara Jusko, his right hand for this initiative (but not of his choosing—she was, after all, a woman) at the Sofitel Metropole Hotel. According to the directions Samuel had scrawled down in his best physician's handwriting, the inn was seemingly located in the Hoan kiem district at 15 Ngo Quyen, which he assumed was the name of the street. Umbridge arranged for a three o'clock meeting. It was already a quarter to, but Samuel was having such a grand old time he decided to keep on walking.

He wasn't sure what he expected to see but a sprawling, vibrant municipality wasn't it. Hanoi, at least that section of it, was a different world than the one Samuel had been trudging through since he arrived in Vietnam. It was a most welcome change of environments. The city seemed to breathe as freely and tenaciously as all those who frequented it. Samuel had always been a city folk, and it felt good to once again be surrounded by the liveliness that only a large urban setting could manufacture. He continued to enjoy his new surroundings, slowly strolling down the bustling sidewalk, smiling at those willing to return the outlook as they hurried on by. He kept following the narrow path for the next 20 minutes until he turned the corner onto Ngo Quyen.

Sofitel Metropole had been a fixture in Hanoi since 1901. The French colonial style inn, which nuzzled up beside the Hoan kiem lake, was steeped in history. Many perceived it as *the* history of Hanoi; Metropole hosted the first motion picture screened in Indochina; it was where Charlie Chaplin spent his honeymoon, and where countless (and purposefully nameless) heads of state and embassy officials resided for years on end. These were just a few of the facility's more outstanding moments, and why it had become one of the most sought after and admired locales in all of Hanoi.

Samuel kept on delighting in the age-old architecture as he walked under the front canopy and pushed his way through the revolving front doors. Inside, he was pleased to note just as much thought had gone into the Metropole's interior; high-polished marble flooring gleamed brilliantly and was perfectly accented with handcrafted wood cabinetry; exquisitely detailed stucco ceilings worked in seamlessly with the countless antique brass ornaments that were positioned all about.

Samuel neared the front desk. The clerk working behind the counter was involved with another patron who was checking out. Leaning on what he assumed was a dark-stained oak countertop, he drummed his thumbs and waited for her to finish.

"Yah. How may I help?"

Samuel breathed a sigh of relief. She spoke English. "I'm looking for…" he trailed off and pulled out the paper with the directions he'd written. "…the Le Beaulieu Restaurant?"

She pointed straight ahead. "Go down the hallway. Your first left."

General Lionel Warren Umbridge didn't like many things and waiting wasn't on his short list of contraries. He looked over to his colleague, Captain Sara Jusko, who appeared to be every bit as uneasy as her superior.

"Where the hell is he already?" Umbridge snarled.

As much as Umbridge didn't appreciate her tagging along, she felt even more uncomfortable being there. The two did share one thing in common—she wasn't fond of many things either, and the general was a definitive inclusion on her list. "He should be here any time now," she said. "I spoke to HQ in Da Nang. They said Dr. Jayne left about an hour ahead of schedule."

"I most certainly did," Samuel said. "Unfortunately, we experienced a bit of a mechanical difficulty along the way."

Both officers looked up to the lithe, unassuming man standing before them.

"Maybe if you took a chopper in like I told you, we could've gotten underway as planned," Umbridge said.

Samuel barely made it out of the Jeep in one piece. He wasn't ready to defy the tumult caused by one of those insufferable whirly birds.

"Yes, well...we're glad you made it here safely," Sara said apologetically, and pulled out the available chair between her and her commanding officer.

Samuel took a seat, still expecting to be introduced. Sara was waiting for the general to go ahead with the preamble, fearing another buttoning-down if she dared supersede him (she'd made the mistake earlier that week when she arranged to set up the meeting without consulting with Umbridge's secretary first). When Umbridge just sat there with his arms folded airtight, she warily stepped in.

"Dr. Samuel Jayne, this is General Lionel Umbridge..."

The general jutted out his hand without taking his eyes off the tabletop.

"And I'm Captain Sara Jusko."

Samuel shook her hand. "It's a pleasure to meet you both."

"Now that we've stowed the pleasantries, let's get down to brass tacks," Umbridge said sharply.

Before they could do that, the waiter arrived. Samuel looked up to the man and noted the anxious look on his face. Obviously, the general had already introduced himself.

"Wha' can I get you to drink?" the waiter said politely.

"What kind of whiskey you got?" Umbridge asked.

The waiter thought about it for a moment. His English was fragmented. Compounding coherence, it was only his third day on the job and he was still learning the menu offerings. "Umm...okay. We got Jameson, Bushmills, Canady Club...no, waitaminnut...Canada Club..."

Umbridge stopped him. "You got anything distilled in the U.S. of 'A'?"
"You mean American?"
Umbridge sighed. "Jesus Christ. Yeah. American…" he pointed out the flag on his uniform in confirmation.
"Umm…okay. Hold it now…we got, lessee…Jim Beam, Jack Daniel…South Comfort…"
"Southern Comfort?" Umbridge corrected.
The waiter nodded.
"Well, why didn't you say so? Gimme a glass of that. Neat."
He looked at Umbridge curiously.
"No ice," Umbridge explained mockingly.
The waiter etched the order down on his notepad. "For the officer lady?"
"Just water, thank you. How about you, Dr. Jayne?"
"I think I'll have a glass of ice water as well. I haven't been feeling well lately, and…"
The waiter didn't wait for Samuel to finish and skipped off to the bar. Umbridge, meanwhile, hunkered down in his seat hoping none of his contemporaries were there to see him breaking bread with those lacking the requisite testosterone to order a proper libation.

Once they'd finished the first round of drinks, Sara ordered the chicken cordon bleu. Samuel's still sour stomach could only handle a bowl of viche sois and Umbridge had a hamburger (he'd lost his taste for all things Parisian ever since he'd gotten back from WWII). Surprisingly, the waiter managed to come back with their meals in a short time. Digging in, the general glazed over the reason why he'd called Samuel down to Hanoi. But it wasn't until the coffee was ordered that he got down to those *brass tacks* of his.
"General Tannenzapf put me on to you," Umbridge explained. "Said you were the best of the best."
"Well…I'm not sure you can categorize neurosurgeons that way," Samuel said modestly, "we're all eminently qualified. But tell the general I appreciate his high praise."
"It's the first thing on my *to-do* list. For the time being, why don't you tell me a little more about Private Rhoe?"
The question hung in the air like one of those Acme anvils in a Roadrunner cartoon. "Emmit?"
"I think that's his first name. Good, strong one at that. Hard to believe he's a Jew."

Sara cleared her throat uneasily. "I think what General Umbridge would like to know is how seriously Private Rhoe was hurt."

"I don't understand. I sent you a detailed file when you requested that information," Samuel said. "Didn't you receive it?"

"We got it all right," Umbridge corroborated, "but for a situation as peculiar as this, I need more than words scribbled down on some papers."

"Well, I'm afraid papers are all I have to offer at this point," Samuel lifted the small case he'd brought along onto the table. He unsnapped the silver latches and started filtering through the contents until he arrived at Emmit's medical file. Pulling it out, he slipped on the pair of cheaters he always kept in his shirt's breast pocket. "Let's see now...ah. Here we are." Samuel grabbed one of the x-rays he'd taken when Emmit was first admitted at 1st Medical Battalion in Chu Lai and displayed it to the officers.

"We've already seen this," Umbridge said.

"You've seen it. But have you appreciated it?" Samuel asked, his eyebrows rising to two rounded peaks.

"That's why we called you here, Dr. Jayne," Sara said.

"Of course. Now, if you'll take a look here," Samuel pointed to the left of Emmit's cranium. "This is where the first bullet hit. As you can see, it merely grazed his skull." Samuel slid his index finger on top of Emmit's parietal lobe. "Now here's where it gets *peculiar* as you put it, General Umbridge."

They all stared at the x-ray. They were so immersed in their study nobody noticed the waiter standing there holding a carafe of coffee. Samuel slipped the x-ray back into the folder while the waiter upturned the china cups already set on the white linen tablecloth. He loosened the top of the carafe and filled each cup. "Anything more?"

"That will do for now," Sara said.

Once the waiter was gone, Samuel drew out the x-ray. He went on with his findings while Sara and Umbridge poured cream and sugar into their coffee.

"The second bullet was lodged eight millimeters deep right here," Samuel said growing more excited. "Right in the parietal lobe."

"Have you ever seen anything like this before, Dr. Jayne?" Sara asked.

"Of course. This war has produced far too many type wounds. But in my experience, they've all proved fatal."

Pulling his cheaters down to the bulb of his nose, Samuel watched Umbridge sink his spoon into his drink, swearing he could see a ragged dorsal fin poking out from the swirling beige liquid.

"Peculiar," the general said. "Very peculiar."

* * *

After Samuel got back to Chu Lai he headed straight for his quarters. Thankfully, the ride back proved much kinder to his delicate sensibilities than the trek to Hanoi. But it had been a long day and his head was aching something fierce. He just wanted to pop a few aspirins, climb into bed, turn out the light and gather his strength for the new day.

Carl Hulce, another neurosurgeon and a longtime friend from Naples, Florida, stopped Samuel before he could sequester himself. "Hey…there you are…" Carl trotted up beside him. "When did you get back?"

"Just now. Look…I don't mean to be rude, but I've got a terrible headache, and…"

"No bother," Carl said. "I just wanted to make sure everything went all right. I know how you hate long drives."

Samuel thanked Carl for his concern and told him he'd fill him in on all the details first thing in the morning.

A few minutes later, Samuel was in his private chamber. He dropped his case onto his bunk, noting he hadn't made the bed that morning. He couldn't remember the last time he'd left without tidying up. *Shame on me*, he thought, and he pulled the sheets and blankets tightly across the well-worn mattress. Once he was through he opened his case and started looking through Emmit's file again. He laid the pages out on the mattress and kneeled down beside the rusted steel frame of the bed. Flipping through the many outputs, he stopped at the x-ray he'd gone over with Umbridge and Sara.

He homed in on the third bullet, which found its final resting place in Emmit's occipital lobe. Samuel had kept his wonderment under wraps during the meeting (to the best of his ability, anyway). He'd gotten into the habit of not trusting military brass. Sara seemed nice enough, however General Umbridge made the hair on the back of Samuel's neck stand at attention. He was almost certain the general was up to no good, at least when weighed against Samuel's moral code. But this was just supposition, a premise Samuel developed. It wasn't until Umbridge asked who knew about Emmit's situation that Samuel knew something bad was on its way.

Though the feeling did pass. For a while. The days went by. Then weeks. Samuel hadn't heard back from Umbridge and the concerns he had regarding the general's intentions started to slip away. Unfortunately, they reared their devious little heads once again early the following month.

Samuel was just finishing up in the OR tending to another head wound. It was a four-hour procedure, and he'd been up for 36 straight hours. He'd barely gathered the energy to stitch the soldier back up, and had to brace himself on the wash basin as he scrubbed the dry blood out beneath his well-manicured fingernails. As he reached for a towel, Carl joined him.

"That couldn't have gone any better," Carl said happily.

Samuel slipped out of his blood-stained smock and said, "Every now and again it happens."

Carl began digging away at the plasma he'd gathered during the operation and suddenly took on a sad tone. "Not for some people."

Samuel looked at him curiously. "What do you mean?"

"You didn't hear? Another suicide bomber hit one of the bases in Cu Chi."

Nothing new there. Suicide bombings were as commonplace as car accidents in this godforsaken place. "How many this time?" Samuel asked fearfully.

"That's the good news. I guess you could call it that since there were only three casualties," Carl explained. "Two grunts from the 35th tank infantry and a field med."

Samuel wasn't sure why, but the mention of the three men's death struck him as oddly sinister.

"You didn't happen to catch their names?" Samuel asked.

"Not the two from the 35th. Why?"

"What about the medic?"

Carl thought about it for a second. "Actually, I think the announcer said his name was Lambert. George Lamb…"

Samuel spun around and ran for his quarters. He fumbled for the deadbolt affixed to his locker and ran the dial through the combination. Throwing the lock aside, he tore the locker door open, grabbed his case and rooted through it for Emmit's file. "Lambert. Lambert…" he chanted, until he came upon the report he was looking for—the one with statements made by those who witnessed the events at the tunnel.

"Allan Winnick…" he said running his finger down to the next column. "…George Franscicus…" he continued until he arrived at…"George Lambert."

All at once the world seemed like a much more dangerous place.

-4-

They'd arranged to meet at Henry's home at one o'clock the following Monday. Henry wanted to *get cracking* as he put it, sooner, but Emmit still had a lot of things to sort his way through, so he stalled the doctor for the next four days.

He still wasn't convinced Henry was who he claimed to be. As guarded as Samuel was about his personal life, Emmit was sure the doctor would have let on that he had a son. Then again, Henry appeared to be in his early to mid-50s, which meant he would have been born years prior to Samuel's military involvement. God only knows what he was up to before that.

This time, Emmit's eyelids didn't flap like a languid butterfly. They snapped open like a Venus flytrap on a mission. He swung his legs over the side of the bed and straightened himself out taking a moment to allow his body to loosen up. It had been a humid night and even though the room was air conditioned, Emmit chose to open the window for a little extra circulation. While it made sleep a lot easier to come by, the cool breeze wafting over him the entire night made his back tighter than Ebenezer.

With a scowl, he reached out for his robe. He slipped into it and flipped the television on to catch the weather report. Dropping the remote onto the bed, he slowly turned around and entered the bathroom.

"Slippers," Emmit muttered as he tiptoed on the cold tiles, "must remember to buy slippers."

Emmit braced himself on the sink and squeezed some toothpaste on his brush. He began jabbing the bristles through his teeth (which were all factory originals he was proud to say) and kept an ear out for the forecast. The meteorologist on Channel 8, the tall, lean, middle-aged man with the impossibly bad comb over, didn't foresee any rain. But judging by the thickening, hoary clouds blocking out the sky, Emmit decided it best to bring along his overcoat.

After he'd finished up in the bathroom, Emmit got dressed—a tan Polo shirt, navy blue chinos and his Birkenstocks. He thumbed through his wallet to make sure he had enough cash.

"On fifty three…four…five," he said then folded the leather case up and slid it into his back pocket.

Heading down the hallway to the elevator, Emmit did his best not to look around at all those sallow, routine faces. When he paid too much attention, he couldn't stop from wandering what was going through their minds— guessing if their collective moods mirrored their dull expressions. For their sakes, he sincerely hoped they did not.

Down in the lobby, Emmit dropped his keys into his coat pocket and fastened the belt tightly. He spotted Frank sitting behind the main desk, going through the day's agenda with some of his colleagues. Emmit slinked on by. He didn't want Frank or any of the others to spot him, fearing another absurd comment regarding his leaving the grounds again. Not that he could blame them for noticing. After all, he'd stayed put for almost four years and all of a sudden he was heading out the door for the second time in under a week.

"Going out again, are we, Mr. Rhoe?" Frank said peering above his clipboard.

Emmit smiled brightly and tapped the desk as he walked by. "I can't speak on your behalf, but I'll be back around five."

Henry lived in Beacon Hill, a well-to-do suburb some 20 miles north of Timberlake. Wherever you looked it was as if Norman Rockwell dropped his paintbrush and picked up an architect's T-square. It was a pleasant, quaint neighborhood with low-traffic, quiet streets and thoroughly preserved 19th century-built houses tidily strung along as far as the eye could wander.

Emmit considered moving the family there many years ago but thought the better of it once Celia's parents moved into the quaint district. It was bad enough having to go to the in-laws every Sunday night for dinner and swallow down that tempestuous chopped liver and brisket with a smile. He shuddered to think of how their unions (and subsequent portions) would increase if they lived across the street from one another.

*   *   *

Stepping out of the cab, Emmit paid the driver. He tipped him five dollars, well over the amount required for the 18 dollar fare. Thanking him heartily in what Emmit immediately recognized as a Saudi accent, the cabbie eased out of the driveway. Emmit watched his ride pull away while he cinched up the belt to his overcoat and started walking up the long, twisting path that led to 346 Chestnut Lane.

It was a large house. Especially considering Henry lived alone. Emmit looked about the impressive abode. It fit right in with its well-groomed shrubbery, impeccably maintained masonry and matching ornamental lamppost and mounted lighting brackets, which all appeared to be forged out of pewter.

Emmit stepped up onto the front porch and prepared to knock on the door. Henry opened up before he got the chance. "Right on time," Henry said cheerfully. "Please...come in."

The foyer had a cathedral ceiling that revealed most of the bottom floor's layout, which looked like it had been recently updated. As Henry walked Emmit through the house, Emmit thought it was much like he imagined— ornate but not overstated. Clean but not fanatically so.

"You didn't have any difficulty finding the house, did you?" Samuel asked.

"Took a cab," Emmit said. "My eyes aren't what they used to be and the DMV thought it best for everyone involved that I hand over my keys."

Henry gently patted Emmit on the back. "Well...let's see if we can't change their minds, yes?"

Continuing along the main floor their footsteps cast a dull, unnatural echo that filled the open area. Henry stopped at the last door on the left which led into his private study. "Please. After you," he said.

Emmit looked at him amusedly. "Age before beauty, eh?"

Like the rest of the house the study emulated Henry's character. It was stylishly appointed but without breaking a sweat. Henry asked for Emmit to take a seat as he sank down behind the antique cherry wood desk sitting in the middle of the room. Emmit found his mark in one of the Victorian crown top balloon back chairs stationed in front of the desk. Reaching into his pocket for his silver case, Henry pulled out a cigarette and looked on at Emmit appreciatively. "So. Here we are," he said with a deep, penetrating smile.

Emmit returned the expression albeit in a toned down edition. "Happy to be here. Though not quite as happy as you by the looks of it."

Henry blushed. "I'm sorry if I seem overexcited. But consider it from my perspective. My father being who he was..." his face returned to its usual pigment as he trailed off to light his smoke. "...having been the engineer to those many atrocities. I've toiled my entire life trying to outrun the dark shadow he's cast and..."

"Say no more," Emmit interrupted. "I understand what it's like living up to unreasonable expectations."

"Indeed. Which is why we're here, yes?"

"So you've said. But before we start in on whatever it is you've got in mind...I need to know what's going on."

"All good things to those who wait, Mr. Rhoe."

Emmit considered telling Henry he didn't care for the *mister* inference, but for some reason he didn't mind it coming from him. "I'm old, my good doctor. But not that old. You don't have to talk to me like I'm your demented grandfather."

"I'm sorry. I wasn't aware that I was."

Emmit's vague smile returned. "Don't worry about it. But please...if you want to know if I want the soup, all you have to do is ask me."

Henry wrinkled his nose.

"Just tell me why I'm really here."

Henry looked Emmit over carefully. Emmit squirmed in his chair knowing right then what a lab rat must feel like.

"You're right, Mr. Rhoe. Of course you are. It's just that I'm so happy to finally have you here, I forgot to consider how you must be feeling."

Emmit told him it wasn't a problem. Not as long as Henry explained exactly what was going on.

Not long after, the term, *be careful what you ask for,* took on an entirely new and horrifying meaning.

"Are you all right?" Henry asked once more. "I've got some ginger ale in the refrigerator..."

Emmit apologized for vomiting on Henry's Oriental rug and wiped his mouth with the paper towel Henry brought in from the kitchen. "This is a joke, right? I mean...it's got to be."

Henry shook his head sorrowfully. "I wish it were. More than anything. But I'm afraid the situation is all too real, Mr. Rhoe."

It was a nightmare. That's what it was. Emmit's most heinous, vile dream come to four-color life. And what that was, was this...

Some 14 years ago the Gulf War (or CNN marketing campaign as many thought it to be), was coming to an end and the world prepared to go about its business as usual. Or so it seemed. According to Henry, several high-ranking Middle Eastern political and military officials made provisions to ensure their homelands would not meet the same fate they had during the Gulf onslaught.

"They'd contacted my father years prior," Henry explained as he started a fresh cigarette. "Before, well...before he met his end."

Emmit felt more uncomfortable than ever. Thinking about Samuel—especially their last encounter—still made him break out in a cold sweat.

Henry could see Emmit was having a hard time of it and asked if it was all right to continue. Emmit waved him on.

"At first they were only interested in his formula," Henry said. "The one he'd started to fabricate when the military concluded what you really were. Or thought you were. Although he hadn't perfected the process, they felt with the proper funding and new technology at their disposal they could see it through to completion."

"But they never did," Emmit affirmed.

"No. Fortunately not. But that didn't stop them from making use of every last piece of data my father compiled on you."

Emmit shuddered inside. Suddenly it was very hot. It felt as though his insides had been scooped out and tossed into a simmering pot.

"Somehow their scientists managed to find a way to complete the process. Not as my father intended, but to the point where the recipients could perform at similarly high levels for brief periods of time..."

And that's when Emmit boiled over.

Henry returned from the kitchen with a dishrag, a roll of paper towel and a bucket of water. He dipped the rag and started dabbing away at the seafood lasagna and Caesar salad Emmit had for lunch. "Are you sure you're all right?"

Emmit nodded, still holding the paper towel over his mouth. He thanked Henry for his concern and told him it was okay to go on.

"I'm afraid I don't know who all the players are. However, the one thing I am certain of is this..." Henry tossed the rag into the trash. "Considering the current political clime, it won't be long before the opposition unleashes a terror that will make 9/11 seem like a warning shot."

September 1966

Samuel had just gotten back to the States. He'd served a full year in Vietnam and much like Emmit, thought long and hard about staying. However, after he found out about Umbridge's most heinous activities (which he had yet to substantiate), plucking slugs out of Yankee soldiers didn't seem nearly as important as the duties that now lay before him.

But before he could get to that, he had to play possum for Umbridge. And to do that, he had to accept Captain Jusko's proposal to work on what she referred to as the most important military discovery since gunpowder.

Samuel told his wife he was coming back to the States on Thursday, though his plane touched down at Logan International Airport on Wednesday morning. Before he headed back home to Florida, he had to stop off in Boston and pay a very special visit to an equally exceptional individual.

Two-and-a-half hours later, Samuel was pacing Emmit's living room, nervously wringing his hands to the point where Emmit feared he might start a fire.

"Just calm down now," Emmit said. "You want a glass of water or something?"

Samuel thanked Emmit for the offer, but was intent on keeping his blood pressure on high.

"You've got to listen to me, Emmit," he pleaded. "They're coming and they're not going to take no for an answer."

When Emmit came out of the laundry room and saw Samuel waiting in front of his apartment door, he was happy as could be. Unfortunately that feeling didn't last very long. Samuel started ranting and raving about Umbridge's most odious deeds, loud enough for all to hear.

Emmit rushed up to his door and fumbled for his keys. "Maybe we should continue this conversation inside," Emmit rested the hamper on the ground. He opened the door, kicked the laundry basket through and ushered Samuel in. Once inside, Emmit looked down the hallway to make sure nobody was about. The last thing he wanted was for his nosy neighbors to catch a whiff of any strange happenings. Especially Mrs. Havercroft. She'd dial 911 just to hear the rotary dial click.

"Did you hear what I said?" Samuel whined.

Confident the coast was clear, Emmit eased the door shut. "Yeah. Three times now," he said as he picked up the hamper and set it on the couch. He started folding his clothes just like the army taught him.

"Then why are you doing your laundry instead of getting the blazes out of here?"

"Look…Dr. Jayne. I appreciate your concern but you've got to admit, it all sounds a little…"

"What? Unbelievable?"

"Well, yeah. Don't you think?"

"This coming from a man who lugged a 200 pound man through ten feet of solid earth while carrying three bullets in his brain."

Emmit laid the T-shirt he was wrapping up onto the couch. "I don't see what that has to do with any of this."

Samuel grinned, though the expression intimated anything but joy. "It has everything to do with this. With you. He killed them…every last one of the people that knew what you'd done."

"Not according to the report."

"Please. I know you're young, but even your naiveté must know some bounds."

Emmit thanked Samuel for the high praise.

"I'm sorry, Emmit. I don't mean to be short with you. But that bastard Umbridge signed the death certificates himself. For your fellow soldiers…that poor medic…even my colleagues who operated on you. I'm certain of it."

Several weeks following the suicide bombing at Cu Chi, Samuel walked into Carl's quarters and found him swinging from the rafters. Three days later, the nurse that helped them during the six-hour operation met her untimely demise at the hands, or treads, of a runaway tank.

"I'm sorry, Dr. Jayne. But I just can't believe that. Any of it."

Samuel shook his head and evened out his tone. "Well, you'd better start trying a lot harder. Because if Umbridge and whoever else involved in this bloody conspiracy have gone to such lengths to ensure you remain anonymous, I shudder to think of what they've got in store."

June 2004

Like the fine men and women at Berkeley's Institute of Cognitive Studies, Samuel uncovered the underlying principle to Emmit's abilities. Where they'd fallen short, Samuel included, was discovering why Emmit's brain functions as it does. According to Henry, he'd finally solved this ultimate riddle.

Emmit arrived at Henry's house at eleven that morning. Henry greeted him with his usual submissive smirk and guided Emmit through the hallway until they reached his study. After a brief session of small talk, Henry ambled over to the bookcase behind his desk. He looked at Emmit knowingly as he pulled out the *Neurology of the Arts* text book. The ground shook ever so slightly and the articles on Henry's desk trembled as the bookcase began to slide open to reveal a hidden entranceway.

"You have got to be kidding me," Emmit said.

Henry, a bit too pleased with himself, stepped aside. "A tad histrionic, I know. But I've always loved those old movies so."

Henry asked Emmit to follow him through the opening. While he was understandably intrigued Emmit couldn't help but hesitate. He stepped up to the entrance and looked inside. There was a spiral staircase laying in wait. Emmit looked down the folded steel steps which appeared to go on forever.

"Please, Mr. Rhoe..."

Ignoring that guarded voice coming from within, Emmit slowly made his way down the narrow steps. Henry followed closely behind. Still not trusting his nemesis' progeny, Emmit took a firm grip of the tubular railing as he continued to navigate the angled steps.

Finally they arrived at the bottom of the veiled chamber. Emmit stepped aside to let Henry past. "You're just full of surprises aren't you?" Emmit remarked.

"Surprises are foolish things," Henry said. "The pleasure is not enhanced and the inconvenience is often considerable."

The quote rang familiar, but Emmit kept his comments to himself as he couldn't quite remember who the original scribe was.

"Fortunately, what I have to show you is considerable only in scope," Henry reached out for the large, flat metal button mounted on the stone wall.

Nothing happened at first. Emmit looked at Henry blankly, asking without asking what was going on. Henry looked ahead just as the wall shuddered and cracked down the middle to open like some ancient gateway.

"Please, Mr. Rhoe..."

"Yeah, yeah. I know. Age before beauty."

*   *   *

Henry and Jane Austen were right yet again. Emmit tried to wipe away his look of surprise but the more he took in the wider his mouth dropped open.

They walked into the main room of the 10,000 square foot laboratory, which boasted the very latest technology had to offer and much more it had yet to publicly cop to.

"Essentially," Henry explained, "I use this lab as a center for basic research to complement my clinical activities."

Henry went on to describe the facility. It was a fully-equipped laboratory, which was supported by numerous common-use areas—a histology room, a tissue culture room for viral and non-viral work, an imaging chamber and a basic laboratory core facility. All of these rooms were connected to the main lab and all totaled, provided the full resources for virtually all aspects of modern neuroscience research.

"So," Henry said with vested pride. "What do you think?"

Emmit wasn't quite sure he had an answer for that. "Wow," he said, immediately feeling idiotic for letting loose with such a dull proclamation.

"Wow indeed," Henry aped. "Now what say we get you dressed for the party, yes?"

Henry showed Emmit to the change room near the back of the main lab. After Emmit slipped into the hospital gown Henry slid under the door, the doctor directed him to the examining table resting in the middle of the room. The area looked like an ultra-modern, oversized OR with overhanging halogen lamps, mounted plasma screen displays, and a host of other impressive looking machinations Emmit couldn't begin to guess what purpose they served.

"What a piece of work is a man," Henry chirped while he tacked on the final pair of sensors to Emmit's temples. "How noble in reason. How infinite in faculty…" once he was sure they were secure, he rolled his chair behind one of the many computer terminals. "…in apprehension how like a god!"

Making sure not to upset any of the wires, Emmit shifted his weight on the cold, cushioned table. A smile came to his face when, this time, he recognized the author of the citation immediately. "If you say so, Hamlet."

Samuel stopped banging away on the keyboard and looked on at Emmit approvingly. "It's heartening to see you've dedicated your acumen to more than lifting heavy objects."

Like he'd done with Samuel many time before, Emmit thanked Henry for the veiled compliment. Henry ignored the sarcastic riposte and keyed in another series of commands. The plasma screens hummed to life. Samuel looked up from the monitor and to his patient. "Are you comfortable, Mr. Rhoe?"

"Not the word I'd use. But I'll do."

"I suppose that will have to do," Henry approached Emmit, stopping just shy of the examining table. "Before we start, I think it would be wise if I gave you a bit of the back story concerning how I discovered what makes you unique."

Emmit transferred his weight again. "Been waiting to hear that for 40 years."

"Well, your patience is finally going to be rewarded, yes? Now…where to begin?"

Henry pulled back to think about it for a moment.

"How about the beginning?" Emmit suggested.

Henry looked at him disapprovingly.

Emmit felt like he was back in the fifth grade catching a hairy eyeball from Mrs. Rumm. "Sorry. You were saying?"

Henry's expression softened. "Thank you. *As I was saying*…there has been much progress made concerning how the human brain functions. But as far as we've come, nobody has arrived at any empirical data to support the concept that we use less than 10 per cent of our brains. Even though this theory has been bandied about in psychological, sociological and scientific circles for over 30 years."

Much like Samuel's chauffer to Hanoi, Emmit tried to stop his eyes from rolling out of his head. The last thing he wanted was to sit through another longwinded, hi-tech sermon. He'd been forced to endure enough of those after he was found out without ever being told what made him tick. But as he said, he'd waited so very long for the truth so another few minutes wasn't going to hurt. At least not too much.

"And that may still be the case," Henry asserted. "Science, after all, is not an exact science. Which explains why my solution does not satisfy those hell-bent on pragmatic statistics."

"In other words, you can't prove jack."

"If by *jack* you mean naught…then yes," Henry said a bit annoyed. "Not insofar as providing concrete proof as to how much of our brains we actually have access to. But it's by subscribing to the hypothesis that I have come to realize why you are so very different."

Henry reached inside his lab coat and pulled out a small, flat object. It looked like one of those newfangled personal organizers Hanna gave Emmit last year for Chanukah. Emmit hadn't seen Henry use his, but he was certain the doctor was able to do more with it than play solitaire.

Henry took hold of the unit's stylus and inscribed a series of instructions on the touch screen. The portable unit was linked to the entire lab's system, functioning much like a wireless Internet connection. As Henry scrawled down the commands, they were relayed to the main server and the information was displayed on the many plasma screens situated about the room.

"What you must appreciate, Mr. Rhoe, is that nobody has been able to produce these facts because there has never been any definitive surgical study of the human brain that tests all physical aspects with intention of mapping total usage."

"Why not?"

"Because such tests can never be conducted. And even if they could, they would not be able to verify the point," Henry looked up to the plasma monitor that hung over Emmit. "Even if you took a random sampling of say…100 people, then tested every portion of their brain against their cognitive usage, the data would still be heavily biased."

"In what way?"

"Culture. Age. Educational background. There are just too many variables. So, the statistical norm would carry such weighted predispositions, no conclusion could ever be accurately drawn."

"That still doesn't explain why I was different."

"Let's keep matters in the present tense, Mr. Rhoe. You are different. But I'll get to the reasons behind your current state in due time. As I mentioned, I want to give you the entire history so you'll better understand how I deduced the root of your power, yes?"

Emmit thanked him for his consideration.

"You're quite welcome. Now, one of the conclusions we have been able to draw is that the brain operates holographically and that memory isn't stored in any one particular place but throughout the entire brain," Henry retook his seat behind the computer terminal. He typed in a quick command, which brought up an image of Emmit's brain on the plasma screen. "Just as conclusively, we've defined what portions of the brain are used for what; i.e. occipital lobes, temporal lobes, frontal lobes. Still, there are large portions of the brain that are a mystery. Obviously, trying to evaluate how much of our brain's capacity we're using when we don't know what certain areas are capable of is pointless."

Emmit winced as he slowly peeled a bare leg off the tacky vinyl cushion. "Which brings us to…?"

"Einstein."

"Easy now, Jr. I may not have your smarts, but there's no need to be impolite."

"Sorry, Mr. Rhoe. It wasn't a jibe. I'm talking about Albert Einstein. His brain usage was actually mapped out," Henry explained. "The one distinction they found in his brain was it had an unusually high number of glial cells circulating in his parietal lobe."

"And glial cells would be?"

"The structural support for neurons which, as you may or may not know, are the cells responsible for conducting nerve impulses," Henry carefully surmised the data appearing on the screens. "High counts of glial cells indicate that Einstein was purposefully using the parietal portion of his brain. Taking it a step further, we believe the parietal lobe facilitates abstract thought, which makes sense in this case because genius is directly related to conceptual thinking.

"As is psychosis."

"Indeed," Henry said, again not pleased about the intrusion. "Back to point, we know for certain that whenever something is learned there are new dendrite connections made between neurons."

"Dendrite connections…?"

"Threadlike extensions of nerve cells. Increased usage of the brain through learning and stimulation creates greater dendrite connectivity. Einstein's brain showed an inordinate number of these connections."

"I'll warrant a guess and say the same goes for me?"

Henry looked up at Emmit and smiled. "You tell me, Mr. Rhoe," he stood up and pointed to the screen above Emmit. "You tell me."

The image of Emmit's brain began to rotate until it stopped at a 3/4 view. Henry snapped up the portable unit and initiated a sequence that caused the view to zoom in, revealing countless hairline configurations.

Emmit craned his neck around and squinted. "It looks like a thousand spider webs set on top of one another."

"Exactly. By some miracle all of these cells are connected," Henry said nearing the screen. He reached into another pocket of his coat, came out with a laser pointer and aimed it at the different portions of Emmit's brain. "Here, here, here…almost everywhere you look."

"I can see that. But what does it all mean?"

"What it means, Mr. Rhoe, is that by my calculations you utilize approximately 68 per cent of your brain's total capacity. This has been an ongoing process. The older you get, the higher the percentage."

"And how could you know that?"

Henry dragged the stylus across the portable unit's screen. The large printer sitting beside the computer terminal he was working at hummed to life and began spitting out pages. Henry collected them and brought them back to Emmit. "You see this here?"

Emmit looked at the page. It was another mapping of what he assumed was his brain.

"This is an image of your brain taken in 1967," Henry said.

"How did you get this?"

"The Pentagon's resolve isn't so strong as to refuse obscene sums of money."

"That's comforting. I guess it's those deep pockets of yours that paid for this set-up, too?"

Henry looked a bit offended. "We're not here to discuss my financial portfolio," he said trying to remember where he'd left off.

"You were going on about those connections," Emmit said.

"Ah, yes. Thank you," Henry ran his finger along the image on the printout. "You'll notice there are far fewer connections here..." he pulled the next page out, which showed the rendering Henry had just taken, "...as opposed to now. If we take another snapshot of your brain in a few years, I'll be able to say the same of this current depiction."

"Sounds great. But if that's true, why can't I do what I used to be able to? I mean...if I still have all of these connections I shouldn't have lost a step, right? What's more, if I keep establishing them, I should be even more powerful than I used to be."

"Of course. That makes perfect sense. But consider this—as powerful as your mind may be, it's just a 1,400 gram lump of tissue and cells if you don't use it."

"Come again?"

"You have made a conscious decision not to play the part anymore, Mr. Rhoe. Just like Einstein, you've deliberately accessed portions of your brain and directed them to do your bidding, dictating your *realm of possibilities* as those warmongers used to put it."

"Sorry. Still not getting it."

Henry dumbed it down a shade further. "Pared down to its barest essentials…you are capable of convincing yourself into performing these amazing biological feats. Just like the Tibetan monks that slow their heart rate to almost nil. Or withstand sub-zero temperatures without a stitch of clothing because they can generate such intense heat within their bodies by pure mental command."

One plus one was starting to equal two. "So…what you're saying is just like I convinced myself I could do all those things," Emmit said while Henry urged him on, "Now I've done the exact same thing, only the other way around?"

"Precisely. Now all we've got to do is find out how we can reverse the process once again, yes?"

-5-

September 1966

While Samuel failed to convince Emmit that Umbridge was up to no good, he was somewhat gratified he'd planted the thought in the young man's head. After all, getting Emmit to believe Umbridge orchestrated those murders was an inordinately large pill to swallow. As such, it would take time, persistence and patience to massage it down Emmit's throat. Until then, Samuel had to play the part as expected by Umbridge, who called for another meeting of the minds for three o'clock the following afternoon.

After 14 years of marriage Samuel's wife, Beth, didn't need much of a hint to realize something was bothering her husband. She watched him sit there at the dinner table hardly moving, speaking even less. She tried to start a casual conversation a few times, but he made it clear he didn't want any part of it. In her experience, she found it best to let silent neurosurgeons lie.

Samuel had always been an emotionally detached person. Even as a child, he found it difficult to express himself on any level. Just like his father, he quickly proved to be a formal soul with an analytical mind to match. Samuel's mother, on the other hand, was quite the opposite. She'd done her best to rear her only child in a loving and caring environment. But it was clear that Samuel would only flourish in a world that challenged his profound intellect.

Samuel's remote nature was a definite asset in his line of work. His skills excelled at a rapid pace because he wasn't mired in emotive issues or circumstances. Unfortunately, it was this same disposition that made his relationship with Beth unbearable at times. She was a lot like Samuel's mother being such a warm and open individual. And even though she and Samuel were polar opposites, she managed to track down that certain, not readily identifiable quality in him that made him desirable enough to hold onto.

The silence was becoming too much to bear, so Beth hoisted herself up and started cleaning off the table. Samuel managed to break his silence just long enough to thank her for dinner. He watched her for a moment then, silently, methodically, thinking thoughts only he could understand, and pushed his chair out. "I'll be in the study," he said softly, "If I don't get through all that paperwork for tomorrow, Umbridge will have my head served on one of your platters."

Beth picked up his plate of half-eaten food. "Would you like me to bring you some coffee?"

"That would be nice," cautiously, he leaned over to give her a sincere if not impersonal peck on the cheek.

Samuel woke up with a stir. Visions of murder, deceit and treachery filled his subconscious.

And something more.

Something worse.

He lifted his head up off his desk and pressed his back flat up against the backside of his executive leather chair, trying to wipe away the horrid images that were tearing away at his psyche. Massaging his temples with either index finger, he let loose a cleansing yawn and turned to take a gander at his reflection in the mirror hanging on the opposing wall. He noticed a piece of paper was stuck to his cheek, and peeled it off as he turned his stare upwards to the clock above the door. It was going on three in the morning.

Umbridge had asked—or told—him to gather all the data he'd compiled on Emmit. There wasn't much more Samuel was able to amass, and that wouldn't change until he could actually get his hands on Emmit to do some real testing. So for the time being, he followed through on Umbridge's request and collected every last stitch of information. After neatly filing all the papers into his briefcase, he tidied up his desk and set off to join Beth to try and get some sleep before his nine o'clock flight to Virginia.

Rather than risk another three hour ride spent hunkered over a stainless steel toilet hovering 35,000 feet aboveground, Samuel went against his own advice and downed some Gravol before the plane taxied off the runway. He was unlike most western-trained physicians (or medicapitalists as he called them) in that he believed in treating the disease rather than the symptom. After all, it made perfect *medical* sense. But monetarily it didn't add up. Not nearly enough for the pharmaceutical and neutraceutical companies who made untold trillions engineering hopped up placebos that only prolonged, not cured, the ailment in question.

As luck had it the Gravol kicked in (it was usually a 50/50 proposition) and Samuel breezed through the flight as easily as the modified 707 cut through the morning sky.

The seatbelt and smoking signs came to life and the near-capacity fuselage jumped up in unison to fill the aisles. Samuel waited for his travel mate (the woman who should have paid a fare-and-a-half since her behind took up her seat and a good portion of his) then got up and snatched his briefcase out of the overhead compartment. Carefully nudging his way into the herd, he shuffled closer to the front of the plane and waved goodbye to the bookend stewardesses.

Forty-five minutes later, the military-issue car pulled up to the main building of the Northwest Naval Security Group. The purposefully inauspicious communications station, which was located in Chesapeake, a backwater town some 30 miles south of Norfolk, was tucked away in the Great Dismal Swamp. Its main function was serving as part of Naval Communications Station Norfolk. A total of 400 people were stationed there, most dedicating their time and efforts to the Naval Security Group in the ComSec Division.

Samuel thanked the driver for the ride and headed in. Before the door could close behind him, a shapely young woman, who introduced herself only as General Umbridge's assistant, greeted him. Samuel followed her into the building, admiring how her suit was barely holding in her Rubenesque figure. Samuel may have been of the scrawny variety, but he had a penchant for the meatier members of the opposing sex. He continued to take in the welcome sight, thinking of how her unquestionably good looks were in no way happenstance. Umbridge's admiration of all things female couldn't possibly go beyond the flesh. And while that just added to the general's lengthening list of ignoble characteristics, Samuel was gratified to have finally discovered some common ground.

"Please, Dr. Jayne…follow me," she said.

They walked through the main lobby and weaved their way down the hallway that led to the conference rooms, stopping when they reached Room 'B'. Umbridge's assistant ushered Samuel in. He tipped his hat and situated himself at the large table near the front of the room. She remained at the door. "Is there anything I can get you, Dr. Jayne? Coffee? Tea?"

Samuel took off his fedora. "No thank you, miss. I'm fine."

"All right then. General Umbridge and the rest should be along shortly."

Samuel thanked her and took in a final eyeful before she disappeared, then took a seat at the huge Formica table sitting in the middle of the room. Resting his hat beside him, he neatly folded his hands on his lap and looked about the room, noting how sparse the décor was. Aside from the table and adorning chairs, all the room sported was a furled projection screen mounted on the wall and pictures of every American president up until the country's present chief. Samuel's eyes kept darting about as he began whistling a surprisingly merry tune when company arrived.

"Good morning, Dr. Jayne," Sara said filing into the room.

Umbridge followed closely behind and a man Samuel had never met brought up the rear. Samuel stood up to greet them. He shook Sara's hand then Umbridge's. "Nice to see you again."

Sara stepped aside to give Samuel a clear view of the tall, handsome stranger. "This is Senator Harold Elias, Dr. Jayne. He'll be joining us today."

"A pleasure," Samuel said brightly.

"It's all mine," Elias said. "I've heard a lot about you, doctor. And I'm very excited about the breakthroughs we'll be making."

"Breakthroughs?" Samuel questioned.

"Settle down, Dr. Jayne. We'll explain everything in due time," Umbridge said unapologetically. "But first…did you bring the materials I requested?"

Samuel returned to his seat and opened his briefcase. He started pulling out the files, which had grown considerably (in width, not depth) since their last face-to-face.

He hadn't thought it possible, but it wasn't long before Samuel discovered the situation was worse than even he feared. *Leave it up to that arrogant sod,* he thought, while Umbridge continued to explain what he and his beloved U.S. Navy had in store for Private Rhoe.

"We want to find out exactly how his systems function," Umbridge said mulling over the medical reports like he actually understood them. "We realize the catalyst to his abilities is still a mystery, but according to the data thus far collected, we're pretty sure it's coming from up here." Umbridge tapped his forehead with his ebony Mont Blanc pen, a gift from President Truman and Douglas MacArthur for his role in helping UN forces recapture Seoul (and a fact he'd relayed several times to ensure everyone knew it full well).

Regarding Unbridge's supposition, Samuel said he agreed, but added Emmit's power tended to manifest itself in a physical manner.

"That's why we need you," Umbridge said, "so we can find out exactly what he's capable of."

Samuel was all too happy to oblige with the fact-finding mission. He would never let on, but he was terminally curious about Emmit and how his mind worked. Even though working toward that goal would help the general and his beloved Core, it was a necessary evil. There was no other way to complete Emmit's puzzle and without that absolute image in plain view, Samuel wouldn't have enough muscle to put a stop to Umbridge and what he called *Project Realm*.

"We came up with the name a few weeks ago," Sara explained. "Based on Private Rhoe's past performance and what we assume he can do."

"I don't understand," Samuel said blankly.

"It's really quite simple," she continued. "Private Rhoe is capable of what should be impossible. To the rest of us, anyway. But to him it's well within his *realm of possibilities.*"

It was a tad theatrical for Samuel's liking, but more secure in its masculinity when compared to a nominate like Mission Tomahawk or Operation Cyclone. Name calling aside, the phase of Project Realm that caused Samuel to break out in an arctic sweat was…

"…and once you've discovered how he works," Umbridge said barely able to contain his excitement, "we can get to work and figure out how to synthesize the process."

Three hours later and 450 miles northeast, Emmit rolled over onto his back and dropped a pillow on top of his face. "Go away," he yelled.

The phone ignored his plea and kept on ringing. On the eleventh chime, Emmit conceded defeat. He leapt out of bed, staggered into the living room and snapped up the receiver. "This better be good."

"I'm afraid it's anything but," Samuel said.

Early the next morning, Samuel eased into the deep cushions of the rear booth at the Bean Village Café. He'd requested a sit-down with Emmit at his apartment, but Emmit insisted on getting together on neutral ground. Mrs. Havercroft had already made comments about Samuel's previous visit, asking Emmit who that *strange man* was. There was no way Emmit was going to risk another outburst and subsequent round of 20 questions.

Chomping down on the last cube from his glass of ice water, Samuel scouted around for Emmit, who was already ten minutes late. Dipping into his blazer pocket, he plucked out a dime for the payphone. Just as he was about to get up he saw Emmit traipsing through the front door.

Emmit tipped his Celtics cap to the pretty girl with the short brown hair, or Celia as he now called her, and looked about the crowded restaurant. He spotted Samuel, who was fervently waving him down like he was trying to attract the attention of an apathetic cabbie. Emmit flashed Celia another toothy grin and warily approached.

"Thank you for coming," Samuel said dutifully.

"No problem," Emmit pulled out a chair. "So long as you agree to stay away from what we were talking about before."

"Of course. I wasn't lying when I said I want to talk to you for another reason."

"Fine. So what's on your mind?" Emmit plopped down in his chair and folded his arms tight about his chest.

There was an awkward pause. Samuel took a deep, cleansing breath. "I had a meeting with General Umbridge yesterday in Chesapeake…"

Emmit's chin dropped to his chest. "I thought we weren't going to talk about him?"

"Please. Let me finish."

Emmit sat silently and waited.

"He wants me to conduct some research," Samuel explained. "On you."

Emmit didn't understand. "On me? What for?"

"It's really quite silly, though not surprising considering the depths of bureaucracy these days. But they feel that if…" Samuel didn't want to divulge everything about Project Realm until he figured out a way to stop Umbridge . "…they just want to put their best foot forward to make sure you're all right."

Emmit didn't know what to think. "First you say they're up to no good…now you're telling me they're trying to make good?"

"I wouldn't put it that way. Not exactly."

Emmit looked at him knowingly.

"Look…I don't trust General Umbridge. And this latest development hasn't changed my opinion in any way. But what's important…at least for the time being…is that we make sure you're all right."

"But it's been almost two years," Emmit said.

"Yes it has. But according to General Umbridge, he doesn't want to take the chance of something being wrong with you."

"Why's he so interested in my well-being?"

"He's not. Not on a personal level. It's just that the extent of your injuries were so severe…and access to medical equipment and supplies isn't exactly up to snuff out there in the bush. You might not know this, but my associate…Dr. Hulce?"

"Yeah…that big guy with the lazy eye. What about him?"

"Well…," Henry went heavy on the thespian. "He made a mistake during the operation. One that could have cost you your life but thankfully did not. But as I said…bureaucracy being what it is and all…"

Emmit's eyes lit up. "Short story is they're covering their asses. Right?"

"In a manner of speaking. Yes. If you were to suffer an injury or worse still, and the cause was somehow related to the mistreatment you received, you or your next of kin could easily sue the military for untold millions."

Okay. All right. Emmit could buy that, he supposed. Aside from the statute of limitations there was no reason to doubt Samuel, save for the odd electrical impulses he was sending out. Emmit didn't know what to make of them since he was still new to the game. But it wouldn't be long before he would learn that, like Samuel said when he called from Virginia the day before, it was anything but good.

July 2004

The next few weeks proved to be an endless series of exercises in futility. Earlier on, Emmit entered into the situation with high hopes. He still didn't trust Henry or who he claimed to be. But it seemed as though the doctor had his shit together, which could translate into Emmit reclaiming what he'd lost.

And that's all that mattered.

Whether or not there was a terrorist threat. Whether or not Henry was good, bad or any shade in-between. If there was some way to squash his depression, to give his life meaning and a purpose to go on, then there was precious little Emmit wasn't prepared to do to make it happen.

He spent nearly every waking hour with Henry, desperately trying to unlearn what he'd learned. Again, the first few steps indicated that they would succeed. Unfortunately, it wasn't long after that that the harder Emmit tried to get back to what he was the farther away he seemed to be.

* * *

Following another long, unproductive day, Emmit slinked back to the change room in Henry's lab to get into his street clothes. Henry could see Emmit was getting frustrated. And he couldn't blame him one bit. But he had to make sure that Emmit stayed on-track.

Failure was not an option.

Emmit appeared from the rear of the main lab. He looked completely defeated, almost like he'd put on 10 years in the past week. Henry smiled assuredly and put his hand on Emmit's shoulder. "I know this is frustrating, Mr. Rhoe. But..."

He'd been trying to pump Emmit up all day. It was getting irritating.

"But what? We've got to persevere? Be patient?" Emmit said sharply.

"There's really no need to take that tone, Mr. Rhoe. No matter how exasperated you may very well be."

"No? Then maybe you haven't been paying attention. We've been at this for what? Almost a month now, right?"

Henry nodded.

"Almost a month," Emmit stressed, "and we're no further along than when we started."

Henry wasn't surprised by Emmit's outburst. It was only natural. But the doctor had to make sure his subject stayed focused and true to their agenda because without Emmit, nothing else mattered.

"Perhaps," Henry offered. "But after all you've been through I don't think it's too far fetched to believe that you'll see yourself through this as well, yes?"

Emmit said that sounded reasonable enough. But he didn't actually believe it. Henry could see that as plain as the nose on his face.

And he didn't give a good god damn.

Certainly not about how Emmit felt about himself, though the session they'd just completed was sure to drastically improve Emmit's POV. While Henry could care less about Emmit's disposition, he was glad that Emmit's soon-to-be Polyanna status was going to make his job much, much easier. And learning everything he could about how Emmit's neurological systems functioned was what it was all about because in this particular case, knowledge had never been more powerful.

Later that evening at Timberlake, Emmit grabbed a bite for dinner. His stomach was a bit sour, a condition, he thought, brought on by the fact that he hadn't eaten up until that point. He barely made it through half his meal before he gave up. He thought about heading out for a walk to clear his head, but he just didn't have the energy. So, he went straight up to his room to sequester himself and his thoughts.

Old habits never truly died.

Stopping in front of the elevator, he caught Angela out of the corner of his eye.

"Shit."

"What was that?" she asked as she stepped up beside him.

"Nothing. Nothing. So…what's new and exciting?"

She cocked her head to one side and looked at him knowingly. "Funny. I was going to ask you the same thing."

"You don't say?"

"I do. You've been causing the rumor mill to spin lately. Much faster than usual, too."

"That's terrific, Angela. Really. But I'm beat and if I don't get a good night's sleep…" The elevator doors stuttered open and Emmit slid in casually but quickly. "I'll see you tomorrow at breakfast, all right?"

Just before the doors closed Angela peaked her head in. "You haven't spoken to that friend of yours about my prescription, have you?"

Emmit felt like every fiber and muscle of his being had been stretched and pulled out of shape. Each move he made, no matter how slight, caused his teeth to grit and his eyes to water. Carefully changing out of his clothes, he ran a warm bath while he sat on the toilet seat.

"I must be out of my goddamn mind," he muttered to himself. "I must be out of my goddamn mind."

Earlier that day when Henry approached him with the idea of Electroconvulsive Therapy, or ECT, Emmit told the doctor he'd have a better chance beating Orson Welles in a pie eating contest. But Henry was persistent and after he explained the procedure and how it could jumpstart Emmit's system, Emmit begrudgingly agreed to give it a shot.

"It's really an age-old process," Henry explained while Emmit stepped out of the change room. "Originally it was used to treat schizophrenia and depression."

"And today?" Emmit asked tying the string of his paper gown.

"Today it's used mostly for people who suffer major depression and are forced to rely on anti-depressant drugs."

"I know I've been down in the dumps these past few years, but don't you think sticking an electrical cord up my behind is a bit radical?"

Henry put his hand on Emmit's shoulder. "It's a bit more congenial than that. Though not by much, yes?"

Emmit's eyes widened in panic.

"A joke, Mr. Rhoe. Now if you'd be so kind...?"

They walked into the main lab and Henry asked Emmit to hop up onto the bench.

"Though when you really think about it," Henry mused, "it's really quite barbaric how the therapy was conducted way back when."

Sitting on the table now, Emmit wondered how low Henry's opinion of him would be if he ran out of there with his paper gown tucked between his legs. Instead he said, "It's a good thing you're a doctor and not a salesman, 'cause Willie Lowman's got nothing on you."

Henry ignored the comment and asked Emmit to lie down. Once he was comfortable, Henry hooked Emmit up to a heart monitor then swabbed the inside of his forearm with alcohol. "A slight pinch now..." he said then inserted the brevital I.V. "And now...if I could get you to count down from 100."

Emmit closed his eyes and began, "100...99...98...97..."

Samuel stepped back and waited for the anesthetic to kick in. Emmit continued to count down and was out before he could crack the eighties.

Quickly now, Henry inserted the succinylcholine I.V. into Emmit's arm. Unlike the brevital connection, succinylcholine wasn't an anesthetic. It was a muscle relaxant to prevent Emmit from breaking any bones once the currents began shooting through his system. With that firmly in place, Henry wheeled his chair to the head of the table and inserted a rubber block between Emmit's neat rows of teeth.

"Can't have you biting off your own tongue," he said. "Whatever would the cat occupy itself with then?"

He then placed a mask over Emmit's mouth to make sure his brain received enough oxygen. With that taken care of, Henry got up to get the conducting jelly that was sitting beside the main computer terminal. Slipping on a rubber glove, he dipped into the jar and rubbed the sticky substance on Emmit's temples then connected the two electrodes.

Henry took off the glove and tossed it into the trash. Approaching the ECT unit, he prepared to begin the treatment. Then he looked at Emmit and marveled.

"How easy it would be," he said with unabridged delight. "To do away with God's most powerful creation…with the simple push of a button."

Henry looked to the machine, which he had custom-made just for Emmit. Regular units had a volt meter going up to 450, but Henry's went to quadruple digits. He was sure Emmit could withstand at least half the full charge, but he couldn't help but wonder what would happen if he pushed matters further.

"All good things to those who wait," Henry chirped, and began the session with a 100 volt charge.

The monitor that displayed Emmit's brain waves jumped and bucked as a 20 second grand-mal seizure wracked Emmit's system.

A good start. But not quite good enough.

Henry cranked the unit to 200 and continued to up the voltage until he reached 500.

Thirty minutes later, Emmit woke up. He was completely disoriented. He didn't know where he was or who was looking down on him.

"Calm yourself, Mr. Rhoe. Everything is just fine," Henry said as he attempted to stop Emmit from jumping off the table.

But even in his average state, Emmit was far too physically imposing for the frail doctor to contain. Emmit shoved Henry aside and the doctor fell hard to the floor. Emmit tried to pull himself up but in his disoriented state, fell off the table and with a dull thud, joined Henry down below.

"Where…where am I…?" Emmit blurted.

"In my lab. You're in my lab and you're going to be fine…"

Slowly, Emmit lowered himself into the tub. The lukewarm water immersed his body and he felt better immediately. He still ached from head to toe but it was the good kind of ache, like the kind you have after working out for the first time in a long while.

Twenty minutes later, Emmit dried himself off with one of the new towels he'd picked up at Target (25% off all towels and linens, don't you know?). He got into his pajamas and slid into bed. It took some effort to find a comfortable position but once he got situated, it wasn't long before he fell into a deep, peaceful sleep.

Thankfully, that night there were no burglars. No suicide bombers. There were no bloodied, battered hostages.

There was just that face.

Those eyes.

And that faint bouquet of Chanel that always worked him into a lather.

January 1967

Celia appeared at the top of the stairs in all her glory. Emmit looked on at her, wondering how he'd managed to exist for so long without her by his side. They'd only been seeing each other for a few months but in that short time they'd grown very close. It was a natural attraction, one that established itself quickly and only grew stronger with every passing day.

Celia walked down the stairs, minding the hem of her new dress while she did. "Hello, handsome."

Emmit was caught up in her vision. He wished there were more steps so he could continue to take it all in. "Hi yourself."

She arrived at the base of the staircase and leaned over to give him a kiss. Their lips met and wouldn't have separated if Celia's mother hadn't appeared right then. "Look who's here?" she said staring Emmit over with taut, fierce eyes.

Celia froze in place. "Hello, mother."

"Hi, Mrs. Katz," Emmit said brightly. "How are you?"

Mrs. Katz, or Myrna as her confidants called her, turned a blind eye to Emmit as she usually did. She didn't care for the young man and just as much, didn't care to hide it. It wasn't like that right off the bat. When they were first introduced, Myrna was under the impression that Emmit was 100% kosher. But when she found out his father was Catholic, she turned downright icy and would be hard pressed to piss on him if he was on fire.

"I didn't know you were going out tonight, dear," Myrna said.

Celia bit her lip. "I told you last week."

"Really? I don't remember. Oh well. I guess your father and sister will have to finish the roast."

Myrna turned around and made her way back into the kitchen.

"Be seeing you, Mrs. Katz," Emmit said, his voice still bright and cheery. "Always a pleasure."

She didn't bother to wave goodbye.

Taking hold of Celia's hand, Emmit gave a little squeeze and opened the front door. "Y'know...I think she's starting to warm up to me."

Celia didn't need 14 years of marriage behind her to know something was bothering Emmit. She'd asked him what was wrong several times during dinner, but he sloughed off her questions saying he was beat from the long hours he'd been putting in down at the paper. As far as she knew, that's where he spent his time when he wasn't with her; working as a cub reporter at the Boston Herald.

Emmit hated lying to her. He hated not knowing what steps to take with her even more. The only upside to the situation was that his uncertainty wasn't instigated by how he felt about Celia. There was no question in his mind that she was the person he wanted to spend the rest of his life with. However, by sharing their lives he felt that that necessitated complete disclosure. And in subscribing to that, he had to tell Celia about the tunnel, Samuel, Umbridge and everything else in between.

He had to tell her about how he'd stopped Ditko and Trimpe from peeling off by lifting their van's rear axle six inches off the pavement.

He had to tell her how he stopped that 2,500-pound support beam from crushing the little girl in that tenement building fire on Massachusetts Avenue.

He had to tell her how he'd *felt* that mob hit was going down, and called the police to put a stop to it before it ever happened.

He had to tell her all that and more if he was going to build a life with her, but he wasn't sure he could because of what her reaction might be. And while the thought of losing her was the one injury he couldn't recover from, keeping his secret was proving to be even more damaging. All of that was even harder to chew on than the charred T-bone he'd ordered for his entrée.

"I've been meaning to tell you this for a while now," Emmit said while he swallowed down another sinewy mouthful, "but I haven't been able to find the right words."

She looked at him curiously. "You couldn't find the right words?"

"Yeah. I know. Not a problem I'm used to having. But I've been thinking about this. Long and hard. And if we're going to take the next step…"

Celia's eyes widened and Emmit felt her heart skip a bit.

"Oh, Emmit."

"Oh, what?"

"Talk about having difficulty finding the right words," she paused and started playing with the clip in her hair. "I like you, Emmit. I might even love you. But if you're going to ask me what I think you're going to ask me…"

It didn't upset Emmit in the least that Celia dismissed what she thought was a marriage proposal. At 24, he was right around the age of most men that entered into wedded bliss. But Celia was only 21. She was still a year away from graduating from Southeastern Massachusetts University. Unlike most women of her generation, she refused to fall under the thumb of her male counterpart and wanted to build her own career before she took on the responsibilities of being a wife.

Emmit didn't bother telling her he hadn't planned on asking for her hand. Not yet anyway. He thought it might embarrass her so he played along, saying he understood and that he'd be there for her waiting with open arms when she was ready to take that step.

Umbridge pulled out all the stops for Project Realm. While the general wasn't sure what Samuel would find, his uncanny sense of intuition told him that it was going to be big.

And if there was one thing Umbridge put faith in, it was instinct, which ensured he got back home safe and sound from the Beaches of Normandy.

It was insight that also saw him through the Battle of the Twin Tunnels in Korea.

And it was gut feeling that assured his continued existence yet again following his last front line assignment; Operation Cedar Falls, in Vietnam.

If the general's hunches continued to prove accurate (and he had no reason to believe otherwise), Emmit was the means in which to ensure America became the greatest force on the planet. The mere possibility of making that a reality was enough of an incentive to outfit Samuel with a state-of-the-art lab, diagnostic equipment, and the greatest minds Berkeley had to offer.

Emmit stared down at the directions he'd written then back up to the two-story, red-bricked building in front of him. There was a sign hanging over the gray steel door that read, *Lonny's Fine Foods*. Puzzled, he looked at the paper again and then back up to the sign when he heard...

"Welcome, Mr. Rhoe. Please come in."

There was a sharp metallic click and the door popped open. Emmit's eyes darted about to see where the voice had come from while he cautiously walked through the doorway.

Inside, Emmit stared down a long, narrow hallway. Neatly strung tube lights lined the ceiling casting a dreary, aberrant glow that turned his skin a pale blonde.

"The door at the end of the hall if you please, Mr. Rhoe. Second last on the right," the voice instructed.

Emmit kept searching for the origin of the tinny voice as he cautiously made his way along the corridor. He arrived at its end, turned to his right and the door opened.

* * *

It was like something straight out of an episode of Star Trek; smooth, clean architecture, lots of flashing, indistinctive lights and intellectual-looking worker bees buzzing about in toning outfits.

Emmit continued to survey his new, ultra-modern surroundings when Dr. Sophie Biernbaum came over to welcome him. "Good morning, Mr. Rhoe. It's nice to finally meet you."

"Ah…the voice behind the mystery," Emmit said.

"Sorry about that. Dr. Jayne is a big Isaac Asimov fan. I guess our facility here echoes that," she said brightly.

"I was thinking more Ray Bradbury."

"Either or, I suppose," she said. "My name is Sophie Biernbaum, by the way. Dr. Sophie Biernbaum. I'll be helping Dr. Jayne oversee this project."

"I guess there's no need to introduce myself."

"No, sir. I know all about you. And before we're through, I hope you'll be able to say the same about me."

Emmit said that sounded pleasant enough, and followed Sophie to the back of the lab where Samuel's office was located.

After 45 minutes Emmit was starting to lose interest. Even though he was finally getting some insight regarding what gave him his abilities the long-winded, systematic sermon Samuel entered into was getting old, fast.

"I believe the discovery was made in the late '20s," Samuel said as he stood beside the light boards mounted to the wall. "They called it a violence center, which is located in the hypothalamus."

Emmit nodded as if he appreciated the rundown.

"The original data was obtained from animal studies," Samuel turned the boards on. They flickered to life and displayed x-rays of Emmit's brain. "They found when the posterior region of the hypothalamus in an animal's brain was destroyed it remained in a permanent state of rage."

Emmit kept bobbing his head like one of those novelty toys with the bird's head and glass bulb end filled with liquid.

"Not long after, it was discovered that in order to yield this reaction, the area of the hypothalamus didn't have to be destroyed, only stimulated."

"And how'd they do that?" Emmit asked, fearing Samuel would pull a Mrs. Rumm and wrap his knuckles with a wooden ruler if he didn't display some sort of curiosity.

"With needle-like electrodes that were inserted into the brain," Samuel asserted while he pointed out the different sections of the x-rays. "Without causing permanent damage, of course."

"Or course."

Samuel retook the seat behind his desk. "So? What do you think?"

"What do I think? About what?"

"About the procedure."

"You're serious?" Emmit's voice shot up an octave when he realized what Samuel was getting at. "You want to stick my head with one of those needles? I thought you were just trying to explain how I'm wired."

"Settle down now, Emmit. It's a virtually painless process."

"You had me until virtually."

"Yes, well…it is invasive. But I don't see any other way to stimulate your mind so we can get to the root of your abilities," Samuel clarified. "I firmly believe that you were able to survive that tunnel collapse and those injuries because you were in a heightened period of tension. As such, this produced a chemical reaction in your brain, which triggered your latent ability."

Emmit's voice returned to its usual pitch. "So you're saying you need to razz me on to get me to come out again?"

"I guess you could say that. Yes."

"I don't think that's going to be necessary, Dr. Jayne."

Samuel's eyebrows climbed a few inches. "No? Why not?"

The good doctor wasn't the only one keeping secrets. Emmit stood up. He started pacing the room while he figured out a way to show Samuel what he was made of. Looking around the modest office space, he considered lifting the filing cabinet (which had to weigh over 200 pounds). *Or maybe,* he thought, *I can focus on that glass and make it slide across his desk.* He thought about it some more until it came to him. "Think of a number," he said.

Samuel's brow remained perched. "What?"

"A number. Just think of a number."

"I really don't see…"

"C'mon. Just do it"

"All right. All right. Let's see…" Samuel leaned back and considered the limitless possibilities. "Okay. I've got one."

Emmit looked deep into the doctor's eyes, focusing all of his energies on the impulses sent out by Samuel's nervous system. A few seconds passed by, then…

"One thousand, nine hundred and twenty one," Emmit said confidently. "Or the year you were born."

Samuel's eyebrows climbed past his widow's peak and crawled back to the base of his spine. "How did you...?"

Emmit sat back down and crossed his legs. "I don't know. That's what you're supposed to tell me."

July 2004

The sun was beginning to set when Emmit turned the corner and headed up the wide, concrete steps leading to the main building. He was still fretting over the fact that he and Henry hadn't achieved all that much. But at the same time, he was starting to feel good about himself and where things were headed. There were several reasons behind his positive outlook, the most concrete being the ECT therapy. While the process still scared the hell out of him, Emmit had to admit that he was feeling a lot better about himself ever since they started the treatments.

Other than that, he attributed his newfound optimism to the fact that he suddenly had something to look forward to other than what kind of coffee was being served for breakfast. He decided to concentrate on that—not the coffee, but purpose. Not only because it stoked his self-esteem, but also because it kept his mind off the terrible things to come.

Or were allegedly coming.

Emmit didn't trust Henry or believe America's Most Wanted had joined forces. Something wasn't adding up. Not yet. Emmit's suspicions weren't brought on by anything Henry had said or didn't say. It was more of a feeling he was getting off of the doctor; some sort of vague, inconspicuous impression he wasn't able to give a name.

Then again, it might have all been in his head. After all he'd seen and done over the years, developing an overblown sense of paranoia was essential. Whether or not Henry deserved to be scrutinized as such remained to be seen.

Emmit walked down the hallway and to the elevator. He cast off a series of half-hearted 'hellos' and 'how-are-yous' to the faces he passed by. It was that kind of lack-luster performance that generated his reputation as an arrogant, distant soul who definitely had something to hide. While Emmit could understand how the others felt that way about him the truth was, he didn't rub elbows with them because it reminded him of what he had become.

Not that that was so bad. Not under normal circumstances. However, Emmit had come from a situation that was anything but normal. He used to bench press Volvos. Now his veins got engorged when he put on his shoes. Not so long ago, he could cover a mile in under a minute. Now his knees filled with fluid from his excursions to the bathroom. It was like Superman suddenly needing the aid of a walker. Or Captain America having to put in his teeth to tear into a steak. It was impossible for Emmit to not feel unequivocally impotent having once been the ultimate man, who was now a senior citizen and a substandard one at that.

Still, he felt bad about treating the other residents like something he scraped off the bottom of his shoe. He resigned himself then and there to try and make an effort, or more of one, to get to know the Timberlake population. If for no other reason than to make them see he really wasn't such an asshole.

Angela's sense of timing was downright uncanny. Again she arrived just as Emmit stepped into the elevator. It was almost as if she was lying in wait; like some rogue predator with infinite patience and absolute hunger. This time she got in with him. They rode in silence as they slowly ascended. Emmit knew full well that she was upset with him because he had yet to contact his fictitious friend's son to fulfill her eyeglass prescription, which was another situation he fully intended to remedy.

"I'm sorry I haven't gotten back to you about your glasses," he said, "I called my friend..."

"You did?" Angela said eagerly.

Just like the first time Henry opened his cigarette case, Emmit's intrinsic sense of self-preservation caused him to shy away. "Umm...yeah. Of course I did. You sound surprised."

"No. Not surprised. I thought you forgot is all."

The elevator stuttered to a stop. The doors opened and Emmit prepared to leave. "Now, Angela...how could I ever forget about you?"

March 1967

The Boeing 727 touched down on the tarmac of the Norfolk International Airport. It was the pilot's maiden voyage at the lead, so the landing was a bit shaky. Inside, the cabin rocked and swayed while the pilot steadied the giant steel bird. The commotion awoke Emmit from his abbreviated nap. He rubbed the sleep out of his eyes and turned to Samuel, whose usual pigment of rose had altered to an incongruously noxious shade of green. This time, the dose of Gravol he'd downed before takeoff didn't quite manage to assert itself.

"You all right?" Emmit asked in between yawns.

Samuel appreciated the concern, but he was having enough problems keeping his stomach at bay without any outside interference.

"Yes. I just need to get out of this blasted sardine tin."

The pilot's voice came over the PA system, apologizing for the rough landing. He then thanked all passengers for their patronage and said how much he and the rest of the crew were looking forward to flying the friendly skies with them again.

Samuel shot up from his seat and pushed by the others, excusing himself along the way until he arrived at the front of the aircraft. One of the stewardesses affirmed the PA's appreciation behind an unfeasibly wide, toothy grin. "The pleasure was all mine," Samuel blurted, and he raced into the terminal to find the nearest restroom.

A few minutes later Samuel was getting through purging himself. After a few dry heaves, he washed his hands and face, combed his hair and rejoined Emmit who was waiting outside the men's room door.

"All better now?" Emmit asked.

Henry nodded. "Yes. Thank you. Now come along…we don't want to keep General Umbridge waiting."

The cab stands were packed with taxis waiting for their impending fares. Samuel and Emmit stepped out onto the curb and looked around for their ride. After being cooped up in that jetliner with a host of travel mates whose personal hygiene was suspect, Samuel was glad to get out into the open, even though the air quality was compromised by the fumes leaking out of all those exhaust pipes.

"There," Samuel said, pointing out the black stretched Chrysler Imperial parked smack dab in the middle of the endless line of yellow taxis.

With their bags in tow they headed for the ebony oversized vehicle, which wore military-issue plates and twin U.S. flags mounted on top of either front quarter panel.

"I thought you said we were supposed to be keeping things incognito," Emmit said.

Samuel looked at the car then out to all the people who were staring it down. "Apparently General Umbridge didn't receive that particular memo."

Samuel voiced his desire several times to step back and take more time to study Emmit, but Umbridge had a fire lit under him and didn't want to wait any longer. So, Samuel came up with a solution that would satisfy both minds, which was putting Emmit through some exercises to showcase his physicality. He was sure once Umbridge gained a sense of Emmit's outwardly capabilities, the general would back off and give Samuel the green light to conduct some real research.

Emmit emerged from the men's change room. He was wearing a pair of cut-off sweat shorts, his lucky Celtics T-shirt and a new pair of off-white Chuck Taylor high tops. He stepped out onto the hardwood floor of the gym, standing at attention before Samuel, Sara, Umbridge and Elias looked on from the table they sat behind near the front of the gymnasium. Behind them two Northwest cadets stood ready.

"That's hardly standard issue Navy gear," Umbridge said pointing out Emmit's raggedy attire.

"If it's any consolation, General Umbridge," Samuel said, "there will be nothing standard about Private Rhoe's performance either."

The gym floor carried a set of free weights complete with bench, barbell and hand weights, an electric treadmill and a series of ropes that hung from the gym's ceiling. Emmit took a step back and waited for instructions.

"Let's start off with the weights," Umbridge said gruffly.

Emmit walked up to the bench and took a seat. The cadets marched over and stood beside either end of the bar.

Umbridge leaned over to Samuel, "What say you, doctor?"

Samuel looked through the latest readouts he'd brought along. "Oh...I'd say three hundred will do to start."

The cadets loaded the bar with four 50-pound plates and an equal amount of 25-pounders, fastened the locks and stepped away. Emmit leaned under the bar and dug his shoulder blades into the padding of the bench.

"Whenever you're ready, Emmit," Samuel invited.

Emmit reached up and took hold of the bar. Tightening his grip, his knuckles turned white as he hoisted it up off its mounts and over his head. He pulled the bar down just inches away from his chest and repeated for a 10 count.

"Okay. Let's see what he can do with five hundred," Umbridge said.

Following the drill session, Umbridge dismissed Emmit in his usual loutish manner. Emmit didn't appreciate the treatment, though he was comforted by the notion that if the mood struck him, he could wipe that smirk off the general's haggard face with but a thought. He went back to the showers (even though the extensive workout failed to cause his pours to leak), and as he washed up and changed back into his uniform, Samuel and the others went through the results.

"This is unbelievable," Sara declared.

"Quite. But according to my studies these numbers barely scratch the surface of his potential," Samuel said proudly.

Umbridge, who for once hadn't said much since Emmit left, stood up and plucked his hat up off the table. With resolute form, he put it on and loomed over Samuel. "That's good to hear, doctor. Best goddamn news I've heard all day."

The flight back to Boston was delayed due to mechanical difficulties, which meant Emmit didn't get back home until after eleven o'clock that night. He'd arranged to have dinner with Celia at nine and wished he could have called to let her know he wouldn't be able to make it, but all passengers were ordered to remain onboard during the repairs. It was the third time in as many weeks he was forced to stand her up. He shuddered when he thought about how he was going to explain what happened this time. But he was too exhausted to worry about that right then and there. For the time being, he just dropped his suitcase to the floor and collapsed on the couch. He just laid there in the darkness enjoying the moment of silence and solitude. He'd been through a lot the past few months. So much that he really didn't have a chance to sit back and think about what any of it meant or where it was leading him.

Samuel's rantings aside, Emmit really didn't feel good or bad about Project Realm. He felt much the same about what he was becoming. Lifting 800 pounds, running a 1:11 mile, leaping from rope to rope with the speed and grace of an anabolic orangutan and reading people's simple thoughts didn't strike him as odd. But considering that—how normal it all seemed—was when he came to realize the significance of it all.

"Well, well, well. Look what the cat dragged in?"

Emmit nearly fell off the couch when he heard Celia's voice. He hadn't felt her presence having been so wrapped up in his thoughts. She turned on the lamp beside the couch and formed a grin that presaged anything but glee.

"Hey. How long have you been sitting there?" he slid over to give her a kiss.

She pulled away. "You ask as if you really care."

The last thing Emmit needed (or was it wanted?) was to get into it with her. But there was precious little he could do when she got *that* way, save for cover up and hope for the best. "Of course I care. What's that supposed to mean?"

"Words, Emmit. They're just words if you don't supply the actions to back them up."

"Look...I'm sorry about this. You know I'd like nothing more than to spend more time with you, but..."

"But what?" she hissed. "You've got better things to do like spend it with Dr. Frankenstein?"

Emmit had told her about Samuel. Not because he wanted to, but because he was going away more and more. There was no way he'd ever get Celia to believe the paper was sending a junior writer out on so many assignments. So, he told her what they told him—the military just wanted to make sure that he was all right. Celia could accept that, though she found Emmit's obvious admiration for Dr. Jayne to be more than a little bit odd.

"He's a nice guy, Celia. If it wasn't for him, we never would've met."

"I'm beginning to think that might not have been such a bad thing."

Emmit wrapped his arms about his midsection. "Please. Stop. My sides...!"

Celia didn't appreciate his sarcasm and let him know.

"I don't mean to be," Emmit said. "I just don't think you should talk about people like that without knowing them first."

She looked at him by design as he'd just validated her position.

"My point exactly," she said, every passing word starting to sound more and more like Myrna. "But if you won't let me in, how am I supposed to think otherwise? How am I supposed to feel otherwise?"

"I'm sorry, baby. I really am, but..."

"Not to put too fine a point on it, but you can stuff your sorry's in a sack," she stood up and slung her coat over her forearm. "I'm leaving now. And I'm not coming back. Not unless you want to include me in your life."

"Of course I do. You know I do."

"No. No I don't," she walked on by. "If and when you're ever ready to grow up, you know where to find me."

All Emmit could do was watch her go. He wasn't ready—and he wasn't sure he ever would be—to tell her what was really going on.

How could he?

He loved her so much. And how could he expect her to return that love if she knew who he was and what was surely to be expected of him? While Emmit didn't know the whole truth behind Project Realm, he was savvy enough to realize that the military could care less about his health. All they were interested in is what he could do and in turn, find out how to best use him to their advantage.

August 2004

Much had changed for Emmit over the course of the year. Or rather, much had returned to what it once was. He was feeling good about himself. He had an objective. And while there was still much work to do and even more to discover, he felt a spring in his step and light in his heart that had eluded him for far too long.

He decided to keep the good times rolling by addressing the personal side of his life. The one mistake he'd made (at least one of the bigger ones) during his earlier days was neglecting his familial duties. It wasn't as if he'd done so purposefully or that he didn't want to play a larger role. But the call of his country was a recurrent conversation. So instead of being present and accounted for during most of his daughters' formative affairs, he found himself slugging it out with strangers in some godforsaken backdrop whose name he could rarely pronounce.

He'd considered biting off more than he could chew by dropping in on Rachel first. His youngest had missed him the most growing up. As such, she carried the largest, sharpest chip on her shoulder. She moved out when she was just 18 and since then, the only time they'd seen one another on a semi-regular basis was when Celia got sick.

Emmit packed a small bag, only the necessities—a couple changes of clothes, toothbrush, floss, antiperspirant and his favorite comb. He mulled it over some more and after a while concluded, *better to begin with Hanna. With her on my side, Rachel will be a much easier nut to crack.*

Nine-and-a-half hours later, Emmit stepped off the train car and onto the platform. Slipping into his blazer, he turned around and waved goodbye to the conductor, who he'd become fast friends with during the trip.

Emmit hadn't traveled by track in nearly thirty years. He'd forgotten what a pleasurable experience it could be. There were no overwrought encounters with customs agents. No rushing to wait for a plane that always turned out to be late. It was a much longer ride than by air of course, but infinitely more congenial. To Emmit, that was a fair tradeoff.

He waited for the porters to unload the baggage from the holding compartments. While he did, he thought about what he was going to say to Hanna. There was no convenient way around it and no words, no matter how baroque, were going to make it any easier.

* * *

By then, it had been going on four years since they'd seen one another in the flesh. Every now and again Hanna would pick up the phone but for the most part, Emmit allowed their relationship to grow stale on the shelf.

She moved from Boston to Bratenahl, a small suburb northeast of Cleveland, 18 years ago. Hanna never wanted to leave Boston. It was where she was raised. Where she'd lived her life and where she planned to spend the rest of it. But her husband, Jamie Wagner, an eminent radiologist from Cambridge, MA, was recruited by Ohio's famed Cleveland Clinic following his brief tenure at Beth Israel Deaconess Cancer Center. It was a tremendous honor and an even bigger stride insofar as his career was concerned. So Hanna banished her personal wishes to the backseat, packed up their belongings and followed Jamie to the Buckeye State to build their new life.

As far as Emmit was concerned, he didn't like the idea of Hanna pulling up stakes even though they were never very close. He cared for the young man who claimed his eldest daughter's hand even less. In his estimation, Jamie was a self-righteous, self-important little shit, who put his needs above all others. Of course, Emmit's disdain for the young man was nothing when weighed against Celia's. Jamie might have been a well-to-do doctor. But he wasn't Jewish. While Celia had made a concerted effort to differentiate herself from her mother as much as possible, she fell into the same holy crisis all the same. Emmit pointed it out to her several times, attesting to how demoralizing it was to be scrutinized based on creed rather than conduct. But Celia simply couldn't get past it, though when push came to shove, she never really tried all that hard.

The fact that Jamie wasn't a card-carrying member of the tribe didn't irk Emmit. How could it? He wasn't a pureblood himself and to snub Jamie for that would be a might too hypocritical. Still, all things being equal (which they never were) he would have preferred it otherwise. *Building a successful marriage is hard enough*, he would say, *without having to deal with the insane complications brought on by religion.*

He wasn't quite sure what to expect when he finally came face-to-face with Hanna but a deep, penetrating hug and full-blown smacker certainly wasn't it.

"Good to see you, too, sweetheart," Emmit said trying to wipe Hanna's lip gloss from his mouth.

Hanna kept hanging on for dear life when a thunderclap rocked the earth. The raucous blast caused Emmit to jump and pull away. Hanna tightened her grip. "You're not getting away that easily," the tears started welling up in her eyes. "Not again."

"It's good to see you, Emmit," Jamie said as he hopped off the front porch and onto the pathway leading to the garage. "It's been too long."

Hanna finally let go allowing Emmit to shake Jamie's hand. He tried not to squeeze too hard. "It most certainly has."

Jamie bent down and picked up Emmit's suitcase, a considerate act that was far and away from his usual character. Just as he snapped up the bags, the sky turned a mean grey and a flash of lightning tore through the thickening clouds. Jamie looked skyward. "We'd better head in before we get soaked."

Emmit filed in with Jamie right on his tail. The rain started to fall as Hanna closed the door behind her. Big, fat drops bounced and echoed off the windows. It sounded like a gargantuan troupe of dancers performing a Scottish reel on a sheet of glass.

Jamie set Emmit's bags down on the hardwood and placed his hands on either hip. "So…what can I get you to drink?"

Emmit considered his options and said, "What've you got?"

"Let's go and see," Jamie said, and they all headed for the kitchen.

Emmit craned his neck looking up and down checking things out along the way. He'd never been to the house before; he'd only heard about it as described by Hanna over the phone. "This is some set-up you've got here."

"It keeps us dry," Jamie said. "We'll give you the grand tour when you've settled in."

"Sounds good. More importantly, though, where are the kids?"

"Nate's at basketball practice. And Hailey's over at a friends place," Jamie said.

"That's too bad. I really wanted to see them."

Then why the fuck did you wait four years to drop by? Hanna thought.

"They'll be back in time for dinner," Jamie assured. "That'll give you some time to catch up with your daughter."

Emmit didn't appreciate Jamie's haughty tone. But he let it slide. He wasn't exactly in the ideal position to make comments on anyone's behavior. Not even his son-in-law's.

"Sure. That would be nice," Emmit said.

Like the rest of the house, the kitchen was massive by design. A large, marble-topped island sat smack dab in the middle of the room. Jamie stationed himself at the head of it then bent down, reached inside one of the cabinets and came back up with a bottle of Crown Royal. He shook it at Emmit, grinning knowingly. "Bought it special today. Just for you."

Emmit kind of doubted that but thanked Jamie all the same.

Jamie poured two stiff glasses. Hanna stuck with water. A few years back, she had a brief bout with the bottle. Nothing major, but she'd fallen into a domestic trap when she left her job to tend to the kids. Since housework didn't eat up enough hours of the day (or put enough of her brain cells to task), she filled the void with sifters of Port.

Jamie handed Emmit one of the glasses. While Emmit took a few baby sips, his son-in-law chugged the entire contents of his glass in one fell gulp. "That's it for me," Jamie said as he snapped up his keys from the hook mounted to the wall. "I've got to head down to the clinic for a deposition." He blew a half-hearted kiss Hanna's way and told Emmit again how good it was to see him. "I'll see you back here for dinner at six."

An hour later and after a quick pot of coffee accompanied by relatively meaningless small talk, Hanna escorted Emmit out onto the rear deck and got down to the proverbial nitty-gritty.

The rain stopped a while back and the clouds were giving way to a pale blue yonder. Emmit gazed up at the beautiful sight as the wind gusted off Lake Erie at a modest pace. He leaned on the rail of the pressure-treated wood deck and turned his attention out toward the tranquil waters.

"You've got a beautiful place here, Hanna. Really."

"Thank you. But you didn't come here to survey the grounds. At least I hope you didn't."

"You've still got your mother's tongue, don't you?"

"I've also got her memory. Where have you been, Daddy?"

This time Emmit gave the words some serious thought. Unfortunately, his reply didn't insinuate any great effort.

"Around," he said.

"Around? Just hanging out at the ole retirement home, right?"

Emmit stalled, sipping his coffee. "It's not a retirement home. It's a..."

"I've been leaving you messages," Hanna said.

He wasn't much better than Debbie Reynolds when it came to using his phone system, and was still trying to figure out the proper procedure for retrieving voice mail. Not that he'd dare mention that as the reason why he hadn't returned Hanna's calls. "Look...we both know I've been terrible at keeping up the relationship."

"Terrible's a bit of an understatement, wouldn't you say?"

"Yes. Yes I would. I didn't come here to argue that," Emmit said apologetically.

"So why did you come?"

"To make up for the past and make sure we have a future."

Hanna's eyes started to fill up with water again. "Y'know...I practiced what I wanted to say to you. I started the second you called and told me you were coming."

"So did I. I even wrote down some notes, I was so nervous," Emmit reached into his pants pocket.

Hanna looked at him as if to say she didn't appreciate the interruption.

"Sorry. So what is it you want to say?" Emmit said softly.

"How mad I am at you. How upsetting it's been for me and the kids that you've turned a blind eye to us."

"I never meant..."

"Meaning and intent are two very different things, Daddy. You taught me that better than anyone."

"No doubt. But you've got to believe me when I say I never mea...I never wanted it to be like this. Especially after your mother passed."

"So why did it? Why did you let it?"

"I wish I had an answer for that. But I don't. Not one that justifies the way I've behaved."

She'd never heard her father talk like that. Not to her. Emmit was a reasonable man but when it came to his children, for some reason or another, his logic system shorted out. But he'd finally recognized the fact and was finally able to do something about it. He just hoped it wasn't too late.

"Look...I could try and justify what I've done 'til my face turns blue but it wouldn't mean much," Emmit folded Hanna's hands into his. "All I want to do is make up for all the time we've lost. If you'll let me."

The rest of the weekend was an extended Hallmark moment. Emmit and Hanna laughed, cried and expressed every other emotion in between. It took Nate and Hailey a while to warm up to their *Zadie*, but when they did it made Emmit wish one of his abilities was turning back the clock.

Sunday afternoon came far too quickly. Emmit was having such a good time, he considered staying around for another few days. But he'd scheduled a meeting with Henry on Tuesday morning, and he didn't want to hear the doctor bitch and moan about a blown appointment. Their relationship had taken on a husband-and-wife dichotomy, and Henry's role was unquestionably caught up in aprons, strings of pearls and rolling pins.

Hugs and kisses all around. Emmit mussed Nate's long brown hair and pinched Hailey's cheek with care. Begrudgingly, he shook Jamie's hand and turned back to Hanna. "You'll make sure to call your sister for me?"

"Tonight," Hanna said. "I doubt she'll go easy…but I think I can get her to fold eventually."

"That will have to do for now," Emmit said and picked up his bag. "I'll make sure to call you when I get back home."

"Promises, promises," Hanna said.

Emmit stepped off the porch and smiled. "Yeah. But this time I intend on keeping them."

-6-

Samuel didn't like listening to lectures nearly as much as he enjoyed giving them. He heard the words coming out of Umbridge's mouth, but discerning their meaning was another thing altogether.

Samuel was too distracted with his recently formed agenda. That, and how ridiculously appointed the general's private office was. Samuel counted eleven American flags, seven mounted certificates, diplomas and degrees, 14 trophies (mostly of the fishing variety) and 27 snapshots of presidents, colleagues and wartime scenarios.

"I called you in here today, Dr. Jayne, because I'm concerned about where things are headed."

"How so?"

Umbridge didn't care for the light tone Samuel was carrying. He let him know and then said, "What's more…I don't think you understand what's at stake here." Umbridge pulled the mini humidor sitting on the well-worn blotter closer to him. "More disturbing still, I really don't think you care."

Since the beginning, Umbridge and Samuel developed a loathing for one another that dare not speak its name. At last Umbridge decided to voice the challenge.

"Up until now, I've been good enough to keep my opinions to myself," the general affirmed as he opened the humidor. He dipped his head into it and took in the aroma produced by the fine cigars within. "Not because I wanted to, you understand. But because the success of the program depended on it."

"Is that why you killed those people?"

Umbridge tried to look insulted, but what was the point? Samuel had taken matters as far as the general wanted (or needed). His usefulness, as limited as it was in Umbridge's estimation, had played out and there was no reason to act coy any longer.

"No. I did it because like you, they compromised the security of this great nation."

Samuel laughed out loud. "You really believe that. Don't you?"

"Of course I do. Just as I don't expect someone like you to understand why."

"Oh...I understand, general. That's why I can't sleep at night."

Now Umbridge laughed. "You're just like the rest of them. Soft. Weak. Just another undeserving heir of the liberties people like me have fought for all their lives."

"You mean slaughtered for, don't you?"

"You say potato," Umbridge said. "Whether or not you appreciate my actions is of no consequence. You've played your role, and thank the stars and stripes that's over and done with."

"As a matter of fact, general, my part has just begun."

Umbridge set in to reply, but Samuel cut him off at the vocal chords.

"You were right when I said I don't understand you or what you've done," Samuel admitted. "But that doesn't mean I'll allow it to continue."

"Allow?" Umbridge said skeptically.

"Yes. After all...how could I ever live with myself knowing someone like you has taken something so beautiful...something so pure...then distorted it to facilitate even more pain and suffering?"

"Your point of view, doctor. And an insignificant one at that."

"Yes, well...we'll see about that," Samuel paused and looked at the general carefully. "So where do we go from here?"

"Why Dr. Jayne, I would think someone of your intellect would have put that together by now."

Umbridge lowered his hand behind his desk. Samuel slowly reached into his blazer's side pocket. Before Umbridge could take hold of the Luger he kept stashed in the top drawer, Samuel whipped out the syringe in his pocket and stabbed the general's forearm. Casually, Samuel sunk back into his seat and watched Umbridge's unadulterated expression of panic and fear.

It was a good look for him.

"What's the matter, Lionel? All out of bold words?"

Umbridge looked down to his arm and took hold of the syringe. He yanked it out and dropped it to the floor. "What did you...?"

"I've injected you with potassium chloride. A derivative thereof, actually," Samuel explained. "I had to modify the mix as I don't believe you would have consented to an intravenous application."

Umbridge's body started shaking and his eyes rolled back. He collapsed back into his high-back chair while Samuel gleefully watched on.

"You see, when someone is given a lethal injection there are three chemicals that are used," Samuel raised his fingers to count down the ingredients. "First, sodium pentothal, or thiopental sodium as it's called in scientific circles. Sixty seconds later, a hearty dose of pavulon in introduced into the unfortunate individual's bloodstream."

Umbridge's entire musculature system began to contract. The pain was too wonderful for words.

"Another minute passes by then the potassium chloride is injected. And after that…"

Without warning, Umbridge's body ceased and desisted. As if someone had just pulled his power cord, he slumped lifelessly back into his chair as the chemical cocktail surged through his system and immersed his heart.

"Well, it appears as though you already know the answer to that."

Some 479 miles northeast and two hours following Samuel's preliminary step toward the *other side*, Emmit was wiping away the thin layer of sweat coating his upper lip and trying to coax his heart back within normal range.

He'd been thinking about this moment for months, feeling that he was finally ready to make the ultimate commitment. It took some doing, but he finally managed to screw up his nerve, decided on the appropriate verbiage and resigned himself to seeing the moment through with aplomb. Of course, that was before he sat down with Celia and looked into her eyes as only he could.

She's still not ready, he thought. *I'm not ready*.

Celia laid out the red and white-checkered blanket onto the neatly trimmed grass. It was a gorgeous day without a cloud to be found. A slow breeze cut the humidity just right, though Emmit still couldn't stop from sweating straight through his cardigan.

As Celia doled out the contents of the wicker picnic basket, Emmit rested on the heels of his hands and looked out onto Frog Pond. He hadn't been cast in its shimmering surface for years. It took him back to a time in his life when things were so much simpler. Times of skipping flat, gray rocks and lacing up his skates for a race to the north corner with his cousins. Times of wandering aimlessly and therefore happily, about. Times of…

"What's on your mind, sailor?" Celia said setting the basket aside.

Emmit turned his eyes to her and smiled dimly. "No more than usual. Well, maybe a little more."

Celia crossed her legs and started fixing Emmit a plate of cold chicken, German-style potato salad and an oversized kosher dill. "Please go on. I'm intrigued."

She set the plate in front of him and waited with baited breath.

"Okay. Here goes," Emmit's voice started crackling like it was being broadcast on his father's car radio. "I thought I knew how to say this. God only knows how many times I've run the words through my head. But..." he stopped while he reached into his shirt pocket. "...maybe this will do."

He pulled out a small pink velvet jewelry box. Trying to steady his hands, he cracked it open to expose the diamond engagement ring that sat regally within.

"OH...MY...GOD...!" Celia shrieked.

"You mean that in a good way, right?"

He took the ring out and offered it to her. Her hands started shaking worse than his, but she managed to reach out with her left arm and extended her ring finger.

"I'll take that as a yes?" he said.

He slipped the ring on her finger. It was a perfect fit. "It's a rose cut...lady at the store said it's a vintage style..." he was speaking so quickly his words strung together like pearls. "...something about brilliant facets arranged in groups that make the stone look like an opening flower which I guess makes sense though I think it looks more like a..."

Celia zoomed in and planted her lips on his. "Just shut up and marry me!"

Two hours later, Emmit hopped the six-foot fence surrounding the rear of his apartment building in a single bound. Spying around to make sure he was out of all sights, he leapt up to the second story balcony that led into his unit.

He waltzed through the sliding glass door and soft-shoed it to the hi-fi in the living room. Thumbing through his modest catalog, he snagged Marvin Gaye's, *Once Upon a Time*. He tipped the jacket of the album over and caught the record as it slid out. Sidestepping to the player in perfect rhythm, he laid the record on the table, flipped the switch and gently lowered the needle onto the vinyl surface. Static played until a few seconds in, Marvin and Kim Weston's velvety voices came on, and Emmit joined the Motown legends as they crooned...

"One can have a dream, baby...Two can make that dream so real...One can talk about bein' in love...Two can say how it really feels..." he grabbed the candlestick holder from the end table and jumped on the couch. Holding the makeshift mic up to his mouth, he continued, "One can wish upon a star…Two can make that wish come true, yeah…One can stand alone in the dark…Two can make the light shine through," just as the chorus started playing, he hopped onto the floor and with gut feeling sang along, "It takes two, baby…It takes two, baby…"

Before Mr. Gaye, Miss Weston and Mr. Rhoe could put the finishing touches on the first stanza the phone started to ring.

"Me and you, just takes two…It takes two, baby…" Emmit reached for the phone and cradled the receiver to his ear. "It takes two, baby…hello?"

"Emmit? Thank God. I've been trying to reach you for hours!"

When he realized it was Sara, he rushed over to the player and pulled the needle off the record. "Captain Jusko. Is everything all right?"

With almost a year of Project Realm under his belt, Emmit didn't have to rely on sight to track Sara down.

He entered the garden and closed his eyes. Deep breaths now—and a determined focus on the unique energy pattern only Sara could transmit. She was wandering about the pond, nervously wringing her hands just a few meters west of where he and Celia had set up their picnic lunch not three hours before,

"I got here as quickly as I could," Emmit said coming up from behind.

She nearly jumped into the water when she heard Emmit's voice. "Oh…Lord! Don't do that!"

Slowly, Emmit walked in front of her. "Sorry. Just trying to stay in game shape."

Sara put her hand over her chest. "That's a good thing…because we're going to need you a bit sooner than we anticipated."

"What do you mean?"

Emmit felt her heart return to its normal rate. But she was still agitated. A bit scared even.

"General Umbridge is dead. They found him in his office a few hours ago," she said.

Her announcement of Umbridge's death didn't do much in the way of moving Emmit. Not on an emotional level anyway.

"What happened…he have a heart attack or something?"

"No. Nothing like that," she trailed off and looked at Emmit knowingly. "They found his body after Dr. Jayne left their meeting."

"Then wha…?"

She just stared at him until he put it together.

"Oh, come on now. You're not serious."

"We won't be certain until the autopsy, but the medics at the scene said he was poisoned."

Emmit still wasn't sure Sara was intimating what he thought she was. "So you're saying…?"

She nodded and turned back to look out onto the pond.

"This is Dr. Jayne we're talking about, right? Emmit said doubtfully. "The same guy that can't take a five-minute cab ride without blowing his lunch."

"I won't pretend to know Dr. Jayne as well as you. But from what I do know about him, I would have to agree that this action doesn't jibe with his character—especially considering how it appears to be such a premeditated act."

Emmit tried to let it all sink in. It didn't add up. It didn't make sense. But when he considered Samuel's certainty regarding Umbridge's involvement in the deaths of George, Allan, the medic and everyone else, the impossible quickly became a much more likely proposition.

Twenty minutes later Emmit was putting the finishing touches on retelling Samuel's conspiracy theory, which was certainly news to Sara.

"I…I had no idea," she said solemnly.

"No way you could have."

Sara thought about the situation and turned to Emmit. "I want you to go home and wait for my call," she said, still running the evolving strategy through her head. "Pack your things and be ready to leave when that phone rings."

"Where are we going?"

"Just be ready."

Thirty minutes later, Sara was at home and contacted Northwest to arrange for the final details that would send Emmit and a select troupe of Naval officers to hunt down Samuel and bring him to justice.

While they got organized, she also issued an APB to the FBI, CIA, and any other law enforcing ellipsis she could think of to ensure every last airport, bus station, train depot and car rental outfit across the state was manned. She felt confident that would prove sufficient to reel in the doctor. After all, he was just a man. And an infuriatingly timid one at that.

It was an accurate assessment, but one of Dr. Samuel Jayne—a man who only existed in name alone. Sara could have thrown a quilt over the entire country. She could have organized every last military faction to join hands and scour the continent. She could have done all that and still this new entity would not be found.

That's because he'd been resolute in keeping that promise he made to himself. He'd played along with Umbridge's scheme and all the while, secretly amassed the requisite knowledge to put a stop to it. But as well-devised as his counter-measure may have been, he failed to take a very important factor into consideration. It was a mistake he and the rest of the world would pay dearly for.

September 2004

Emmit squeezed a handful of the translucent green shaving gel into his left palm. Wiping the steam off the mirror, he dabbed his cheeks and chin with the lotion watching it turn white as he rubbed it into his skin in a circular motion. Extending his index finger, he ran it along his upper and lower lip and wiped away the excess.

He carefully dragged the razor over the two days worth of stubble, noticing how much he was starting to look like his old self again. But for the first time in a long while, he recognized another person living within those features; a man he'd tried his best to forget, but couldn't wipe out of his consciousness no matter how hard he tried.

His father.

The old man was in Emmit's eyes. He was in his mouth. That dimple riveted into Emmit's chin was also an express donation. The old man was in Emmit's deeply-set brow and receding hairline, as well as that near-perfectly rounded skull.

Emmit squinted, trying to obscure the image staring back at him. All that did was make him look mean, like when his father got his drunk-on and took his frustrations out on his only son with whatever hard, blunt object that came in handy. Emmit opened his eyes—wide—and continued running the blade across his features.

Stepping into the bedroom, he laid out his clothes for the day—a fire engine red polo shirt, dark chinos and the new pair of Sperry topsiders Hanna gave him when he visited the previous month.

For once, he was running ahead of schedule. There was plenty of time before his meeting with Henry and his couch that afternoon, so he headed down to the main floor for a bite to eat.

* * *

Emmit was happy to have finally settled matters with Hanna. He was even happier he'd soon get the chance to do the same with Rachel, which he expressed to Henry as the doctor continued to probe about Emmit's prodigious psyche later that day.

"That's terrific, Mr. Rhoe. Truly," Henry said gladly.

Emmit was a bit surprised by Henry's cheerful response. It wasn't like the doctor. Not in the least. There was too much emotion in that voice. Emmit didn't know Henry had it in him.

"Yeah. It's been a long time coming," Emmit said, trying to peel away the layers of Henry's mind.

"It certainly has. And I think it will do you more good than you realize."

"How's that?"

Henry shifted in his chair. The leather-wrapped seating surface let off a flatulent squeal. Henry's face turned beet red. "It was the chair," he blurted.

"Of course it was," Emmit teased. "You were saying…?"

Henry cleared his throat and went on. "I was saying…what was I saying?" he thought it over. "Oh yes…reuniting with your family. Good. Very good. For your personal life as well as our purposes here, yes?"

"How so?"

"Well, it's always been my belief that you have reverted to the mental and physical state of an average 60-year old man…"

"61," Emmit corrected.

"I thought you were 60?"

"Had my birthday last month."

Henry wished Emmit a happy birthday, adding how sorry he was to have missed it.

"No worries. And thanks. Please continue."

"Of course. I was saying that I firmly believe one of the reasons you've become *normal* is because over the course of nearly 40 years you've been repressing your emotions."

Emmit looked at him guardedly. "You're not going to get all Freudian on me now, are you?"

"As a matter of fact that's exactly what I'm going to do. Because it's only by subscribing to Freud's theory concerning how unconscious factors control our actions that we'll arrive at a solution to our dilemma."

Henry went on as he tended to do when matters of the mind were concerned. Emmit sat across from him on the matching leather chair, again trying to seem interested.

"You see, Mr. Rhoe, most people are unaware of the internal conflicts they face. More often than not, they misconstrue the reasons behind these adverse feelings and employ a series of defense mechanisms to combat them."

"Such as…?"

"Denial. Rationalization. And of course…regression."

"And the plot thickens."

"Broth to spackle would be an apt analogy in your case, Mr. Rhoe. Now, most people, yourself included, like to think they are in control. Of themselves and their environments. Knowing what you are and what others are up to is a comfort obviously. But…"

"We're not. In control, I mean, right?" Emmit offered.

"No. Not even someone with your abilities can hope to be in complete control of themselves or those surrounding you."

"I never thought I tried."

"We all do, Mr. Rhoe. Remember—we're dealing with the subconscious mind, yes?"

"Yes. I mean, sure."

"Very well. I presume that this issue of control represents one of the reasons behind your current state."

"There's more?"

"There usually is. And to get to the bottom of it, I'm afraid we need to touch upon a rather delicate subject."

"This one sounds like a doozy."

"Please, Mr. Rhoe. If we're going to make progress, it's going to require your complete and undivided attention."

"Sorry."

"Don't be. Now…as much as I know about you and as much time we've spent together these past months, I have yet to hear you talk about your family. Other than the mention of your recent reunion with your daughter just now."

Emmit's body started tightening up. "I knew you were going to start up with this."

"And what might that be?"

"My father. Right? You're going to start asking me about my relationship with my father."

"Yes. And no. I was going to broach the paternal issue, but not the one you had with *your* father."

Tight turned to rigor mortis. Emmit knew what was coming now.

"Judging by your expression, it's safe to say you know whom I'm referring to."

Emmit nodded.

"Fine. Based on my understanding of the relationship you had with your father, which is not very deep, would it also be a safe assumption that it wasn't close-knit?"

"That's putting it a tad lightly. But that's the gist of it."

"Of course. That explains why you developed such an affectation for my father."

"Come again?"

"I'm referring to earlier on. Realizing that you had no relationship with your own father so to speak, it makes perfect sense that you unconsciously tried to establish a father/son relationship with my father."

"I really don't think…"

"I really do, Mr. Rhoe. Because our childhood experiences have much to do with who we become in our adult lives, yes? And knowing this, it's reasonable to assume that when you finally found the father you so desperately craved…then you were abandoned by him…"

"Abandoned? Is that what you call what he did to me?"

"I'll ask you to remain calm, Mr. Rhoe."

Emmit bolted up from the couch. "And I'll ask you to go fu…" he halted mid-word. "Your father…that psychopath…did a hell of a lot more than just abandon me!"

"Of course he did. I never meant to diminish…"

"But you did. Just like you always do! You think you know it all…about me, what makes me tick. You think you know every last inch of me and lead me down whichever path you choose hoping I'm gullible enough to follow…" Emmit stepped up to Henry. "…I'm sick of this. Understand? I'm sick and tired of you telling me what's what and what I should do about it."

"If that's the impression I've cast, I apologize, Mr. Rhoe. And believe me when I tell you that I never meant to imply your relationship with my father was anything more—or less—that it actually was."

Emmit pulled back. He didn't want to lose control. Not in front of Henry.

"All I was trying to get at," Henry said calmly, "is that believing in my father as you did, then witnessing him become all you abhor? Well, that sort of thing would damage the heartiest of souls."

Retaking his seat, Emmit crossed his legs and fought back the tears. "That's...not what made it so hard."

Henry managed to keep his next opinion to himself and let Emmit continue.

"I was devastated when he turned. I mean, I don't agree with your father figure theory. But I did look up to him. In more of a Florence Nightingale sort of way, I guess. But what really killed me was I never saw it coming."

"You can hardly blame yourself for that, Mr. Rhoe."

"No? Why not? After he told me about Umbridge...how be believed he killed all those people. How could I not see something like this on the horizon? Especially when I'm supposed to be able to see all these bad things before they even happen?"

"It's easy for me to say this...but you can't hold yourself accountable for that. You can't blame yourself for not being able to stop m..."

Emmit cocked his head to one side. Henry, meanwhile, tugged at his collar as he stopped himself from topping off that last consonant with the second vowel as opposed to sometimes 'y'.

January 1969

Once the lab report came back to confirm Umbridge had indeed been poisoned, Sara sent Emmit back to Norfolk for an impromptu training session with a Navy SEAL team. The duration for the all-encompassing instruction usually took months. But Emmit recently discovered his physical form could function photographically, which allowed him to tear through the excruciating physical fitness standards in less than two weeks.

The first phase of training began with a 50 meter underwater swim, underwater knot tying, a drown-proofing test and a basic lifesaving trail. Like all markers for the training regimen, it was either pass or fail (or in this case sink or swim).

Emmit set records for all of these exercises in both time and accuracy.

Phase One continued with a 1,200 meter pool swim with fins (Emmit didn't need or want them, but rules were rules), a one-mile open water swim, a one-and-a-half mile open water swim and a two-mile swim.

The finishing touches were put on Phase One with a four-mile timed run and a sprint through the obstacle course, where Emmit proved yet again that timing is everything.

After this initial series of tests, SEAL wannabes were treated to a sabbatical of sorts, which was affectionately referred to as Post Hell Week. These seven days held a 2,000 meter conditioning pool swim (without fins to Emmit's delight), a one-and-a-half mile night swim in open water, a two-mile open water swim, another four-mile timed run (Emmit beat his last record-setting pace by a full eight seconds) and another dash through the obstacle course.

By this time, the SEALs were growing a bit weary of Emmit's cockiness, though in their private thoughts, each marveled at how easily and assuredly the raw recruit made his way through the tortuous workouts.

It was on to Phase Two, which threw much the same unrelenting challenges Emmit's way and a few more, including a three-and-a-half and five-and-a-half mile ocean swim. By this point, even Emmit was starting to get winded. But he refused to give the SEAL trainers any hint of his mounting exhaustion. He'd made his supercilious bed and now he had to lie in it.

With the Third Phase underway, Emmit gathered what strength he had left and beat his own personal records for the obstacle course and two-mile ocean swim. He faltered during the 14-mile run (he tripped halfway home and tore up his knee pretty bad). But it wasn't enough of a delay for him not to beat the previous record by over six minutes.

The SEALs put him through all those paces (and several more to see what it would take to break him). But they just couldn't do it.

They couldn't even come close.

It had been over seven months since Samuel murdered General Umbridge. Even though the evidence was set in non-porous stone and he had plenty of time to accept the sickening notion, Emmit still wasn't convinced the doctor committed the crime. He wasn't sure why he was having such a hard time coming to grips with the situation. And he wouldn't for some time. All he could recognize was his mounting frustration. That and the sudden realization of what he was involved with.

Emmit hadn't appreciated the weight of it all until Sara ordered him to join the SEAL team. Up until then it all seemed like some sort of game, just a diversion that would peter out on its own accord. But with every day that passed him by, it was becoming clear that this was far from the case. National security was on the line and if he didn't pull his weight, people were going to die.

* * *

The SEAL team filed into the small conference room. Like a meticulously-maintained timepiece, they stood at attention until Sara and General Charles Tannenzapf, the true leader of Project Realm, joined them.

Tannenzapf was the first to come across Emmit's medical reports. Much unlike Emmit, he immediately grasped just how amazing the situation was, and he was just as fast to set Project Realm into motion. As crucial as the matter was, though, Tannenzapf didn't get directly involved. Early on in his military career, he discovered that it was much easier to lead peripherally. Not only that, but by assigning others significant duties, they came to trust their respective managers all the more, which always improved the quality of the final product.

It took a bit more time and effort to decide who should lead the secret op. There were many choices, though none of them seemed to instill him with confidence until Umbridge's name came to mind.

Tannenzapf didn't have much in common with Umbridge. Truth be told, they were so far apart Tannenzapf sometimes wondered if they belonged to the same species. But as much as they diverged on every moral, political and personal opinion, Tannenzapf recognized that Umbridge was a man who got things done. He was also the type who, unlike Tannenzapf, was on a perennial hunt for a spotlight.

But with Umbridge gone, Tannenzapf had no choice but to step under those hot lights. For a brief stint, he considered allotting the responsibility to Sara, but she just wasn't experienced enough. She was also a woman, which didn't bother him in the least, though he was certain his colleagues wouldn't share in his gender-based indifference.

Before coming to Norfolk, the trio of SEALS—Vernon Mills, Aubrey Jones and Percy Rawlings, served in Vietnam as part of an underwater demolition team, or UDT as the contraction went. They'd been hand-picked by Tannenzapf six months ago. Not just because they were the very best of their kind, but also because he'd served with Vernon's and Aubrey's fathers in Korea. There was no shortage of well-trained soldiers to choose from. But the selection dwindled insofar as whom Tannenzapf could trust to keep Project Realm strictly under wraps. He wasn't sold on Percy as he didn't know him from a hole in the ground. But Vernon vouched for him, so Tannenzapf agreed to bring Sergeant Rawlings along for the bloody ride.

The SEALS saluted the officers in perfect unison. Emmit was a few seconds behind with his gesture. He was too busy admiring his new colleagues, marveling how men that utilized a mere 10% of their brain's total capacity moved with such precision.

"Thank you, gentlemen," General Tannenzapf said politely. "You may be seated."

They all took a seat and awaited further instructions. Tannenzapf strode back and forth before them, looking pleased as he did. Another few revolutions and he took a seat at the head of the table. He turned to Sara and said, "The floor is yours, Captain Jusko."

"Of course, General," Sara made her way to the front end of the room.

Stretching out as far as her five-foot-five frame allowed she reached for the projection screen that hung from the wall, which proved to be just out of reach.

"Sergeant," she said looking Percy's way, "if you would be so kind."

Percy straightened out to reach his full six-and-a-half feet, walked up to Sara and easily pulled the screen down flat against the wall.

"Thank you, Sergeant Rawlings," she said and waited for Percy to retake his seat before she started in on the briefing.

Just over an hour later, Sara pulled the last of the maps off the projection unit. She turned the machine off and rejoined the others at the table. "We believe Dr. Jayne has been in Toronto for the past month or so," she revealed. "Intelligence claims he's established his base of operations there and…"

"Excuse me. Base of operations?" Emmit said skeptically.

He'd been fending off the urge to break down in hysterics from the beginning of Sara's session, but managed to keep his amusement to himself up until that point.

General Tannenzapf shot Emmit a critical glare. He didn't have any patience or understanding for soldiers interposing on their superior officers. Not even a soldier as singular as Emmit.

"Yes," Sara said taking note of Tannenzapf's tapering expression. "We believe this is the location where Dr. Jayne is planning and organizing a major terrorist initiative."

Emmit stifled his laughter again. "Dr. Jayne? Terrorist initiative? Look, captain…I wouldn't dream of questioning intelligence, but…"

Sara and all the rest shook their heads, wondering how someone who used so much of his brain could be so stupid.

"If you all wouldn't mind," General Tannenzapf cut in, "but if you could give Private Rhoe and I a moment alone?"

They all filed out as requested. Tannenzapf closed the door gently behind them and turned his attention to Emmit. "Trying to figure out what's going on up here?" he said drumming his temple. "Don't bother. Before Dr. Jayne jumped off the deep end, he taught us all how to stop you from getting inside our heads."

"Sorry, general. I wasn't trying to…"

"Of course you were. We didn't do a very good job training you otherwise. But that's not why I wanted a word alone." Tannenzapf took the seat beside Emmit. "I realize this is hard on you, son. A lot harder than you're letting on. But I can't have you questioning an officer. Especially in front of the other men."

"I'm sorry. I didn't mean to. But this whole story of Dr. Jayne just strikes me as…" Emmit stopped in mid-sentence. He looked on at General Tannenzapf and felt the warmth coming from him. "I just find it hard to believe is all."

"Given your close relationship with Dr. Jayne, that's completely understandable."

"I feel a *but* coming on."

Tannenzapf's jowls sagged. "May I continue?"

This time Emmit made good use of that magnificent intellect of his and kept his mouth shut.

"If we're going to have any chance of bringing Dr. Jayne in, you're going to have to set your personal feelings aside," Tannenzapf said, his tone now hard and to-the-point. "And please understand…I sympathize with your situation. But as much as I do, I can't have you compromising the lives of those men you're about to go into battle with. Is that understood?"

Emmit nodded timidly.

"I said…IS THAT UNDERSTOOD?"

Emmit shot up straight as a nail. He flattened his hand to a sharp edge and saluted the kind general. "Sir, yes sir!"

Two days later, Emmit was packing the last of his things into his duffel and getting ready to leave for Logan International. He was scheduled to meet the SEAL team at the Northwest hangar where their plane would take them to a Canadian military airfield 25 miles north of Toronto.

He still couldn't help but feel the entire situation was ridiculous. But he was able to take General Tannenzapf's words to heart and in so doing, managed to get Private Emmit Rhoe's—the soldier's—sentiments and priorities to outrank Emmit Rhoe's—the concerned citizen's.

With that in mind, Emmit snapped up his bag and headed for the door. Before he could close up the phone rang. He jammed the key in the lock trying to ignore the incoming call, but he'd never been one to leave a telephone ringing. He sidestepped back into the living room and picked up. "Hello?"

"Good afternoon, Emmit."

When he placed the voice he nearly had a full-blown coronary.

"Dr. Jayne?"

"The one and only," Samuel hummed.

There was an unnerving pause, the sort two ex-lovers have when they unexpectedly bump into one another at the mall.

"I can hear you breathing," Samuel said melodically.

"Yeah. I'm still here."

The Celtic emblem on Emmit's T-shirt rose and descended with every exaggerated gulp of air as he tried to creep into Samuel's head for any scraps of useful information.

"Now, now. I can't have any of that," Samuel said. "Not until we get a few things straight between us."

Emmit backed off. "Did you do it?"

"Did I do what?"

Emmit gritted his teeth and tried to play it calm. "Did you kill Umbridge?"

"Well, I wouldn't put it that way. Not exactly."

"You did, didn't you? I know he was an asshole…but you didn't have to kill him."

"I didn't kill General Umbridge, Emmit."

"You sure as hell didn't serve him tea."

"No. I served him justice."

Samuel's fulsome stance took on peacock proportions.

"You say potato," Emmit said.

"Now where have I heard that one before?"

"What do you want, Dr. Jayne?"

"Want? I don't want anymore, Emmit. I take. But that's not why I'm calling. I just felt I owed you the courtesy of letting you know."

"And what's that?"

"As much as our relationship has deteriorated over these past months, I still think we share a special bond," for a scant second he sounded like his old self. "I feel foolish saying this but I believe what we have, or had, may still be salvageable. Considering that, I thought I owed you the courtesy of telling you that no matter how well-prepared you and the others think you may be; it will not be enough."

"I guess we'll have to wait and see about that."

"I guess we will."

Emmit still had much to learn about his capabilities, however, he was savvy enough to pick up on the impulses Samuel was sending out. He could taste them and it would only take a few more licks before he could savor all the ingredients. But Samuel was very protective when it came to his recipes.

"You're more naïve than I ever imagined. I hadn't thought that possible until now," Samuel said while he continued to fend off Emmit's mental advances.

"I think you're confusing terms. I'm not naïve. I'm sane."

"Perhaps you're a bit of both. Be that as it may, you can't believe I'd risk contacting you without being properly prepared?"

"No. I don't think you'd ever start something up without figuring out all the angles first. I also think you believe Umbridge killed those people. More than that, I think you still have hopes that I'll start believing it, too."

"An insightful appraisal. But not that insightful. It's true I had a lingering hope that you would grasp the severity and true nature of the situation we're both embroiled in. But I never believed that you could be swayed. Not to that extent."

"So why are we having this conversation again?"

"As I said…I wanted to tell you. I wanted to give you fair warning that hell is on its way and there is nothing you or any of General Umbridge's gofers can do to stop it."

-7-

November 2004

During the past four months, Emmit was resolute in his efforts in becoming a more obliging presence within Timberlake. Overcoming four years of his contrary behavior wouldn't be easy, but it appeared as though the other residents were already starting to warm up to him.

It was getting to the point where he could actually attach the names to the faces. For instance, that pallid yet up tempo gentleman who stationed himself in front of the big screen for most of the day watching Jeopardy and Card Sharks reruns on the Gameshow Network was Robert Cryer. The Lilliputian lady with the unrelenting enthusiasm for those floral arrangement and macramé classes was Cecile Hunnicutte. And the alarmingly attractive, yet expressively reprehensible woman with the all-embracing collection of jeweled lizard broaches was Tammy Stein.

With a spring in his step, Emmit went on with his greetings and salutations, until he arrived at the person he'd spent most of his time trying to avoid.

"There she is," he said merrily.

Angela looked up from her cards. She was in the middle of a game of gin with Alice Brannicky from 235. "And there he is," she said curiously then laid down her cards. "Gin."

With a most vigilant eye, Alice looked over Angela's hand. She was having a hard time believing a card player as bad as Angela managed to take her down three games in a row.

"How are you, Emmit?" Angela asked.

"Fine. Great," Emmit dipped into the pocket of the new red argyle cardigan he'd bought at the Nordstrom's in Copley Place.

As Alice tried to lay off as many of her cards as she could, Angela pulled her cheaters down to the bulb of her nose and looked Emmit over from head to toe. "There's something different about you," she said. "Something very different."

"Maybe you'll have an easier time figuring out what that is with these," Emmit brought out Angela's new pair of bifocals and waved them at her.

"You...you got my glasses?"

"Sure did," he said and handed them to her. "I got the invisible ones...bifocals, I mean. So you can't see the lines. Hope you don't mind."

She took off her cheaters and placed them on the table. Alice watched on with a frown (she'd only been able to lay off three cards). "Are we still playing?" she asked.

Angela didn't answer. She was too pleased admiring her new eyewear. Alice braced herself on the arms of her chair, minding her bionic hip along the way. She thanked Angela for the game, bid Emmit adieu and started scouting about for a new victim. Emmit took her seat and smiled on at Angela as she slipped behind the glasses and started looking about the room. "They're perfect," she said excitedly. "Just perfect."

"That's great. I was hoping you'd like them."

"They're perfect," Angela reaffirmed. "I love them."

A bit later on, Emmit and Angela enjoyed a fine lunch of lobster bisque, angel hair pasta with marinara sauce and a dark, Splenda-sweetened chocolate mousse.

They didn't talk about anything specific during the meal; just chit chatting about what the other was up to as of late. It wasn't until they stepped off from the patio and onto the garden path that either decided to delve into some more interesting topics.

"You know...as long as you've been here, I really don't know anything about you," Angela declared while she cinched up the collar of her overcoat.

Emmit did the same with the zipper on his parka. It was only November, but the temperature had dipped down to the mid-December variety. "I'm afraid I'm not very good at sharing myself. I've been trying to get better at that lately."

"And so you have. In fact, you've been doing such a good job you've become the talk of the Timberlake town."

Emmit smiled. "Really?"

"I suppose it's no surprise, though; that you've finally decided to come out of your shell."

"And why is that?"

Angela pulled back like she suddenly remembered she wasn't supposed to be talking about it. "No. I shouldn't. It's none of my business."

"What's that?"

"I've said too much already."

"Then there's no point in holding back."

She wrestled with her conscience for a few seconds more, until…"Well, a lot of people have been wondering where it is you've been going for the past three or four months."

"Yourself included?"

"No," she said with a faint trace of resentment.

"C'mon now, Angela. It's only natural to wonder about these types of things. I mean…I spent four years pacing my room. Then all of a sudden, I'm disappearing for a day here and a day there. I'd be wondering where you were off to if the roles were reversed."

Angela's expression softened. She looked into Emmit's eyes and couldn't help but smile. "So…?"

"So what?" Emmit said coyly.

"Where have you been going then?"

"I'll tell you…but first, I'm interested to know what you and all the rest have put together."

Angela thought about it. She began to blush. "Considering how happy you've been…we all just assumed it was…you know?"

Emmit waved her on.

"A woman…" she looked up at him over her bifocals for confirmation.

"I guess that adds up. Makes perfect sense. Though it's not the case."

Inside, Angela's grin distended and her heart started to hum. "At the risk of being even more of a snoop…"

"I've been seeing a doctor," Emmit explained.

The song in Angela's heart faded to white noise. "A doctor? Is everything all right?"

"It's nothing like that. I'm healthy as a horse. From the neck down anyway."

Angela was confused. Enough so that her face told Emmit she hadn't caught what he was throwing.

"I've been seeing a psychologist," Emmit clarified. "Three times a week."

"A psychiatrist," Angela said a bit startled. "I never would have expected that."

"Why? You don't approve?"

"No, no. It's nothing like that. It's just my generation…our generation I guess you could say," she was seven years Emmit's senior, "well, we never really believed in such a thing."

"I know. Our kids were the first to start blaming their parents for all of their troubles. And I was a lot like you not long ago. I never would have put much, if any, faith in a head doctor."

"So what made you change your mind?"

"I was unhappy. With myself. With how I was treating people…friends and family alike."

"I didn't know you were so miserable."

"Well I was. A lot more than I'm even letting on. But I covered it up. By acting like an outsider looking in."

"Well, I'm just glad you've allowed yourself to shine," Angela said. "I knew there was something special about you. I always told the others that you were something else…something more than what you wanted us to see."

"You have no idea," Emmit said. "You have no idea."

March 1969

For Emmit, the past 14 months were a whirlwind of activity.

He'd tied the knot with Celia.

Eight months later they welcomed Hanna into the world.

But the biggest event (in Emmit's estimation) was that he'd finally come clean about what he was and what he was doing.

"So…what do you think?" Emmit said slinging Hanna over his shoulder.

Celia was dumbfounded. "What do I think? I don't know what to think."

Emmit started patting Hanna on the back. She unleashed a burp that blew his hair out of place.

"It's not everyday your husband tells you he's been contracted by the military to use his super powers to battle terrorism on a global scale."

"That's a bit of an exaggeration, but…"

"What about the paper?"

"What?"

She gave him a cold, hard look. "Your job, Emmit."

"What about it?"

"As *super* as you may be, you can't possibly be working there and doing this at the same time."

Emmit rubbed the back of his neck. "Well…here's the thing about that…"

"You never worked there, did you?"

"No. I mean yes. I did. For a few months anyway. But once I started up with them, they arranged it so I kept getting the checks."

"So it's a cover?" Celia asked/said.

"In so many words. Yes."

"So how is it when I call you there, you're able to answer?"

"General Tannenzapf…he's the one who organized this whole thing…he arranged to have an agent at the paper. Whenever you call, it's relayed to me."

"Sheila is an agent?"

"I think she was way back when. She's retired now and does this for a few extra bucks."

The situation was so fantastic Celia wasn't having nearly as difficult a time with it as she should have. She'd have plenty of time for gaping and gawking later on and for years to come. "Why didn't you tell me?"

Emmit pulled Hanna down and rested her on his lap. "I wanted to. God only knows how much. But I was afraid of what you'd say. More than anything, I didn't want you to worry."

Celia laughed nervously. "Worry. Right."

"It's not as dangerous as it sounds. Believe me. More times than not, I'm just sent in to talk. You know…negotiate with them."

Celia raised herself up from the coach and prepared to finish cleaning up in the kitchen. "So let me get this straight…they're using you for your powers of persuasion?"

"C'mon, Celia. There's no need to…"

"I don't mean to be rude, but if that's the case and based on this conversation…a lot of innocent people are going to die."

Emmit didn't expect Celia to understand. Nor approve. He just wanted to let it all out in the open and give her the chance to get used to the idea (if that were even a possibility). And that's where he left things.

For the time being at least.

He'd given her more than enough to chew on and she'd worked it down remarkably well. A lot better than he could have hoped for, which is why he elected to leave out one small detail.

"You're shittin' me," Percy said reloading his Kimber .45 automatic. "You didn't tell her about Jayne?"

"No. What was I supposed to say?"

"Ohh...I don't know. Maybe something like—honey...y'know how I can leap tall buildings in a single bound? Turns out the guy that showed me how to do that just happens to have a Lex Luthor complex." Percy slapped in the fresh clip and took aim at the paper target dangling 50 yards ahead.

"Good of you to take this so seriously."

Percy fired a shot then another, hitting the image of the silhouette in the neck and forehead. "I could say the same of you."

The sergeant got ready to squeeze off another shot but Emmit snatched the gun from his hands. "What's that supposed to mean?"

"Look, I know you're supposed to be the fiercest creature walking God's green earth...but you ever dream of grabbin' my firearm away from me again and..."

Emmit didn't blink. "What did you mean by that?"

"What did I mean by what, motherfucker?!"

Emmit's eyes tapered to two furious slits.

"You can stare me down 'til your eyes start to water," Percy said behind clenched teeth, "but that won't change the fact you know I'm speaking the gospel."

Emmit handed him back the .45. "You seem like an honest enough guy. Haven't given me a reason to mistrust you yet. But I have absolutely no idea what you're going on about."

Percy snapped his left eye shut and focused on the midsection of the target. "You know exactly what I'm going on about," he nailed the target dead center in the abdomen. "And if you don't, you're not half as smart as I was led to believe." he squeezed off another shot, this time hitting the target just a few inches to the left.

Emmit reached for Percy's gun again. This time the sergeant was too quick for him.

"What'd I tell you?!" Percy barked as he threw a solid right at Emmit's chin.

Emmit was so surprised Percy actually made contact, nailing him square in the jaw. It was a good hit. Good enough that Emmit felt it.

"Why you miserable..." Emmit yelped and before Percy knew which way was up, Emmit had him pinned to the floor.

Wrenching the gun out of his hand, Emmit slid it out of reach. Percy tried to wrestle free but Emmit locked in good and tight. "You keep squirming and you're likely to break your arm," Emmit said. "Now what did you mean by that?"

Percy kept struggling. "Fuck you!"

"Not until you spill it. That and a nice candlelit dinner maybe."

Percy failed to see any humor in the situation. And while he was never one to give up, it was obvious, and painfully so, that even he was well overmatched. Appreciating that, he relaxed his body, allowing Emmit to loosen his vice-like grip.

"You were saying?" Emmit eased up some more.

"I was sayin'…" Percy took a deep gulp of air. "…you'd best start treating this situation with the respect it deserves…instead of acting like it's some kind of amusement park ride."

Emmit let go completely, allowing Percy to stand up and gather himself. While he rubbed the feeling back into his arm he went on. "As if that weren't shameful enough, you go on acting like just 'cause you can do what others can't, you can afford to take it all in stride."

Percy dusted himself off and bent down for his gun. Stepping back into the booth, he opened both eyes wide and true and raised the weapon, positioning it slightly to the left and shot the target's left breast. "You're wastin' all that time doing that when what you should really be doing is giving us all you've got…heart and soul." Percy turned to Emmit and handed him his sidearm. "And once you're done with that, you should consider doin' the same with your wife."

Samuel had been a busy bee since he last spoke to Emmit, making good on his promise by devoting his considerable efforts and equally expansive fortune toward funding a multitude of terrorist factions and operations.

He'd bankrolled the bombing of the United 747 at LaGuardia killing 57 people.

He'd financed the abduction of three American senators, whose body parts were still being mailed bi-monthly to the Pentagon.

And most recently, he sponsored the complete and utter annihilation of the American Consulate building in South Korea, which provoked the burial of another 18 citizens.

All the while, Emmit, the SEALs, CIA, FBI and countless other government and military agencies chased Samuel and his foreign tails around the world, trying not to look too foolish as they failed to bring him in.

It was coming up on two in the morning. For the first time in three-and-a-half weeks, Emmit managed to stay firmly planted on solid ground for more than a few consecutive minutes. He crept up the front porch, trying his best to stop the front door from squeaking. As he slowly closed the door behind him, the trio of brass coated hinges disobeyed his direct order and squealed sharply. Emmit pressed his index finger across his lips and told them to *shush*. As he clicked the lock in place, he slowly turned back around and jumped out of his skin when he saw Celia sitting there on the stairs.

"Whoa! Hey! What's up?"

Celia grabbed the banister and pulled herself up. "I thought you said you'd be home by six?"

Emmit dropped his bag on the Oriental rug and stretched his arms out wide. "I'd be willing to get into this any other time. But I've been up for two days straight now, and…"

"You missed the party."

Emmit's head dropped right beside his duffel. "I know."

"She was looking for you."

"Y'know…It's great that you're not trying to make me feel any worse than I already do."

"She started to cry…"

"Jesus Christ, Celia! Of course she started to cry. She's all of 12 months old. That's what she's supposed to do!"

Much like Emmit, Celia often forfeited one emotion for another. She was scared to death when he was sent out to the four corners of the earth, and since he was gone more often than not, found herself habitually terrified. But she couldn't own up to it. She wouldn't own up to it. She refused to give her husband the satisfaction. Celia came from a poor but proud family. Before her father managed to scrape up enough money to buy their first home in Beacon Hill, putting food on the table was a daily crap shoot. Even after his tailor shop started earning significant dollars, Celia stuck to her wartime survival routine, and she wasn't about to give up on it just yet. So, instead of paying tribute to her true feelings, she veiled her fear with an unremitting house-frau routine, which she'd learned from the best of the best.

Through it all Emmit couldn't piece it together. As brawny as his intellect may have been, it was still male in conception. As such, he wasn't capable of peeling away the portico of Celia's female psyche in order to arrive at the layers of truth.

Dealing with the pressures of capturing Samuel was bad enough without having to face Celia's wrath. But that's not what bothered him. At least not the most. What ate away at the lining of his stomach was that he didn't have anyone to talk to. Not about the trauma he experienced on the job, and not at home about the responsibilities of being a husband and father.

As odd as it seemed, Samuel had been Emmit's outlet. The two had grown close during the time they spent together and just like Henry said, Emmit developed a paternal relationship with Samuel. And again just as Henry observed, the formation of this relationship was in no way surprising because Emmit never had any sort of liaison with his own father.

But that relationship had disintegrated, and again Emmit found himself with nobody to turn to. Nobody to rely upon. It was him against the world, and no matter how strong he was, or pretended to be, he was no match for such a laudable rival.

It was only a matter of time before he cracked. But unlike most people (or was it all?), he couldn't afford to break down. He couldn't let up, not for an instant because the fate of the free world rested on his shoulders.

December 2004

Considering how slowly (more inert, actually) the going was for he and Henry, Emmit couldn't wait to hop on the plane and get to Hanna's place for the holidays. He hadn't spent Hanukkah with his kin for what seemed like forever, and he was licking his lips in anticipation for good times rekindled.

He planned on staying the entire week. Hanna asked him to hang tough until the New Year, but Emmit didn't want to risk wearing out his welcome. He still didn't feel completely comfortable in his reactivated role as a father figure, and he wanted to make sure that he did things the right way.

After he unpacked the last of his things, Emmit washed his hands and face, ran a comb through his hair and scuttled down to the kitchen where Hanna was putting the final touches on dinner.

"Mmmm. Smells terrific," he said, taking a load off on one of the stools by the breakfast counter.

Hanna removed the thermometer from the turkey, closed the oven and joined him. She looked at the temperature reading. "Should be ready in about half an hour," she shook the thermometer and gently placed it on the counter beside the oven. "You want something to drink?"

Emmit thought about what would tickle his fancy when Jamie came wandering in, passing Hanna by like she wasn't there. "I've got it," he dipped down to grab the bottle of Crown, which Emmit assumed was the third or forth incarnation since his last visit.

"With a little bit of ice if you don't mind," Emmit requested.

Jamie doughtily saluted his father-in-law. He set the bottle down on the countertop, spun around and opened the fridge. After scouting about for a minute or two, he finally paid Hanna some mind. "We're out of ice?"

"Machine's on the fritz again," she said, "but I picked some bags up this morning. They're in the freezer down in the basement."

"Ah'll bee bahk," Jamie said in his best Schwarzenegger.

Emmit smiled politely and waited for him to leave. He much preferred talking to Hanna when Jamie was out of earshot. He waited until his son-in-law's footsteps faded until he asked, "A bit early to be courting the bottle, isn't it?"

Hanna bit her lip. "He's been under a lot of pressure at work."

Emmit could see Jamie's indulgence was a raw issue with Hanna. She knew too well how easy it was for addiction to arrive at a ten count. "I see," Emmit said deciding to cut her some slack by changing the conversation. "So…what's new and exciting?"

"Not much. Same as usual. How about you?"

"I can't complain, I guess."

Hanna wiped her hands on her apron and leaned on the island countertop. "You look good, Daddy. Better than I've seen in years."

"Meaning what? I've looked like hell until now?"

Hanna turned back around and opened the refrigerator door to look for a bottle of Diet Coke. "Leave it to you to turn a compliment into an insult."

Emmit held up his hands in surrender. "You know what they say about old habits."

"Yeah. They're a pain in the ass," Hanna spotted a half-full bottle, popped the cap and turned back to Emmit. "But we're not about the past anymore, are we?"

Emmit looked on at his daughter and felt his heart beat strong and proud. It skipped a beat when Jamie returned with a bag of ice in tow, along with a fresh bottle of Absolut.

He laid the items on the island beside the Crown Royal and snagged two clean glasses from the cupboard. While he cracked open the bottle of vodka, Hanna opened the bag of ice and dropped a few cubes into one of the glasses.

"Actually…I think I'll stick with a Coke," Emmit said.

"You sure?" Jamie asked a bit surprised.

"Beyond a doubt," Emmit said.

Hanna went ahead and fulfilled her father's request. Jamie, meanwhile, filled his tumbler to the brim. "Here you go, Dad…" he slid Emmit's drink across the countertop like he was some tavern extra in a John Ford film. "Enjoy."

Emmit's heart sank further still. He hated it when Jamie called him that.

A few hours later, Emmit had forsaken his soft drink pursuits and was polishing off his third glass of bourbon. It was going down smooth, though he was having a bit of a hard time keeping his eyes open and stopping his speech from slurring. He'd never been a hard drinker but in his natural state, he could suck down every last bottle out of Kentucky and survive it with little more than a buzz.

He might have been well past drunk, but he still noticed Hanna was acting peculiar. She was quiet, distracted; like she was holding onto something she couldn't wait to be rid of. Jamie wasn't acting like himself either, not that Emmit cared. But it was unsettling nonetheless.

The further along the evening progressed the stranger they both seemed to get. Hanna grew increasingly anxious. She looked like she wanted to tell Emmit something, but couldn't find the courage to let it loose. It wasn't until Nate and Hailey went upstairs to bed that Emmit decided to broach the subject.

"You okay, sweetheart?"

"I'm fine," Jamie said with a shit eating grin.

Emmit flashed him his toothy version then returned his attention to his daughter. "How about you?"

Before Hanna could rebut there was a knock at the door. They all turned around to see who it was, though Hanna and Jamie knew full well the identity of the person standing on the other side of the door.

"I'll get it," Hanna jumped out of her seat and raced to answer.

Now Emmit's radar was screaming incoming. He shifted in his seat uneasily when he figured out who it was.

"Hi."

Emmit took a double take at the woman standing before him. He looked down at his glass, thinking perhaps the bounty of alcohol in his system was causing him to hallucinate.

"Hi, yourself," he finally said to Rachel.

Hanna tapped her husband on the shoulder and motioned for him to join her in the kitchen. He didn't take her hint until she flicked his ear.

"Hey!" he yelped.

Hanna motioned towards the kitchen again.

"Guess we'll be going," Jamie said, and he and Hanna were quickly out of sight.

Rachel stepped toward the dining room table. She didn't sit just yet. She wasn't sure she'd be staying that long. "Always said he was the dumbest surgeon I've ever met."

Emmit laughed.

"So…how are you?" she asked half-interested.

"A lot better now."

After withstanding an onslaught of name-calling (Rachel's vocabulary was a lot muddier than even Emmit recalled), Rachel calmed herself down, allowing Emmit to finally get a word in edgewise.

"I had no idea you felt that way," he said. "Not to that extent."

"For someone who uses so much of his brain, you sure can be dense."

Emmit could hardly be upset with his youngest for her sarcasm. It was the one quality she deemed worthy enough to inherit from him. "Funny. I've never been told that before."

Rachel said she kind of doubted that.

"You sound like someone I know," he said.

"And you sound like someone I don't."

"I've been trying my best to change," Emmit explained. "For the better, I hope. And like I told your sister—I want to make up for all the time we've lost. Especially with you."

"Crawl, old man. Before you start a full-out sprint."

They peered through the floor-to-ceiling windows overlooking the lake for a quiet moment thinking their private thoughts, until Emmit turned to look at her with somber eyes. "How about a brisk stroll?"

Rachel laughed. Anxiously, but it was still music to Emmit's ears.

After he'd done flossing, Emmit gargled a capful of Listerine, then another. Reaching into his toiletry bag, be grabbed up the travel-sized bottle of Tylenol and took a triple dose. He packed it all away, zipped the case up and tucked it under his arm. Carefully, he took hold of the banister and just as cautiously took one step at a time down below. Hanna stepped out of the kitchen, cutting him off from the clear path leading to the guest room. She'd been cleaning the china, a process that usually didn't take so long, but she was stalling on Emmit's arrival.

"So...?" she asked hopefully. "Do I have to ask?"

"Not now, sweetheart. We'll talk about it in the morning."

"Yeah. Right," she took her father's arm and pulled him into the guestroom.

"C'mon, now...I'm tired and I drank too much," Emmit protested even though he knew it wouldn't do him any good.

"Tell it to someone who cares," Hanna pushed him into the room and pointed to the bed. "Okay, old man...spill it."

"Why does everyone keep calling me that?"

Hanna's stare kept stern and true.

"All right," Emmit conceded. "Jesus...I was spared from the ire of Rhoe women for the better part of a decade, and in the past five hours I've been brought right back up to speed."

Hanna didn't seem too concerned with Emmit's dilemma.

"Yeah, yeah, yeah. I know. Save it for someone who cares," he said.

He sat down on the stiff mattress, sliding toward the headboard. He grabbed one of the pillows and propped it up and carefully rested his head. Meanwhile, he took the time to think about how he was going to retell the conversation he had with Rachel. The last thing he wanted to do was over dramatize the matter, especially since Hanna was prone to tears. He'd shed enough that night for the both of them.

"Before I get into it, I'd like to ask you something?" Emmit said.

"What's that?"

He ran his tongue along his lower lip while he kept figuring how to downplay it. "What did you think of me when you were growing up?"

"What do you mean?"

"About what I did. And I'm not talking about when you were knee high. More into your teens...when your mother and I told you what was really going on."

"What's this got to do with you and Rachel?"

"Just answer the question please."

Now Hanna pulled back to surmise. It was strange but all of a sudden it occurred to her that she really didn't have an answer. "I don't know...I guess I felt like any other kid."

"Really?"

"Okay. Maybe that's a bit off the mark. I felt like...I felt okay. I worried about you of course, but I felt like you were doing something worthwhile. Something noble, you know?"

"So you weren't…ashamed?"

Hanna's mouth gaped open. "Ashamed? Of you? Why would I ever feel like that?"

Emmit's chin sank into his chest.

"Is that what she told you?" Hanna said gallingly.

"Calm down now. She didn't put it like that. Not exactly."

"Then how did she put it? Exactly?!"

"Oh…you know what she can be like. Her liberal views and all."

"So you watch Fox and she tunes in to CNN. That's no reason for her to say she's ashamed of you."

"I told you…she never said she was ashamed."

"Then what?"

Emmit closed his eyes. Not a good move. The room started spinning like a runaway Ferris wheel. He opened up and went on. "I…I've been…" A rush of bile raced up his throat.

"Are you okay?" Hanna raised herself up, ready to escort Emmit to the bathroom.

Emmit held up his hand. "Just…gimme a minute," he swallowed the acid-laced flow back, wincing horribly as he did. "There. That's a bit better. Where was I?"

"You said you've been *something.*"

His eyes widened to two near perfect realizing circles. "A soldier," he said with any and all traces of pride distinguished. "For most of my life. And a soldier follows orders, whether or not he agrees with them."

"You were a good soldier, Daddy. And like you used to say—a good soldier follows orders."

Emmit nodded. "Mmhmm. But a great one knows when to ignore them."

Hanna shot her father a curious look. "Where is this going?"

"I've done some things…things I'm not proud of. And I was never sure how much you or your sister—even your mother—knew about the operations I was involved in. But after tonight it appears as though you knew a lot more than I ever imagined."

Emmit's chin dug down further still.

"We knew what we needed to know, Daddy. No more. No less."

"In this case, less is definitely less."

Hanna sidled nearer to her father and put her hand on his knee. "We knew what was important…that you were trying to do the right thing. I knew it. Mom knew it. And whether or not Rachel ever admitted it…she knew it, too."

Emmit smiled. "She certainly has a funny way of showing it."

"She usually does. But I want you to know that we were always proud of you. No matter what was in the papers. No matter what color the networks painted you. We always knew that you tried to make the world a better place. And that's more than any of us had the right to ask for."

-8-

September 1969

It had been nearly four years since Samuel pitched his rebel's flag. In that time, Emmit and the SEAL team chased him around the world a dozen times over, and all they had to show for their efforts was an overflow of frequent flyer miles (well, they would have but the incentive program was still another 24 years away from being introduced to airborne consumers).

When the hunt began, Emmit made the cardinal mistake of getting caught up in his personal feelings. He was hurt, confused and angry. More than anything, though, he felt foolish because he should have seen it coming. He should have been able to detect this new menace just like Samuel taught him, and put a stop order on it before it ever had a chance to pick up steam.

But he didn't.

In his most private thoughts, Emmit assumed he'd missed the signals because of his involvement with Samuel. He clung to the notion that his strong feelings for his mentor blinded him to the diabolical doctor's true intentions. However, when he considered determining an individual's intent was his greatest attribute, the aforementioned rationale held about as much water as a ramshackle sieve.

While Emmit's ability to access well over 60% of his brain's total capacity allowed him to perform some amazing physical feats, his most impressive ability was cognitive in nature. The fact that he could clean and jerk a prop plane or outrun the B-train was merely icing.

So why then, had he not uncovered Samuel's true intentions? The question had been tugging away at him since he learned Samuel murdered General Umbridge. But again, when he delved into the infinite recesses of his consciousness where fiction was banished and fact ruled sovereign, Emmit pinpointed how Samuel managed to shroud his purpose.

The discovery wasn't nearly as remarkable as it was frightening.

* * *

Emmit didn't discuss his revelation with anyone. Not Tannenzapf or Sara. Not even Percy. He kept it to himself because they were wound tight enough already, and their hopes were riding curb high. Telling them that their adversary—the one that was already eating their collective lunches—was someone much more powerful would only make a bad situation worse.

Infinitely.

So, he put it on the mental backburner and focused all of his attention and efforts on bringing Samuel back to the States.

He'd come oh-so-close in Brazil on September 3rd when Samuel teamed up with MR-8, a Marxist revolutionary militia. While Emmit managed to take down the leader of the group, Samuel again tiptoed around the mine fields.

After tracking him down at the Paysandu Hotel in Rio de Janeiro, Emmit stormed into Samuel's suite, only to find him coolly sifting through the daily news. Before Emmit could get within a half-dozen yards, Samuel stomped his foot down and the remote control plunger in the heel of his loafer activated the bomb he'd planted in the wall between his room and the adjacent suite. The targeted impact caused the shared 3,500 pound patrician to crumble, and Emmit could only watch Samuel casually wave goodbye as he desperately held it up so the family next door would live to see another day.

July 1970

Ten months later, Emmit and the SEAL team were breathing down Samuel's neck in Montevideo, Uruguay. The doctor touched down with the Tupamaros terrorist group to kidnap Daniel Mitrione, an advisor for the U.S. Agency for International Development.

Following a brief but heated exchange with the Tupamaros squad, several of its members escaped with Mr. Mitrione in tow. Emmit hadn't seen Samuel yet but was sure he was somewhere close by. For the next month, Emmit and the SEALs continued to hunt down the Tupamaros terrorists and Samuel. They gave up their pursuit when they found Mitrione's battered, bloodied body. To add insult to injury, Samuel tacked one of Umbridge's stogies to the ex-advisor's forehead along with a note that read, "Close, but no cigar."

July 1972

As it turned out, terrorism was hard work. Samuel enjoyed the frights of his labor thus far, but he decided to take a well-deserved vacation. Exhaustion wasn't the only reason he took two steps back. Emmit had been getting a bit too close for comfort the last few encounters, and Samuel thought it wise to let things cool down for a spell before he unleashed his next offensive.

Besides, even though he was catching headlines and making Emmit and all the rest look like unabashed morons, he wasn't really making a difference. Not enough to change things. If Samuel was to make good on his lofty ambitions, he needed to make a really big splash. But he couldn't let his passion override cold, hard reason. Samuel appreciated that patience was indeed a virtue, and terrible things most certainly came to those who waited. Though he still wasn't sure how he was going to make the world stand up and take notice. And he wouldn't until it finally occurred to him. Every operation he was involved with, any assault that had been directed at the U.S., was executed on foreign soil.

That was the key.

Watching bodies being carted off on television made for spirited water cooler banter. Reading about the widows and children of eviscerated emissaries made you appreciate the finer things. But it was still a secondary threat—a far, far away peril that certainly could never find its way back home. But what if Samuel carted the chaos and bedlam into people's backyards? What if he made them turn off their sets, put down their papers, and look out their windows to see it with their very own eyes?

Now that would be something, wouldn't it?

It was a delicious prospect. But one that would have to wait. Samuel already had numerous other plans in the works, and those partners involved were definitely not in the habit of being disappointed.

So, Samuel busied himself with amassing the funds to see his next string of commitments through, the first of which was joining forces with the Irish Republican Party to bomb raid Belfast on what was coined Bloody Friday. The attack killed 11 people and injured another 130.

Emmit and the SEALs picked up their trail earlier that morning. For the next 10 days they kept up with their hot pursuit until they caught up with Samuel and his IRA counterparts 60 miles northwest of Belfast in the village of Claudy. Not long after their arrival, Samuel organized a series of car bomb attacks, which took the lives of six citizens. During a bloody standoff with the

IRA members, Emmit abandoned the pitched battle when Samuel bolted to catch a plane waiting for him at a nearby airstrip. Emmit chased down the single-engine prop plane. But just as the small craft started to ascend, he ran out of gas and again he could only watch as Samuel escaped to terrorize another day.

Phase one of the trilogy that would lead to Samuel's magnum opus was complete.

September 1972

Another close call came and went 46 days later in Germany during the Munich Massacre. The operation was near and dear to Samuel's heart as he believed the deaths of the 11 Jewish Olympic athletes would strike an inordinately poignant chord with Emmit.

Truth be known, Emmit didn't care what God Samuel's victims paid homage to. The thorn that stuck deepest in his side was that the West German authorities disallowed his and the SEALs' participation in the rescue effort. Emmit didn't blame the local powers that be for leaving them out (at least not wholly and not at the outset). After all, they'd barely managed to slow Samuel down let alone stop him. But when the German's botched the rescue effort and nine hostages and five terrorists were planted as a result, the finger Emmit was pointing straightened out considerably.

Reel two was in the can.

December 1973

On the morning of December 17th, Emmit and the SEAL team arrived at the Leornardo da Vinci International Airport in Rome. General Tannenzapf received an anonymous tip the week earlier informing him there was going to be a major strike in the vicinity. While he was certain it was another one of Samuel's attempts to get his SEAL team off on another chase, the General couldn't risk not having his team there. Innocent lives were at stake and worse still (on a PR level) the media had been eating Tannenzapf alive. His failure to capture Samuel was attracting all the wrong kinds of attention and the longer the mad doctor remained at large, the uglier things were going to get.

That was bad enough without having to contend with Emmit's recent conduct. Tannenzapf had been ignoring the problem for too long, foolishly believing the heart and soul of Project Realm would work his way past his issues. But Emmit wasn't dealing with the problem in any way that helped anyone. Instead, he let his anger dictate his actions and his rogue behavior was starting to endanger team members, not to mention innocent bystanders.

Tannenzapf wasn't sure how to remedy the situation, though he was certain another head-to-head confrontation with Emmit wasn't the answer. He'd broached the subject with Private Rhoe several times already and was starting to come off like a nagging parent. Since Emmit turned a deaf ear to him, Tannenzapf concluded another voice needed to make itself heard.

Two hours before Emmit and the SEALs were to take off for Rome, Tannenzapf called Percy into his office. The general was aware Percy and Emmit had grown close since they began serving together, and if anyone could talk some sense into Emmit, it would be the sergeant.

"So, what do you think?" Tannenzapf asked as he carefully looked Percy over from behind his desk

Percy thought about the question in silence until he said, "I think these things have a way of working themselves out, general."

"I'm sure they do. And please…don't misunderstand my meaning. I trust your judgment. But you've got to appreciate the ramifications of Private Rhoe's actions. How they reflect our operation and more importantly, how they can compromise all we've worked so hard to achieve."

Percy appreciated that all too well. But the question Tannenzapf originally posed still hadn't been answered.

"So I ask you again, Sergeant Rawlings," this time, Tannenzapf's voice was completely devoid of empathy, "what are you prepared to do should our extraordinary colleague step out of line again?"

Percy wasn't sure what to do when Emmit decided to go freelancing again. And even if he was able to formulate a plan of attack, he was certain there was nothing he could do to execute it. He did, however, know exactly what to say to Tannenzapf. "Whatever it takes, general. Whatever it takes."

The first stage of the Rome assault began when five terrorists pulled out weapons from their luggage in the terminal lounge. They set their sites on anyone unfortunate enough to be frequenting the area and in the process killed two people.

Emmit and the SEAL team brought along a new member to the squad, Carl "Boom-Boom" Othello (who'd earned his nickname based on his expertise with explosives rather than his veneration of Freddie Washington). The chopper carrying the SEALs touched down just as the terrorists attacked a Pan American 707 bound for Beirut and Tehran. The aircraft was summarily obliterated with incendiary grenades, laying 29 people to rest including four senior Moroccan officials. Also killed in the melee were 14 American citizens who were employed by ARAMCO, the world's leader in crude oil production.

The E-2C Hawkeye helicopter set down on a discontinued runway; just shy of two miles west from where the aircraft was destroyed. As they stepped out of the chopper's bay, Percy pulled Emmit aside for a few words before the guerrillas hit the fan. "How you feeling?" he asked, inspecting the clips of his side arms.

Emmit didn't reply. He just wringed his hands and closed his eyes, trying to round up the energies that coursed untamed inside him.

"I know you hear me talkin' to you!"

Emmit's eyes popped open and he gave Percy a hard, cold look. "You raise your voice any more and I won't be the only one hearing it."

Slipping the .45 into his left ankle holster, Percy put his hands on Emmit's shoulders. "Just be careful out there. Okay?"

Emmit pinched Percy's cheek. "Why Sergeant Rawlings. I didn't know you cared."

The SEALs jogged through the terminal ordering the crazed passengers and airport workers to vacate the area. The further along they got, the more manic the atmosphere became confirming they were headed in the right direction.

They neared the entrance of the adjacent terminal when an explosion rocked the building. Large chunks of debris dropped from the high ceilings. Percy just managed to sidestep a falling light fixture as his team stopped in front of the shattered windows that looked out onto the runway.

Long, jagged spears of fire shot high into the air and dense clouds of thick, black smoke blotted out the tarmac. Airport workers scurried about like a horde of cockroaches caught in unexpected light while Emmit and the SEALs wafted through the carnage and spotted the terrorists, who were hustling off some 50 meters ahead.

Percy and the others noticed the change in Emmit back in Belfast. Up until that point, Emmit kept his astonishing facilities in check and only flexed as much muscle as necessary to get the job done. Killing was a last ditch resort and one he never aspired to frequent. But back in Claudy, he submitted to his most feral nature. It was the first time he'd ever put on a display of his full power. While it was a most frightening exhibition, just between Emmit and the lamppost, it felt good.

Really good.

A lot better than trying to fight it anyway. So when he caught up with one of the IRA members who attempted to speed off in a car he'd boosted, Emmit tore the engine out of the vehicle then performed a similar operation on the terrorist's jugular.

The SEAL team assumed his aberrant conduct was brought on by Samuel's treachery, and it had finally pushed Emmit over the edge. It was an accurate assessment, but a bit misguided because they believed Emmit could control himself. All it would take was a little effort and self management. But Emmit's anger was beyond his control. Perhaps if he were more experienced he could have kept himself at bay, but he was still learning the ropes. His exasperation prompted a chemical reaction much like blood in the water triggers a shark into frenzy. And just like nature's perfect killing machine, the only way to get Emmit's pulse down to normal was by eliminating the agitating agent.

Percy took the lead as the SEALs followed their targets across the blacktop. The terrorists were making a beeline for the Lufthansa airliner that was already filled with fuel, passengers and crew members. Amid all the commotion, the SEALs managed to keep their presence anonymous. Not one of them intended to introduce themselves until they could piece together a viable offensive.

At that moment, Emmit didn't consider himself a member of that particular committee.

Percy and the rest found cover behind one of the large luggage carriers positioned not far off from the plane. The sergeant peaked around the corner of the carrier and saw the terrorists snap up five hostages who were attempting to flee the aircraft. The SEALs kept watching, still searching for that elusive counter measure when Emmit strode past them and out into plain view.

"Hey…where the fuck're you going?" Percy yelped.

Emmit turned around without breaking cadence. "Putting an end to this massacre."

Tannenzapf's question ran through Percy's mind over and over again as Emmit put it into overdrive and covered the 20 meters between him and his targets in a heartbeat. The SEALs watched in awe (and equal amounts of terror) as Emmit flanked their enemy. He grabbed the tail man and spun him around.

"This ends now," Emmit muttered.

He hoisted the 175-pound man up off the ground and threw him against the hull of the plane. Emmit heard a sharp *crack* as the terrorist's spine splintered like a bolt of deadwood. He landed back onto the tarmac in a lifeless heap. Emmit didn't sense any pulse or read any thoughts but he was through taking chances. He stepped up to the terrorist and brought his boot heel down hard on his head, crushing it to an off-pink paste.

"Jesus. What the fuck was that?" Aubrey mewled while his stomach began turning cartwheels.

"I dunno, but I don't think he's done," Vernon pointed towards Emmit as he turned his attention to the next terrorist in line.

This fanatic caught an elbow to the kidneys. The organ exploded like an overfilled balloon and as he turned to face his executioner with a mouth full of blood and bile, Emmit drove his fist through his nose, past his brain and back out the posterior of his skull.

The remaining terrorists took note of their fallen comrades and opened fire. Emmit's flack jacket rang like a bell as a slue of bullets bounced off the reinforced Kevlar plating. His hand was still stuck in the terrorist's face and before he could wrench himself free, caught a bullet in the meaty part of his right shoulder.

The SEAL team snapped out of their wonder and opened up with an encompassing round of cover fire. Emmit seized the opportunity and spun around to hustle back to rejoin them. He settled beside Percy, slapping his back flat against the fascia of the luggage carrier.

"You okay?" Percy shouted.

"Just a flesh wound," Emmit wiped his hand clean of the bits of bone and brain.

"I'm not talking about your shoulder," Percy said.

Emmit gritted his teeth and dug his fingers deep into the bullet hole. After a bit of exploratory surgery, he located the slug, yanked it out and proudly displayed it to Percy.

The SEALs continued to rain a hail of gunfire down upon their enemies. Unfortunately, the terrorists proved to be considerably more proficient than Emmit, Percy or any of the others would have liked. They were organized and worse still, motivated. They held off the counter attack rather easily (they had the advantage of higher ground), gathered their fresh batch of captives and boarded the Lufthansa airliner.

The turbines of the craft started to churn. There was nothing the SEALs could do but watch and wait.

"Anyone got any bright ideas?" Percy asked.

Emmit stood up and walked back towards the plane. "Just one."

Percy lunged at Emmit and grabbed hold of his jacket. The sergeant's fingers were nearly torn out at the knuckles in the process.

"Let go or you'll never be able to count to 10 again," Emmit snarled.

Percy held firm until he looked into Emmit's eyes, or what had been his eyes. His irises and pupils vanished, making way for two pitted black coals that burned so fiercely Emmit's eyelids started to smolder.

The sergeant relinquished his grip and detected the faint aroma of burning flesh. He rubbed the feeling back into his fingers and watched Emmit dart off after the jetliner, wondering what he was going to tell Tannenzapf once he got back to Northwest for the debriefing.

Adrenaline scorched Emmit's veins like battery acid. He picked up his pace to a full out sprint. He hit 30, 40, and redlined at just over 50 miles per hour until he caught up with the 336,000 pound jet, which was preparing for lift-off.

In perfect stride, Emmit jumped for the landing gear. He just cleared the rear wheel and hopped up onto one of the struts. As the 707 grabbed air, he held on tight while the landing gear retracted into the thickened juncture where the wing met the fuselage.

Inside, Emmit steadied himself while the enormous airbus broke for the open sky. Some 3,000 feet below and a mile east, the SEALs craned their necks upwards and watched the 707 disappear behind the pale cloud line.

"This is bad," Percy lamented. "This is so fucking bad."

Vernon checked his weapon's magazine. "Keep it together. Emmit'll be okay."

Still half-loaded, he slipped the clip back into his weapon, got up along with the rest of the team and started checking the area for survivors.

"He's not the one I'm worried about," Percy said.

The 707's 130+ foot wing span carried it further into the atmosphere until it reached its cruising altitude of 38,000 feet. Emmit was tucked away in the cargo area, trying to get a bead on the terrorists' energy signatures. Their numbers and sheer exasperation made it difficult, but Emmit was still able to dig into their frenzied psyches and establish a rough understanding of their plans.

They may have been experienced but Emmit was relieved to discover they were also scared. Fear could be a powerful catalyst, prompting a host to pull off some amazing deeds. But it also compromised reason.

Emmit could use that.

He closed his eyes and pushed out the rest of the world. The only two people in existence were him and the leader of the terrorists; the tall, lean bearded man with the Popeye-width forearms.

Pushing past his men, Popeye entered the cockpit. He pulled his modified Sten Mk V machine gun front and center, pressed the barrel hard against the pilot's temple and screamed in broken and battered English, "You will fly this plane to Beirut, or I will send you to hell."

Emmit felt the sinews in Popeye's wrist swell and constrict around the handle of his weapon. He sensed his index finger tighten and twitch around the half-oval shaped cobalt trigger as Popeye impatiently waited for the pilot to redirect the plane.

"Just do it, for chrissakes," Emmit whispered.

The seconds ticked by. Popeye's trigger finger tautened. It wouldn't be long before the hammer pulled back and the pilot's inner workings were sprayed on the windshield.

"Okay! All right!" the pilot shrieked.

He pulled the yolk back and to the left and they were en route.

Four hours later the pilot, who had long ago soiled his Hanes boxers, (according to the stench, Emmit surmised he had some sort of fish for lunch) called in his arrival to the Beirut International Airport. Emmit was still tucked away in the cargo bay, listening intently when the Lebanese official on the other end of the transmission told the pilot that he would not allow them to land.

Emmit was fighting off the urge to bust in on the terrorists and take them down as hard and fast as he could. But he'd used the fly time to the best of his advantage. He'd calmed down, treating himself to a bout of rational thought, which hopefully wouldn't wind up being drowned out in a sea of blood.

Meanwhile, the terrorists fought their fears and vied for an equally cunning proposal by keeping their hostages alive. Dead captives made for poor bargaining chips, and they'd need all the leverage they could wrap their deviant hands around to make it out of the debacle alive and kicking.

A decision had to be made. They couldn't land in Beirut. They couldn't kill the hostages. If Popeye was half as clever as Emmit thought, he'd arrive at the only option available, which was…

The 707 landed in Athens six hours later. Emmit waited for the jetliner to come to a complete stop before he made his stand.

Carefully now, he peered around the corner of the cargo bin and looked out toward the passenger cabin. The hostages were bundled together near the front of the plane. The terrorists were holding a tight vigil, jabbing their weapons and shouting out Arabic platitudes. Popeye, meanwhile, was calling out his demands over the plane's radio. Rather than embarrass himself by stringing together another barely coherent command in English, he demanded to speak to someone who spoke Arabic. At first the only reply he got was feedback, but then the Athens Airport official said in her thick Macedonian accent, "Please to hold…we are contacting our translator now…"

Another few impossibly tense moments came and went, until the radio chirped an incoming call. Popeye picked up the handset and was greeted by a voice every bit as caustic as his own. The translator asked what Popeye's demands were. Emmit leaned in and heard Popeye say, this time in his native tongue, that he wanted two of his brothers released from their wrongful imprisonment. He gave the translator their names and to ensure compliance, ordered one of his men to kill a hostage.

Before even Emmit could react, the underling stabbed the barrel of his weapon into the back of one of the hostage's heads (the short, rotund man in the pale blue leisure suit and matching shirt). Praising Allah, the terrorist pulled the trigger and blew the back of the hostage's head clean off. One of his mates opened the hatch and he threw the man out onto the tarmac for the entire world to see.

The remaining hostages screamed and ranted, forcing the cabin to endure a lot more pressure than it had taken on at its highest altitude. The terrorists, already on edge, began beating them down with the butts of their rifles, until Popeye stormed out of the cockpit. Once he settled them down, he returned to the craft's command center and told the translator that when his brothers were released, he would fly to Damascus for fuel and food and then on to Kuwait. He pledged his eternal soul that if his demands were met and everything went according to plan, he would release the remaining hostages.

That's what the stories in the papers read. It's also what the television and radio stations reported as fact. But the Tannenzapf spin machine had to be put into action again, because once Emmit discovered *He* was on board, all bets were off.

Two days later, Emmit arrived at Northwest. The SEAL team touched down the day before. They were already waiting outside of General Tannenzapf's office when Emmit came walking down the hall. Tannenzapf was debriefing them one at a time to find out what really happened in Rome. But more than anything, he wanted to ensure they were all on the same page if and when they were approached by reporters.

Emmit sensed the tension and anxiety ripping through the team the moment he entered the building. Although, he didn't need access to over 60% of his brain's capacity to catch the strange vibe they were sending out. Their tight, pale expressions told the story. "Fellas. What's the good word?" Emmit stopped in front of Tannenzapf's door.

"Lots of words," Aubrey said somberly, "not many of 'em good, though."

Emmit patted him on the back and leaned on the wall between him and Carl. They stood there for a while staring into nothing, until Emmit noticed that one member of the team was absent. "Where's Perc?" he asked.

Aubrey pointed to Tannenzapf's door.

"Ah. Guess I don't have to ask what this is all about then, do I?"

They waited in relative silence until Percy came through the door. He half-smiled to the team, the kind you give at a funeral. He stopped in front of Emmit and shook his head. "Good luck," he said and looked on to the others. "C'mon, guys. Let's go grab something to eat."

They all left without so much as a goodbye. Before they could turn the corner, Tannenzapf's ample figure filled the frame of his open doorway. He called out to Percy, thanking him for his time and candor, and waited for the sergeant to leave until he even looked at Emmit.

"Inside," Tannenzapf nudged his head towards his office.

Emmit passed him by, kind of slouching like an elementary school kid who knew he was in for a hell of a time in the principal's office. Tannenzapf eased the door shut behind him. He passed Emmit and made his way behind his desk and took a seat. "How's the shoulder?"

Emmit rubbed his wound. "It's all right. Practically healed already."

"Excellent. Now that we've done away with the pleasantries, I'll ask you if you've read this morning's paper."

"No, sir. I've been in the air for most of the day."

Tannenzapf grabbed the copy of the Washington Post sitting on the corner of his desktop and slid it to Emmit. "Here."

Emmit looked down and read the headline printed on the front page, *"Special Military Operation Foils Terrorist Plot in Rome."* He looked back up to the general. "Catchy."

"It certainly is. But if you'll take a moment to read the story, you'll notice a few discrepancies."

Tannenzapf waited for Emmit to sift through the copy. Emmit's eyes darted through the article. He wasn't really reading. There was no need. He knew how the story ended. He also knew what Tannenzapf was getting at.

"And they all lived happily ever after," Emmit slid the paper back to the general.

"Yes. At least according to this ink. But we know better, don't we?"

"Look...I know what you're going to say and I can appreciate your position, but..."

"The time for buts has passed us by, private. Long ago. You must know this considering your ranking hasn't ascended since you started on with us."

Emmit looked down to the single stripe adoring the upper portion to the sleeve of his uniform. "I had to make a decision," he said, kind of excusing his words to come. "And fast."

"Of course you did. As did all of your teammates. That's what you're trained for."

"There's no training that could prepare us for the shit we've been trudging through, general."

Tannenzapf's expression hardened. "I understand that. And I would appreciate it if you wouldn't use that sort of language in my office."

Emmit apologized and waited for Tannenzapf to get his mad-on.

"Do you realize what you've done, Private Rhoe? Can even your mind grasp the scope of this situation? People died. And they died on account of your recklessness."

Emmit's blood started to boil. All he could see was red water. He had to stop himself from slapping the teeth out of Tannenzapf's head.

"You've been trained to circumvent these dangerous situations," the general explained. "To diffuse them and protect the innocent. What you haven't been trained for—not by this facility—is take matters into your own hands."

"Like I said, sir...beyond my control."

"Beyond your control? Just like the political and moral pitfall you've created for me and my staff!"

Emmit had never heard Tannenzapf raise his voice. He wasn't aware the bear-of-a-general was even capable.

"While we're at it, I might as well tell you I don't appreciate your forcing me to cover your behind by fictionalizing these reports. For God's sake, I'm not Mickey Spill..."

"He was there," Emmit said softly.

Tannenzapf didn't hear him. He kept rambling on until Emmit said a bit louder, "He was on the plane!"

Tannenzapf started in on the next sentence, but stopped midway and asked, "What was that?"

"Dr. Jayne. He was there. On the plane."

Tannenzapf's face turned back to its usual color. "What do you mean? In Athens?"

"He was on that plane," Emmit said, his voice returning to a barely audible pitch.

"Why didn't you tell anyone?"

"Because I knew what was going to happen...that you would think I acted out again without thinking. I wanted to tell you face-to-face so you would understand that I did what I did because I had to."

The general leaned in closer to Emmit, folding his hands on top of his desk "Of course. But...where is he then?"

February 2005

Upon closer consideration, Emmit chose the barker recliner over the couch. While he was exhausted and sure the sofa would be more comfortable (which was especially important since Henry tended to go on in these types of situations), the decorative and plush settee was a tad cliché for Emmit's liking.

As always, Henry asked Emmit to begin with a retelling of the past few days since they'd last seen each other; what he was up to, how he was feeling, general inquiries and going overs that Henry used as tent poles for the weighty issues to come.

An hour or so later, Emmit was going over the Rome briefing with Tannenzapf and what happened between he and Samuel.

"So you told General Tannenzapf the truth?" Henry questioned, dipping his view just above his reading glasses.

Emmit looked around Henry's office, which had recently been redecorated. Nothing matched. Not the colors, fabrics, shapes or sizes but somehow it all worked perfectly together. "Of course. I was saving that part for him like I said."

"But why?"

"Because I was becoming a detriment. A liability. I knew it and I couldn't do anything to stop it. So I had to substantiate my actions and I wanted to make sure Tannenzapf heard it from my lips and not some half-baked headline."

Henry said that sounded logical enough then asked, "What happened on that plane, Mr. Rhoe?"

"You know what happened," Emmit said grimly. "About as well as I do."

A bit uneasily, Henry said, "All I know is what I've read, yes? But now that I've got the horse at my trough…"

Emmit wasn't in the mood to fend off Henry's psychosomatic advances, so he got straight to the point. "I was hiding out in the cargo bay…trying to figure out how to get those hostages out of there when…" he trailed off as the memories hit him like a runaway freight train.

"When what?"

"I felt him there," Emmit continued. "I wasn't sure at first…he'd always been able to mask his presence from me. But right then, I could read his signature as clear as day."

"Which triggered another reaction, yes?"

"It was like those other episodes I'd been having over the past months. When I'd set my mind to the objective…try as hard as I could to push out all those bad feelings. But the harder I tried, the worse it got."

"We've discussed the causes of your reactions, Mr. Rhoe. Even you are susceptible to emotional stimulus, be it positive or otherwise."

"Yeah. So you've said. But I should've been able to control it. 'Least a lot better than I did."

"No. I don't think you could have. But that's neither here nor there. Now, you were saying you were in the cargo area…?"

Emmit un-crossed his legs and cupped his hands over his knees. He began swaying to and fro at a gentle pace. "As soon as I knew he was on that plane, I felt the power start building inside me. It was like…hell, I don't know what it was like. Almost as if I was some sort of remote control toy and there was some sadistic kid out there with the remote."

"You were a Manchurian Candidate," Henry explained while he continued to jot down notes with his stylus.

"Yeah. Sort of. But not entirely. Because I knew what I was doing. I made the decision, whether or not I believed it was the right one. Don't get me wrong…most of those men deserved what they got. But after a while, I couldn't help but notice that they were a lot like me, you know? Men who were thrown into a situation…forced to fight for a cause whether they believed in it or not."

"I really don't think you can compare yourself to those animals, Mr. Rhoe?"

"No? Why not? A terrorist is only as much of an animal as the papers and T.V. stations portray. And I can see why they have to go that route…won't sell many papers or get good ratings if you focus on all those widows and orphans, right?"

Henry cleared his throat. His grip on the stylus tightened to the point of it snapping in two. "Which brings us to?"

"I tore out of that cargo bay like the devil was on my back," Emmit said, paying closer attention to Henry's reactions. "They didn't know what hit them."

"You killed them all?"

"Butchered them is more like it. And like I said—I knew what I was doing. I didn't black out and come to once it was all over. I made the choice to rip them to shreds. I made the choice to sacrifice those few hostages so that the others might survive."

"Which they did."

Emmit mulled it over. "Mmhmm. But what's that mean when you weigh it against the fate of the others? General Tannenzapf was right when he said I was trained to diffuse dangerous situations. Not light them up."

"Drastic times call for drastic measures, Mr. Rhoe. I believe you were the one to tell me that."

"More of an excuse than code of behavior, I'm sad to say."

Henry let Emmit regain his composure as he was getting a bit overwrought, or at least that's what Emmit wanted him to believe. He kept rocking back and forth, his hands on his kneecaps, until he took a deep breath and closed his eyes tight.

Henry looked at him curiously, though he was pretty sure he knew what Emmit was trying to do. "What happened after you killed the PLO members?"

Slowly, Emmit opened one eye, then the other, and looked at Henry just as inquiringly. "Who ever said they were PLO?"

Henry looked like a kid caught reaching into the cookie jar. "The reports. They claimed…"

Emmit shelved that glitch right alongside the others and went on. "The reports claimed a lot. But I'm not sure they were PLO. If they were, their higher-ups refuted the fact."

Somewhat relieved Henry said, "All right. Fine. What happened after you killed the *terrorists*?"

"That's when your father traipsed through the cockpit door."

The anger was still a living, breathing thing and on the lookout for reparations. But Emmit kept his emotions in check as he described how Samuel so offhandedly made his presence known.

"The son of a bitch was there all along. Just laying in wait," Emmit said, voice low, even and sure. "But for all he did…all the pain…all the suffering he'd caused, I still couldn't bring myself to do it."

"It?" Henry asked.

"Yeah. IT. I couldn't kill him."

"So why didn't you simply detain him and bring him in so justice could do its work? Surely he was no match for you. Not in a physical sense."

Emmit's head bent to one side and he smiled wryly. "You think your old man would've agreed to come along for that ride? Above ground, I mean?"

Henry tapped the stylus on his chin. "No. I suppose not."

"You suppose right. So…I did the only thing I could do, which was wait for him to make his move."

"He'd planted a bomb in one of the turbines if I'm remembering the report correctly."

"There and in three other places. I'm not sure where exactly."

"Three bombs. One homicidal maniac. And one choice. What did you do?"

"Listen for yourself," Emmit placed either hand on the arms of the chair. His legs were feeling heavy as was his heart, but he managed to pull himself out of the lounger and walk over to the coat hanger standing beside the door. He shuffled through the few coats hanging there until he found his windbreaker and came back with an audio tape in hand.

"What's that?" Henry asked.

"I realize I'm a bit behind in the technology department, but it hasn't been that long since tapes, has it?"

"You know what I mean, Mr. Rhoe."

"Sure. Sorry," Emmit returned to his seat. "This, Dr. Jayne, is your father's last words."

"How did you…?"

"General Tannenzapf had the whole team wired for sound. Said it helped him better understand what we were doing right and what we were doing wrong. Personally, I always thought he just wanted to cover his own tail in case things turned sour."

"You taped my father?"

"Sure did. And you can hear it for yourself if you have a player handy."

"O...of course. Here..." Henry dropped the PDA onto the coffee table and quickly got up.

Emmit was taken back. It was the first time he'd ever witnessed Henry at a loss for words. The doctor stuttered a few more syllables, none of which Emmit could make out, and reached inside his desk. He rummaged through the contents until he came upon a small black recorder. "There you are," he said and returned to his seat. "Before the world went digital, I used it to record my sessions," he held out his hand to accept the tape.

Emmit passed it over—carefully—like he was handling a fussy explosive device. Henry took it but didn't put it in the recorder right away. He just held it up parallel to his line of sight and stared it down like it was some alien thing.

"What's the matter?" Emmit asked.

"What? Oh...nothing. I just can't seem to get my hands to stop shaking."

"Allow me," Emmit leaned over and opened the recorder. He took the tape from Henry and slid it in, still mindful while he did. "The reception is all out of whack, but you should be able to make out most of it."

Emmit pressed the *play* button and a succession of pings and pops filled the room. A low murmur followed. It sounded like a human voice, one that was trying to speak but couldn't find the strength to wrap his or her lips around the words. That went on for a minute or two, until a terribly proverbial voice cut through the electronic chatter.

"...all comes down to this."

Henry stiffened at the sound of his father's voice. Then, Emmit's voice came on-air. He sounded a lot like he did at the present but not quite as gravely certain. "I'd ask you if you're going to come along quietly, but I don't have time for rhetoric."

"Simmer down. The auto-pilot is engaged," Samuel said. "We've got plenty of time to reminisce."

Emmit said he didn't have time for that either.

"Then make it," Samuel ordered.

A grating, scratching sound caused Henry to jump in his seat. Emmit explained that was the point where one of the hostages tried to get to her feet. Suddenly, a loud BANG came on.

"And that's where your father shot her," Emmit said.

The tape continued. "Consider that a warning to the rest of you," Samuel said to the two remaining hostages. "I don't appreciate interruptions." A long, drawn out pause and more static until, "Now…where were we? Oh yes…history. I've always thought it to be the best teacher. Apparently, you don't agree."

Emmit, the way-back-then on-tape version, took a step toward his ultimate quarry. "You're coming with me, Dr. Jayne. Peacefully or in pieces. You decide now."

"Clever as always my dear boy. And just as pointless," Samuel said and then…

"What was that?" Henry asked.

"A surprise," Emmit sat up straight as a pin. "And the reason why your father was able to always stay one step ahead of me and my team."

"What are you talking about?" Henry asked. His tone didn't match his supposed perplexity. He sounded more fascinated.

Emmit pressed his finger flush against his lips. "Shhh…"

"Since you're so obviously out of your depth, I might as well tell you," Samuel said. "I'm not the person you knew, Emmit. Not the same at all."

"Yeah. Now you're a full-fledged psycho," Emmit's audio persona proclaimed.

"Opinions vary. However the distinction I'm referring to is up here."

Emmit explained to Henry that Samuel tapped his temple.

"You see, when I learned of General Umbridge's most heinous activities," Samuel said, "I took it upon myself to ensure he nor anyone else involved in Project Realm would ever be able to do so again. As irony had it, Umbridge gave me the means to accomplish just that."

Regrettably, Emmit's hypothesis turned out to be right on the mark. "You didn't?"

"I most certainly did. And gladly, I might add…"

The transmission ended right there and the recorder clicked itself off. Emmit leaned over and popped the tape out of the recorder and slipped it into his shirt pocket. Henry, meanwhile, awaited some sort of explanation.

"Ran out of tape," Emmit said.

"What was he about to say?"

"Why, Dr. Jayne. I would've thought someone of your intellect would have pieced it all together by now."

Henry's head cocked to one side. "You almost sounded like my father for a moment."

"Impressions aren't my thing," Emmit said reveling in that he was finally the one with the answers.

"Please, Mr. Rhoe...now is not the time for levity."

"All right. All right. Keep your pants on," Emmit cleared his throat. "That process your father developed...the one that was supposed to give other soldiers by abilities?"

"Yes. Of course. The one he never perfected. The one he sold to those middle-eastern villains."

"That's the one. Anyway...he thought he was a lot further down the road than he was and made the mistake of volunteering to be his own guinea pig."

"He used it on himself?"

"Mmhmm. And it worked out pretty well if you look past the fact that it drove him out of his gourd."

"Of course," Henry said, his voice and meaning now matching up identically. "That makes perfect sense. That's why he was able to mask his thoughts from you."

"That's what I figured."

"So what happened after he told you?"

"He went on like he always did...something about this being the final part of his plan that would lead to his greatest accomplishment. I couldn't make it all out...the blood was pounding so loudly in my ears."

"And then...?" Henry was on the edge of his seat.

"I jumped him. As fast and hard as I could. I hit him and hit him until all that was staring back at me was a bloody pulp."

"Which explains why nobody reported that he was on that plane, yes?"

"A bit of a bonus. As far as our PR campaign was concerned anyway. Before the clean-up crew arrived, I threw his body on top of the terrorist pile and told 'em he was just another member."

"What about the bombs?"

"There weren't any. Your father may've been crazy as an outhouse rat, but he wasn't so far gone that he'd sacrifice himself," Emmit decided the time was right to test his evolving theory. "Besides...as smart as he was, he was still a coward."

Emmit trailed off and took a long look at Henry, whose expression curdled ever-so-slightly.

-9-

Not so long ago all Emmit had was time. That's all, just endless waves of days and nights left to think, wonder and consider how uncompromisingly meaningless his existence had become. There was precious little he wouldn't have given to change that. But now that that's precisely what had happened, he was reminded of the fateful saying, *be careful what you wish for*.

Trying his best to think happy thoughts, Emmit dried himself off and stepped out of the shower stall. He tied the thick terrycloth towel around his waist and stood in front of the mirror. It was steamed up to a smoky haze (Celia often wondered what was hotter—those red and white blood cells that were spawned by his Catholic legacy or his showers), so he ran a flat palm from side to side until that familiar but somehow different face came into clear view.

He recognized *this* man.

He had a long face that was worn but not battered.

He had steel-blue eyes that dimmed some over the years, but were still sharp and knowing.

The memorable but singular man winked to Emmit, telling him the future may have been in doubt, but somehow, someway, everything would work itself out well enough. Emmit didn't know whether or not to believe him. But he'd pulled Emmit out of some pretty nasty scrapes in the past, so Emmit didn't see any reason to stop trusting him now.

After he slipped into a fresh button-down, tan jacket and pair of slacks, Emmit noticed it was already past six. He'd gotten off to a late start. From sleeping in that morning and arriving one hour past due at Henry's, dinner was now well underway. If he wanted to fill his belly, he'd have to get a move-on.

A few minutes later down in the dining hall, Emmit quickly but graciously sifted through the room, zigzagging between the circular tables until he arrived at the buffet. Luckily, some of the decorative serving trays still had something to offer. Usually if a body wasn't there when the dinner bell was rung, they'd have to put a call into Dominoes.

Biding his time and minding his churning stomach, Emmit finally arrived at the front of the line. He'd been scouring the buffet's contents from the moment he arrived, so there would be no hesitation once he finally arrived. He knew exactly what he wanted—a few strips of seasoned brisket, half-cut potato wedges, a couple of spires of asparagus and a modest helping of brown rice.

After Emmit was through loading up his plate he looked around for an available seat. It was very busy and most spots appeared to be occupied. With his plate firmly in hand, he kept up his vigil when he spotted Angela, who was hunched over a group of ladies sitting at table #8 while she played the household *yenta*.

"Looking good, Mrs. Yablans," he said passing on by.

Angela straightened out and caressed the rim of her glasses. "Seeing even better, Mr. Rhoe."

The dining room was so packed Emmit began his meal standing up. It wasn't until he polished off the bounty of his entrée that he nailed down an empty seat.

It didn't take him long, maybe another minute or two, to reveal the pattern of his plate. Making sure to save his place by slinging his blazer over the back of his chair, Emmit left to grab another helping of brisket along with some of that wonderful looking cherries jubilee. He was back in a flash and devoured the replenished offerings just as quickly as his initial serving.

Slurping down the last of the jubilee, Emmit excused himself from the table to go and refill his coffee mug. Before his behind left the seat surface, Angela dropped by for her expected visit. "May I?" she asked and without waiting for a reply, slid into the lone available chair Mrs. Kleinsausser just vacated.

"I'm sure nobody would object to some more company," Emmit looked around to the others at the table.

Nobody said a word. They were too busy watching Emmit and Angela out of the corner of their cataracts.

"I see I wasn't the only person who enjoyed dinner," Angela pointed out Emmit's bare plate, which was so clean it looked as though it had already been run through the dishwasher.

A bit embarrassed, Emmit reached for his mug. "Can I interest anyone in a refresher?"

"You read my mind," Angela said.

Emmit grabbed up his coat, and they made their way to the coffee bar where he filled Angela's cup with the decaf blend. He then reached inside his blazer and pulled out the Armagnac he'd bought on the way back from Henry's. He showed Angela the bottle much like David when he unveiled his bottle of Jack. Angela smiled approvingly.

"Why don't we take a load off in the sunroom?" Emmit suggested.

It was a beautiful evening. The sky was a perfectly clear cerulean with countless stars poking holes of brilliant, focused light through the dark environ. Angela and Emmit sunk into one of the coaches situated in front of the tall windows that overlooked the gardens. They talked about this and that, nothing in particular, sipping their spiked drinks and looking out onto the snow-capped grounds. They continued with the small talk until Emmit said, "You want to know a secret?"

Like he had to ask.

He set his mug down on the table and played it up a bit—looking back and forth, lowering his voice, everything except donning a trench coat and standing in the shadows of an underground parking garage.

"Ever wonder what people really are around these parts? I mean…before they came here?"

"It's a safe bet I already know," Angela claimed humbly.

Emmit's eyebrows raised and the corners of his mouth curled. "Think so, huh?"

He wasn't sure why he decided to tell her *his* story. Maybe it was because he'd kept it inside for so long. Or perhaps he just wanted to see what sort of reaction it would yield. Most probably, though, it was spurred by the grape cognac he'd poured to halfway fill both his and Angela's cups, which lowered his inhibitions to limbo-champion proportions.

Ten minutes later, Emmit had completed his tale. He sank back into the couch, picked up his drink and waited for Angela's reaction. Then he waited some more.

She didn't have a word to say.

She just looked at him trying to envision him as he'd described himself. She tried again and again, but she couldn't match the two up.

"You're not serious," she finally said.

"As a heart attack, my dear."

She couldn't reconfigure that disbelieving expression off her face. It reminded Emmit of Daffy Duck's manic look once he realized he was going to get mowed down by that bus that came out of nowhere.

"So...you're *him*?"

Emmit nodded.

"The super soldier," Angela continued, "the one they always used to write about in the newspapers?"

"Mmhmm. Though I never thought of myself as such. Super, I mean."

"If any of those stories were close to accurate, I'd say super was a fair enough description."

Emmit took on a serious tone. "You won't tell anyone will you?"

Angela looked insulted. "Of course not. Who do you think I am?"

He shot her an incredulous glare.

"Okay. I deserved that," she conceded. "But you can rest assured your secret is safe with me. I wouldn't want anyone here thinking I'm crazier than they already do."

Emmit looked at her curiously. "It almost sounds like you don't believe me."

"Not as far as I can throw you, my dear."

"Fair enough. I guess it is a pretty tall tale. So how can I make you climb it?"

Angela scratched her chin and she looked up to the ceiling. "Meet me in my room in half an hour," she said. "If you really are *him*, there's one way to find out."

Before Emmit set off to meet Angela in her room, he made a pit stop back at his place to freshen up. After he doused his face with some cold water, he took a few swigs of Listerine and ran a comb through his hair. "Here goes nothing," he whispered.

A few minutes later, visions of spiders, webs and hapless flies crept and crawled through Emmit's mind as he cautiously approached Angela's door. *This is how rumors get started*, he thought as he looked down the dimly lit hall. Certain he was alone, he wrapped on the door gently and heard Angela call out from inside, "I'll be right there."

Again he peeked down the corridor. He didn't see anyone, but he heard a familiar noise coming closer. He spotted Cal Spooner arduously pushing his walker ahead of him. Cal was only a few years older than Emmit, but you'd never know it by looking at him. He appeared to be at least 20 years older than his birth certificate would admit. Considering he'd been laid out on an operating table more times than even he could remember, though, it was impressive that he was still alive. Cal was having a tough time of it as usual; the diminutive wheels mounted on the front of the walking aid couldn't quite surmount the heavy carpeting. Stepping away from Angela's doorway, Emmit waved to him feeling safe that Cal wouldn't think it strange for him to be there since Emmit's room was only four doors down. Cal lifted one of his hands off the walker and waved back, almost tumbling to the ground while he did.

"Well…don't just stand there looking obvious," Angela's sudden presence caused Emmit to jump. "Come on in."

The room was crammed with odds and ends—*chatchkas* as Celia used to call them. Vigilantly pushing his way past the Royal Doulton figurines sitting on the coffee table then past the hutch lined with a menagerie of crystal animals, Emmit stopped in the middle of the room and surveyed his total surroundings.

"So…what do you think?" Angela asked with a glint of hope in her eye.

A barbed question if ever there was. "I think," Emmit surmised, "I think it's you."

Angela smiled deeming his answer to be kind enough. "Thank you," she pointed out the sofa with the clear plastic cover. "Please…sit,"

Emmit sat down thanking the heavens he wasn't wearing short pants. He'd lost a couple layers of skin on his Aunt Ruthie's similarly wrapped sectional back in the smoldering summer of '71. "Okay. I'm here. Now what?"

Angela walked past and picked up the large cardboard box she'd taken from her closet just before Emmit knocked. She let out a faint grunt bending down to lift it up. Emmit raised himself off the couch and asked if she needed a hand.

"No thank you," she braced herself, took a deep breath and hoisted it up all by her lonesome. "I'm a lot stronger than I look."

Emmit sank back in and said he used to be able to say the same thing. Angela looked at him suspiciously and took a seat in the loveseat facing the couch. "We'll just see about that," she said laying the box on her lap.

"What is that?"

She pushed the worn flaps aside, "It's a box, silly,"

"Of what?"

"Ohh…this and that. But mostly it's about you. Or who you say you are."

Emmit bent forward to grab a closer look.

"Ut, ut, ut. No peeking," Angela scolded. She pulled the box tight against her chest. "Sit back down now."

The soldier in Emmit was out of sight but not forgotten. He followed the order and sank back down into the thick cushions. Angela watched him carefully then opened the box and started pulling out pale yellow file folders—one after the other—until the rug underneath the glass-topped coffee table disappeared.

"What's in there?" Emmit asked, his insides starting to quiver.

She laid the last folder down and slipped on her glasses, "Information. But never you mind about that. I'll be asking the questions from here."

"Sure. You're the boss."

Angela adjusted her glasses and leaned over the table, looking through the many folders until she spotted the one she was looking for. "I'm not sure if I ever told you this…but my husband, Hank, was a sergeant in the Marine Corps," she opened the folder and looked down to the files within. "He…well, he was killed in action in '92 in Kuwait. He was a helicopter pilot and there was some sort of malfunction."

"Geez…I'm sorry, Angela. I didn't know…"

"That's all right. I knew what I was getting into when I said, *I do*. That's why I refused to give in to the fear. Of losing him, I mean. In lieu of that, I got involved in the details. More lost actually. Before I knew it, I'd become a full-fledged military-phile."

"Which brings us to…?" Emmit's stomach churned and roiled. He thought perhaps he'd swallowed down too much cognac, but…

"This," she raised one of the pages and shook it at Emmit. "We're going to have a little Q&A session, you and I."

"Are we now?"

"Mmhmm. Unless you want to come clean?"

Emmit said he already did.

"Fine. So we'll go ahead. I'll ask you a question. A question only you and a handful of others could possibly know the answer to and…"

Emmit held his hand up to stop her then slapped it down on his knee when he noticed his leg was shaking. "C'mon, Angela. How am I supposed to remember what color socks I was wearing or…"

Now Angela cut him off. "It won't be anything that trivial," she explained. "Are you through stalling?"

Emmit waved her on. She adjusted her glasses again (one of the arms was loose, but she didn't have the heart to tell Emmit), and began scrolling through the contents of the page.

"Let's see…let's see. Ah. Here we are. Are you ready?"

Emmit nodded.

"Okay…here goes. What was the name of the medic that tended to your wounds following the tunnel collapse in Cu Chi?"

"How did you get that?"

"Didn't your mother ever tell you it's not polite to answer a question with a question?"

"But…?"

Emmit backed off. He'd learn soon enough how Angela got her hands on the classified information—information that had allegedly been buried alongside General Umbridge.

"What was the question again?"

"The name," Angela said sternly, "of the medic that tended to you following your injury."

"Christ. That was a long time ago…40 years…"

"Thirty-nine actually. Now what was his name?"

Emmit sunk deeper into the couch and ran his index finger along his lower lip. "Hold on. Gimme a second."

Angela waited impatiently, drumming her freshly French-manicured fingernails on the side of the file folder."

"You mind?" Emmit said.

"Sorry."

He thought about it some more, sorting through nearly 40 years of history until he arrived at…

"I have absolutely no idea."

With as much satisfaction as regret, Angela folded the file on her lap and looked on at Emmit like a disapproving mother.

"What? He never told me his name," Emmit said in his defense. "And even if he did, I'd been shot three times!" he pointed to his head. "How in the hell am I supposed to remember the name of the guy that stitched me up in the middle of the jungle after something like that?!"

Angela opened the folder again and ran down to the paragraph that detailed Emmit's injuries.

"How many times did you say you were shot?"

"Three."

"Interesting," she said. "Very interesting."

She closed the folder and looked at Emmit thoughtfully. "You wouldn't happen to recall the names of the two soldiers that carried you into the helicopter, would you?"

He couldn't take it any more. That sick feeling, those memories and the energies that flickered and sparked deep within but just couldn't ignite. It was all too much for Emmit and he needed to let it all out before it consumed him. "This is bullshit!" he practically leapt off of the couch and got right in Angela's face. "I trust you with my deepest, darkest secret and you treat it like some parlor game!"

A bit taken back but not all that surprised, Angela took a lyrical tone. It was the same voice she used with her father in the latter stages of his Alzheimer's. "I'm sorry, Emmit. I didn't mean…"

"Didn't mean what, Angela? To reopen old wounds? Or to pour salt in them?"

"Of course not. I would never."

"Well you did all the same."

Angela apologized again but Emmit wasn't in the mood to forgive. "How the hell did you get your hands on this information anyway?" he said. "Your husband couldn't have…"

"Couldn't. And didn't. I came across these files by accident if you must know."

Emmit tried to calm down but the images of his painful past wouldn't allow it. "Is that a fact?!"

"Yes. It most certainly is. Hank had nothing to do with it."

Emmit ordered her to clarify.

"I know you're upset, dear. But I didn't put up with my husband barking at me like one of his soldiers, so I don't imagine I'll accept it from you."

Taking deep breathes—in through the nose and out through the mouth—Emmit calmed himself and retook his seat.

"That's better," Angela said as she nudged her glasses until they butted up against her brow. "Now…as I was saying, Hank's aunt, Emilia, was married to a man you knew only too well. Lionel was his name. He was a general in the U.S. Navy."

"Lionel Umbridge?"

"One and the same. Judging by your voice, I'd say my dear uncle didn't save his nasty disposition just for family."

Emmit said he'd never attended one of Umbridge's family affairs, but it sounded like a fair assessment.

"Mmhmm. Before he was bumped from major to general, Hank and I used to joke the only word that should be inserted after his rank was asshole," Angela said sort of blushing while she did. "As you can imagine, nobody was too overwhelmed when they found out he'd been murdered. Although I did feel for Aunt Emilia. She was such a kind and gentle soul." Angela stood up and started gathering the folders. "Anyway, a few months after Lionel's funeral she passed on. Natural causes. The old dear was fortunate enough to go in her sleep." She put them all back into the box, folded the flaps shut and offered it to Emmit. "Long story short, Hank and I were the only family Aunt Emilia had left. So we were the ones to go to the house and clean it out. And that's where we found this."

"What are you doing?"

Angela's smile returned. It made Emmit feel better just like when David used to curl his lips in his direction.

"I believe this is yours."

He didn't know what to do.

"Go on now. Take it," she said.

"No. I can't. It was your aunt's, and…"

"It wasn't her's. It was his. Truth be known, I'll be happy to be rid of it. There are enough assholes in this world without being reminded of one every time I open the closet door."

December 1998

Samuel was gone. But not forgotten. Emmit was reminded of him every time he came face to face with the newest terrorist on the block. While his resolve never faltered, not even for an instant, he was growing weary. He'd been going strong for over 25 years, and the more blood he got on his hands, the more he realized it was never going to wash away. But there was something else that was bothering him. Something that came from the inside. It was very similar to the feelings he used to get when his true self started to emerge; almost like someone else was trying to break free.

Emmit had just returned from Occra Hills in Sierra Leone. It was there that the AFRC, or Armed Forces Revolutionary Council, kidnapped 33 United

Nations reps. The hostage count was high but miraculously, Emmit and the anti-terrorist squad he was leading managed to talk the AFRC members into submission without so much as a shot fired. He was excited to finally be able to tell a story where his powers of persuasion were actually put to the test. He couldn't wait to get home and tell Celia all about it, as he was sure she'd get a good laugh out of that.

He paid the cab driver, tipping him 10 dollars, and raced up the front walk. He stormed through the door and called out for Celia.

"Honey! I'm home!"

There was no answer. *Probably in the bathroom*, he thought. He yelled out to her again racing up the stairs taking three at a time.

Still no reply.

"Celia?" he peeked through the doorway of their bedroom. She was sitting on the corner of the bed.

"Hey. There you are. Why didn't you answer?"

She didn't look up at him or say a word. Emmit was so caught up in the moment he didn't notice anything was wrong. He walked up to her and started telling her the AFRC story, and didn't stop until she put her hand on his and looked up at him with swollen, tear-filled eyes.

"We have to talk."

Being such a private person, Celia hadn't mentioned anything. Since Emmit was away so often and had enough to contend with, she thought it best to take care of the matter on her own. Besides, she wasn't even sure there was cause for concern.

Until then.

She'd gotten the news earlier that day after she met with Dr. Leeza Eden, her gynecologist. As soon as Celia told Dr. Eden about the bleeding, the doctor insisted on taking a biopsy from the lining of Celia's womb.

"She used this tiny telescope…a hyper-something-or-other she called it," Celia explained while Emmit lifted the kettle off the stove. "I didn't want to say anything to you until there was a reason to, but…" she started to sob.

Emmit put the kettle on a cozy and sat down beside his wife. He reached out with a tissue and dabbed her cheeks dry as she went on. "I'm scheduled for a hysterectomy the week after next at Brigham and Women's Hospital."

Eleven days later (which seemed more like an eternity) Celia pulled through the operation with flying colors. Laid out in one of the recovery rooms, her eyes finally opened. The first person she saw was Emmit, who'd been sitting by her bedside for the past two hours.

"Well, well, well. Look who finally decided to wake up?" he reached out to brush the hair out of her eyes.

Still groggy, Celia looked on at her husband. "How…how did I do?"

"Emmit smiled, a nervous reaction, and said, "Perfect. You did absolutely perfect."

According to the most recent statistics, the five year survival rate for Celia's specific type of cancer was upwards of 70 per cent. A high number but unfortunately not one that applied to her case.

They hadn't caught the disease in time. When Emmit found out the tumor was gestating in his wife's womb for over half a year, he wanted to grab her and shake her. He wanted to tell her he was right about always nagging her to go see her doctor for regular check-ups. While his abilities also made him effectively immune to all diseases, they also instilled him with a fortified sense of concern for the weaker members of his clan. Celia appreciated being worried over. But she never really trusted doctors and felt that if she was feeling fine, there was no reason to solicit any of their member's services. Emmit, meanwhile, kept his opinions to himself and focused on making Celia feel as comfortable and confident as humanly possible.

They'd carved out the largest mass and were relatively sure (not a term Emmit ever liked to hear especially under the circumstances) the surrounding tissue was free from infection. But Dr. Eden prescribed chemotherapy anyway, even though there was no clinical evidence to support it was an effective treatment for uterine cancer. Compounding matters, since the cancer was so advanced, all chemo would do was slow it down. And even that wasn't a sure bet.

But that's all they had. The disease was backstroking through Celia's bloodstream and even though they didn't detect any more cells, a fresh batch could materialize any time and practically anywhere.

Two years. That's what they gave her. It took all of Emmit's resolve and strength to put on a brave face. It took even more of a concerted effort to keep it from slipping off. But inside where all disguises were rendered transparent, he was irrevocably devastated and beyond reassurance.

Surface reasoning had him believing that he felt as such because Celia's life was being cut so short. But there was more to it than that. He was used to stepping in and making a difference. He was accustomed to achieving when all others failed. He'd traveled around the world more times than he could remember, saving people whose names he didn't even know. Now that it was time to come to the rescue of the most important person in his life, his hands were tied tight.

For the first time since he realized what he really was, there was absolutely nothing he could do.

Nothing, save for make the most of the little time he and Celia had left.

Later that night after Celia fell asleep, Emmit tiptoed downstairs into the living room. Plopping down on the couch he put his feet up and just lay there, not thinking or feeling anything in particular.

He was exhausted—physically and even more so emotionally. It was all he could do to reach out for the phone and remember Tannenzapf's direct line. He wasn't sure if the general would be in so late at night, but appreciating his unrelenting sense of dedication and resolve, it was a safe bet.

He hadn't told Tannenzapf about Celia. Emmit was a lot like Samuel in that he kept his private life private. More than that, he didn't want people to pity him. So, all he mentioned was that he was feeling a bit burned out and that he needed a few weeks for his batteries to recharge. As coincidence had it, Percy asked for the same time off and he'd asked Emmit to join him on a canoe trip to the Ozarks. Emmit acted as though he was thinking it over, then kindly declined saying he wanted to spend some quality time with his wife (he didn't feel too bad for saying that, as it was partially true).

Like most of Emmit's actions, there were multiple reasons behind this particular one. He hadn't mentioned Celia's mortal condition in the hopes that the diagnosis would somehow be rescinded. Stranger things have happened, after all, and Emmit lived his life beating the odds. No reason to exclude Celia on the proceedings. But now it was clear. She wasn't going to be around for much longer and Emmit had to let Tannenzapf and the rest know.

After a bit more thought, the number came to him and Emmit plugged in Tannenzapf's direct line. He pressed the receiver against his ear and waited. The general's voice came on following the fourth chime.

"General Tannenzapf speaking."

Emmit didn't know what to say. His mouth opened, but nothing came out.

"Hello? Is someone there?"

"Hey…general. It's Private Rhoe. Emmit."

"Hello. I didn't expect to hear from you until next week."

"Well, that's the thing, sir. I wanted to ask you if it'd be all right if I extended my leave."

"Is everything all right?"

Emmit gripped the phone tightly. The thick plastic casing cracked at its seams. "No. No it's not."

He told Tannenzapf about the operation. He told him about how long they gave Celia. Surprisingly, it felt good to get it out in the open. After Emmit was through venting, the only reply he got was a faint murmur of static.

"General Tannenzapf?"

"Yes. Yes…I'm still here," by the timbre of Tannenzapf's voice, he took the news harder than Emmit.

"I…I don't know what to say," Tannenzapf finally choked. "I had no idea she was even sick."

Tannenzapf hated to lose Emmit, but he would never dream of trying to persuade him to stay. To him, there was nothing more important than family. Anthony, his youngest son, died after an eight year battle with leukemia and he understood all too well what it felt like to lose someone you love more than life itself. He also knew that nothing could be more vital—not even the sanctity of his country—than spending the precious time you had remaining with that special someone.

So, he wished Emmit and Celia the best of luck and should they need anything, he and all the resources of the U.S. Navy were at their disposal. Emmit felt like saying the only thing they needed was a cure. Sadly, a remedy for cancer wasn't one of the clandestine technologies Tannenzapf and his peers kept tucked away under their hats.

"Really, Emmit…anything you need, please don't hesitate to call."

"I appreciate that, General Tannenzapf. Really," Emmit said. "I'll keep you posted."

Emmit went to hang up the phone. As he lowered the receiver onto the base, he noticed he'd damaged it. "Pick up a new one…" he said, his voice cracking, and…

For the first time in 50 years, Emmit began to cry.

June 1999

Celia had a rough time of it during her four-month chemo treatment—thinning hair, fatigue, depression and a substantial amount of weight loss were the major side effects.

All things considered, though, she got through it well enough. If Celia was anything, it was tough and a tapering hairdo certainly wasn't enough to put a dent in her armor.

For the life of her she couldn't remember when it happened but before she knew it, she'd almost gotten used to it all. *Funny*, she thought, while the nurse inserted the intravenous catheter into her arm, *how the most bizarre and unpleasant experience can become part of a person's life.*

Once the I.V. was secure, the nurse injected the tube with the drugs for that day's session. Celia hated being stuck and prodded, but it wasn't so bad on that particular day because it was her last session.

The nurse went on to take a complete blood count and Celia was led into the *room*. She hated that place. More than any other she'd ever known. It was cramped and conspicuous. Cold and calculating. She'd spent too much time there and it had gotten to the point where those four walls had developed respective personalities. And Celia didn't like any one of them, so she was all too happy knowing it would be their last encounter.

The chemo treatment was an intravenous infusion drip as apposed to a pump/push variety. Dr. Owen Warne, her oncologist, had recommended the first treatment, appreciating her form of cancer was especially aggressive and the infusion drip ensured the noxious chemo toxins flooded her system completely.

Unfortunately, the process took several hours, forcing Celia to sit there staring at those churlish walls for all that time. Sometimes she'd bring along a book or some magazines to pass the hours. But mostly, she just sat there and counted down the seconds. For her, that was one of the hardest things to cope with. Not the pain. Not the discomfort or fault-finding side effects.

It was the waiting.

Just as bad, though, was realizing that as soon as she started to feel better, as soon as she felt like, *Okay. I made it through this again*, she'd have to do it all over again.

After Celia was done with her final treatment, Emmit drove her home and she went upstairs to the bedroom. "I just want to clean up," she said. "We'll have lunch in half an hour."

"You sure?" He said/asked. "Maybe you should take a nap?"

There will be plenty of time for that, she thought, but instead said, "Don't be silly. I'm fine. I'll be down before you know it."

Emmit placed an open hand over his mouth and blew her a kiss. "Sounds like a plan."

Waiting by the base of the staircase he watched her go. She stopped halfway and turned to face him. "I'm capable of climbing the stairs without a spotter," she said.

Emmit gave a shucks-gosh air kick and told her he'd always enjoyed watching her perform on a staircase.

Upstairs, Celia headed straight for the bathroom. She closed the door behind her and stepped up in front of the mirror. Looking herself over, she suddenly noticed something strange.

She was smiling.

Not out of nervousness. Not out of prolonged anxiety. But out of actual happiness and contentment. For the first time since she was diagnosed she felt good. Aside from the bouts of lightheadedness she'd been experiencing the past day or so, she'd never believe herself that she was sick.

It was cause enough for celebration, which she would have preferred to do solitarily. But when Emmit suggested that they go down to Abe & Louie's, she just couldn't say no. After all, they'd been going there for years. They'd commemorated untold anniversaries, birthdays, graduations and other special occasions there, even before it became a faux dive for the local three-pieced masters of the universe. While it had become one of *the places to be* in Beantown, Celia didn't actually like it all that much. The lighting made her look heavy and it was quite expensive. But Emmit loved their rib eyes nearly as much as he did her, so she didn't put up a fuss when he suggested it.

Later that evening, Celia was adjusting her wig for what must have been the hundredth time. She started losing her hair after the third chemotherapy session, so she and Emmit went out and bought the best looking piece they could find. It cost $2,400, but the human-hairpiece made Celia feel good and to Emmit that was priceless.

"You about done with that?" he asked slipping into his new navy blue 46-long Brooks Brothers blazer.

Celia looked in the mirror again and pulled the wig back ever-so-slightly. "I think so," she said and turned to face Emmit. "What do you think?"

He hadn't seen that light about her for a long time. The wig didn't look too bad either. Emmit was hard-pressed to discern it from the real thing.

"You look beautiful," he brought his eyes up to his reflection as he fastened every last button on his blazer.

Celia sighed. Her husband was many things, but a fashionista was certainly not one of them.

"I don't know how many times we have to go through this," she spun around on her stool and took hold of his jacket's lapel. "You're supposed to leave the last one undone."

She unhinged the bottom button and turned back around for a final look.

"That makes absolutely no sense," Emmit grumbled. "If you're not supposed to button it up, why the hell did they put it there in the first place?"

Celia waited by the side of the driveway while Emmit backed the STS out of the garage. He eased on the brakes as she climbed in and he waited for her to fasten her seatbelt.

"You called back and made it for five?" she asked.

Emmit groaned. "Yeah. Unfortunately they had the space."

"Let's just try and have a good time, hmm?"

When he first made the reservation he'd instinctively made it for four—Celia, Rachel, Hanna and himself. Jamie wasn't a consideration. Emmit had quickly fallen into the habit of disregarding his eldest daughter's husband. It was a lot easier than thinking of him as part of the family. He leaned over and pecked her on the cheek. "You're the boss," he leaned back into the heavily bolstered seat and backed out of the drive.

"You really should try and be nicer to him," Celia said.

Emmit stopped to allow an oncoming car to pass. "This coming from the woman who affectionately refers to him as *Dr. Strangelove.*"

Both Celia and Emmit were convinced Jamie was seeing someone on the side. They couldn't prove anything, though, and until they could, decided to keep the theory to themselves. Still, Celia was hard on him. Harder than anyone else. But she'd promised herself that, along with many other things, was going to change.

"I've made a resolution," she said doggedly, "to start treating him as family. He is the father of our grandson."

"Fair enough," Emmit eased the Cadillac out into traffic. *But he's still an asshole*, he thought.

Abe & Louie's was on Boylston Street—a 10 minute walk from Emmit and Celia's home. But Celia insisted on driving. It was rather windy and she didn't want to risk upsetting her painstakingly crafted hairdo.

Slowly (and painfully so), Emmit squeezed the car into one of the few available parking spaces. It wasn't that small of an opening, but he'd always been careful when driving his Caddy. It was more than just a car. At least it was to him. The 3,500 pound pile of molded metal, plastic and wood was a symbol of achievement. Even more than that, something his father had always wanted, but could never bankroll on his plumber's salary.

Satisfied that the cars on either side were a sufficient distance away, Emmit skipped around to the passenger side to let Celia out.

It was a Saturday night and the joint was jumping. Emmit and Celia entered the busy restaurant hand-in-hand. Emmit looked over to his wife then out to the crowd. It felt like someone had taken the clock and wound it back 30 years…like when they first started seeing one another.

How many times had they walked up that parking lot and into that building? How many times had they scrimped and saved…every last nickel and dime, just so they could enjoy a night out? Way back then, the food always seemed to taste better. The music always sounded sweeter. Emmit leaned in close to her, his lips almost touching her ear and said, "I love you."

Celia didn't reply. It didn't bother Emmit. He knew how she felt without her ever having to utter word one.

Celia waited while Emmit headed for the reception area. Politely, he pushed past the masses until he stepped up to the maitre-d, an attractive older woman with long, tussled blonde hair. She was stationed behind a wooden podium, a phone cradled between her ear and shoulder. Emmit stood and waited for her to get off the line.

"All right. We'll see you at nine-thirty," she hung up and directed her attention to Emmit. "Yes sir. How can I help you?"

Emmit took in another eye-full and felt like telling her she already had but instead said, "Rhoe. Party of five."

His stomach clenched when he spit out the number. The maitre-d looked down at the monitor embedded in the mahogany fascia of the podium. "Rhoe…Rhoe. Here we go."

She looked back up to Emmit. "Two of your party has already arrived, sir. I'll have someone show you to your table."

"No bother," Emmit said. "I know this place like the back of my hand."

It felt good to be in familiar surroundings. More than that, an environment that didn't stink of antiseptic or wasn't frequented by people wearing white coats. Ever since Celia started chemotherapy, the only two locales either she or Emmit frequented were the hospital or home. Neither had much of a chance or the inclination to step out, which made that evening out such a welcome event.

Emmit ducked under the looming torchieres as he and Celia brushed past the people waiting for their tables. The room was quite dim as most steakhouses tended to be. But the vaulted ceiling ornamented in gold-leaf washed the room in a pleasant, warming tinge, which made Celia look more vibrant than Emmit had ever seen.

Hanna and Jamie were seated at one of the leather-wrapped booths just off to the center of the main dining area. Much like her parents, Hanna had been looking forward to the evening very much. Nathan was just six months old and the newborn put up ear-shattering protest if his mother ventured any further than the end of the hallway. So, Hanna asked her cousin (begged was more like it), to watch Nate for the weekend so she and Jamie could fly in from Cleveland to spend the weekend with her mother.

"This is nice, isn't it?" Hanna said sidling in closer to Jamie

"What's that?"

"This," she purred, looking out across the room. "Being out in the public eye. Sitting down for more than thirty seconds at a time."

Jamie said it was, though he couldn't quite relate since he'd acquiesced the bulk of the baby-tending chores to his wife.

"Sure. I guess."

Jamie got like that—disinterested with a chaser of surly—whenever he was forced to break bread with his father-in-law. He knew Celia didn't care for him either, but he was willing to cut her some slack seeing she was dying and all.

Emmit spotted them and waved. He and Celia approached the head of the table and Jamie and Hanna stood up to welcome them. Hanna pecked her father on the cheek then pushed him aside to wrap Celia up in an all-inclusive embrace.

"You look amazing," Hanna pulled away, her hands still resting on Celia's shoulders. "Really."

"Thank you," Celia said feeling a bit uncomfortable.

Emmit cringed when he and Jamie shook hands. Whenever he took hold of the young doctor's palm, it felt like he was being greeted by a damp, cold trout.

Hanna kept gushing about how terrific her mother looked as Emmit and Celia took their seats. After they worked their way past the obligatory *how've you beens* and *what's new and excitings,* Emmit looked down the chair to his left and noticed it was still empty. "Where's Rachel?"

There was a discomfited hush until Hanna cleared her throat and said, "She's not coming. Said she couldn't get off work."

"She couldn't get off work?" Emmit snarled. "Not to have dinner with her mother?"

Celia took Emmit by the hand. "Please. Not tonight."

"She managed to find the time to hit the slopes in Vale a few months ago. Took more off to be with that boyfriend...what's his name?"

"Alex," Hanna said.

"Yeah. Alex. She booked off more time to go down to Mexico with him last month, right?"

"It was the Caribbean," Hanna corrected.

"Whatever. She's got all the time in the world to go and do whatever she wants with whoever she wants. Except of course if that person's her mother...!"

Celia squeezed Emmit's hand as hard as she could. He barely felt it, but he stopped anyway.

He hadn't mentioned anything; about the change he'd seen in Celia. She was feeling so good after she got through the chemo he didn't have the heart. But a few weeks ago, Emmit noticed that there was a slowness to her speech; an awkward, disjointed undertone to her movements. He wasn't too concerned by the behavior at first because he was certain it was brought on by the chemo sessions. It was a poison and irradiating someone's system with such toxic material was enough to make anyone a bit dizzy in the head (save, perhaps himself).

He didn't realize something was terribly wrong until after dinner when Celia fell beside the car while she was trying to get in. He didn't even notice she'd gone down until he slid in behind the wheel and started jawing at the empty seat beside him.

"Jesus!" Emmit got out and raced around the back end of the STS. "Are you all right? What happened?"

Celia was more embarrassed than anything. "Just...lost my balance..."

Emmit hoisted her up off the parking lot ground and brushed her coat off. "We're calling Dr. Warne when we get home."

162

March 2005

There was something strange going on. Emmit could feel it as surely as he felt the mid-March wind stick it to his neck like a thousand barbed needles.

Henry was hiding something.

There were too many issues floating errantly about and Emmit had to sort them out and put them in their proper place. Add to that the continual resurgence of his power (it was trickling in at a sap's pace in April now), and it was all he could do just to stop his head from splitting right down the center.

He needed to get away. To think. To evaluate the situation without anyone tugging away at his coattails. More than anything, though, he needed to reestablish control (or at least some semblance of it) to figure out a way to best position himself in case things headed south.

He couldn't think of any place better to do that than down at the harbor.

Wandering around the many piers of Boston Harbor with his father was one of the only happy memories Emmit had of the old man. Okay—it was THE only happy memory. But he couldn't feel too sorry for himself, because having one positive recollection of the sadistic lush was one more than he ever would've given his maker credit for.

After mulling around for an hour or so, Emmit looked up from the wooden planks and noticed he'd arrived at the front doors of Boston Harbor Cruises. For as long as he'd lived in Beantown, he'd never taken one of the expeditions. It was a tourist affair, after all, and he was definitely not one of those sore thumb sightseers intent on taking snapshots of anyone or anything that didn't frequent the place they called home. But he was growing tired of circling the piers. And even though he felt hypothermia knocking, he still didn't want to go back to Timberlake and face Angela. Not yet. He was still embarrassed over the way he behaved following their impromptu session of *What's My Line*.

Thirty minutes later, the voice broadcast over the ship's PA system came on-air. She went over some safety precautions and mentioned the cruise was a two hour affair. Since it was so cold, there were only a handful of people, a half dozen or so, that dared venture onto the unprotected deck. Emmit was the last to step up and as he found a spot near the front of the craft, the announcer's voice came back on to tell everyone they were casting off.

* * *

The boat cut through the choppy waters heading for Stellwagen Bank, an 840-square-mile stretch of open water that served as a sanctuary for marine life. The announcer called everyone's attention to the stern, where three finback whales had just been spotted. Emmit and all the rest crossed the ship's platform and saw the huge beasts break the surface of the water, then slip back out of sight. The largest of the three, the one with the chunk of flesh missing just above the fluke of its tail, popped back up and neared the boat. The announcer went on to describe the species, its diet and habitat. The others listened on, but Emmit didn't hear a word. He'd locked onto the 45-ton beast. It locked onto him.

"What's that?" Emmit asked.

He could hear it. Feel it inside his head. It wasn't talking. Not in any language Emmit could come close to dispelling. But it was communicating with him.

"That must've hurt," Emmit said as he looked over the large wound. "I've suffered my share of scrapes and bruises over the years, too."

The whale sidled right beside the ship. It was so close that its body swiped the rusted steel hull. Emmit leaned over the railing and cleared his mind while the creature continued to rant.

"I know what you mean. Though I've always said whatever doesn't kill you makes you stronger. Am I right?"

The great sea creature seemed to nod its immense head, though Emmit could see the undulating waves caused the agreeable movement.

"And if that's true, I guess I am the strongest thing on this planet."

The whale slapped its tail on the surface of the water. A foamy stream shot into the darkening sky.

"Okay…" he conceded, "one of the strongest."

Another tour goer, a woman wrapped up in a dozen layers of sweaters, turtle necks, coats, jackets and scarves, tilted her head and noticed Emmit was speaking to someone. She leaned back to see who was standing behind him. When she saw he was by his lonesome, she looked down and spotted the whale. Emmit turned to her and tipped the hood of his parka. "We went to high school together. Just catching up."

She looked back down to the whale and quickly shuffled to the other side of the deck.

"Guess she doesn't like whales," he said as he watched the woman scurry off. "Though judging by the size of her, I'd say that's a bit hypocritical."

The whale backstroked several meters away. Emmit swore he could hear it laughing.

"Yeah. You take care," the creature slowly sunk below the surface, disappearing beneath a foaming cover of bubbles. "Stay strong."

Once the boat was securely docked, Emmit stepped off the walkway and back onto the pier. He smiled at the layered woman, who smiled back (or was it gas?), and raced to the parking lot without turning back.

Emmit didn't know what to do next. It was only six o'clock, which meant Angela would still be roaming about. So he couldn't go back home. *Better to stay put*, he thought. And that's just what he did until the sun settled behind the dissipating dark cloud line to the east.

Even though he was wearing gloves, the bitter chill numbed Emmit's fingers to the bone. He massaged his hands together to get some of the feeling back and pulled the hood of his parka further over his beet-red ears.

If he was back—all the way—he could have easily called upon the energies at his command to raise his body temperature, much like he'd done in Chechnya during the winter of '97. Emmit was called in to aid a small cadre of Russian servicemen, who were stationed outside a dormitory. Unfortunately, he wasn't able to stop the Chechen guerilla attack, which collapsed the building right around their collective ears. He managed to dig himself out of there, but was stranded for the better part of two days all by his lonesome. When the sun went down, the temperature dropped to sub arctic numbers. Emmit was only able to survive by fashioning a crude shelter out of the rubble, then coaxing himself into a deep trance and raising his body's temperature up as much as ten degrees.

At the moment, though, his system wasn't outfitted with a pre-heating mechanism, so all he could do was rub his mitts together hoping sheer friction would be enough. He continued to furiously rub away until he came upon a small marina. The doors to the main hangar were open revealing a dozen or so boats. Most were rather small; outboard models used for fishing and traveling short distances along the harbor. For a brief while, Emmit flirted with the idea of buying a vessel. Not some four-man fishing dingy, but a 30 or 40-foot cruiser he and Celia could take out and discover the world in. Unfortunately, she got sick before he could snap up his check book.

He wandered onto the property without really knowing it, minding the icy puddles that were scattered all over the grounds. As he neared the stored boats, a man walked out of the mobile office that was erected next to the hangar.

"Is there something I can do you for?" the man slipped a checkered flannel overcoat over the wide shoulders he'd built spending a lifetime working on playthings for the rich.

Emmit hopped over another puddle and said, "Just looking around. That okay?"

The man nodded, cupped his hands and blew into them. "No problem. Take as long as you like," he extended his right hand. "Name's Lyle, by the way."

"Emmit. Pleased to meet you," Emmit shook his hand then turned to face the boats again, looking up and down the four storey structure they were housed in.

"You looking to buy?" Lyle asked.

"No. Not really. Once upon a time I thought about it, but the wife..."

"Say no more," Lyle said with a hacking smoker's giggle. "You're one'a the smart ones by the sound of it."

"Come again?"

"You listened to the little lady," Lyle looked at the many water crafts. "Y'see that one up there...the 15-foot Merry Fisher?"

Emmit nodded, though he wasn't quite sure which boat Lyle was going on about.

"Belongs to this accountant, I believe. Or maybe he's a lawyer. Whatever the species, he came on down with the missus just this year with that look in his eye. She had one, too...though I don't mind sayin' it was a look of a different kind." Lyle cast off another grisly chuckle. "Got at least 10 or more fellas couldn't find the capacity to back off and listen to their significant others. He said yes. She said no. He went ahead and coughed up the dough anyways."

"Not too bright," Emmit said.

Lyle shook his head. "Nope. For as much as they got to enjoy themselves with the missus nagging the flesh clean off'a their bones."

"Well, you don't have to worry about adding my name to that list," Emmit said with a tinge of sorrow.

"Yeah. You don't look the type anyways. 'Least not from where I'm standing."

"And what type is that?"

"The sea-faring type," Lyle explained. He took a step back and looked Emmit over very carefully. "You know how I can always tell?"

Emmit was fascinated. "How?"

"It's all in the pegs," Lyle neared Emmit and hunkered down in front of him. He tapped Emmit's right knee. "You don't got the pegs for nothing more than dry land. Straight pegs don't get the job done out there…" Lyle stood back up and gazed out towards the water.

"I've never heard that one before," Emmit said, half wanting to tell Lyle about the dozens of missions he'd run over and under every last square kilometer of sea and ocean across the globe.

"Apparently most haven't. But that never stops 'em. Doesn't even stall 'em," Lyle reached into the chest pocket of his jacket and came back out with a crumpled pack of Chesterfields. He plucked one in his mouth and offered another to Emmit.

"No thanks."

"Been tryin' to kick myself. Never cared for the damn things. Though they seem to like me quite a bit."

Emmit laughed. Lyle did, too.

"Anyway…they come strolling in here," Lyle said in between drags. "Year after year…knocking on my chamber door, straight pegs and all. They slap their cash down all swollen with pride like they've accomplished something worthy of retelling."

"Captains of industry don't necessarily make good captains," Emmit mused.

Lyle looked at him curiously. "Don't know much about that, but most'a the folks I rub elbows with wouldn't cut it as squid gutters."

Lyle kept the lit cigarette firmly tucked between his lips and vigorously rubbed his hands together. "I suppose it's just human nature, though."

"What's that?" Emmit asked.

"People trying to be what they're not. Trying to latch onto what they don't got."

Emmit didn't think much about the comment. Then it dawned on him and it was amazing. In the past three-plus hours, a marina manager and a whale managed to shed more light on the human condition than Henry had been able to in months.

"I always thought this world and any other'd be a much brighter place," Lyle continued, "if folks were content with what they had and what was staring back at them in the mirror, y'know?"

Emmit nodded. "Too well for my own good, I'm afraid."

"You're one'a the few. Anyways…I've gotta lock up. Feel free to look about some more. I'll come'n fetch you once I'm outta here."

Emmit said that sounded good enough. Lyle waved to him as he headed back into the office space and before he slipped inside said, "You just keep being you, you hear? 'Cause no-one else can do it better."

"Will do," Emmit said.

"Besides…" Lyle pitched the cigarette to the gravel. "Nobody else wants the job."

June 1999

Much unlike Samuel and most other physicians, Dr. Owen Warne had a tendency to grow close with his patients. It wasn't as though he was an overly warm or sentimental type. But unlike the majority of his contemporaries, he was human and the oncologist had taken a shine to Celia. Being in that type of relationship—the healer and the terminal—was like putting the union in a time compressor. Very quickly, each gets to know the other's character, wants, desires and fears. Owen fancied himself fortunate to meet someone like Celia. But at the same time, he couldn't help but feel cursed because she wasn't in any position to commit to their budding friendship on a long-term basis.

As soon as he heard about what happened at Abe and Louie's, Owen told Emmit to bring Celia down to the hospital immediately.

Not hours later, Emmit packed their bags, stowed them in the STS and got ready to take Celia in. She was sitting on the bench beside the front door, watching her husband frantically milling about.

"Are you all right?" she asked.

Emmit didn't answer. He snapped up his keys and looked around the hall trying to remember if he'd grabbed up everything they needed. "You ready to go?"

"I am. Are you?"

After Emmit had a moment to think about what was going on with Celia, it dawned on him that the cancer could have very well spread to her brain. While she'd displayed all of the symptoms (especially over the past two or three days), it never occurred to him before. That's because Dr. Warne explained Celia's type of cancer—where it originated from—dictated any migrating cells traveled east or west. The chances of a north or south journey were minimal.

Dreadfully, minimal turned out to be surefire. Emmit and Celia sweat it out in Owen's private office while the doctor pulled out the display from the CT scan he'd run and pointed out the three tumors nesting in Celia's head.

"The largest growth is here," he pointed out the walnut-sized mass attached to the periphery of Celia's brain. "The other two, which as you can see are significantly smaller in diameter, are here."

It felt like the end of the world had been declared. Again, Emmit desperately tried to put on a brave face but looking over at Celia, he couldn't stop the tears from streaming down his face.

"I know this is hard," Owen said. "But it's not the end of our road. The larger tumor can be taken out surgically…"

"And the other two?" Emmit asked.

The Taussig Center was one of the top medical facilities for cancer treatment in North America. It was part of the Cleveland Clinic and like its parent body, Taussig was renowned for blending discoveries from the laboratory with clinical cancer treatment, creating innovative trials for most common forms and variations of the disease.

One of the more innovative treatments Taussig introduced into its repertoire was called the gamma knife. Neither Celia nor Emmit ever heard of it before, even though both had been fastidious in their research of cancer treatments over the past half year. To Emmit, gamma knife sounded like some half-assed military operation. But Owen spoke highly of it so he and Celia didn't hesitate to visit Dr. Mora Tobolowsky at Taussig early the following week.

They'd been waiting in the treatment exam room for almost 20 minutes. Not very much time, but when your fate is being decided a second can seem more like infinity. Emmit gripped Celia's hand tightly. "You want something to drink?"

She shook her head.

"Hungry?"

She hadn't had an appetite since she collapsed at Abe & Louie's. He doubted she'd eaten a complete meal all total since.

"No thank you," she said flatly.

He asked again just to make sure, but before Celia could refuse the doctor walked in. Dr. Mora Tobolowsky was around Emmit's age, just a few years shy. She was an attractive woman, with medium length light brown hair and what appeared to be a decent figure hiding underneath her white lab coat. She seemed pleasant enough upon introductions, and was every bit as congenial when she began talking about the new radiation therapy.

"The instrument is really quite amazing," she said hopefully. "We use it to treat arteriovenous malfunctions mostly. And certain types of brain tumors. The best part is it does away with having to make a single incision."

"You keep referring to it as an instrument," Emmit said while he stroked Celia's hand, "but it uses radiation, correct?"

"Yes. Basically, the gamma knife uses a highly concentrated dose. It's derived from a Cobalt-60 source that's used primarily to damage abnormal tissue."

"Cobalt 60?" Emmit questioned.

"It's a radioactive material. The main application is to kill bacteria and other pathogens in food without damaging the actual product. That makes it ideal for our purposes as well."

Emmit said that sounded good enough and let the doctor continue.

"Insofar as the gamma knife is concerned, it uses 201 beams of intersecting radiation that are focused on the target area."

"You mean the tumors?" Emmit said.

"Exactly. Now, what you must understand is that even though the gamma knife is incredibly accurate it still uses radiation."

Emmit steadied himself for the pitch. "Meaning what exactly?"

Mora's voice lowered. "Meaning…there are side effects. People that have undergone the procedure have displayed signs of fatigue, skin reactions, hair and appetite loss…"

Emmit's insides tightened. "I feel a big AND coming on?"

The doctor paused while Emmit handed Celia a tissue. "It can also damage normal brain tissue, causing a failure or decrease in brain function. There's also the risk of swelling of the brain, but we'll keep a close watch on that during Mrs. Rhoe's recovery."

Two days later, Celia was convalescing in intensive care. Dr. Tobolowsky got out of her operating gear and headed out for the waiting room where Emmit was wearing the carpet thin for the past two-and-a-half hours. When he saw Mora coming through the glass door, he nearly jumped her to find out what happened.

"How is she?!"

The doctor retreated until Emmit took the hint and backed away a few steps. "She's fine, Mr. Rhoe. Couldn't be better under the circumstances. The tumor practically fell out on its own."

Emmit sat down and turned his eyes up to the ceiling, thanking whoever was looking down on him. He'd been fighting the feeling all day—the feeling that Celia was going to die on that table.

Celia was given another few weeks to recover before they started the gamma knife therapy. Again, it went well enough and the following month the CT scans showed the tumors had shrunken significantly. But just as Mora forewarned, the procedure took its toll on Celia and after her brain was exposed to the highly-concentrated radioactive material, she was never the same.

-10-

March 2005

When Emmit suggested they meet somewhere other than Henry's house, the doctor was clearly suspicious. But Emmit didn't really care. Okay. He cared, but not enough to falter on his wishes. Still, the last thing he wanted was to tell Henry what was on his mind in a private setting. Finding a nice, crowded forum was as good a way as any he could think of to diminish the likelihood of getting slapped in the face.

"You know…for a change of pace?" Emmit said cheerily.

The phone line went dead save for the intermittent crackling of static until…"Certainly," Henry said. "Where do you have in mind?"

Emmit suggested they hook up at Kanes Donuts in Saugus. It was a rundown, grimy little hole-in-the-wall of a place. But they made great éclairs and the coffee was even better. Emmit should have known the manicured and meticulously-mannered doctor would never agree to such a common setting. Instead, Henry recommended Café Paradiso out on Hannover Street. Emmit had never been there and judging by the name, he was sure he wouldn't be sorry if he never did.

Emmit made it to the café ten minutes early. He still wasn't sure what he was going to tell Henry and he wanted the extra time to prepare. Unfortunately, Henry arrived five minutes before that and was already working his way toward the end of a double espresso.

Emmit waved to him as he walked over and took a seat. "You're early."

"So are you," Henry said, wincing from the sheer might of the coffee blend.

Emmit looked at the clock on the opposite wall. "Yeah. Traffic can get out of hand around these parts. Didn't want to be rushing so I headed out a bit early."

Henry said he'd thought much the same.

172

"So…what's up?" Emmit asked.

"You tell me, Mr. Rhoe. I'm not certain, but it sounds as though you've got something you want to tell me."

Emmit didn't want to start in on his speech until he had some caffeine poured into him. He looked around for the waiter and hailed him down.

"Yeah. I'll have a large coffee. Double-double if you please."

The server looked at him quizzically. "What type of coffee would you like, sir?

Emmit aped the waiter's confused stare.

"They have many different kinds here," Henry offered.

"Such as?" Emmit asked.

The waiter went on to decry innumerable blends and roasts until Emmit butted in. "Why don't you just give me something that isn't too strong. Still double-double. Okay?"

The waiter nodded and turned to Henry, "And how are you doing, sir?"

Henry raised his cup of espresso which was nearly empty. "I'll have another. Thank you."

Emmit didn't get into it until he slurped down his first cup. He ordered another, then straightened himself out and took a long, hard look at Henry.

"So? Out with it then," Henry demanded.

Emmit took another sip even though he'd bled the cup dry. "Sure. But before I do, I just want to say how much I appreciate all you've done for me during the time we've spent together."

Henry returned Emmit's concentrated gaze. "You're quite welcome. Although I didn't do it for you as you well know."

Emmit said he did and went on. "I don't know how to tell you this so I'll just tell you—I think we need to put a stop order on what we've been doing."

Henry didn't look surprised. More irritated. "So that's why you wanted to meet me here. Breaking up is much easier to do in a public setting, yes?"

"Actually, I wanted to meet at Kanes. But that's not the point."

"And what is the point, Mr. Rhoe?"

Emmit wasn't sure he had one, though he was certain he had to get away from Henry. "I'm not sure. And that's the point. I mean…who are we fooling? We're not getting anywhere, right? We've been running for months and we're still at the starting line."

"I disagree. While your progress hasn't been prompt by any means, I firmly believe that if we keep at it, we can bring you all the way back. It's just a matter of time, yes?"

"As a matter of fact—NO. Even if I did come back…and that's a really big *if*, I don't think it would make much of a difference any which way."

"Forgive me if I disagree with you again, Mr. Rhoe, but your presence is not a luxury. It's a necessity."

"For what?"

"For the continued well-being of our democratic way of life for one."

"C'mon now…you don't actually believe that, do you?"

"I most certainly do."

"Well, you're going to have to forgive me because that is the stupidest thing I've ever heard."

Henry crossed his arms. "Is it?"

"Mmhmm. You know as well as I do what kind of dent I made in the grand scheme of things. As powerful as I ever was, I never made things any better."

"I don't believe that's the correct way to look at things, Mr. Rhoe. If you…"

"If nothing. My participation hurt just as many people as it helped," Emmit did his best not to get upset. He stood up and folded his jacket over his arm. "There's nothing I can do to help. I wish there was, but I've been around the block enough times to know better."

Later that evening following a brief bout of dinner (the shrimp cocktail proved to be every bit as disagreeable as Henry), Emmit headed straight back to his room. He wanted to be alone for the moment and think things through.

A few days earlier, he'd put in a call to Captain Jusko to see what she knew, if anything at all, about the supposedly good Dr. Henry Jayne. Emmit hadn't seen or heard from her or the rest of the Project Realm team since Celia passed. Most had attended the funeral. Emmit was touched that they made an appearance, and while he appreciated their display of compassion, the only officer he completely trusted other than Percy was Sara. Since Percy didn't have access to the information he needed, he dialed up the ex-captain instead.

There were two messages waiting for him. The first was some marketing communiqué sponsoring what the telemarketer claimed to be the most radical advancement in carpet cleaning history. Emmit recently learned to master the nuances of voice messaging and he proudly tapped the '3' button on the phone to fast forward, then the '7' to erase the message. He waited for the second recorded call to come in, which turned out to be Sara.

"Hi, Emmit? I hope this is the right number…" she sounded just like he remembered. "God…I can't believe it's you. We haven't spoken in what…three, four years? Anyway, it was great to hear from you. Give me a call when you get this…if this is your number. I'll be up until eleven."

Emmit pressed the '9' on the phone pad to save the message then hung up. He activated the handset's call-display and tapped the control strip twice until Sara's number came up. He pressed the *send* button and waited for the phone to dial her number. Before the auto-dial could get to the sixth digit there was a knock at the door. Emmit thought about not answering, but he'd made such an effort to make everyone see he wasn't such a miserly old Spartan, he hung up and went to see who it was. Not that he had any doubt about who was standing on the other side of that door.

"Hi," Emmit said brightly.

Angela, who looked a might uncomfortable for some reason, kept her eyes on her feet. "Can I come in?"

"Of course. Please…"

Angela stepped in. Emmit eased the door shut. "So…what's up?"

Angela's lips began to part but no words were forthcoming. She just stood there and looked on at him with a dull grin.

"What?" Emmit asked.

"You're not even upset, are you?"

Emmit wondered what she meant. "About…?"

She sidestepped him and neared the couch, asking if it was alright to sit just before her backside met the cushion.

"Suit yourself," Emmit said and once more asked what she was talking about.

"Oh…I was so worried. After you left me that night, I thought about what happened. And, well…I don't blame you for being so upset."

"More embarrassed actually," Emmit said. "I know you didn't mean anything by it…it's just sometimes I…"

"Sometimes what?"

Emmit took a load off in the Lay-Z-Boy. "I don't know. Even though it was so long ago…a lifetime it seems like…but it still gets to me. I still have a hard time dealing with it."

"Well, I had no right to bring up the past like that. And I'm sorry. Really."

Emmit said she had nothing to apologize for.

"You have no idea how relieved I am to hear that," she gently patted her chest. "After I hadn't seen or heard from you all this time, I thought you were avoiding me."

"Nothing like that. Just taking care of some personal affairs."

"All right then. Let's just forget any of it happened at all."

Emmit said that sounded like a plan. They sat in silence thinking their private thoughts until Emmit's eyes settled on Angela. For the first time, he noticed what an attractive woman she was; long brown hair (dyed, but who cared?) tidily held in place with a scarlet clip; a full-figure but not to the point where she was spilling out of her one-piece floral print dress; and a simple, smooth countenance that belied her 67 years spent out of the womb.

It was amazing to him that he'd never appreciated just how lovely she was. *Maybe,* he thought, *it was because she was always running off at the mouth.* It was a mannerism he never cared for, and it was all he could recognize before he took the time to get to know her.

"What are you staring at?" she asked with a tinge of whimsy.

Emmit snapped out of his daze. "Huh? What's that?"

"Why, Mr. Rhoe. I do believe I've been ogled."

Emmit's face turned as red as the clip in Angela's hair. "What? No. I would never…!"

"Settle down. There's no need to be embarrassed," she raised herself off of the couch.

Emmit got up as well, his face still displaying a full-burn-blush. "Look, it may have seemed like I was…*ogling* you as you put it, but…"

Angela reached out and pressed her index finger across Emmit's lips. "There's no need to get uptight. I liked it,"

Before Emmit could stop her, she pulled her finger away and replaced it with her full lips.

It was surreal—standing in the middle of his room, lip-wrestling with a woman that made him cross to the other side of the street mere months ago. Even stranger, it felt pretty good.

"Whoa! Okay now," Emmit said as he wrenched himself free. "That was weird!"

He stepped away until his back met the wall.

"Weird nice, though. Right?" Angela asked hopefully.

"Umm, yeah. Sure," Emmit stammered and he quickly excused himself.

It wasn't until he was halfway down the hall that he realized he'd left his own room.

Early the next morning, Emmit was drawn out of his deep sleep by a strange noise. Pulling himself up by the headboard, he listened for it again. It sounded like a grizzly giving its last rites. Another murmuring growl and he discovered it was his stomach.

He was starving. Ravenous.

After washing up and getting dressed in record time, he raced down to the main floor of the building. It was early, not yet eight o'clock, but he still didn't want to risk bumping into Angela. Even though he felt like he might pass out at any second from hunger, he left the grounds. *Better to grab something on the outside,* he surmised, *clear my head and go see her once I've got it all sorted out. But first...*

He didn't tell Sara what he really wanted to talk about; just that he'd been meaning to get in touch with her for some time and it would be great if he could see her.

He'd called her up after Angela left his room the other night. It was after 12 in the morning and Emmit thought twice about calling her. But it was very important that he got a hold of her so he risked it. As it turned out, Sara was still wide awake and after a bit of catching up, she happily agreed to meet with Emmit. "You can come over to my place tomorrow. I'll make us some lunch and we can go over the bad old days."

Sara lived in Somerville, a middle-class suburb 20 miles northwest of downtown Boston. Before he set off for her place, Emmit scarfed down a none-too-pleasing breakfast at Charlie's Sandwich Shoppe in Beacon Hill. The eggs were runny and he wasn't sure what was burnt worse between the toast and coffee, but he finished it up anyway. As famished as he was, he would have eaten something that would make a Billy goat shake its hoof at the cook.

It seemed as though time had passed Sara right on by. Emmit looked her over from head to toe; she hadn't aged a single day. She was still slim, with a full head of blonde hair and a complexion you could bounce a quarter off of.

After she showed Emmit around the place, they settled in the living room for a cup of coffee. Emmit was glad to see her and all, but he wasn't interested in wasting any time and got right to the point.

He told her Henry had contacted him and how he wanted to reinstitute Project Realm so they could thwart the impending terrorist attack.

He told her things weren't going very well and that he'd broken off ties with the doctor because he felt like Henry was up to no good.

He kept going through the motions until Sara finally stopped him and said, "What are you talking about? Dr. Jayne didn't have a son."

Emmit wasn't quite sure he'd heard her correctly. "Say again?"

"He didn't have a son, Emmit. How couldn't you know that?"

"How could I?"

"I thought the two of you were close."

"We were. But our relationship never went past Northwest."

"Well, according to our information, Dr. Jayne didn't have a son. Just a daughter. Corrina was her name."

"That can't be right. He…he looked just like him for chrissakes!"

Sara didn't know what to tell him, but she did have a ballpark theory. "Have you considered the possibility that it was her?"

"Her who?"

"Corrina."

Emmit gave her a deadpan look. "You're serious?"

"Haven't you ever watched Maury Povich?"

All things considered maybe it wasn't too far of a stretch. Henry was definitely on the feminine side of the masculine scale. He was quite thin and neat and was always immaculately put together.

"No. No way. I just don't believe it," Emmit said.

"Well, I don't know who else it could be."

Emmit decided to shelve the matter for the time being. "What about this attack? You hear anything on that?"

"No. But that doesn't mean it isn't so. I don't speak to many people involved in those sorts of things anymore. Too many bad memories."

All the life seemed to leave her then. Ever since she picked up Emmit's message, she was doing her best to come off as bright and positive. But it was plain to see how she really felt. Sara may have removed herself from Project Realm, but its effects on her were still strong.

Other than Emmit, Samuel's treachery left the worst taste in Sara's mouth. She had no more right to blame herself for the doctor's actions than Emmit. But she couldn't help but feel that she was the one most responsible for the creation of the most malevolent despot since Adolph Hitler.

Emmit was well aware of that, but he called Sara anyway. He really didn't want to drag her down that pothole-ridden memory lane, but he couldn't think of anyone else who might be able to give him the information he needed. If there was the slightest chance she would be able to help him in any way, it was worth forcing her to relive some painful memories.

Unfortunately, putting Sara through the emotional wringer didn't yield any positive returns. Following a light lunch, he thanked her and headed straight back to Beacon Hill to pay Henry a visit.

This time Emmit didn't bother tipping the cabbie. Nor did he notice the driver's middle finger as he raced up the front path leading to Henry's house.

"Open up…!" Emmit shouted pounding on the door. "Open this goddamn door or I'll…!"

Emmit continued to bang away until the thick wooden door separated from its reinforced hinges. He backed away, looking down at his clenched fist.

The change was taking place. He could feel it picking up steam, but he didn't know he was so far along. Not until that very moment. Carefully now, he pressed up against the door and pushed it through its frame.

The place was cleaned out—every last stick of furniture, picture—even the light switch covers. Emmit whipped through the house, screaming out Henry's name until he arrived at the doctor's private study. Like the rest of the house it was bare, including the bookcase Henry used as the trigger for the hidden opening to his below-ground laboratory. The place smelled of fresh paint, an oil base by the stench of it. Emmit tried breathing through his mouth and looked dead ahead, trying to remember where the doorway was.

"The hell with it," he said and rushed the wall full-steam.

It took him a couple of tries but he managed to plow through the freshly dry walled section. Dusting himself off and trying to ignore the sharp pains in his shoulder and side, Emmit scurried down the spiral staircase. At the bottom, he reached out for the button on the wall. That's when he noticed the purple envelope taped to the steel balustrade.

Emmit slid his hand along the cold stone wall until he reached the reinforced banister. This time when he took hold of the envelope, it felt as light as a bald feather. The blood pounded in his ears as he tore the flap open and unfolded the note nestled inside. He took a deep breath and started to read:

Dear Mr. Rhoe,

It is with much sorrow and disappointment that I write you this letter. It was my greatest wish for matters not to come to this, but it is clear now that I must take charge of the situation to ensure the future of our way of life. I am sorry you felt that you could not help in this regard, though I still have hopes that you will see things differently. However, I cannot risk the lives of countless thousands, perhaps even millions, on merely hope. That is why I must regrettably take these next steps. While you have no reason to believe me, I hope my actions do not cause you too much pain. In time, I am certain you will find that what I have done was for the greater good. Until that time, I wish you all the best.

   Henry

-11-

May 2000

Anything Emmit was ever forced to suffer through paled to watching his wife disintegrate before his eyes. Celia had been on a steady decline for the past six months. The gamma knife had done its job by shrinking the tumors in her brain, but as per Dr. Tobolowsky's warnings, the radiation also damaged healthy tissue.

Before Celia started her treatment at Taussig, Emmit rented a townhouse a few miles from Hanna in Bratenahl. The miniscule but upscale community wasn't that close to the clinic—it was about a 25-minute drive door-to-door. But Emmit thought it more important to be closer to Hanna, and the rental put Celia practically in her backyard.

It was pretty big for a townhouse—three bedrooms, full kitchen, living and family room and a finished basement. It came furnished, though Emmit sprung for a bigger television when he discovered the only set there was a 20 inch Zenith. He also brought the sectional couch Celia had custom-made for them a few years back. And that's where she spent most of her time, curled up in the corner while she watched T.V.

She was very weak and in a constant state of disarray. Emmit didn't want her going up and down the stairs, especially since she'd taken a few spills over the past few weeks. So he stationed the big screen Sony up in the living room instead of the basement.

Celia was nestled in her usual spot that afternoon, while Emmit was in the kitchen reading the paper. Nothing but bad news. He folded it up, tossed it in the recycling bin and headed into the living room.

"Where are you going?" Celia asked.

"Nowhere. I told you I'm staying home all day with you today."

"Good. I'm glad you're staying," she said, snuggling deeper into the thick cushions. "I wouldn't want you to miss our special lunch."

181

Emmit sat down beside her. He looked down and noticed she'd taken her feet off of the ottoman, which caused her legs to swell up again. The condition was known as lymph edema, yet another unfortunate side effect of the radiation treatment. The potent toxins damaged Celia's lymphatic vessels, which could not longer contain the accumulating lymphatic fluid tissue. The steroids she was taking impeded the process but on bad days, her feet and shins still ballooned to twice their normal size.

"You've got to keep your feet up, Hon," Emmit said, gingerly lifting and lowering her legs back onto the ottoman. "Remember what Dr. Tobolowsky said?"

Celia nodded without taking her eyes off the television. She was watching CNN, something Emmit had asked her not to do.

"And why are you watching this again? I thought we said you weren't going to watch this anymore?"

She was having a hard time discerning between what was real and what wasn't. A few days ago, she'd woken Emmit up in the middle of the night screaming bloody murder that an Al Qaeda militia was breaking down the door. To assuage her fears, he went around the entire house checking to make sure every last door and window was secured. He even went outside to inspect the yard and garage as she directed him with a flashlight.

He wasn't sure where she'd come up with the idea until he caught the broadcast on CNN the following day, which informed viewers that CIA intelligence caught wind of an imminent Al Qaeda strike. Celia interpreted it a bit differently, much like she had innumerable other reports, which was why Emmit didn't want her watching the news anymore.

"C'mon now…let's see what else is on," he took the remote and flipped through the channels until he arrived at *Love is All Around*, the pilot episode of the Mary Tyler Moore Show.

Before Mary could sign the lease for her new apartment, Celia and Emmit had fallen fast asleep. If it wasn't for the chime of the doorbell, they probably would have made it through the entire night.

Emmit stirred and his eyes snapped open. He looked over to the front door then back to Celia, who was still sawing serious logs. He didn't want to wake her, so as quietly as he could, eased himself up off the couch and flitted to the door. He assumed it was Hanna so when he saw who was standing there with a fresh-cut bouquet of lilacs, he was a bit taken back.

"Senator Elias!"

"Hello, Emmit."

Emmit just stood there staring at the politician, not quite believing it was him.

"May I come in?"

Emmit shook the cobwebs loose. "Wha...of course. Sorry. Please..."

Emmit stepped aside to allow the senator in. "These are for your wife," he said and tendered the flowers to Emmit.

"Thank you. Thank you very much," Emmit said appreciatively.

He took the bouquet and quietly led Elias into the kitchen. Emmit pressed his index finger against his lips then pointed to Celia. Elias nodded and tiptoed behind Emmit into the kitchen.

Unlike most of his contemporaries, Emmit developed an affectation for Senator Elias. He was a kind man and honest to boot—two attributes that proved to derail his attempt to further his political career. Even though Elias was one of the few, if not the only, political figures deserving of admiration, Emmit didn't believe for one minute that he'd dropped by just to see how he and his ailing wife were doing.

"You look good, Emmit. All things considered."

"I'm hanging in there. How are things in Washington?"

Elias said it was the same as usual, although the climate had grown increasingly tense lately. "I don't know. It seems just when things can't possibly get worse that's exactly what happens."

"It's the way of the world, senator."

Elias looked up from his cup of coffee. "Please...we've known each other long enough to stow the formalities. Call me Harry."

He'd said it himself—the red tape was in dire need of cutting, so Emmit decided to jump on him with both feet. "All right, Harry. Now that you've seen how I am and asked about my wife, why are you really here?"

"A pessimist to the bitter end, eh?"

"Not a pessimist. A realist," Emmit explained and carted his mug to the sink.

"Semantics. But at the risk of owning up to a lesser character, I have come for another reason."

The senator straightened himself out and went on to describe the latest terrorist action, which began three weeks prior on May 1st. A band of Revolutionary United Front militants kidnapped over 20 members of the United Nations Assistance Mission in Makeni, Sierra Leone. They went ahead and opened fire on a UNAMSIL facility, killing five UN soldiers.

Emmit had a side-line understanding of the event from the press reports he'd read, which turned out to be accurate for once.

"They swept the country grabbing up 300 more peacekeepers," Harry said. "A few weeks later in Liberia they released 139 of them."

Emmit returned to the kitchen table and sat down. Calmly, he folded his hands on the place mat in front of him. "Sounds like a real mess."

"The story doesn't end there, I'm afraid. Just yesterday they…"

"I'm sorry, *Harry*. But I don't see what any of this has to do with me."

"You don't, eh? Well let me tell you…"

"No. Let me tell you," Emmit had to be careful. Elias requested a first name exchange, but Emmit was sure he wouldn't suffer any disrespect. "That chapter of my life is written. You know that. I've got other matters that need my attention now. More important ones."

"General Tannenzapf wasn't very cryptic about his feelings when I suggested we contact you, Emmit. And I agreed with him that it was in bad taste considering your circumstances."

"Yet here you are."

"Yes. Here I am. Which should give you a pretty good idea of how badly we need you."

"I can appreciate that. But my answer is still no."

"Even if I told you there are indications of a massive assault on American soil?"

"What are you talking about?"

"I've been working closely with the CIA and FBI—counter-terrorism measures. Intelligence recently came to us with a very disturbing piece of information regarding an as-of-yet determined initiative. We believe its members of the Al Qaeda."

"Sounds ferocious," Emmit said.

"I'm glad you think it's funny."

"I don't. And I'm sorry for making light of the situation. But come on…did you forget who you're talking to?"

"Meaning what?"

"Meaning, I know how the game is played. Well enough to know how you all go on and act as though you *think* you know what's going on, when you know it all for certain."

"I'm glad you have such faith in us, Emmit. But we're still learning as we go."

"Well…you'll have to excuse me for saying this, Harry…but I don't believe that. Not for a second."

"Please, Emmit. If you'll just let me explain…"

Emmit held up his hand. "You have my answer. Accepting it is up to you."

He hated to be short with Elias. He respected the man and what he was trying to accomplish. Though he didn't feel nearly as reverent about the way he went about it.

Conversely, the senator would never admit to it (not in public), but there was no doubt in his mind that Emmit was spot on when he said Intelligence knew about each and every terrorist operation in existence. Not thought, surmised, guessed or gathered. They were certain—about who all the players were, what they had up their sleeves and precisely when they planned to roll them up. The only thing left to contemplate was acting upon said information, and whether or not congress was good enough to supply them with the funds to do so.

Half-an-hour later, Emmit saw Elias to the door.

"If you ever change your mind," Harry said, "you know where to reach me."

Emmit said he did and that he wouldn't.

There was a stack of dishes in the sink that needed to be stowed in the dishwasher. Emmit had been putting off the chore for the last few days, which was why their numbers had climbed past the rim of the sink. He wandered back to the kitchen to take care of it. Before he could make it there, Celia raised her head off the couch and asked, "Who was at the door? Was it her?"

Emmit leaned over and gave her a kiss on the forehead. "It was nobody, Hon. Go close your eyes."

"All right. But you make sure and let me know when she gets here for our lunch, okay?"

Emmit looked her over curiously. "Her who?"

Without a doubt, Celia said, "Oprah, silly."

Emmit bit his lip and swiped his hand along Celia's cheek. "You'll be the first to know," he said and left to finish up with the dishes.

April 2005

With all that was going on Emmit considered canceling. But it was Hailey's birthday on the 6th and he wanted to make sure he and the motorized Barbie Corvette he'd bought were there for the celebration.

The driver offered to carry the large box into the house for Emmit, but he was feeling so good he had no problem lifting the box out of the airport limo's trunk even though it weighed over 60 pounds. Cradling it under one arm, he carted the toy car onto the textured concrete porch. He did his best to knock while he held onto the large box, but he couldn't manage it. Gently resting it on the ground, he prepared to go for the door again until he noticed something strange.

It was quiet. Very quiet.

But it was after four. The party was called for three-thirty, yet you could hear a pin drop. Hanna mentioned she was expecting over 20 kids. Such a large gathering of young ones would surely be loud enough to be heard all the way out onto the I-90. Yet there was nothing in the air, save for the errant barking of a dog and some light traffic coming from Green Lane.

Making sure not to do any damage this time, Emmit tenderly wrapped on the door. There was no answer. He knocked again and waited. Again no reply.

He picked up Hailey's gift and headed for the backyard. Out of the blue, he thought about the letter Henry left him. He dropped the box and raced for the rear of the house and...

They were dead. Every last one of them. Mothers. Fathers. Children. He hadn't seen wholesale slaughter like that since he and that paratrooper squadron touched down in Kosovo in '96. Most unnerving of all—it was an organized hit. That was obvious by the precision of the entry wounds and the minimal damage to the surrounding area.

Emmit frantically sifted through the bodies for his family. "Hanna?! Hailey?! I'm here!" he cried like he expected someone to answer.

He tossed through the grisly remains until he came across his worst nightmare. It was Nathan. It appeared as though he'd been shot four times. It was hard to tell. There was so much blood. Emmit pulled the handkerchief from his pocket and wiped his grandson's face clean. He looked at him for a moment, willing his grandson to open his eyes. But even Emmit wasn't that powerful. He kissed Nathan on the cheek and rested his body on one of the built-in wooden benches.

A few minutes later he found Hanna slumped on top of Hailey. Intuitively the scenario ran through his mind—*they came through the sides...flanked them in tight...they opened fire...everyone panicked...except for Hanna who tried shielding Hailey with her own body.*

He picked them both up, slinging them under his arms. Laying them beside Nate, he cleaned their faces off and gave them each a final embrace.

And that's what finally lit the fire.

Before it was just a spark; when Emmit knocked Henry's door down; when he crashed through the study wall. But at that moment, his turmoil triggered the transformation much like it had in that tunnel. That's what Samuel, Henry, the boys and girls at Berkeley and all the rest never came to understand—Emmit's power not only derived from his mind, but it was also managed by it. On a subconscious level, he chose to manifest his abilities in a purely physical fashion. After all, he'd grown up as a rather meek, feeble sort who jumped at the sight of his own shadow. What a dream come true it would be to step out of that anemic skin and into a coat that was so powerful and confident, so vibrant and full of belief. While that made Emmit the most powerful creature ever to walk the earth, it was just an indication of what he could do. It wouldn't be until he harnessed the full power of his mind that he displayed his true power.

For the moment, though, he just stopped.

From loving.

From caring.

From feeling anything that could dilute his pain. Like some construct he stood up and looked all around. He took a mental snapshot. Every body. Every expression. Every detail no matter how painful or damaging. It stoked the fire. Made it burn white hot and fierce, giving instinct reign over rational thought. That was good. Because even Emmit didn't want to think about the scene he was going to create when he caught up with Henry.

-12-

February 2001

Emmit had brought up the notion of taking Celia to a hospice several times, but the mere mention was enough to drive her to tears.

But her condition was growing worse every day.

It was getting to the point where homecare was difficult and it wouldn't be long before it became impossible.

He'd hired Maddie Franklin a month ago to clean the house, cook the meals and keep Celia company. While Maddie was more than capable of looking after all that, she too said it was getting harder and harder to properly care for Celia. They were running out of options and as much as it pained Emmit, he had to make the decision.

Dr. Tobolowsky recommended the Hospice of the Western Reserve. It was the ideal choice (if it could ever be considered that) since it was on 185th street, which was just a few miles away from the townhouse and not too much further from Hanna's.

By then, Celia wasn't able to walk on her own so Emmit had to carry her to the car. He carefully lowered her into the back seat and did up her seatbelt. While he made sure she was in nice and tight, Maddie came out with Celia's suitcase. "Here you go, Mr. Rhoe."

He took it and slid it in beside Celia. "Thanks."

Emmit ambled 'round the nose of the Seville he'd rented the week prior (they were all out of STSs) and got in. He slid the key into the ignition and the 300 horses whinnied to life. Emmit sat there just staring through the windshield until Maddie knocked on his window.

"You take care now, Mr. Rhoe."

"You too," he said faintly. "You packed her pajamas? The yellow flannel ones?"

Maddie nodded. "Yes, sir. Her slippers and robe, too."

Emmit put the car into gear. "Thanks for all your help, Maddie. We couldn't have done it without you."

She said she was only doing her job then looked over to Celia and knocked on the window. "Stay strong, Mrs. Rhoe. You hear?"

Celia didn't answer. Like Emmit, she stared dead ahead into nothing.

"We'll do our best," Emmit said and slowly eased the car out of the drive.

Several of the staff members were waiting for Celia at front reception and they welcomed her with open arms and a wheelchair. Emmit helped them lower her down into the chair then excused himself to go fetch Celia's things from the car. While he did, the nurses wheeled Celia to her room.

Emmit shuffled back to the car and parked it in one of the visitor's spots. He reached back to grab the suitcase, got out and locked up. Before he went into the building, he leaned on the hood (minding the studs on his jeans didn't scratch the paint) to take a moment. He'd been so busy tending to Celia he really hadn't had a chance to think about things. Not in any detail. It wasn't until he looked out towards the main building that it finally hit him.

"She's going to die," he whispered. "She's going to die."

Stepping onto the rubber mat, the glass-faced entranceway to the hospice slid open and Emmit ambled inside. Still moving at a snail's pace, he carefully took in his new surroundings.

There was an antique desk just off to the right of the doors. A volunteer was sitting there going through the latest issue of People, carefully surmising which celebrity made the grossest fashion faux pas that month. Emmit walked up to the aged woman and said he was the husband of the woman that was brought in moments ago.

The woman raised her finger as she finished the final paragraph. Folding the rag on the desktop, she looked up at Emmit over the rims of her cheaters. "Just sign here, dear," she slid the sign-in binder in front of Emmit. "Your name and the time please."

Emmit put Celia's suitcase down and took hold of the pen attached to the binder. He scrawled in the requisite information. "Where to from here?"

"Straight ahead and to your left, dear. You'll need to sign some papers at the nurses' desk."

* * *

For a hospice the Western Reserve was pleasant enough; lots of flowers, well-kept furniture and decorative appointments that gave it a homey, personal feel. But there were no floral arrangements or furnishings fragrant or pleasing enough to mask the true ambiance of the place.

Emmit entered the sitting area. Like the other sections it cast off a welcoming appeal. There was a piano sitting smack dab in the middle of the room. The sun shone in from the windows affixed to the top of the 30-foot elevated ceiling, flooding the room in a pastel yellow light. There were several tables positioned all about with thickly padded chairs neatly lined around them. To the left there was a green leather couch and matching loveseat. Over to the right, there was an identical set along with a rear projection television. The nurses' station was ahead and to the left of the twin ten-foot-long fish tanks, which were filled with colorful, exotic looking specimens.

Emmit neared the nurses' desk. There were two women sitting there, the one with the powder blue uniform was typing away on a computer, while her colleague decked out in a pristine white outfit was filing her nails with an emery board. Emmit put the suitcase down and rested his elbows on the countertop. Neither Blue nor White acknowledged his existence. Finally, Blue, who finished banging out her sentence, shot a dirty look over to White. Focusing back on the tall, handsome stranger before her, Blue put on a diminutive smile and said, "Sorry about the wait. What can I do for you?"

"Yeah. My wife was just admitted and I was told to come here and sign some papers."

"Your name?"

"Rhoe. Emmit Rhoe. My wife's name is Celia."

Blue bent down and pulled a clipboard out from one of the cabinets. She dropped it in front of Emmit and asked him to sign. After he was done, she directed him to where he could find Celia.

It was a nice room. A bit small, but it had everything Celia needed, including a decorative, dark-stained armoire with a T.V. and VCR. The bed was just opposite and beside that, a reclining chair with wheels affixed to its legs. Off to the right there was a bathroom. It had no door but instead a thick plastic accordion patrician. Over on the parallel wall, there was a twin set of leaded glass doors, which opened up to a small patio overlooking Lake Erie.

Celia was still in the wheelchair, not saying or looking at much. Another nurse, this one larger than life, was preparing the bed. Emmit walked in and set the suitcase beside the lounger. "Hi."

The nurse turned around. "Hello. Are you the husband?"

"Mmhmm."

"My name's Shanice," she said fluffing one of the pillows. "I'll be takin' care of your special lady."

"Her name is Celia."

Shanice pulled the blanket away from the top of the mattress and shimmied towards Celia. "I know. We already introduced ourselves. Didn't we, young lady?"

Celia looked up at the caregiver, which was as much of a reaction as she'd given anyone those past few days. Shanice smiled brightly then turned back to Emmit. "She'll warm up to me soon enough. Don't you worry about that."

Once Shanice had Celia all tucked away, she neatly folded and stowed the rest of Celia's clothes in the narrow closet in the armoire. All the while, Emmit paced about the room, trying not to think about where he was or where things were headed.

"There we go," Shanice said all finished up. She went for the door. "I'll leave you two be now. Don't be shy to ask for me if you need a thing. Okay, darlin'?"

"Hmm...what's that? Oh yeah, sure. And thanks."

"Uh-huh."

He eased the door shut behind her, wondering why each and every Ohioan gave off the discourteous-sounding reply whenever someone thanked them.

Emmit spent the next few hours by Celia's side. She seemed to be comfortable and had even spoken a word here and there. But he was still holding up the bounty of the conversation until Hanna and Jamie arrived.

"Knock, knock...?" Hanna said cheerfully.

Emmit was relieved to have some company, even if Jamie was included in the mix.

"Hi, guys," he bolted out of his chair and hugged Hanna tightly. "Where are the kids?"

Hanna broke free and turned to Celia. "I didn't want to bring them yet," she leaned over her mother and kissed her on the forehead. "Maybe tomorrow."

Jamie extended his hand. Emmit prepared himself for that limp, icy impression.

"How're you doing, dad?"

Emmit didn't know what he hated more; the way he shook hands or when he called him *that*. "Fine. I'm not the one that's sick."

Hanna shot her father a wicked glare. As always, Jamie let Emmit's hostility wash over him like a spring rain.

"I was really hoping you'd bring the kids," Emmit said as he retook his seat. "Your mother would've enjoyed it."

Hanna sighed and said with a slight hint of irritation, "Tomorrow, Dad. All right?"

April 2005

Eight years ago Rachel settled in Covington—a half-horse town some 65 miles south of Cincinnati. Emmit always found it odd, if not ironic, that his youngest daughter chose such an insular post to hang her hat since she'd always pined for urban splendor.

He didn't tell her he was coming. He didn't have the time or luxury to bicker. While they'd cleared the air (at least enough to see through it) back at Hanna's, it was going to take much more than that to reestablish any sort of viable relationship.

As much as they didn't get along, though, Emmit still loved Rachel with all his heart and he was going to do everything in his mounting power to make sure Henry didn't take that away, too.

Back in February, Emmit took the time to get his license reinstated. It was part of his rejuvenation program, the one that had him picking up the pieces of his life and becoming a vibrant, necessary citizen once again. Along with his driving privileges, he'd become a registered voter (for the first time in his life), filed his taxes; he'd even gotten a library card.

The Chrysler Sebring he'd rented at the Lunken Airport Hertz was certainly no Cadillac, but it still felt good to get behind the wheel again. According to the map, it was a three-inch journey (or 45-minute ride) from the airport to Rachel's place. Time was running desperately short and he already frittered enough away nailing down a flight and getting the car. As quickly as he could (which wasn't easy since the rental counter girl seemed to utilize 4% of her brain's total capacity) Emmit signed the car out and peeled off for the interstate.

Half-an-hour later, Emmit took the ramp leading off the highway and pulled onto the side of the road. The one skill of his that never attained uncommon proportions was his sense of direction. Trying to keep his cool, he reached into the glove compartment and unfolded the map again.

"Ullery Street...Ullery Street..." he recited while he slid his finger along the printout. "Ullery Street!" he stabbed his finger on the roadway, which was only a half-inch away now. Stowing the map back in the glove box right on top of the .38 he'd brought along, Emmit checked over his left shoulder and pulled back into traffic.

Continuing west on East Bridge Street, he made the right onto South High until he arrived at Ullery. He made the left and parked in front of one of the many dilapidated buildings lining the street. *Hope the inside's nicer than the out*, he thought as he got out of the car and jogged for the apartment's lobby.

It was close, but the interior turned out to be more pleasing than the outside of the building. The wallpaper was hanging at the corners and the flooring was chipped and faded. But at least it was clean, or clean enough by the smell of things. Just as Emmit stepped up to the directory hanging beside the elevator, he heard that familiar voice.

"...meet you after I put the groceries away," Rachel said. And then she saw him.

She nearly dropped the two brown paper bags she was carrying. The woman she was talking to steadied the parcels. "Who's that?"

"My fucking father," Rachel whispered, though Emmit could hear her clear as day.

He walked over to his daughter and said hello.

"What are you doing here?" Rachel said.

"Not here. Can we go somewhere and talk?"

Emmit turned to the woman and smiled a stranger's smile. She did likewise and introduced herself. "I'm Alexis. But you can call me Alex. Nice to finally meet you."

"Same here," Emmit said all wide-eyed and obvious.

Rachel passed the grocery bags to Alex and took Emmit by the elbow. "Come with me."

* * *

Much like Angela's room, Rachel's apartment fit her personality; it was sparse, disconnected and neutral.

"Nice place," Emmit said looking all about.

"Why don't you do us both a favor and get to the point?"

So much for chitchat.

"Fair enough," Emmit peaked behind the curtains and opened a closet door. "You haven't seen any strange bodies around lately, have you?"

"Other than you, you mean?"

"I'm being serious, Rachel. I need to know."

She acted as though she was thinking it over; scratching her head and running her tongue along her bottom lip just like Emmit did when he was searching through his mental files. "Nope. Can't say I have."

Emmit stepped back and pushed the curtains aside again. He peered through the window and looked down to the alley below. "You sure?"

"What am I? An idiot?! I said I haven't and I haven't. Are we done?"

He kept staring down into the alley, absorbing and sampling the energies.

"So that was Alex. huh?"

Rachel's voice hardened. "Yeah. So?"

"No need to get defensive. I'm glad I could finally meet *her*."

He was stalling. For the moment he couldn't care less whether Alexis or Alex or whatever she liked to be called peed with the seat up or down. He kept on-topic because he needed the time to figure out what was going on.

There was something, or someone, out there. Whatever it was it didn't belong. Another quick sampling and Emmit put it together. He whipped back around to Rachel. "We've got to get out of here. Now!"

"What the hell are you talking about?"

"I SAID NOW!"

There were three of them. All wearing nondescript outfits and toting considerably more distinctive Interdynamic KG-9 assault pistols with 30 round magazines.

Emmit and Rachel stopped in the hallway just shy of the grimy window overlooking the alley. Emmit took a deep breath and pulled the .38 out from his beltline, suddenly wishing he'd brought along something that didn't look like a prize he'd snagged from the bottom of a cereal box.

"What's the best route to the street?" he said.

"The way you came in. Who's down there?!"

Emmit peeked through the window and watched the trio make their way down the alley and head for the laundry room door dead ahead. He recognized the lead man. It was Michael Pocci, an ex special ops agent. Emmit had run a few missions with the sergeant a decade back in Kashmir then another in Jerusalem. He was a good soldier. Smart. Efficient. But a bit too much of a firebrand. Like so many others, he didn't get in to the game to prevent suffering, but to administer it. From what Emmit heard, Pocci had gone rogue tendering his deadly services to the highest bidder.

They took the stairwell. Down two flights, Emmit ducked back behind the wall. "This way. Quietly now…"

Meanwhile, Pocci and his men entered the building as Emmit and Rachel continued to worm their way out. There was another door at the north end of the alley, which was where Emmit and Rachel were headed. Unfortunately Emmit's car was parked on the south side.

"Who are they?" Rachel asked.

"I'll tell you later. Right now I've got to figure out a way to get to my car."

"Where'd you park it?"

He pointed towards Pocci and his men. "On the other side of the alley."

Emmit held firm for a minute, allowing Pocci and the other two soldiers to go deeper inside the building. Arriving at the north door, Rachel was all set to burst through but Emmit caught her and held her back. "Not yet."

He waited some more. Enough to make sure Sergeant Pocci and the others were far enough along so that even if they spotted them running down the alley, they wouldn't be able to catch up until Emmit put the Sebring into gear.

Pocci was a bit smarter than Emmit gave him credit for, though. He'd ordered one of his men to stay down below as he and the third man went upstairs to check out Rachel's apartment. Emmit was in such a hurry he hadn't considered the possibility. Foolishly, he pushed Rachel through the door and they started bolting down the middle of the alley. Pocci's man saw them and cocked his weapon.

As hard as Emmit was breathing, he heard that unmistakable sound of metal sliding along metal. Instinctively, he shoved Rachel to the ground. She landed hard but unscathed in a pile of overstuffed garbage bags.

Pocci's man opened fire. Emmit found cover behind one of the banged up dumpsters, but not before he took a bullet just above his left forearm.

He was well on his way to coming back, but he certainly wasn't far enough along to take on someone of Pocci's caliber. He had to take down the lone man before the sergeant and his cohort joined the fray. Since Emmit didn't have the ability, he'd have to rely on cunning.

Pocci's man stepped out into plain sight. Like a good soldier, he stayed low and close to the wall, bobbing up and down amid the piles of garbage. "C'mon out, old timer. You don't put up a fuss…I promise I'll make it quick."

I just bet you will, Emmit thought as the man slithered his way ever closer. Emmit leaned back behind the dumpster, desperately trying to figure a way out of the jam.

Then it came to him.

He'd devised the scheme after he saw *The Empire Strikes Back*, when the still petulant Luke Skywalker was captured by the wampa ice creature. The slobbering, white haired monster had stuck young Skywalker's feet in the ceiling of its ice cave and prepared to devour him as the Jedi-in-training hung upside-down and helpless.

Or so it seemed.

Using his still-marginal understanding of the Force, Skywalker called forth his lightsaber, which was sticking out of the snow just out of reach. Miraculously, the Jedi's weapon started to shake until it lifted out of the snow and sailed into its master's hands.

The soldier continued to weave his way towards Emmit. It would be only seconds until Pocci and his other minion would arrive.

Emmit closed his eyes, focusing all of his energies outwards and into his assailant. Just like Skywalker's lightsaber, the soldier's Interdynamic KG-9 started to shake until it broke free of its master's hands and fell a dozen feet in front of him. Emmit popped out from behind the dumpster and opened fire. He was sorely out of practice, which explained why it took him five shots to hit his target. The soldier collapsed. He'd taken the care to slip into a flack jacket just to be on the safe side, but one of Emmit's bullets found its mark in his jugular.

The soldier clutched madly at his throat trying to plug the geysers of blood shooting out of his body. But it was a mortal wound and in a few seconds, he was gone. Once Emmit was certain the immediate threat was nullified, he called out to Rachel. "You okay, baby?!"

Rachel popped up like a groundhog in early February. "Yeah. I think so."

Trying to remember how many shots he had left, Emmit shoved the .38 back into his beltline. He dashed across the alley and scooped Rachel up, and they tore down the remainder of the path, through the laundry room, up to the lobby and back out onto the street where Emmit parked the rental.

By then, Pocci and the other soldier had come back down. They were right on top of Emmit and Rachel and opened fire just as Emmit started the car. He stomped on the gas, the car's two front tires squealing and smoking as they gripped the road for traction. The rear window shattered while the two soldiers-for-hire jumped into the middle of the street and continued to pelt the vehicle with armor piercing rounds.

"Get down!" Emmit barked.

Rachel the groundhog didn't forecast Spring coming any time soon, so she dipped her head below the dashboard. Emmit eased off the gas, not much, just enough to hug the corner onto South High Road and they were gone.

July 2001

The previous week Emmit put a call in to Dr. Warne asking him if he'd be kind enough to attend the festivities for Celia's birthday. He felt a bit awkward making the request and didn't want to put Owen on the spot. But Celia had taken such a shine to him Emmit thought she'd perk up if the doctor could find his way to attend.

"If you can't make it there's no hard feelings," Emmit said again. It was the third time.

"Don't be silly. Of course I'll be there," Owen affirmed. "It will be my pleasure."

"Terrific," Emmit said excitedly. "And don't you dare think about reaching into your pocket for the flight. It's on me."

Five days later, Emmit picked Owen up at the airport. The doctor hardly got the chance to grab a seat before Emmit stuck the car in gear and tore off for the hospice. He made it there in record time—only 20 minutes as Emmit proclaimed, though Owen wasn't quite sure why Emmit was so impressed with the deed.

After signing in, Emmit hurried Owen to Celia's room. The door was closed, so Emmit held Owen up as he cracked the door open to see what was going on. Emmit's eyes adjusted to the darkness and he saw that Celia was sound asleep. He turned back to the doctor. "She's out."

"Why don't we let her rest," Owen suggested.

"Nah...she'd love to see you," Emmit opened the door and cleared the way for Owen to enter.

Emmit flipped on the lamp resting on the nightstand as he explained how Celia was barely talking as of late. "'Cept to some of the staff members from what I've been told."

"I wouldn't let that upset you," Owen said as they looked on at Celia. "It's a common thing."

"What do you mean?"

"I've seen it many times before...when a terminally ill person cuts off communications with loved ones."

Emmit thought about it for a moment until he said, "Shanice...she's one of the nurses here...Celia's favorite. She said Celia talks to her all the time."

"To her. Yes. But not those close to her. It's a psychosomatic reaction— a way that person better copes with losing those they care for the most."

"Then I guess she really does love me," Emmit said.

They talked a bit more, waiting for Celia to open her eyes. After 15 minutes, she was still sound asleep, so Emmit asked if he could interest Owen in a cup of coffee. The doctor said that would be nice and after Emmit flicked the lamp off, they headed out for the kitchenette.

Emmit filled up two plastic cups and they walked down the hall and into the main room. One of the residents was playing an old tune on the piano while a small group of residents watched on.

"I dunno," Emmit said. "For as long as we've been dealing with this...I thought it would get easier, you know?"

Owen shook his head solemnly. "It's never easy. Not when it's sudden and especially not when it drags on."

They took a seat at one of the tables off to the side of the piano. While they sipped on their cups, they watched the woman as she stroked the keys. Instinctively, Owen started tapping his foot in rhythm. Emmit leaned back and rubbed the sleep out of his eyes. "So what do you think?"

Owen kept swaying with the merry tune and said, "She's gotten worse. There's no denying that."

"How long do you figure?"

Owen looked at Emmit and shook his head. "I'm not going to give you another prediction. Celia has made a fool of me too many times."

Owen never liked to put a timeline on these things. But Emmit wouldn't let up with his queries, so he reluctantly gave him his projection. Based on the rate of her decline, Owen initially called for Celia's demise six months ago. After that, he said it would be a miracle if she lasted another few weeks. He wasn't willing to put Emmit through another false prophecy, though, no matter how insistent he became. He liked him far too much for that.

"Thanks for coming in by the way," Emmit said. "Celia really enjoys seeing you whether or not she shows it."

"I know. I like seeing her, too. She's a wonderful person."

Was a wonderful person, Emmit thought. "Hanna and the kids'll be here at two. I set up the cake and the rest in the dining room."

"That sounds nice. I'm sure she'll get a kick out of it."

Celia's reaction to her party was much the same as it was to everything else; nonexistent. Even Nate and Hailey couldn't bring a smile to her face. Emmit had been relentless in his requests for his grandchildren's attendance. He knew it was beginning to irritate Hanna, but having them there was the one thing Celia looked forward to (at least it had been once upon a time). Hanna appreciated the fact, so she bit her lip and carted Nate and Hailey to the hospice nearly everyday. She didn't feel too bad bringing them along. There was a playroom at the west end of the building where they could read, play video games and watch television. Emmit would wheel Celia there in the lounge chair where she could sit comfortably and watch her grandchildren tear the joint up.

That ended a week ago.

Being laid out on her back for the past five months, Celia developed a nasty bed sore. A few days ago when the nurses were draining and cleaning it, Emmit caught a glimpse and swore he saw Celia's tailbone glinting by the light of the silvery moon. Her hands and legs had gotten a lot worse as well. Emmit could hardly wrap his hands around hers anymore, and her feet looked like something out of a Warner Bros cartoon.

Hanna served up the cake. She barely got the chance to set a plate down in front of Nate before he sank his fork in deep. The kid was always a big fan of the sweet stuff. It was only his seven-year-old metabolism and unbridled enthusiasm that allowed him to remain so lean and mean. Hailey, on the other hand, liked playing with her food far more than she did eating it. That's just what she did as she rolled the cake off her plate and smeared it into her hair and the tablet of the highchair.

Hanna cut another piece and handed it to Owen.

"No thank you. Dr. Atkins would have my head if he found out," he said while he rubbed his sides.

Hanna redirected the plate and offered it to Emmit. He took it and sat in front of Celia, who had closed her eyes. "Hi, hon. You want some?" he raised the plate up to her eye level.

Celia didn't make a move.

Emmit offered again but she'd fallen asleep. Shrugging his shoulders, he dug in as did the others, while Hanna began to clean the table off.

Emmit scooped up the last bite and slowly lifted himself up out of his chair. It was getting harder—lifting himself up, sitting down, going to sleep, taking a breath…everything was becoming a chore. "Here…let me help," Emmit said wiping the icing from the corners of his mouth.

He started grabbing up the paper plates. Hanna looked on at her father in disbelief. She couldn't remember him ever offering to help clean off the table, let alone actually seeing it through.

"Where do these go?" he asked.

Hanna was putting the remainder of the birthday cake back into the box. "Garbage is over there," she nudged her head to the left.

Emmit opened the large black plastic bag and threw the plates in. "Jamie couldn't make it, huh?"

"You don't see him here, do you?"

"No. No I don't," Emmit said and stood beside her. "How are you doing with all this?"

Another disbelieving glance and Hanna said, "As well as can be expected, I guess. Making the best of the worst."

After Owen was picked up by the airport limo and Hanna and the kids left, Emmit closed the door and sat down beside Celia. She was still sleeping, breathing heavily now with the aid of the oxygen unit kept hidden under the sliding picture frame behind the bed. He sat there looking on at her, remembering what she had been—how she had been—before all of this happened.

He remembered how he finally talked her out of her poodle skirt and how she scrambled to get back into it when Myrna came home early from her weekly game of Mahjong.

He remembered rushing back from San Paulo to the hospital when she was giving birth to Hanna.

He remembered throwing that party for their 25th anniversary and getting so drunk they slept through the entire weekend.

He thought about all the good times and some of the bad; how they'd built a life, and how it was all being taken away as heedlessly as those animals took the lives of those he'd sworn to protect.

Emmit got so lost reliving those moments gone by he hadn't noticed Celia's labored breathing trailed off. It wasn't until he got up to put on his windbreaker that he saw she wasn't breathing at all.

-13-

Emmit was stepping so hard on the gas he nearly pushed his foot through the floorboard. He kept the accelerator buried until he hit the I-75. Heading south, he merged onto the westbound I-70 that would lead them to Indianapolis.

His arm was throbbing something fierce, even though he'd cleaned and dressed the wound a few hours before he and Rachel hit the interstate. He assumed it was the poison coated bullet that was causing him the undue comfort. It was a Pocci trademark of sorts, something he came up with to ensure all of his intended targets graduated to fatality. Pocci said it was a final *fuck you* for his contracts, though Emmit always believed the sergeant coated his ammunition because of his piss-poor aim.

From what Emmit could recollect, Pocci used an arcane mixture, which was fuelled by the bulbs of the amaryllis plant. While it wasn't a very potent concoction, when introduced into the system of a weakened individual, say, a gunshot wound victim, it would finish the job the slug started a few hours prior. Emmit wasn't too concerned, though. The poison was more of an irritant to him. Painful, yes, but he'd survive it easily enough.

"I think you can slow down now," Rachel said.

Emmit looked down to the speedometer. The needle was perched at just below the 100 M.P.H. mark. He eased off until the six cylinders settled down to a nearly-legal 75.

Neither had said much since their narrow escape, but settling in for the 100 mile stretch before they reached US-52, Rachel started up the inevitable conversation.

"You want to tell me what's going on now?"

Emmit's knuckles turned white as he strangled the wheel. "You wouldn't believe me if I told you."

"Try me."

Repositioning his grip, he noticed he'd crushed the portion of the wheel he was holding. "Okay. Here goes."

He explained it all. Everything. Every last detail.

From the moment he first met Henry at the Boston Public Garden.

About the alleged terrorist invasion and how Henry tried to bring him back to combat the threat.

He told her about Henry's lab that seemed to be a set inspired by James Whale, and how Henry discovered why Emmit could do what he could do.

He told her he'd found out Henry wasn't who he claimed he was, and that he was the one who sent Pocci and his mercenaries to kill her.

The one thing he decided to keep to himself for the time being, however, was that Hanna, Nate, Hailey and Jamie were on a slab at the morgue.

It took Emmit over 95 miles to tell the tale and after he was through, Rachel turned to him and said, "You were right. I don't believe you."

Emmit said that was fair enough and took the exit leading to US-52.

Four hours prior, just before leaving Covington, Emmit pulled into a BP station for gas and to stock up on some food and drink for the long ride to come.

He'd wrapped his forearm with one of the T-shirts he'd brought along, but it had already been completely soaked through with blood and he needed to properly dress the wound. Scouting about, he spotted a pharmacy across the street.

Emmit pulled up to the last available pump, still surveying the surroundings to make sure Pocci hadn't managed to pick up their trail. When he was certain they were clear, he let Rachel out of the car and she headed for the pharmacy.

"Don't forget the gauze," Emmit said.

Rachel nodded. "Yeah, yeah, yeah. You told me a million times. Anything else?"

Emmit thought it over. "Can I borrow your cell?"

She turned back around, scooted up to him and tossed the phone over. "Here…"

Emmit caught it and waited for her to cross the street. He waved to her as she went in then put a call into another old friend.

It took him a few tries (Emmit wasn't quite sure which was the *send* button), but he eventually connected with his intended party.

"Jesus 'H' Christ. I can't believe it's you," Percy said in that unmistakable Midwestern brogue of his.

Emmit didn't want to tell the ex-SEAL too much. Not over a cell phone. All he mentioned was that he was in trouble and that he needed to stow Rachel there for a few days until he figured a way to work it all out.

"That's what friends are for," Percy said. "You just let me know when you're coming and I'll have Janice make up the spare room."

Six hours later they were nearly halfway to Percy's place in Minneapolis. Emmit considered forging on but it had been a long, terrifying day and his batteries were long overdo for a decent recharging session. Even though she was putting on a brave front, Emmit could see Rachel didn't have much left in the tank either.

They were approaching Madison, Minnesota. Emmit trudged on for a few more miles until he spotted a sign for a Holiday Inn Express. Flipping the turn signal on, he followed the navy blue and orange logo into the parking lot.

There was one suite left with two queen-sized beds. Emmit pulled his wallet from his back pocket and thumbed through his credit cards when he thought it better to use cash. He rummaged through the wrinkled bills and handed the man behind the counter the $65 for the room.

"C'mon," he said to Rachel. "Let's grab some shuteye."

The room was every bit as plain as the Express following Holiday Inn intimated (and considerably less well-kept). But so long as there was a bed, a shower and a toilet, Emmit didn't care if the place was swimming in beer and semen.

He collapsed on one of the queen-sized mattresses. Rachel was dog-tired, but she was still on edge. Enough that she wasn't ready to call it a night. Meandering about the room, she opened a drawer here, a door there, until she arrived at the floor-to-ceiling window. She took hold of the cord, pulled down and was treated to a grand vision of the parking lot. "Nice view."

"We're not here to see the sights," Emmit said as he sat up with a grunt, "just to stay the night and first thing in the A.M., we're off to Percy's in Minneapolis."

Rachel let go of the window covering and sat down beside her father. "It just occurred to me, you know?"

"What's that?"

"Don't you think we should call Hanna? To make sure she and the kids are okay?"

With all that had happened, Emmit nearly forgot. Rachel pulled her cell from her pocket and began to dial her sister up, when…

"That won't be necessary," Emmit said.

"What are you talking about? We've got to warn her…"

It took him over an hour to get Rachel to calm down. He wasn't able to do so all on his own, but once he threw half a Valium down her throat, he managed to stabilize her.

It didn't seem like the appropriate time, but neither of them had eaten since early that morning, so Emmit picked up the phone and called down for some room service. He ordered a club sandwich for himself and a Greek salad for her.

They were both hungrier than they let on. Rachel finished her salad in minutes, while Emmit did almost as good a job with his sandwich. Exhaustion took over soon after and they both fell fast asleep. They were so tired neither was bothered by visions of any kind, and it wasn't until eight o'clock the next morning that Rachel began to stir. Groggily, she lifted her head up off the spongy pillow and looked around to gain her bearings.

It wasn't a dream.

Images of her sister, niece and nephew flooded her mind as she slid off the bed and arduously made her way to the bathroom.

It wasn't like she and Hanna were close. Not since they were very young. But they were still sisters, and Rachel had grown to adore Nate and Hailey even though she only saw them a few times a year. Most who knew her thought that to be out of character—her tight-knit relationship with her sister's children. Especially considering she and a maternal nature had a similar working relationship to oil and water. And while that may have been true, the real reason behind her feelings was that her lifestyle didn't make it easy, if possible, for her to have children of her own. Not unless the state of Ohio deemed same sex partners as worthy adoption candidates. That, or she suddenly developed the ability to produce sperm.

Rachel turned the faucet on and doused her face with a handful of cold water. She did it again trying to shock herself awake, when Emmit knocked on the door.

"You decent?"

"That's a matter of opinion. But you can come in if you want."

Emmit opened the door and stood behind her. He dwarfed her in size; she was just over five feet and hadn't yet managed to coax the scale past 100 pounds even though Krispy Kreme and Big Macs were her absolute favorite food groups.

"How're you holding up?" he asked.

"Okay."

Emmit reached over her and grabbed one of the larger towels form the chrome tube rack bolted to the wall beside the shower. "We'll get through this. We just have to stay strong."

He wanted to lean over and hug her; kiss her; tell her how much he loved her. But he didn't have it in him. Not yet. "Let me know when you're done in here. I need the shower," he said and closed the door behind him.

Rachel dried her face with a hand towel and looked at her reflection in the mirror. "I love you, too."

After a quick bite, Emmit and Rachel hopped into the Sebring and back onto the highway. It was still over 350 miles to Percy's. While Emmit wanted to get there as soon as possible, he was glad he had some time to work out how he was going to deal with Henry.

"Where are they?" Rachel asked from out of nowhere.

"Where are who?"

"Hanna and the kids? You said…" she trailed off choking back the tears. "You didn't just leave them there, did you?"

"Of course not! I called the police before I left. I'll call them again when we stop off."

He still didn't want to risk using Rachel's cell phone.

"You really don't think much of me, do you?" he said.

Rachel chewed it over for a spell. "No. I guess I don't."

Silence then. A bit unpleasant but a lot more comforting than the conversation they were entering into.

"I tried my best, you know. Whether you want to believe it or not, I always did my best to be there for you…for everyone," Emmit said.

Rachel looked at him skeptically. "Should've tried harder."

He tightened his grip on the wheel, this time minding he didn't squash it. He looked over his right shoulder to make sure the lane was clear then eased off the accelerator and pulled onto the shoulder.

"What are you doing?" Rachel said.

"I'm putting an end to this right here and now."

Once the car was stopped, Emmit jammed the gear stalk into park and turned to his sole surviving daughter. "I've been putting up with this nonsense for longer than I care to remember. And I won't have it anymore. Especially not now!"

Rachel smiled. It was what she did when she got nervous. "What do you want, hmm? You want me to forget all about the past? Just set it aside and give you a big sloppy kiss?"

"No. I don't expect you to forget. Never did and I never will. All I ever asked of you was to try and understand."

"Understand? Okay. Sure. But before I do…why don't you ask Hanna if she can do the same? Ask Nate and Hailey when you're done with that."

Emmit slumped down in his seat. "I never meant for any of this to happen. I just wanted to protect my family."

"Well, you did a bang-up job," Rachel said, her voice starting to crack. "Grade-fucking-A!"

Emmit pulled up onto Percy's driveway just before five that afternoon. It started to drizzle when he got off the interstate and as he and Rachel stepped out of the car and walked up to the house, it began to pour. Soaked to the bone, they found shelter under the front awning. Before Emmit could reach to knock on the screen door, Janice, Percy's wife, came through.

"I don't believe my eyes," Janice said looking on at Emmit.

"Sight for sore ones, am I?" Emmit couldn't move quick enough to dodge as Janice practically jumped him.

"Your certainly are," she said.

Emmit struggled, but Janice had a pretty strong grip. She gave him another solid squeeze before she let go. A bit embarrassed, Emmit introduced Rachel. "Janice Rawlings, I'd like you to meet my daughter, Rachel."

Rachel stuck out her hand.

"Oh…we can do a lot better than that," Janice wrapped Rachel up in another bear hug. "Any daughter of this big lug is a daughter of mine."

Rachel froze like a deer caught in gas-powered, xenon headlights. She didn't try to wrangle herself free, though. It felt good to be held.

"It's…nice to meet you, too," Rachel said.

Janice stepped back and looked at them both. "My, but you do look alike, don't you? Well, don't just stand there like a couple of dogs caught out in the rain. Come in."

Janice kept gabbing it up as she led them down the front hall leading into the kitchen. "I still can't believe you're here," she said excitedly. "Percy said you'd be coming...but I still don't believe it!"

"Where is he anyway? Emmit asked, though he could feel the retired sergeant coming up quickly from behind.

"Right on top of you, you old fart!" Percy shouted.

He jumped onto Emmit's back and clamped on for all he was worth. Emmit acted surprised, lunging forward with the sudden 220 pounds strapped to his back.

"You settle yourself, Percy Rawlings," Janice yelped. "He's not so young in this day and age."

Percy kissed Emmit on the top of his head and hopped off. "He isn't at that," he said as he walked around to face his longtime teammate. "Not by a long shot."

"I'd watch those words. You're sporting a few wrinkles there yourself," Emmit said in his defense. "And what's this?" he pointed out to Percy's tightly shorn haircut. "Getting a little singed around the edges, too?"

Percy returned the sentiment, running his fingers through Emmit's thinning do. "Wouldn't get into much detail on the matter, 'specially seeing how you've blown a few feathers yourself."

"That's enough of that," Janice hollered. She turned to Rachel and winked "That's men for you. Haven't seen one another for nearly five years and all they can do is jab one another in the ribs."

Percy said that was because Emmit gave him so much ammunition. Emmit didn't get a chance to launch a rejoinder as Janice stepped in again.

"You stop that, Percy. Right this minute," she took Rachel by the elbow. "You come with me, sweetheart. I'll show you to your room." She led Rachel out of the kitchen. "You boys take the time to catch up on whatever it is needs to be caught. Dinner's at six. And that's sharp!"

Half an hour later, Emmit and Percy were holed up in the study Percy set up in the basement. Before Emmit got down to business, he wandered about the cramped room, taking in all the familiar sights. Percy had a collage of snapshots from Vietnam framed and hung on every wall. Emmit was familiar with a lot of the faces staring back at him. Those he didn't recognize Percy was quick to give a name.

Once Emmit was through with his tour, Percy poured them both a stiff drink and they took a seat on the tan leather sofa resting against the back wall of the room. Emmit went into story-mode again, though this version held quite a bit more details. Thankfully, Percy was a lot easier to convince than Rachel, though he wasn't willing to accept the proposition that Henry wasn't who he claimed to be.

"How's she so sure he's not that son of a bitch's boy?" Percy said pouring Emmit another glass of Chivas.

"What, Sara?"

"Yeah. I know she and Umbridge kept close tabs on whoever was involved in the program, but Dr. Frankenstein was out from under their thumbs not after long. Who knows who or what he was pokin' during that time out?"

"I thought about that. But the numbers don't jibe." Emmit took a modest sip of the liquor.

"How so?"

"I'm no carnie, but Henry or whoever he is has to be in his mid-50s. If Dr. Jayne had another kid after he went section-8…well, that was halfway through '68, so…"

"Maybe he just looked older'n he was," Percy offered. "First time I saw his daddy, I thought he was 103."

Emmit shook his head. "Maybe. But I doubt it."

July 2001

Celia had always been well-liked, but even Emmit was surprised when the Stanetsky Memorial Chapel filled to capacity.

He was milling about in a private room overlooking the chapel, peering through the smoked glass as more people filled up the room. Hanna was sitting with Jamie on one of the coaches and Rachel was staring through another window that looked onto the main room. "There's got to be over 300 people out there," she said.

Hanna dried the corners of her eyes with a fresh tissue and told her sister they weren't charging admission, so she could care less about how many times the turnstiles spun.

Celia's casket was sitting at the head of the chapel between two high-polished wooden podiums with flaming copper bowls mounted on top. A large Star of David was engraved on the top portion of the casket's lid, which was made of a similar wood—not as glossy, but the same color.

Once the main doors were closed, another member of the chapel came through to greet Emmit and the rest of the immediate family—Hanna, Rachel, Jamie, and Celia's younger sister, Gertie. He led them out of the private sitting room and showed them to the front bench stationed to the left.

Hanna decided to leave the kids at home with one of the neighbors. *No reason for them to be here for this*, she said when Emmit asked her if they were coming. *They have their entire lives to learn about death.*

Rachel, too, had left someone behind. She'd considered bringing Alex along, but thought the better of it at the last minute. It was one thing having to deal with her father's dirty looks. But she wasn't sure she could handle the multitude of conservative, stone-aged questions the rest of the family was sure to pose.

Emmit told the rabbi, Huntzinger was his name, that he didn't want him going on and on about what a noble, selfless and kind person Celia was. Even though all of the descriptions were a custom-fit, he didn't want an absolute stranger going on about his wife like they were intimates.

Not long after, Huntzinger was putting the finishing touches on his vague declarations. The attendees started raising themselves from their seats and formed two lines allowing Emmit and the other mourners to pass between them. As they did, the rabbi chanted, "Ha-makom yinakhem et-khem betokh she-ar aveilei tziyon veyerushalayim."

Once the mourners disappeared behind the door of the private sitting room, Huntzinger approached the microphone and instructed those who would be attending the burial service to leave the chapel and wait in their cars. "Please keep in mind that even though we have a police escort, you must obey all traffic signs and signals."

It was a 20-minute drive from the chapel to the Adath-Jeshurun Cemetery in West Roxbury. If Emmit had his druthers, he would have chosen the new memorial park in Cambridge since it was a lot closer to home. But most of Celia's family was buried at Adath-Jeshurun. He knew that's where she'd want her final destination to be even though she wasn't on speaking terms with most of her kin during their above-ground days.

"It was a beautiful ceremony," Jamie said as he limply held Hanna's hand. "Mom would have been happy with the turnout."

Emmit chomped on his tongue and looked out the window of the stretched limo. *Like you know what would've made her happy*, he thought.

Rachel clamped down on her tongue as well, minding the silver stud she'd recently pierced it with. *You're such a schmuck*, she thought. *Mom hated most of those people with a passion.*

The 56-strong convoy led by the grey hearse eased past the green rod iron gates that led into the Adath-Jeshurun grounds. Celia's plot was located in one of the newer sections, which was nestled near the back of the property. The bulk of her family was in the Beth Tikvah congregation, one of the original sections situated at the front. Emmit would have liked to bury Celia there with the rest of them, but he wasn't a member of the synagogue. Without the $3,500 annual membership fee, it was made abundantly clear that Celia's presence was not welcome.

The hearse slowly rolled through the winding narrow gravel roadway and parked a few meters shy of the plot. There were two grubby looking characters stationed there standing on either side of a tall mound of earth. Each was wearing mud-soaked coveralls and holding onto earth shovels.

The limo driver nudged up close to the hearse and stepped out to open the door for Emmit and the others. They all thanked him (save for Jamie, who reckoned that sort of thing to be an inalienable right rather than a courtesy).

Rabbi Huntzinger's 5-series BMW was third in line. He got out and walked to the open grave, never taking his eyes off the Sidor resting in his palms. Emmit stared him down and thought how glad he was to help the man of God with his lease payments by shelling out $400 for his services.

One of the men who worked at Stanetsky's, the short, chubby gent with the sorely out-of-date double-breasted dark brown suit, popped the rear hatch of the hearse and slid Celia's casket out into the afternoon sun. The other cars parked on the sides of the path and the drivers and passengers got out and began congregating near the mouth of the open grave. The six pallbearers Emmit chose—Percy, Vernon, Carl and Celia's cousins Max, Steven and her nephew, Jonathan, stood three strong on either side of the coffin and raised it up and out of the hearse.

Huntzinger started reciting his prayers as the pallbearers carried Celia towards the trimly fashioned 6-foot deep rectangular hole. Gently, they lowered it onto the thick green straps positioned on either side, stepped back and waited for the rabbi to finish his entreaty.

Most of the people at the memorial service found their way back to Emmit's. Rather than worrying about setting out all the food themselves, Emmit sprung for a few hired hands to help out. All was ready when they got back and everyone dug in to the food and drink.

Emmit didn't care for the majority of the people. Most resided on Celia's side of the family; cousins, uncles, aunts, nieces and nephews. Truth be told, he didn't really know most of them. Not well anyway. But what little he did know he didn't like and he made sure to keep his distance.

A few hours later the crowd finally started to thin. Emmit appreciated everyone coming (well, a few of them anyway), but he was glad that he would soon have a few minutes to himself. It had been a rollercoaster ride those past few days, and he was sorely in need of some alone time.

An hour later, Emmit filled another Styrofoam cup, this time with decaf. He wasn't exactly sure when it began but lately the pure stuff had been keeping him up at night. He'd never had that problem before, nor did he ever have to suffer through the host of everyday nuisances that seemed to be popping up lately; he couldn't make it through the night without getting up to take a piss; he couldn't pick up a book without also snapping up a pair of reading glasses; and he couldn't add much more than salt and pepper to his meals without reaching for the Gaviscon. These were all standard practices a man of his age was forced to withstand. But Emmit and normal weren't two words that ever collided in the same sentence.

Not until then.

With his cup in hand, Emmit slid the glass door open and strolled out onto the deck. It was just after five o'clock and he wanted to seize the moment because it wouldn't be long before people starting filing back in for the evening's minion.

It had been a beautiful day and it was shaping up to be an equally lovely night. It wasn't too hot or cold. A lazy but refreshing breeze came off the ravine that the backyard led out to and rustled Emmit's steel-grey hair. He stood there enjoying the moment until Jamie stepped out to join him.

"You mind some company?"

He did, but it wasn't the time or place to voice such an objection. "Knock yourself out," Emmit said and Jamie took a seat on one of the chairs of the patio set.

"It's a beautiful night, huh?"

Emmit nodded and sipped on his coffee.

"I love it out here this time of year. Reminds you what life's all about."

Emmit's inner dialogue kicked in; *like you have the faintest concept of what that is.*

"How are you holding up?" Jamie asked.

Emmit said, this time out loud, "All right. Like Hanna said—making the best of the worst."

"Well, if there's anything you need—I MEAN ANYTHING—don't be afraid to ask."

Jamie got up and in a reassuring attempt, put his hand on Emmit's shoulder.

"I appreciate it," Emmit said.

The minion started right after dinner. Emmit was worried they wouldn't have enough people (10 was the least God allowed). As it turned out, though, the living room was barely large enough to contain all those who came.

More food, more friends and more well wishes were heaped upon Emmit for the next few hours. Again, he appreciated it all, but he was exhausted and all he wanted now was to turn in and get a good night's sleep.

Emmit carted in the last of the cutlery from the dining room and brought it into the kitchen where Carla, one of the women he'd hired to help out, was rinsing off the serving trays. Hanna was sitting at the table, just drinking her water and relaxing for a spell.

"Where do these go?" Emmit asked.

"You don't have to do that," Hanna said. "Let her take care of it."

"Just trying to pitch in for once."

Hanna put on an admiring grin. "You can put them in the sink."

He did and then took a seat in one of the high chairs under the counter attached to the island. He turned to Hanna and looked at her, marveling at how much she reminded him of Celia. While she didn't look much like her mother (save for her deep blue, steely eyes), Hanna and Celia shared many of the same mannerisms; the way they crinkled their noses when they were confused, or how they hit that specific high note when a bee was buzzing underneath their bonnets. Upon first glance, you'd never know the two were related but if you stepped back and watched carefully, it quickly became apparent that they were one in the same.

Emmit kept his watch over his eldest daughter, thinking about Celia as he did. Hanna looked up from her bottle of water and noticed his eyes on her.

"What?" Hanna said.

"What, what?"

"What are you looking at?"

"Can't a father look at his daughter without getting the third degree?"

Hanna brushed the hair out of her eyes just like Celia used to. "I guess not."

Emmit smiled faintly. "Well, I think that does it for me. I'm turning in."

Hanna took one last swig from the bottle and got up as well. She stood beside Carla, washed her hands and grabbed one of the dishtowels hanging underneath the sink. She noticed the bottle for the large cooler was running on empty and turned to Emmit, "Do me a favor before you go…?"

"What's up?"

"The water cooler is empty. Can you put a fresh bottle in so it'll be cold for everyone tomorrow?"

Emmit scouted around for a new bottle.

"You do live here, don't you?" Hanna asked.

"Your mother was the organizer. I just did the heavy lifting."

Hanna nudged to her right. "Under the desk over there."

Emmit got up and reached for the cooler. He grabbed the bottle with both hands and shook it loose. "Where do you want this?"

"Just leave it there. The guy's coming tomorrow to pick up the empties."

He placed the drained bottle on the floor beside the cooler and went to pick up a full one. Grabbing it by the neck, he pulled up and…

He couldn't lift it.

He tried again but could barely tilt it off the floor.

"What's the matter?" Hanna asked.

"Nothing. Just lost my grip," Emmit gritted his teeth and at last managed (just barely) to hoist the 35-pound water bottle up off the hardwood.

-14-

October 1993

He'd first met Osama Bin Laden eight years ago in Somalia during the Battle of Mogadishu. Mohamed Farrah Aidid, the resident warlord, brought the two together realizing that if they combined their forces and funds, there was no limit to what they could accomplish.

While *He* and Osama couldn't have been more disparate both geographically and spiritually, they did share much in common. Both came from privileged backgrounds—*He* the son of a wealthy industrialist and Osama the offspring of a flush entrepreneur. Both were highly educated—*He* graduated at the top of his classes at Harvard and Johns Hopkins and Osama earned his degree as a civil engineer at King Abdul Aziz University of Jedda.

Most of all, though, they shared a passionate resolve to uphold the well-being of their respective countries and political schemas, and there was nothing they wouldn't do to preserve them. Aidid was certain either man's infinite veneration would make them fast fiends, which in turn would serve his immediate political agenda very well.

The Battle of Mogadishu pitted forces from the United States against Somalian guerrillas, who had pledged their allegiance to Aidid. The fur started flying when a U.S. Army Special Forces team traveled from their compound to the outskirts of the city to capture the leaders of Aidid's militia. The strike was modest in scope—19 aircraft, 12 land vehicles and 160 men all told. The Americans weren't expecting their enemies to be quite as well-armed or prepared as they turned out to be, which explained how the Somalian guerrillas blew two of the U.S. helicopters out of the sky with rocket-propelled grenades.

Most of the members of the American team were able to hightail it back to their compound, however, several were trapped back at the crash sites.

It wasn't until the ground battle began that things got really messy. The fight raged on throughout the night. Early the next morning, the joint task force arrived, which included soldiers from Pakistan, Malaysia and the U.S. 10th Mountain Division. The task force quickly assembled 60 vehicles, including Pakistani tanks, Malaysian Condor armored personnel carriers and U.S. AH-1 and UH-60 choppers.

The task force bulldozed its way through to the initial crash site and led the trapped soldiers to safety. They didn't fare nearly as well at the second site. It was overrun and a lone American soldier was taken hostage.

When the smoke cleared, 18 Americans were killed and another 79 wounded. Two Malaysian soldiers joined the 18 U.S. soldiers six feet under, as did hordes of Somalis (the exact numbers were never recorded, but estimates put it at 500 to 1,000 dead Somali militia and civilians and another three to four thousand injured).

Holding Aidid accountable for the event was a natural conclusion to draw, but it wasn't long before Osama put a call in and took credit for orchestrating the attack. *He* was also behind the Battle of Mogadishu, having funded Aidid's guerrillas. But *He* held back and played silent partner, allowing Osama to revel in the moment.

It wasn't *His* sense of modesty that prompted anonymity, though. *He* stayed in the shadows so *He* could freely plant the seeds for a future endeavor, one which the world would never forget no matter how hard it tried. In order for *His* plan to be successful, *He* needed a figurehead, or scapegoat, and Osama was shaping up to be the ideal candidate. While the leader of Al Queda was a shrewd and intelligent man, the one characteristic that overrode all was his vanity. *He* could see that the moment *He* laid eyes on the Afghan, and *He* would use that weakness to *His* greatest advantage.

September 2001

On the morning of Tuesday, September 11th, *His* master plan was set into motion when the U.S. was attacked in New York City and Washington.

The first leg of the assault was consummated when four jetliners were hijacked. The first two struck the World Trade Center. The third was flown just outside of Washington to the Pentagon. The forth plane was the only one to miss its mark entirely and crashed in an empty field in Pennsylvania.

After an initial outburst of panic, confusion and fear, all trading on Wall Street was stopped. The Federal Aviation Administration called down every plane in the nation for the first time in its history. The U.S. military was placed on high alert, while President Bush addressed the nation as he vowed to, *Find those responsible and bring them to justice.*

It was a good start, in *His* estimation. But *He* wouldn't find cause to smile from ear-to-ear until the end of the month.

The next day, residing New York Mayor Rudolph Giuliani warned the citizens of his fair city that the death toll would be in the thousands. Bush, meanwhile, branded the attacks as acts of war and proceeded to ask Congress to pledge $20 billion for the rebuilding efforts. As per *His* carefully laid plans, Secretary of State Colin Powell I.D.'d Osama as the prime suspect. In turn, Paul Wolfowitz, Deputy Defense Secretary, promised the U.S. would respond with a sustained military campaign.

The corners of *His* mouth started to curl.

On the 14th, President George Jr. declared a national emergency and bequeathed his military to activate 50,000 reservists. In the meantime, the Justice Department (a most inaccurate and undeserved designate in *His* opinion) released the names of the 19 hijackers. Later that afternoon, Bush led four former presidents and citizens of the United States in prayer at the National Cathedral.

He hadn't seen a performance that schmaltzy since Barbara and Robert hooked up in *The Way We Were.*

Not quite 24 hours later, Bush pledged to send U.S. troops to hunt down the terrorists in a long, unrelenting war, citing the American people's desire for not only revenge but an end to the barbaric behavior. The State Department also chimed in, warning all governments *they will be no friend of ours* if they tolerate or assist terrorist groups. Nearly wetting its pants, Pakistan agreed to the complete list of U.S. demands regarding a possible attack on neighboring Afghanistan.

His lower lip started to quiver with delight.

On September 16th, Bush kept beating his gums as he vowed that a crusade was coming to rid the world of all evil-doers. The president also dismissed reports made by Osama that he was not behind the attacks. A Pakistani official stated a senior delegation would be sent to Afghanistan to deliver the U.S. message—*hand over Osama bin Laden or risk massive assault.*

He'd never been a fan of television, but even *He* had to admit that month's programming was must-see TV.

He'd played it out perfectly, right down to the finest detail. Osama was Enemy Number One. The U.S. was becoming the most hated nation in the land. And all those raggedy, disordered mutineers were on the run, clearing the path wide open for *His* next move. But that would have to wait, because the final installment of his promotion was just about ready to hit the American public right between the eyes.

With as much resources and manpower at its command, the U.S. still failed to flush Osama out.

He made sure of that.

Bush was starting to look like a fool (a much bigger one) and the figurehead of the most powerful nation on earth desperately needed to give his constituents a reason to believe in him and his cabinet again. After some careful thinking and instigating what little imagination at his command, George Jr. redirected his agenda on terrorism westward, declaring war on Iraq and Saddam Hussein's regime.

Right on cue.

On March 12th, 2003, General Tommy Franks returned to his forward headquarters in Qatar. Firmly clenched in his hand were very specific orders, which were to go on the offensive the following day. Unlike '91, this proved to be a war rather than a marketing tactic, and the U.S. soon found itself embroiled in a bloody and uphill battle. Of course, even though the campaign was no cakewalk, the outcome was never truly in doubt. Mr. Hussein's regime was brought down not one month later, and even though his defeat was met with mixed reviews, Bush had managed to nudge the spotlight off Osama, his oily benefactors, and all those responsible for the September 11th tragedy.

He'd played it like a master puppeteer, stage-managing his marionettes without anyone in the audience—not a single one—ever knowing *He* was pulling the strings.

Because of *Him*, Bush was able to convince his many lemmings that Saddam was harboring weapons of mass destruction without ever having to back it up.

Because of *Him*, the U.S. populace's disinterest was cemented, even though anti-terrorist intelligence had implied (on several occasions) that an attack on American soil was imminent.

Because of *Him*, the world's suspicions and indignation were laid to rest, even though Israeli intelligence publicized Iraq had no apparent ties with the 9/11 terrorists.

And finally, because of *Him*, Bush and his whipping boy, British Prime Minister Tony Blair, were under hellacious fire concerning the possibility they misled their people in order to justify *their* war.

November 2001

It was gone. Emmit didn't know how. He didn't know why. But his power had disappeared just the same. Strange as that was, even more peculiar is that he wasn't all too upset about it.

Maybe that was because without it, Elias, Tannenzapf and all the rest would have no cause to beat down his door. Or maybe it was because he didn't have to feel guilty about turning them down anymore. Whatever the reason behind his apathy, Emmit could finally be afforded a normal life. The only problem now was finding out what to do with the remainder of it.

It was customary for the grave marker to be put in place and for an unveiling ceremony to be held after the Kaddish period, which was 11 months for parents and 30 days for other close relatives. While most families tended to wait until the full year elapsed, Emmit didn't want to put it off any longer than he had to.

After the rabbi removed the cloth from Celia's headstone and completed the El Maleh Rachamin Memorial Prayer, Emmit, Rachel, Hanna and Gertie went ahead with the Mourner's Kaddish. Their Hebrew was rusty at best (Gertie could make out a word or two, but that was all) so they cordially welcomed the phonetic version the rabbi tendered.

In unison they read, "...sh'lama raba min sh'ma-ya, v'ha-yim aleynu v'al kol yisrael, vimru amen. Oseh shalom bim-romav, hu ya-aseh shalom aleynu v'al kol yisrael, v'imru amen."

Everyone gave an *Amen*. The rabbi shook Emmit's hand, again offering his condolences.

And that was that.

* * *

After Emmit, Hanna, Rachel and Gertie thanked everyone for coming, they headed back to the winding path and made their way to the STS. Without warning, Emmit turned to Hanna and said, "Here. You drive." He tossed her the keys and headed for the passenger side of the vehicle.

Along the way to the cemetery, he'd been having a tough time making out the street signs and signals. His eyesight wasn't what it used to be—not by a near or far shot.

"You want me to drive? She asked. "Your car?"

Emmit nodded. "Just feeling a bit tired. You don't mind, do you?"

"Not at all," she said as she took the keys and opened the doors with the remote.

Rachel opted for the backseat even though it meant riding shotgun with Aunt Gertie, who reeked of Chanel #5 and whitefish. She tried her best to breathe through her mouth until Hanna pulled up to the front of her aunt's building. Making sure the old gal was safely on her way in the lobby, the rest waved goodbye and Hanna eased the Caddy back onto the street. Rachel closed the window, sunk deep into her seat and slipped on her Discman.

"Thanks for making that speech by the way," Emmit said. "Mom would've like it very much."

Hanna said she would have made it without being asked. Emmit looked behind to Rachel. "Would be nice to have two daughters that felt as such."

Hanna sighed. "Can we please not get into that right now?"

"I'm just saying."

"Well don't. Let's just change the subject. All right?"

Emmit backed off and considered another line of conversation. "Did you think about what we were talking about before?"

"What? Moving the dining room set to my place?"

"You know what I'm talking about."

He'd heard about this place called Timberlake a few months back from a friend of a friend. Emmit didn't really deem such a locale as a viable living option for himself at this stage of life. He was, after all, not even 60. But when he learned Timberlake was more of a live-in hotel where middle-to-late agers could spend their days without worrying about cleaning up after themselves or turning on a stove, he brought it up to Hanna just to see what her reaction would be.

Hanna didn't think it was a good idea, putting it lightly, even though she knew Emmit was a terrible cook and an even worse housekeeper. She thought

Timberlake and any other place like it were suitable for the incontinent and whose relatives referred to them in the third person even when they were in the same room.

"So?" Emmit asked.

"So what?"

"What do you think?"

Hanna gripped the wheel tightly. "I think you're old," she said, "but not that old."

She stopped at the light and waited to make the left onto Massachusetts Avenue.

"It's not that kind of place," Emmit said a bit defensively.

"No? What kind of place is it then?"

The advanced green came to life and she cautiously directed Emmit's STS through the light. She looked at him without turning her head to make sure he was comfortable with how she was driving.

"Look…why don't we just go and check the place out?" Emmit asked.

"I don't see why you need me to do that."

"I don't need you. I just want you there with me is all."

How could she refuse that?

"What about moving in with us?" she said.

When Emmit first brought up Timberlake, Hanna suggested that perhaps he would consider taking residence with her, Jamie and the kids.

"I really don't think that's such a good idea," Emmit said.

"Why not?"

He looked at her knowingly.

"He's really not that bad, Daddy. You just have to get to know him."

Emmit said that may very well be true, but if it was all the same, he'd appreciate her visiting Timberlake with him. "So? What do you say?"

Hanna thought about it some more and said, "What time?"

Two days later, Emmit and Hanna strolled through the main entrance of the Timberlake Retirement Villa. Upon first glance, it looked like some three-to-four star hotel.

They parked the car and surveyed the grounds for a spell. The place was a bit bland in nature. Well-kept, but it just didn't seem to be able to muster any sort of workable personality. Hanna said the panorama was the equivalent to a mayonnaise sandwich.

"Let's just go inside," Emmit said, a bit annoyed.

Inside, they continued to take in their new and thankfully more stimulating surroundings as they approached the main reception area. One of the Timberlake staff was sitting behind the desk working away on a computer. Hanna and Emmit stopped in front of him when he held up his hand before either could speak. A series of keystrokes later and he greeted the new guests.

"Sorry about that. I was right in the middle of something. How can I help you?"

"Yeah…we're here to see," Emmit looked down at the piece of paper he'd written the directions on. "Francis. Francis Albertson. We're a bit early."

The worker looked down at the computer monitor and accessed the day's agenda. "Mr. Rhoe?"

"That's me."

"Frank will be with you in a moment. Can I get you anything while you wait—coffee, water?"

"I'm fine, thanks."

"How about you?"

"I'll do," Hanna said.

Ten minutes later, Frank's rotund figure turned the corner. Emmit and Hanna were sitting on the couch overlooking the marble water fountain. Since they were the only two people the head orderly didn't recognize, he assumed they were his two o'clock. "You must be Mr. Rhoe," he said brightly.

Emmit stood up and shook Frank's hand. "That's me. But please…call me Emmit."

"Gotcha. And who might this lovely young lady be?"

"I might be his daughter, Hanna."

"It's a pleasure to meet you both. My name is Francis Albertson. But you can call me Frank," he said.

Hanna stood up beside Emmit as Frank waved them on. "If you'll please follow me."

Frank began the tour by showing them around the common areas of the building—the dining hall, entertainment rooms, gym and so on. Hanna still wasn't convinced Timberlake was a good fit for her father, but even she was impressed by the facilities thus far. After Frank pointed out the sun room, he guided them back into the lobby and went on ahead to the elevators.

"So what do you think so far?" Frank asked reaching out for the *up* button.

"Nice. Very nice," Emmit said. He turned to Hanna. "How about you?"

Hanna's eyes narrowed. She didn't appreciate being put on the spot like that. "So far so good."

The private room was the little sister to the rest of the place—immaculate and convivial.

"Of course, every guest is welcome to bring along his or her own decorations and furnishings," Frank explained turning on the light to the bathroom. "At Timberlake, we don't just try to make it like home—it is home."

"Nice pitch," Hanna said just barely loud enough to hear.

Emmit jabbed her side and walked into the bathroom. "Looks more like a condo than an old age home."

"We prefer the term worry-free living facility. And to your comment, this section of Timberlake has been especially designed to feel just like a condominium. All residents on this floor are more than capable of taking care of themselves."

"So why join up?" Hanna asked.

"Every person has their own reasons. Most just want to live somewhere where they don't have to worry about preparing their own meals, doing their own laundry, or taking care of the basic upkeep of their home."

Emmit stepped back into the room, looked around some more and said, "So…when can I move in?"

Emmit deliberated over the matter until his head ached, but he finally decided to get rid of all the furniture—save for the bed and the new reclining seat Hanna bought for him. Too many memories were locked away underneath all that veneer, polish and paint. He was starting a new life and that necessitated being surrounding by new things. He'd even sold the STS. It was too much car for him, and he would feel foolish meeting his end by doing something as trivial as wrapping himself around a lamppost.

He gave Hanna the dining room set; the one Celia's parents gave them for their wedding present. He also gave her the crystal chandelier, couch set, matching Persian rugs and end tables, which were finished in the same stain as the dining room furniture. He'd considered offering the dining room set to Rachel, but her place was far too small to accommodate the 12-piece arrangement. Besides, Rachel said (in no uncertain terms) that she didn't want a thing. That didn't surprise Emmit. She'd always been stubborn and she certainly would never sacrifice her principles just to get her hands on some antique fixtures.

With all that taken care of, Emmit bought a new couch, 36" Sony Wega and a coffee table. He would have loaded it all into the U-Haul trailer himself but by then, he was having difficulty raising his eyebrows.

He was still trying to convince himself it was a good thing; that he was normal now and that would facilitate his new lifestyle. But there was no denying it was starting to get under his skin.

Rather than load up by himself, he asked one of his neighbors, Estelle Bousmalis, if her son Justin could lend a helping hand.

"That should do it," Emmit said while Justin pushed in the coffee table. "Thanks for the help."

Justin said it was no problem and waited for a little something to cement his good nature. Emmit took the hint and dipped into his pocket. "Here," he said pulling out a twenty.

Justin palmed the bill and waved goodbye. Emmit waved back as he rolled down the door of the trailer and continued to pump himself up for the first day of the rest of his life.

February 2002

Not so long ago, Emmit could lift mountains. Now, he couldn't lift his own spirits. The depression set in somewhere around the second week after he moved in. At first, he thought he was just homesick. He hadn't felt that overcome with anxiety and sorrow since his first year of sleepover camp.

Moving into Timberlake was an even bigger transition, and it would take time to get properly acclimated. Add to that he was still reeling from Celia's death and the WTC tragedy, and it was no wonder he was fending off the urge to shave his wrists.

It all made sense. Added up well enough. But there was something else behind his misery. Something that he recognized but refused to validate.

He'd been spending most of his time locked away in his room. Frank and some of the other staff tried to get him involved in the various activities and outings, but Emmit made it clear that he wanted no part of it.

Angela had her eyes on the tall stranger from the moment he first waltzed through the door. He certainly wasn't making her sightseeing duties easy. But if Angela was anything it was persistent, and she was going to make sure the newest member of Timberlake knew she was alive.

She watched from afar (what other choice did she have?) as he ate, walked and roamed about the grounds all by his lonesome. He was a sight all right— six feet tall, trim and proper and a full head of hair (or one striking toupee). He stood out from the rest of the Timberlake men, that's for sure, and Angela wasn't going to let herself go unnoticed.

She had a habit of coming on too strong. She knew that. *Men might claim to like aggressive women*, she would say, *but the truth of the matter is, a woman who knows what she wants and isn't afraid to ask for it scares the pants off them.*

It had been quite some time since Angela managed to frighten the khakis off anyone, so she decided to play this one out a bit differently.

His name was Emmit, she found out. He was in his late 50s, recently widowed and just like her deceased significant other, was a military man.

It's kismet, she thought. *We were meant to get together.*

Even though she was convinced all the stars were in alignment and the gods were smiling upon their imminent union, Angela was intent on keeping her cool. She'd do everything she could to gradually embrace him with her charms instead of strangling him with her charisma.

So she waited.

Then she waited some more and while she did, continued to watch from the sidelines. She saw that Emmit was a quiet man who kept to himself. The other residents quickly pegged him as standoffish, but she knew his type all too well. He just needed a little bit of help to open up, to reveal his true nature. And who was better suited to help him blossom than Angela Yablans?

A few months into his stay, Emmit forfeited his better judgment and joined one of the Hearts tournaments. It wasn't too bad at first. He was actually having a pretty good time of it, having won the first game then the second. Unfortunately, the good times came to a screeching halt during the third match when Herb Fleischman threw down his cards and accused Emmit of cheating. Rather than beat the old, wrinkled bag of skin into submission, Emmit thanked him and the others kindly for the game and went back up to his room to hide.

As usual there was nothing on TV. Emmit was halfway around the horn when there was a knock at the door. Nothing unusual about that, save for the fact that no-one had bothered to wrap on his gate for weeks. Emmit waited for another knock before he lifted himself out of his chair. He wasn't so sure he hadn't imagined the first one.

And there she was. Emmit recognized her, though he was at a loss for her name. She remedied that right away.

"Hi. I'm Angela," she said. "Angela Yablans."

Emmit stared at her dully. "Bond. James Bond."

Judging by her reaction, she obviously wasn't a George Lazenby fan so Emmit told her his real name.

"It's nice to finally meet you—Emmit. I've been meaning to stop by for a visit, but you know how it goes."

That's it. Play it cool. Don't scare him off.

"It's nice to meet you, Angela. But I was just getting ready to turn in and…"

"Don't let me stop you. I just wanted to make the introductions and maybe when you have some time, we can get together for lunch?"

"That would be…nice," Emmit said and quickly closed the door.

Things between Angela and Emmit went on like that for the next year. She would knock on his door, sit at his table, walk by his side—just try and get next to him and invite him to get to know her a little bit. And every time she did, he politely declined.

Playing it cool might have worked with penguins, but Angela could now see that Emmit was a tropical creature and would only be comfortable in a considerably more sultry environment.

Or perhaps not.

Angela's rainforest approach proved to be every bit as successful as her arctic tundra routine. In fact, Emmit seemed even less interested (if that was even possible). So she backed off. Far off, trying to forget he ever existed. The way Emmit removed himself from everyone and everything at Timberlake, that wasn't a hard thing to do at all.

June 2005

It had been some time since downtown Boston saw Emmit's shadow. Even before he entered Timberlake, he'd kept to the suburbs. The older he got the less he cared for the traffic, congestion and rapid pace of the core. But he couldn't go back to Timberlake. And he didn't want to stray too far from home. So, he settled in to the busiest neck of the city hoping he could buy himself enough time before he'd have to pop up and reveal himself.

He found a small motel on Lansdowne Street. Aesthetically, the place was a nightmare but logistically it was perfect because it was just a half-mile away from the Massachusetts Turnpike that bled into the I-90.

Once he'd settled into his room, Emmit headed out to look for a pay phone. He wanted to call Percy and see how Rachel was doing. He hoped his daughter was behaving herself. Not just because of the reflection it had on him, but for her sake as well. Janice was one of the nicest, most generous people you'd ever be lucky enough to meet. But get on her bad side and you'd learn firsthand that hell's fury truly pales by comparison.

After scouring the neighborhood for the better part of an hour, Emmit found a working phone at the corner of Brookline Avenue and Jersey Street. Before he dialed, he rummaged through the change in his pocket to make sure he had enough to cover the long distance charge. Scrimping together nearly three dollars, he plugged in the initial change and dialed Percy up. After the third ring Janice answered and following a brief chat, she handed the phone over to Rachel.

"How's it going?" Emmit asked.

Rachel said she didn't like being cooped up in that small house with Percy, and Janice's attendance didn't make the situation any better.

"I know it's hard, but you won't be there much longer," Emmit said assuredly.

"I hope so," Rachel whispered. "That old broad is driving me nuts."

Emmit hoped Rachel couldn't sense he was smiling. "She means well. Just bite your tongue and I'll have you out of there as soon as I can. Okay?"

After he got off the phone with Rachel, Emmit asked if he could have a word with Percy. Rachel dropped the phone and went to fetch the ex-sergeant, and a few seconds later...

"Yeah. What's up?"

"How is she doing?" Emmit asked.

"Well enough. Just between you'n me, though, that kid of yours got some mouth on her."

Emmit didn't care if Percy knew he was grinning. "Has she been foolish enough to open it up to Janice?"

Percy echoed Emmit's cheerful air. "Sure enough. Though she learned better the next time around."

"I'll just bet she did."

Percy got serious then. "How're you doing?"

"Me? I'm fine," Emmit said, hoping his voice didn't hint at his true feelings.

"Yeah? You sound tired."

"I'm old, my friend. I'm always tired."

Percy understood the feeling all too well. "How's that other thing coming along?"

"Not too well. I spoke to Sara again. Thought maybe she would've dug something up by now. But she's still as lost as I am."

"Well, at least you don't have to fret about your baby girl. So long as she's hanging here, you can bet she'll be safe."

Emmit hadn't been back to Timberlake since he dropped Rachel off in Minneapolis. He'd made sure to call Frank, explaining he would be spending a few days in Palm Springs with an ailing uncle. He also put a call in to Angela, telling her the same even though he was sure she knew something else was up.

The only public appearance he'd made was back in Cleveland for Hanna's, Jamie's and the kids' funeral. Rachel had demanded she attend as well, but Emmit managed talking sense into her and got her to stay put with Percy and Janice.

While it made perfect sense keeping a low profile, Emmit was quickly growing tired of acting all Sam Spade. He hadn't made any progress playing the game that way, so he decided it was time to change the rules.

But that would have to wait because he was close, very close, to getting back to his old self. He felt stupid not admitting why he'd lost it up until right then, hindsight and all. But now that he'd thought about it—really thought about it—it was the only possible conclusion that could be drawn, even though it matched up to Henry's prognosis, which was…

Emmit's brain quickly proved to be the most powerful weapon on the planet. It allowed him to do anything he thought possible. And that turned out to be the key.

If he believed he was capable of broad jumping the Golden Gate Bridge, he'd step up onto the shoulder, tense his calves and quads and clear it without a second thought. If he thought he could beat out a Peterbilt in a tug-of-war, he'd spit on his palms, dig in his heels and pull it over the line. His heightened brain capacity made his aspirations a reality. By channeling what was closing in on 70% of his mind's total area, any ambition he formulated, no matter how lofty, was a foregone conclusion.

But that was him. If, say, Angela had access to 67% of her brain's capacity, she would aspire to something completely different. Perhaps she'd drop 20 pounds overnight. Or maybe she'd regain her 20/20 vision or finally get a peak at some gams by charming the pants of any man that caught her eye by self-manufacturing an irresistible pheromone.

That's how it worked, and that's why Emmit reverted to an average man of his age, physical attributes and intelligence. The process began long ago when he started to get disillusioned with the operations he was involved with. Slowly but surely, his mind started to bend to his wishes. Then, when he wasn't able to help Celia the objective was finally attained.

He wanted a normal life. At least that's what he thought he wanted. Whether or not it was his true desire was irrelevant, as his subconscious mind only reacted to stimuli of a cognizant nature. Like his wish to break Henry in two pieces over his knee, or his need to catch up with Pocci and his mercs and bleed them dry through their assholes. As advanced as Emmit's brain was, it was still ruled by instinct and desire. Because of that, he was every bit as susceptible to emotional cravings as anyone else, which again jibed with Henry's analysis.

He was almost there.

Sitting on the corner of the bed in that fleabag motel, Emmit closed his eyes tight and reached out for the energies that lapped up his insides. They were wild and hot, but he had 40 years of experience behind him and he didn't break a sweat directing them to precisely where he wanted them to go.

"In through the nose," he murmured, "out through the mouth…"

And on to Timberlake to gather a few belongings, say goodbye and finish things once and for all.

-15-

That Morning

The first thing Emmit did when he got back to his room was peel out of his clothes, wrap them up in a tight ball and skyhook them into the trash. He'd been wearing the same outfit for the better part of the week and even though he'd run them through the sink a few times, had long since wandered down the road leading to rank.

He hopped in the shower. Immediately, he appreciated the water pressure a lot more after using the motel facilities, which couldn't muster a stream hearty enough to poke a hole through humidity. He shaved while he shampooed, brushed his teeth and as he towel dried, combed his hair (just like Michael Douglas in Wallstreet, a style he hadn't worn since the same era the movie was released).

He slipped into his maroon short-sleeved button-down, the one Celia bought him for father's day the year before she passed. As he buttoned up, he stepped in front of the mirror hanging above the dresser. The person staring back at him was nearly spot-on now—tall, lean and confident. He had that unmistakable look, the kind that showed he was the sort who knows what he's doing, what he wants and most importantly, how to get it done. All the while, Angela dipped in and out of his subconscious, much like she had even through the past week while he fought for his and Rachel's lives.

He thought of how she tried to be someone she wasn't just to make him feel comfortable.

He thought of how she tried to play it nonchalant, when all she wanted was to show him and the rest of the world how passionate she was.

He thought about how strange it was to think—and feel—like that about anyone not named Celia.

* * *

She was sitting comfortably on one of the couches overlooking the gardens, talking with two other female residents. Emmit recognized the lady to Angela's left—the one who always wore the pale yellow shawl. Her name was Esther Something-or-Other. He couldn't place the bag of bones piled up on the right, though he was sure she was the one who always left the coffee carafes empty without telling the wait staff to refill them.

Making sure to come up from behind so Angela didn't see him, Emmit declared, "And how is everyone this beautiful morning?"

Angela stiffened at the sound of his voice. "We *were* enjoying it just fine."

Emmit didn't care for the past tense reference. "How about now?" he asked, taking the available cushion beside Mrs. Something-or-Other.

"Getting worse by the moment," Angela said stiffly.

He couldn't blame her for being upset. After all they'd been through lately and how he took off without a word of explanation. But once he let her know what was going on, he was certain she'd lighten up.

"I don't mean to be rude ladies, but do you think it would be all right if Mrs. Yablans and I had a moment alone?"

They didn't wait for him to finish his sentence before they were up and gone. Esther turned around and shaped her hand like a phone and jiggled it beside her ear. Angela nodded and folded her arms tightly across her chest.

"That good, hmm?" Emmit slid closer to her. "Do you mind?"

She did but didn't voice it. "What happened to you?" she said, pointing to his forearm.

"Scraped up against a fence," Emmit explained then immediately switched conversational gears "Look…I know you're mad. And I guess I'd be too if I was in your shoes. But you've got to believe me…"

"I don't have to do anything. Not as far as you're concerned."

"Fair enough. But maybe once you've heard me out, you'll understand that the last place I wanted to be for all this time is away from you."

That was enough to get her arms to loosen just a little and her mind to open a bit—enough to get her to listen anyway.

His explanation went as scripted. "I didn't want to go to Palm Springs, but Uncle Isaac is on his last legs. He was always there for me…when nobody else was, so I felt it only right that I be there for him, too."

Angela looked him over suspiciously. "Why didn't you tell me you were going?"

"There wasn't time. Jonathan called me, and…"

"Jonathan?"

Think fast now—who's who and what's what.

"Uncle Isaac's son. My first cousin," Emmit blurted. "Anyway, Johnny called and told me Uncle Isaac had taken a turn for the worse, and if I wanted to see him again I'd better make it quick."

"So how is he?"

"He who?"

Angela's wary glare intensified to the point where the temperature in the room shot up several degrees. "Uncle Ike," she said.

Emmit had so many things running through his mind he was finding it difficult keeping pace with his white lies. "Not good, I'm afraid. Like I said…"

"Last legs," Angela added.

"Right. Anyway…I just came back to pick up some things. I'll be heading back to Palm Springs this afternoon. But I'll be back in a week or so."

All at once, Angela's tight features gave way to their usual soft, satisfying façade. Emmit felt her pulse even out as she took his hand into hers. "Have dinner with me…tonight?"

Emmit would have loved to on any other occasion, but he'd risked enough coming to Timberlake in the first place. Henry and his well-armed associates could have been running a tail on him for all he knew (actually he sensed nothing, so he was confident he was out of harms way for the moment). But the longer he stayed, the more likely someone who didn't deserve it was going to get hurt.

But how could he say no, especially after Angela had been kind enough to let him back into her good graces?

"Can we make it an early one?" he asked, puppy dog eyes set to stun.

That Evening

Setting his powder blue button-down and black dress pants on the bed, Emmit sat down beside his outfit and started spit-shining his black loafers. Once he saw his smiling self in the leather's reflection, he went into the bathroom for a final grooming session.

As he pulled his hair back as far as it would go, he noticed it was already getting thicker and a bit darker as well. The liver spots on his hands and knuckles were also starting to fade and according to the notches of his belt, he'd shed an inch or three from his waistline.

"Looking good," he said almost singing as he buttoned up his shirt. "Feeling even better."

Then it happened...

He felt it. Right before it hit. Just seconds before it tore through the building's foundation. And while the sheer thought of it was enough to scare a precious year's life out of him, what really frightened him was that he could've stopped it.

Cursing his own name for lingering, Emmit got dressed as quickly as he could and went for the door. Just as he reached for it, the first wave struck. The walls buckled and the windows shattered. Emmit picked himself up off the floor, steadying himself on the dresser. He just managed to kick the door open before the next strike.

Slowly but surely, he headed down the crumbling hall. He didn't get a dozen steps before he felt the floor tremble, ushering in the next shockwave. He braced himself and watched as the other residents were thrown around like some bratty kid's unruly rag dolls. Emmit pulled himself away from the wall, picking other residents up off the floor as he went along. He hoisted Deborah Kantor up and pushed her towards the fire exit. "Outside," he ordered.

Once she was out of sight, he turned his attention to the remaining stragglers—Mr. Garrison, Mr. Babbet and Mrs. Justin. "Take the stairwell," Emmit barked, "nice and easy now."

He watched them go—slowly—out the door. Once they were safely on their way, he turned around and raced back to Angela's room. In all the commotion, he wasn't sure if she had gotten out to safety. He hadn't seen or felt her, and he wanted to make sure that she got out of the building.

He stepped in front of her door and slapped his hand palm flat against it. He could sense something moving inside but it wasn't a human signature. "Angela! You in there?!"

There was no answer. Emmit took hold of the brass knob and turned. It was locked.

"I'm coming in!" he shouted and pushed just hard enough to ram the door through its frame.

"Angela?!" she wasn't in the bedroom but he heard the water running in the bathroom. "Angela...you in there?!"

She was on the floor, not moving. He raced to her side and knelt down beside her. "Hey...you okay?"

A sickening feeling washed over him—*she's dead*, he thought.

"Is it…six…already?" she said, her mouth barely able to shape around the words.

Paying special mind to her head, Emmit picked her up. She'd sustained a nasty head wound. Streams of blood were running down the sides of her face. He looked at the sink and saw some blood smeared on the dull corner. As always, the scenario ran through his mind…*she lost her balance during one of the explosions, tried to steady herself…but knocked herself out cold on the counter.*

"Just relax now," he said calmly. "You're doing great."

He wanted to take the stairs and get her out of there. But he could feel them now. Even smell them. There was no time to get her out. He stopped in the middle of the hall thinking about his next move.

The fireplace, he thought. *She'll be safe there for the time being.*

The sitting areas were outfitted with large cobblestone fireplaces. Large enough for most bodies to stand in. Emmit jogged down the hall and stopped in front of the open hearth. He lowered Angela, laying her flat on the ceramic flooring. Then, he grabbed a few cushions from the chairs that sat on either side and he propped her head and legs up.

They were almost there.

Emmit leaned in tight and brushed his hand along Angela's cheek. "You wait for me. Understand?"

She nodded. Before Emmit could take off, she reached out and took hold of his shirt. "Kiss…?" she said faintly. "For good luck?"

Emmit laid her hand by her side and leaned over. He gently pressed his lips against hers. She tasted like cherry blossoms and something else; bitter and antiseptic—like medicine.

Making sure Angela was comfortable, Emmit got up and left to face the transgressors. He tore down the hall, made the left and stopped just shy of the elevators. There was still some time, maybe a minute or two. Just enough to clear his mind and completely reclaim what had once been his and his alone.

The seconds ticked by. That long-past-due feeling started tickling his insides. It wasn't long before it began roiling deep in his mind. It sprouted tendrils that shot throughout his nervous system penetrating every last cell of his system. He was right there—grazing the surface of his most accomplished potential when they finally made their grand entrance.

"There you are," Colonel Hummerbert snarled. "We've been tearing this joint apart looking for your decrepit ass."

Emmit opened his eyes. "You didn't have to go to such bother. I'm listed in the directory."

The colonel grinned like he was privy to some dirty little secret. He lowered his weapon and looked Emmit over from head to toe. "Damn...*He* was right," he said while his men filed in a perfect line beside him. "You got fucking old."

Emmit thanked him for the kind words and stretched up to his full six feet. He was almost ready. It was just a matter of swindling the ex-military hero, now mercenary-for-hire, into giving him that extra little bit of time. Hummerbert had always been a sucker for flattery, so...

"I've got to admit," Emmit said. "The years have been a lot kinder to you, colonel."

Hummerbert slung the strap of his AK-47 around his shoulder. "Sorry I can't say the same to you."

"You're looking good yourself, sergeant," Emmit said to Pocci, who stood right beside Hummerbert. "Let's see what we can do to change that, hmm?"

"You just say when," Pocci hissed.

Hummerbert pushed Pocci aside. "Pissing contest over now, boys?" he waited for the reply he knew wasn't coming. "Good. Let's get down to it then."

Hummerbert was the most brutal man Emmit had ever been unfortunate enough to cross (he'd witnessed the colonel use his hunting knife to flay a prisoner like an oversized trout and hang his entrails around his ears as a final humiliation). But as nasty as Hummerbert was, Emmit couldn't help but admire the man. He was an excellent soldier. The best. And he never allowed anything—man, animal or element, get in the way of seeing a mission through to completion. In all fairness to those now in attendance, though, he'd never faced a noun quite like Emmit.

Hummerbert reached for his vest. He took hold of one of the concussion grenades he and his men had been igniting all throughout the lobby downstairs and pulled it free. "I'd like to reminisce with you, but I'm not getting paid by the hour. So if you don't mind...?"

Hummerbert pulled the pin and tossed the explosive. It hopped and rolled towards Emmit's feet. Emmit bent down, noticing any trace of his sciatica was gone and picked up the grenade. He looked on at Hummerbert and his men as he wrapped his hand around it just before it went off.

A muted bang filled the room. Emmit clenched his fist hard, his teeth even harder, trying not to let on that it felt like he'd dipped his hand into a vat of industrial-strength acid. Even he couldn't withstand such an impact (most of the skin on his hand melted down to the bone and his index and pointer fingers were shredded down to two jagged nubs). But it was worth the hurt because now Hummerbert, Pocci and all the rest knew *who* they were dealing with.

"Is that all you've got?" Emmit wiped the powder and blood onto his shirt.

"Hardly," Hummerbert said.

In perfect harmony the soldiers cocked their weapons. On Hummerbert's command they took aim and…

It was too late. Emmit was back.

Before Hummerbert could formulate the thought to squeeze the trigger, Emmit was already behind him. He wrapped his forearm around the colonel's neck and slapped his good hand firmly behind his pumpkin-sized head. Emmit turned them both around clockwise to face the others.

"Drop 'em, kids. Or poppa gets torn a brand new behind."

Of course, being trained by Hummerbert, they would never consider relinquishing their weapons. So Emmit had a decision to make. Did he dip into the mercy fund and hand them over to the authorities just so they could break out and kill for the highest bidder? Or did he take advantage of the opportunity and make it their last encounter?

When Emmit felt *His* presence, the decision was made for him.

Applying a few more pounds of pressure per square inch, Emmit snapped Hummerbert's neck like a dehydrated chicken bone. He dropped the colonel's body and before it hit the ground, rushed the others.

Aside from Hummerbert and Pocci, there were four more. They were well-trained but young and inexperienced. *Cheap bastard*, Emmit thought, *wouldn't shell out for seasoned troops…even for me*. Emmit almost felt bad about tearing into the young bodies. But when he imagined how many innocents they'd fit for toe tags, his reservations evaporated.

Pocci took the lead with two men by his side. The other two spread out and opened up to spray the area with cover fire. Emmit easily sidestepped the barrage then flanked the two men in the rear. He was moving so quickly they lost sight of him and didn't reestablish a visual until he came to a screeching halt behind them.

"Lose something?" Emmit hoisted one of the men up over his head.

He threw the 200+ pounder at his mate, who fired away until his magazine was empty. The only person he managed to hit was Mr. 200+ and before he could reload, Emmit popped his head off like he was opening that bottle of Chanoine Grande Reserve at his retirement party.

Three down. Three to go.

Emmit was feeling good. Better than he could ever remember, though he was a bit lightheaded, a side effect of all that adrenaline pumping through his system.

Or so he thought.

He set his sights on the three remaining soldiers. The mercs scattered the area with gunfire, while Pocci took hold of a flash grenade.

"Fire in the hole!" the sergeant shouted, and the room filled with a most brilliant and discombobulating light.

Pocci intended to catch Emmit by surprise, disable him for just a moment then cut him in two. But Emmit was beyond surprise. He'd tapped into Pocci's head—along with the others—and knew what they were going to do before they did.

"Sad," Emmit said grabbing the tailbone of one of the men. "Just pathetic."

He dug his fingers into the young soldier's flesh, took a firm hold of the end few vertebrae and tore his spine clean out. With wide eyes and a frenetic heartbeat, the other soldier watched the life seep out of his mate. Emmit took the opportunity and broke him in half over his knee.

Tossing the carcass aside, he turned to face Pocci. "Next."

He could feel Pocci's pulse quicken and the blood course through his veins like a tidal wave. The sergeant was scared. But a good soldier's training always overrides fear, and Pocci stood his ground ready to fight.

"Your daughter…she begged for her life, you know," Pocci taunted as he took aim. "Like the bitch mongrel that she was."

Pocci secured his finger on the trigger and got ready to drain the magazine.

"You're empty," Emmit hissed.

Pocci pulled the hammer back. The weapon clicked hollowly.

Just like back in Rome, Emmit's eyes began to smolder as he walked up to Pocci.

Slowly. Deliberately.

Pocci widened his stance. He tossed his weapon to the ground and reached into his vest for his Kershaw blade. Emmit stepped closer still and Pocci took a jab at Emmit's midsection. Emmit didn't bother trying to avoid the attack and the hardened steel sunk deep into his stomach.

He didn't even notice.

Pocci pulled the knife out and swiped for Emmit's neck. The well-honed steel carved a path through Emmit's worn skin. Geysers of blood shot high into the air.

Emmit could care less.

Needless to say, Pocci was a bit taken back but he still managed to prepare for another strike. Emmit, however, was done playing pin cushion. He grabbed Pocci and pulled him in nice and tight. The sergeant tried to get his hands free so he could take another stab, but Emmit's grip was far too tight.

He kept applying pressure. Doubling it. Redoubling it. Slowly, mercilessly, he kept squeezing until Pocci's insides ran out of real estate.

His kidneys popped, his liver was squashed to paste and his heart exploded. Emmit watched the streams of blood run out of the sergeant's eyes, ears, mouth and nose. Pocci screamed out in exquisite agony, still trying to break free.

"Did she sound anything like that?"

Pocci wasn't in any condition to answer. Emmit held him for another moment then threw his lifeless body to the floor. It was a bit melodramatic, granted, but like he'd done with the grenade, needed to put on a show for his final guest of the evening.

Emmit stepped back, admiring his handiwork. He turned to face the elevator and said, "You can come out now."

He stepped out from behind the mounds of rubble, brushing up against one of the flaming piles. Amusedly, *He* looked down at Hummerbert's body and all the rest. "Well. That wasn't so hard now was it?"

Emmit was fighting the urge to jump *Him*. To grab hold of *Him* and rip *Him* to pieces. Before, when he'd found the bodies of his family, he'd relinquished control, this time willingly to give vengeance free reign. But now that he was face-to-face with the man (or was it the woman?) responsible for all his pain, he wanted to know why. Once he had that answer, there would be plenty of time to send him to Hell.

Emmit did his best not to think about Hanna, Hailey or Nate. He reached inside himself, desperately trying to wipe his memory clean so he could approach the situation objectively. But it wasn't easy, and not just because of the emotions that tore through him. All of a sudden, he noticed his vision was blurring and his head ached badly. Trying to home in on the matter-at-hand, he cautiously took a step closer. "You did this."

He wasn't quite sure what was more intriguing—Emmit's grasp of the obvious or his ability to so easily take down a cadre of highly-trained killers. "I suppose you could say that. Though Colonel Hummerbert and his men were the ones who actually saw the deed through."

"But why? Do you know what...?"

He raised *His* hand and pulled out a handkerchief to wipe the dust off the shoulder of *His* coat. "Please. The time for frivolous annotation has long since passed us by. Cutting to the proverbial chase—you were not performing, so I was forced to present you with the proper incentive, yes?"

"Incentive? Is that what you call this?!"

He laughed. This time the schoolgirl was gone. In her place was someone—something—much more ominous. "Of course. What else would you call it?"

"Oh…I don't know. Murder? Massacre? Misguided hostility at the least."

Emmit didn't think it appropriate to make light of the situation. But he needed to buy himself a moment so he could figure out why his head was pounding to a jungle beat.

"Interesting," *He* said. "Is that your professional psychological evaluation? Or is it simply your opinion?"

"A little of both."

"I'm sorry you feel that way. Though it is heartening to see that I have succeeded."

Emmit was all set to cough out another objection when he processed what *He* said. "What are you talking about?"

"You're not playing possum, are you? You really haven't figured it out?" *He* plucked a cigarette between *His* full lips. "Well, I suppose I should come clean. It's only fair that you know."

Emmit clenched his teeth and again submerged his urge to rush *Him*. To crush *Him*. To be done with *Him* once and for all. As it turned out, he couldn't even if he wanted to because the closer he got, the more his head throbbed. Another step in and it felt as though his brain was going to implode.

"I'm afraid I haven't been completely honest with you," *He* said lighting up. "For I am Dr. Jayne, you see…though my first name is not Henry."

Emmit could barely make out the words. He was in such pain he was finding it hard to concentrate on anything else. Even though, he was able to reach into *His* mind and extract *His* true identity.

Samuel let his guard down just for the occasion.

"No…that's not…"

"Possible?" Samuel questioned. "I've never been one to judge, but I don't think you should be the first in line claiming what is and what is not possible, yes?"

"But…I killed you."

"You killed *someone*. But it certainly wasn't Samuel Jayne. If memory serves, I believe it was that fine-looking young Austrian businessman wearing the three-pieced Armani."

Emmit stepped back. The pain subsided, but his stomach took a churn for the worse.

"I made you see what I wanted you to see—cast an illusion in that tremendous mind of yours, which is something only an equally powerful mind could ever realize," Samuel said winking by design. "By-the-by…if you're wondering why it feels as though someone has taken a pickaxe to your skull," he reached into his pocket, "it's because of this." He waved a small vial at Emmit. "It's a little invention of mine. I won't bother getting into the specifics. Suffice to say, it's a tranquilizer…an anti-psychotic actually. And according to my estimates, you should be passing out in oh…" he looked at his watch.

Emmit's knees buckled. He tried to stay upright but the chemical cocktail Samuel somehow managed to inject into his system was too powerful. Still fighting, Emmit fell to the ground and the world turned black.

"Right about now."

That Night

Emmit reached out. His arms were pinned. He tried lifting his legs. He couldn't get them to budge. As his eyes focused and his mind cleared, he looked to see if he could find David but…

No. David was dead. He wasn't in Vietnam. Nor was he trapped in that collapsed tunnel. That was years past. A lifetime ago. This was the here and now. Somewhere else altogether.

Somewhere much worse.

"Welcome back," Samuel crooned.

Emmit tried to turn his head, but like the rest of his body it was trapped tight. He kept struggling anyway.

"Just settle down now. No need to make this any more difficult than it has to be," Samuel said soothingly.

He hung over Emmit like a vulture in a pristine white lab coat. Emmit looked up at him with contempt so thick and conceptualized he could see it standing there alongside the mad doctor.

His vision clear, Emmit could see that he was in Henry's/Samuel's lab. It was a bit different, a new locale, but most of the same equipment was there.

Emmit wasn't a metallurgist, but he could tell the straps that bound him to the reinforced steel examining table were encased in titanium. That's the odor they were giving off anyway.

Samuel had tied Emmit down while he was out. He'd also dressed Emmit's wounds on his hand, neck and midsection, which according to that annoying itching sensation, were already starting to heal. Emmit couldn't see them, but he could feel a pair of sensors attached to his temples.

The potent tranquilizer that had taken Emmit down had nearly worn off, though he still felt a slight sense of euphoria, a side effect of the potent narcotic. "How did you…?"

"How did I what?" Samuel asked brightly.

"How did you…dope me up?"

Samuel smiled. "It wasn't me, my dear boy…"

"It was me," Angela said stepping into the room.

She stopped in front of the table and reached up to her mouth. Carefully, she pulled off the clear membrane Samuel FedEx'd her the previous night.

"Peachy Sheen from Maybelline," she said.

"With a touch of bupropion," Samuel added.

"Thought it tasted more like cherry," Emmit said.

Samuel reached down and snapped up a small trash can. Angela pitched the membrane into it. "I know you don't believe it…but I am sorry," Angela leaned over Emmit. "But I really didn't have any other choice." She kissed him lightly on his forehead.

"There's always a choice," Emmit said trying his best to get mad. "You just made the wrong one."

Angela looked like she was about to cry but Samuel stepped in. "So says the man strapped to the table. Though I do admire your bravado."

She pulled a tissue from her purse and dabbed the corners of her eyes.

"Perhaps this will assuage your tears, my dear," Samuel handed her a fat envelope. "You may count it if you wish. But if you don't mind, please do it elsewhere. I'd like some time alone with Emmit now."

She wiped her eyes again and waved to Emmit as she headed for the door. Emmit could twist his head just enough to watch her go. Once she was out of sight, he turned his attention back to Samuel.

"That's how you got to her? Money?

Samuel nodded.

"Not very original."

"Perhaps. But effective nonetheless, yes?"

Emmit chuckled. "Appears so."

"If it's any consolation, she didn't agree to help me right away. She's quite taken with you, you know?"

"Apparently not enough."

"Ah, yes. Cupid may be the God of love but cold hard cash is the deity of all. Especially considering her husband's pittance of a pension wasn't enough to keep her at Timberlake for very much longer. In lieu of spending the rest of her days in a facility featured on 60 Minutes, she decided to take me on."

The euphoric effects of the tranquilizer were still going strong. Coolly, Emmit tested the strength of the straps just to see what it would take to break free. "Where do we go from here?"

"I think you already know the answer to that," Samuel charged. "But before we get there, I think I owe you a bit of an explanation. After all I've put you through it's the least I can do."

"After all you put me through, that is definitely the least you can do."

"Yes, well…that's your perception. It has been no matter how hard the truth ever sought you out."

"You mean *your* truth."

"No. My perception. Truth is just a word. One that doesn't have any place in today's vocabulary. But perception?" Samuel took hold of the strap fastened over Emmit's chest to make sure it was secure. He did the same with the others. "That's what it's all about in this digital day and age, isn't it? Casting the right impression to make people feel safe and secure. Creating the illusion that everything is just fine—whether the hounds of Hell are nipping at your heels or you're floating on cloud 9."

"You're insane."

"Am I? Or am I speaking a truth that scares even you? You can't argue that ours is a society built upon appearances. And I suppose that makes sense considering reality is far too depressing and traumatic for most people's liking."

"Including yours."

"Certainly. That's why I've dedicated myself to the greater good," Samuel claimed proudly. He took a seat behind the main computer workstation and activated the power terminal. Within seconds, all of the monitors and plasma screens hummed to life, bathing the room in a drab electric glow.

"I'm sorry. Did you say good?"

Samuel looked up to Emmit. "Of course. Don't you consider it good to admonish evil-doers? Is it not good to wrest power away from those who abuse it?"

"I've said it before and I'll say it again—you're out of your goddamned mind. You were back then and you are now."

Samuel smiled. It ran a chill down Emmit's spine. "And you're every bit as naïve," he lit a cigarette and blew streams of smoke through either nostril. He looked like Satan himself. "But I didn't come back to try and make you understand what it is I'm trying to accomplish. I wouldn't dream of beating my head against that wall again."

"Then why have you come back?" Emmit asked not really caring. At least not insofar as content was concerned. He just wanted to keep Samuel monologue-ing long enough until the drug wore off so he could focus and break free.

"I've come back to finish what I started and to do that, I needed you to come back as well."

"Me? What do you need me for?"

Samuel's smile widened to the point where Emmit thought the top of the doctor's head would fall off.

"As you now know...my mind is every bit as powerful as yours. Unfortunately, it didn't get that way on its own."

"Neither did the color of your hair."

Samuel ran his fingers through his wiry chestnut strands. "Though my stylist has done a better job than Mr. Clark's, yes?"

"If you say so."

As hard as he tried, Emmit still couldn't find the strength to bend the armored straps. Perhaps if his head was clear and his desire pure, but Samuel's drug was blurring the lines—reality bowed to fiction. It was almost like Emmit was sitting in his Lay-Z-Boy and watching the scene play out on his Sony.

"I can understand why it bothers you," Samuel said.

"What's that?"

"That I've ascended to a place where only you've been."

"The only thing that bothers me is I haven't been able to tear your heart out of your chest."

"No. I think there's more eating away at you than just that. After all, a unicorn is just a horse with a horn sticking out of its forehead when there's more than one, yes?"

"No."

"Let's just agree to disagree then," Samuel said. "Back to my point…I was able to devise a procedure granting myself access to a much greater portion of my brain. According to my estimates, I'm only a few percentage points behind you." The screen hanging over Emmit displayed an image of his cranium. "But when all has been said and done it is still an artificial state. As such, it needs to be replenished over time."

"Which is why you need me?"

Samuel tapped the end of his nose with his finger. "It's also why I brought along our little friend," he pulled the portable device from his lab coat and ran the stylus across the screen.

An ominous hum filled the room. It sounded like a swarm of killer bees on its way from Tijuana. Loose articles on tabletops started jumping and the ceiling opened up, revealing a huge construct that slowly descended until it hovered a few feet directly above Emmit.

The tube-shaped base, which was made of a lucent polymer/plastic compound, split open like a banana to reveal a most intricate series of spinning servos and hydraulics that whined and whirred. A slender steel arm with a sequence of colored plastic tubes wrapped around it extended out of the base until it stopped only inches short of Emmit's forehead.

Still in the joyous throes of the tranquilizing agent, Emmit amusedly stared at the huge machine. "Ever the drama queen, eh?"

"I see you're still feeling the effects of the anti-psychotic," Samuel mused. He entered another command with the stylus. "Let's see if we can't change that, yes?"

The tip of the arm opened up much like the base, and three eight-inch long needles poked out.

Emmit looked at the most menacing-looking spikes and smiled. "Where's my cookie?"

"It's not your blood I'm after," Samuel approached his captive patient. He looked down at Emmit as he ran his finger along the side of one of the needles. "Well…not literally."

Carefully studying the image onscreen, Samuel returned to the main terminal and keyed in a series of commands. The arm rotated counter-clockwise until the needle with the red tube attached to it jutted out past the others.

As high as Emmit was, even he was starting to appreciate the magnitude of the situation. He started struggling in earnest, though the straps still wouldn't give way one bit.

"Don't try and fight it. It will only make it worse," Samuel said dutifully. "Just try and relax and it will all be over before you know it."

The needle started spinning like a drill. Once it reached full r.p.m.s, Samuel pressed a button on the keypad and the needle stabbed closer to Emmit until it entered his left temple.

Even with a 50 horsepower hydraulic engine egging it on, the needle had some difficulty penetrating Emmit's thick skull. The stench of burning bone filled the lab, until the reinforced titanium tip found its way past the dense obstacle and proceeded to pierce Emmit's occipital lobe.

After the sample was attained, the biotic material sluiced through the hose and a jet of pressurized air shot it up into a hidden containment vessel within the body of the machine. The other needle spun into place to extract a sample from Emmit's temporal lobe then the final needle did the same with his frontal.

With all the samples safely stowed away, Samuel typed in a command and the entire unit disappeared into the ceiling. He stood up and approached Emmit with a look of undeniable accomplishment. "There. That wasn't so terrible now was it?"

Emmit was writhing in absolute agony. Samuel watched on, amused at how he'd incapacitated the most powerful creature on the planet.

"This...isn't...over..." Emmit puffed.

Samuel investigated the trio of punctures in Emmit's head. "Of course it isn't over, my dear boy. If I wanted it to be over, would I have gone to all of this trouble? If all I was after were samples, I could have just done away with you and that would be that."

"So why...?"

"Because I won't have *them* destroy such a beautiful thing. That's why." Samuel said a bit annoyed.

"Destroy...what?"

"You, of course. You are beautiful, Emmit. A bit misguided and confused, but beautiful all the same. You are the next step in human evolution, and all they wanted to do with you is create another weapon...another tool to destroy rather than create."

"How're you...any different?"

Samuel took a deep breath. "You're referring to the actions I've taken part in, I assume?"

"Actions…mass murder. Give it a name."

"Well, if you didn't insist on ignoring history and all it's taught us, you'd realize that my actions were absolutely necessary."

"For what?"

Just to be safe, Samuel checked out Emmit's bindings. "If a man kills a single person, they call him a murderer. But take that same man…and have him kill a million…what do they call him then?"

"Samuel?"

A giggle squirted out between Samuel's lips. "I was going for king. But that will do."

Convinced Emmit was still firmly held in place, Samuel went on. "Now, you take that same man…this homicidal majesty…have him wipe out the entire population and what has he become?" This time he didn't wait for an answer. "A God. My point, if it isn't quite crystal yet, it that again it's all a matter of perception."

"You still…haven't answered my question," Emmit said.

"What was that again?"

"What do you want?"

"I thought I just told you."

"Save it…for the strangers. I know you. I know…there's more to all this than your unbridled sense of…humanitarianism."

"Well…I suppose there's no harm in telling you," he said with a tinge of guilt (or was it virtue?). "If you must distill my desire, the one word I would use is competition."

Emmit looked at him curiously. "What?"

"Competition, my dear boy. I needed some competition."

Samuel waited a few moments while Emmit tried to add it up. "What the hell are you…talking about?"

Samuel's smile took on sinister proportions. "I don't mean to strut, but someone of my caliber—my abilities—needs a worthy adversary, yes? Saving this mud ball from annihilation can be tedious work after all. So why not have a bit of fun in the process? It's for this other reason—and I realize it's a tad selfish, that I chose to reinstate Project Realm."

"You're serious?"

"Of course. Let's be honest now. Without you, all that stands in my way is the F.B.I., C.I.A., S.W.A.T, SEALs…nothing more than catchy acronyms whose value is relegated to placement on T-shirts and baseball caps," Samuel grabbed a cigarette from his case and lit up. "Then of course there are the task forces, Bureau of Diplomatic Safety, Counter-Terrorism Program. It sounds impressive enough, but they couldn't combine forces to put a stop to a bad check."

"That's why…you're back?"

"Partly. As I've said, I came back because I needed those samples," Samuel reconfirmed. "Being afforded the opportunity of defeating you…utterly and completely…is merely a bonus, yes?"

"So all of this…this Middle East conspiracy nonsense. It's…"

"Nonsense. Indeed. I thought given your bloated sense of patriotism, perhaps that would have been enough to bring you back. But when it didn't…even after the electro-shock therapy and hypnosis sessions, you can understand why this was necessary."

Emmit flexed as hard as he could. The straps tightened and crackled with the strain but held firm. "Sorry to disappoint you…but all the glial cells in the world…won't help me understand something…like this."

"Then look at it from more of a narrative point of view. We are, after all, actors fulfilling their respective roles, yes?"

"Don't you ever…shut up…?"

Samuel ignored Emmit and continued. "The way I see it…this country doesn't merely crave heroes. It needs them. On screen. On paper. In the flesh. Just as much, it needs nemeses. Or those they believe to be worthy of such nominate. After all, where would the free world direct its sense of moral outrage and indignation without the likes of Adolph and Saddam? What good would come out of the great pains taken to develop those wonderfully contrived and disingenuous ethics if individuals like Osama and Fidel weren't there to violate them?"

"…think I've had just about…enough of this," the words dropped out of Emmit like weighted things. "Maybe I can't understand why. But…even you're not so far gone to believe…I'd actually let you go."

"Of course not. A true enthusiast of all things pure and noble would never fall into such an apathetic stance," Samuel stepped back to the table behind him, palmed the ashtray and returned. "Just as someone with equally righteous objectives would never leave home without ensuring the back door is unlocked." He rested the ashtray on Emmit's chest. Shuffling backwards again, he picked up the portable transmitting device and dragged the stylus across the bottom portion of the screen. "You'll understand what I'm getting at once the end credits have rolled." Dropping the device into his coat pocket, he crushed his smoke out into the ashtray and prepared for his finale. "For the time being, you'll be delighted to know that the bindings will be automatically unlocked in three hours. Just enough time for you to clear your head…and enough for me to get where I have to be going."

Emmit tilted his head up and watched Samuel daintily wave goodbye.

"I took the liberty of having your uniform dry-cleaned. You can pick it up at Lucky 7 Martinizing in Cambridge."

And with that, Samuel was gone.

Printed in the United States
61284LVS00003B/203

9 781424 137152